THE
HAWK
ENIGMA

J.L. HANCOCK

ISBN: 978-1-7371501-1-4 (paperback)
ISBN: 978-1-7371501-0-7 (ebook)

Class Five Press

Edited by Sandra Haven
Cover by 100Covers

For Chris
LLTB

AUTHOR'S NOTE

This writing has been submitted to the appropriate authorities prior to publication to avoid any unintentional disclosure of sensitive information. Any resemblances to real persons, dead or alive, or other real-life entities, past or present, is purely coincidental.

Finally, as a disclaimer, this novel includes subtle sexual references, violence, kidnapping, and confronts the trials of post-traumatic stress.

CHAPTER 1

It Ends Where It Begins

BUNKYO CITY
TOKYO, JAPAN

Bam! Bam! Bam!

B A fist pounded on the door, punctuated by the repeating jingle of the apartment doorbell.

The cacophony ripped Dr. "Taka" Hawkins from her computer game–induced trance. She yanked her gaming headset off her head and rubbed her eyes as they readjusted to reality. Her mind, however, had no desire to readjust.

Most nights, she would be deep in a coding binge, her fingers orchestrating syntax, projecting scores of code like a cyber-Mozart. Instead, the music hall of her mind remained quiet tonight—no symphony, no opera, only the mind-numbing escape of a virtual fantasy world. She had been consuming the digital content of the role-playing game for the past three hours. A Michelin-starred chef at a cheap buffet restaurant. Just the fix she wanted, not the fix she really needed.

Bam! Bam! Bam!

She spun to face the front door.

"*Taka-chan, Ichikawa desu. Hayaku doa akete kudasai!*"

Dr. Hawkins sighed and shook her head. It was her mentor, Dr. Kenzo Ichikawa, the last person she wanted to see. *Maybe I can ignore him?* A glance at the clock: 1 a.m. *What could he possibly want, or be able to say after what happened today?*

She reluctantly traversed her small living space and spied through the peephole to see Dr. Ichikawa outside in a huff. With a click and a creak, she opened the door.

"Taka-chan, I'm so sorry to barge in on you like this. Has anyone come by tonight or tried to get a hold of you?" He wrung his hands, his eyes wide. Sweat stained his blue dress shirt. His typically well-combed hair was a mess, and he appeared to have lost his rimless glasses.

"No." She frowned. She wanted to just slam the door on him, the way she did earlier that day when she stormed out of their lab, but Dr. Kenzo Ichikawa always exhibited consistency and stability. Tonight, nothing about him seemed consistent or stable. "What's going on? If you're here to change my mind about quitting—"

The elderly Dr. Ichikawa waved off her words, stumbled through the entryway, flipped off his black dress loafers, and scurried inside.

The studio had a compact kitchen, an adjoining bathroom, a living space with a two-cushion couch, and a shelving unit built into the wall that held her futon and a television. A tiny desk hugged the far side where a gaming computer framed the frozen image of the paused game. The small and sparse quarters suited the scientist, who devoted her life to her work.

She folded her arms, both decorated in tattoo mosaics of birds, crashing waves, and the Anasazi god Kokopelli, and prepared herself for some elaborate attempt at reparation. Dr. Ichikawa indecisively fidgeted then settled on the couch, cradling his bag on his lap. At nearly six feet of height, Dr. Hawkins towered over him, glaring.

"I...I have something important I need to tell you." His voice quivered. "I have made a grave mistake, and I fear I have put you at risk."

"Put *me* at risk?"

"Well...someone. I have been keeping something from you even though the dreams told me this is inevitable."

Dr. Hawkins blinked. *Nothing is inevitable.*

"Did you run the algorithm again or—"

"I ran it again and again. Nothing changes. I can't... It won't..." He shook his head, then seemed to plead, "You know, everything we have done has been to help people...but I've gone too far." His eyes drifted across the intricate blue and white oriental rug that overlay the tatami where she lays her futon each night. His countenance carried acceptance and defeat. He took a deep breath and shifted his remorseful eyes to meet hers. "I need you to trust me...as a colleague, as a friend, as a—"

"Don't even finish that sentence. After what you—"

"I know, I know," he said with his hands raised in surrender. "Just trust me one...last...time, please." He swallowed. His heavy words clung to the air, pressing down on both of them.

Dr. Hawkins paused.

"What...what is it? It's not who I think it is, is it?" she asked, her brow furrowed. *Perhaps he does have a foot in reality... Just one.*

He reached into his brown messenger bag.

"I need you to sit and face toward the kitchen. I don't want you to see what I have in my bag until I'm ready."

"You're not making any sense. What do you have in the bag?"

"I just need you to trust me...please. Everything will make sense in a moment."

"Fine," she conceded, flinging her folded hands free. She knew deep down Dr. Kenzo Ichikawa held no malice. He was a troubled man after all. She had always known that. He was troubled in the way that peasants and commoners in mythology are troubled by meddling gods—troubled by tragedy, troubled by gifts, troubled by time, of which Dr. Kenzo Ichikawa seemed to have too much, too many, and too little. So, she sat, settled in with her back to her mentor, her knees together, and her hands on her lap. Black yoga pants hugged her legs, and a baggy T-shirt with the print of some heavy metal band's skeleton mascot holding a gun defended her torso. Her long, dark honey-colored hair folded behind her ears and flowed along her tall, thin frame like water pouring from a pitcher.

"Ow! What the—" She spun and grabbed her left shoulder. In his right hand, Dr. Ichikawa brandished a spent syringe.

"I'm sorry. I need to keep anyone from getting it. And this is the only way I knew how to do it." He scrambled away from her, cowering from her anticipated anger.

"Kenzo! You sonofa—"

She rubbed the point of injection on her shoulder.

He shoved the syringe back into his bag as his phone pinged. He scanned the text message, his face turning pale.

"I have little time. I must go. Thank you, Taka-chan. When all this is over, let history be kind to me." A faint smile quickly bent the edge of his lips before dissolving. His seventy years of life passed and vanished in that simple expression. It wasn't an apology, it was a farewell. He rushed to the door, speared his shoes with his feet, and sprinted off into the rain.

"What're you talking about? What did you—"

In a rush of emotions, her initial confusion shifted to waves of anger.

Dr. Hawkins, or Taka-chan, as she was known to her Japanese colleagues, suddenly understood. *Our lives are in danger...*

She popped up to run after him and stumbled when the room started spinning. She bobbled at the step before the entryway, one hand holding the door open, the floor pulling at her. She propped her other hand on the wall to catch herself as her eyelids grew heavy. She dropped clumsily on the step; the front door closed...then her eyes.

CHAPTER 2
The Shrine

ather, I had a wonderful dream, the voice of his daughter said in his mind.

Dr. Kenzo Ichikawa entered the Koishikawa Korakuen Gardens. To the east, the Tokyo Dome loomed overhead. The man-made glow of spotlights illuminated the outline of the white, pleated, egg-like shape of the massive sports complex above while a forest of dense deciduous trees cast the park in darkness below. Tall buildings stood as sentries around the island of life in the concrete jungle of downtown Tokyo.

He rushed along the path of tiny stones. Water mixed with the gravel and muted his steps in the rainfall. It was late, and the hour meant he should be alone. The rain should reinforce it. And yet the dream...

Kenzo slowed to a stop beside a koi pond in the middle of the park. Raindrops disturbed the water and amplified the sparkle of the city lights encapsulating the garden under the overcast skies.

An island sat quiet in the pond. On the south side of the island, a trail of round, gray, water-worn river rocks meandered through ginkgo trees and bushes. The gray stones were in stark contrast to the greenery of the fauna and the stagnant brown water. In the center sat a tiny, red, boxlike Shinto shrine.

Shinto shrines pay homage to the many gods of Japan as part of the traditional religion of the Japanese. According to Shintoism, Izanagi and Izanami were the first gods to come to this earth. They dipped their spears, swirled them around in the oceans, and thus created the islands of Japan, the lands farthest to the east. Their daughter, Amaterasu, the goddess of the sun, the greatest of all the gods, brought light to the islands. Thus, Japan became known as the land that first greets the sun, or Nihon, the "origin of the sun." At night, however, the island and the shrine appeared as shadows as Amaterasu slept.

I knew the end from the beginning, Dr. Ichikawa thought. *And now the end begins.*

Kenzo Ichikawa held his umbrella over his head and clutched his bag. He prayed that his foolhardy effort to involve Dr. Hawkins would somehow absolve his mistakes and save their work. He also hoped to keep his other colleague, Dr. Naomi Shimoda, out of the fray.

"*Honto ni kuru to omawanakatta ze*," a throaty voice said to him. Like an arctic wind, the air around Dr. Ichikawa blew frigid. He shivered.

"I didn't think I would come either. I also knew I didn't have much choice," Dr. Ichikawa replied in Japanese. He turned to address the voice, but nothing greeted him except shadows under the tree near an unlit rock lantern. He thought of the dream that told him of tonight and this very moment. *I'm not ready.* Fear pumped through his veins. He knew what needed to happen.

Can anyone ever truly be ready for their own death? Especially when they know it's coming. His knees trembled.

"Do you have it?" the voice asked.

"I...I don't." The rain hitting his umbrella now pounded like rocks on a roof, the erratic drumbeat stoking his desire to run. But he held fast.

"Where is the algorithm?"

"I was hoping we could find another solution to our problem." There wasn't hope in trying to reason with this man. There was less hope in trying to hide from him.

"Without the compound or the algorithm, there is no arrangement," the voice warned.

"I know that I said I'd give them to you, but I just can't let you have it yet. I still don't know how it works, and I don't know what you'll do with—"

Icy steel slid across his right shoulder, slicing his jacket, filleting his skin beneath. A sharp, splitting pain filled his arm. He spun around to see the silhouette of a man in a trench coat. A long, bloodied blade extended from his right arm.

Thunder crashed from the growing storm overhead.

I'm not ready!

Dr. Ichikawa's legs gave out and he collapsed at the sight of the hulking figure, scrambling backward like a crab before rotating to his feet.

Outside of a scuffle with a neighbor when he was eight, Kenzo Ichikawa had never raised his fist at a soul. His was a life dedicated to science and helping others. But it was also a life of loss: many footsteps down a lonely path where he eventually lost his way. He had known the risk of dealing with men like this, but his desperation and zeal had led him here.

To a mistake. And tonight would not be the moment mistakes found forgiveness.

He pivoted to escape along the trail. The silhouette cut him off. Dr. Ichikawa's thoughts filled with panic. With no other choice, he leaped into the pond, flailing as the water and terror deepened.

Dr. Ichikawa kicked his legs and slapped his arms frantically until his hands contacted the algae-covered rocks in the shallow water on the opposing bank. He scrambled onto the island, up the pathway, and into the small forest around the shrine. Blood poured down his shoulder from the horizontal slash deep in his muscle. He ditched his bag as he treaded up to the little red Shinto monument. His foot caught a rock, and he fell to his knees in a heap.

A blade pierced through his left shoulder from behind. He winced, then wailed. Rain trickled through the leaves above his head. A heavy wind shoved the branches, and the trees groaned. Above them in the night sky, the Japanese god of thunder, Raijin, pounded on his taiko drum. Tumultuous crashes of thunder echoed through the clouds.

Before him, the wooden shrine, as the eyes of the past gods, stood in observation, in judgment, saying nothing, as gods always do.

The chilled blade twisted inside Ichikawa's shoulder. He cried out. A bolt of lightning lit up the skyline.

"You are the first of three then."

"Leave them out of this! They don't know the truth about the compound," he lied. "They don't know what it can do!" His body froze as the blade continued to tear through muscle and tendons.

"Even if you die, they'll tell me what you refuse. A debt will be paid."

"I'll find your money if that's what you want. I'll sell everything I own!"

"You think this has anything to do with the money? You do not understand who you borrowed from...who you have taken from. And not just you...all of Japan!" The blade ripped out of his shoulder. The man grabbed Dr. Ichikawa by the hair and pulled him up to his knees then released. Ichikawa arched his spine, arms widespread. The rocks dug into his knees.

Kenzo had told Taka-chan that tonight was inevitable. The dream. The algorithm.

And now it comes...

The light from the Tokyo Dome peeked through the shadows, exposing the pond's clay mud as it mixed with the bright red blood pouring from his shoulders.

"Dr. Kenzo Ichikawa, before the shrine of your ancestors, you receive the judgment of the ancient gods...for defying the gods of the future."

The assassin reached around him from behind and slid the blade into Kenzo's stomach like an assassin's Heimlich, puncturing his diaphragm. Kenzo stopped breathing. The killer extended the evisceration.

Unable to scream, unable to cry out, unable to pray, Dr. Ichikawa lifted his head and closed his eyes tightly in a final repentant gesture. Images from his dream filled his mind with the face of his daughter. A thousand cranes circled the sky, and the torrent of a raging river flooded his thoughts.

Father, I had a wonderful dream.

CHAPTER 3
The Hunt

Voodoo squinted through the green glow of his night vision goggles as he compulsively thumbed the safety of his rifle. To his right, a soldier manned the crew-served machine gun mounted to the riverine craft. Its barrel tracked the shoreline. The boat's motor throttled, cutting a wake in the river that was still as glass.

Voodoo's armored craft crept away from the Basra Palace Complex and headed north on the Euphrates. The Iraq invasion left the elegant building intact but structurally unstable—a shadow of its former opulent glory. Like the palace, the city of Basra, Iraq, still fought to maintain appearances. The orange glow of streetlights reflected off the water of the river. It contrasted with the empty desert on the opposing bank where Iran lurked in the distance. A blinking Ferris wheel gave the impression that, for some, normalcy endured.

But it didn't.

Buildings were sheared in half, bullet holes peppered crumbled walls, and black waste-filled water pooled between homes. The smell of burning feces in fiery earthen pits hovered in a haze.

Oil processing facilities burned off excess gas and lit the horizon with fifty-foot flames.

The riverine craft trolled through the murky waters of the Mesopotamian river and delivered its cargo. Voodoo jumped onto the beach and bounded up a small embankment toward the remains of Basra.

Keep your head down, *Voodoo thought.*

Kitted with the latest military duds, he crept forward, ignoring the sweat saturating his hair from the humid summer air. Voices crackled from the radio connected to his headset as he carried his rifle at the ready.

He reached the top of the riverbank and caught movement in the corner of his eye. He emerged from the darkness of the Euphrates twenty meters from two men. They held hands in off-white cultural garb known as dishdasha, which soldiers called "man-jams" as they resembled pajamas for men.

Harmless, *he thought.*

Voodoo let out a sigh of relief and headed to the rally point. The ground shook, then he saw them. Three matte tan armored personnel carriers called RG-33s pulled up. The vehicles looked like the Frankenstein love child of an SUV and a tank. Built to withstand the blast of land mines and IEDs, the V-shaped hull and reinforced armor transformed the vehicles into mobile fortresses. The back door of the lead RG-33 flew open, and a massive block of muscle that masqueraded as a human being with a gun jumped out to check the perimeter.

Stu stared down the two men as he scanned the area. Voodoo chuckled to himself as they darted off, seeking refuge in a nearby alley. At six-seven, Stu had traps that bulged from his shoulders to his ears. The XL plates for his body armor barely covered the center of his chest and exaggerated his exposed midsection. Though a horrifying sight to the enemy, his size made his body armor and weapons seem like they were made for a child, the proportions comical. He would have looked more appropriate lugging around chain mail with a Crusaders' cross tunic and a bastard sword.

Stu glanced over and gave Voodoo a nod. Voodoo jumped into the RG-33.

"The air asset was diverted. We're gonna need to use the ground box if we're gonna get the target," Stu said as he climbed in behind Voodoo and slammed the door shut.

"Roger that," Voodoo said. He settled into the back of the crowded vehicle and opened his Toughbook CF-19 laptop. The regional task force was notorious for stealing reconnaissance air support.

Every damn time, *Voodoo thought.* How're we supposed to fight a war if they keep stealing our resources?

Voodoo revived his computer. Even through his gloves, the familiar plastic feedback of the keyboard brought Voodoo comfort—it grounded his focus on the task at hand. The Toughbook displayed the graphical user interface to the system everyone called the "PFM box." Voodoo used specialized technical equipment to hunt targets. Any time someone asked him about it, he would inundate them with radio frequency theory and computer science jargon. He told them just to call it the PFM box, and no one questioned what it meant. Voodoo always laughed to himself knowing that it stood for "Pure Frickin' Magic."

"Voodoo, this is Frisco. I have the last grid coordinates. Let us know when you're ready, buddy," Frisco called out over radio comms from his position riding shotgun in the lead vehicle.

"Hit it!" Voodoo replied. The RG-33 rumbled down the road. The size limited movement, but Frisco navigated their vehicle, Vick One, with ease. Ten minutes later, the hunt began.

A familiar chime pinged on Voodoo's laptop. Like Pavlov's dogs, shooters in the vehicle adjusted their weapons, leaned forward, and salivated in anticipation.

"Got 'em!" Voodoo called out. His heartbeat intensified.

"All stop," Frisco ordered. The convoy came to an abrupt halt in the middle of the city.

"First Base. Dismount," the platoon chief pushed out over the radio. The platoon of eighteen shooters and Voodoo exited the RG-33s. Another set of vehicles arrived, and twenty Iraqi military personnel dismounted as well. Despite their lack of discipline, indigenous partner forces filled a critical role in operations as US forces coordinated a transition of power. Drivers remained in the vehicles along with the Common Remotely Operated Weapons Station, or CROWS, operators. Fifty-caliber machine guns were mounted on top of the RG-33s connected to video cameras inside the vehicle where the CROWS operator controlled the gun turret via a joystick.

Dust billowed as the point element broke away from the group and stood ready. Voodoo positioned himself in the front, identifying Stu, Frisco, Heath, and Bobby by their silhouettes and the unique ways they configured their body armor—the monochromatic green night vision making it hard to differentiate them otherwise.

"Everyone up?" the ground force commander asked. After several radio check-ins, the platoon chief patted his helmet and gave the thumbs-up, signifying a positive headcount. "Do your thing, Voodoo."

Voodoo punched in some numbers on a small black box connected to a camouflaged antenna strapped to his chest. Under his helmet, he wore Peltor electronic earmuffs.

A unique screeching sound dumped into Voodoo's ears, sending a warm wave rippling through his body. I love that sound.

He tilted his head toward Frisco, nodded, and gave a knife-hand gesture with his gloved hand to move out. They broke into a dead sprint with the rest of the assault force following behind.

Move, *Voodoo thought.* Speed is safety.

As the point element, they would be the first to face an ambush, first to find an IED. After four combat deployments, hundreds of combat operations, God knows how many enemies captured or killed in action, yet another awaited. But there was always a chance. There was always something waiting. And, once again, Voodoo rushed headlong into the fray, chasing the tone in his ear, and the tingling sensation in his fingertips that made him feel alive.

Voodoo stopped at an intersection in the shadows beside a wall at the end of the street. Frisco took point, presented his M4 assault rifle, and gave Voodoo cover. Voodoo moved his body left to right, tracking the tone in his ears as it changed. The rest of the element fixed their barrels at the buildings in the periphery and waited. They knew not to rush him.

• • •

SAN DIEGO, CALIFORNIA, USA

3:43 a.m. Voodoo lay in his bed, salt crusted on his forehead from another late workout, still in his running shorts. He could have showered before bed, he could have changed into something different, he could have gone to sleep before 2 a.m., but he never did. At least tonight he made it to the bed. The couch was the usual place. Sometimes he slept at work.

A picture sat on the nightstand. A happy couple smiled as a gray C-5 Galaxy—a "big daddy plane," as his niece called it—loomed behind them. It was just before his first deployment.

In the kitchen, a disassembled microwave, soldering irons, wires, Raspberry Pis, circuit boards, and lithium polymer batteries littered the kitchen table he had painted by hand in the garage. She wanted it white.

She's the reason he never slept in the bedroom. It smelled like her. Heavenly Eau de Parfum. Everything in that bedroom was hers. Her comforter. Her Shanghai Tang dress in the closet. Her set of keys. Her Ray-Bans. Her long, amber-colored hairs that still turned up. Her spiral notebooks for her scribbling. Her wedding band.

Everything except the nightmares.

Those were all his.

He ground his teeth, arched his back as he tossed and turned. He knew what was coming.

• • •

Voodoo patted Frisco on the shoulder and pointed left. They headed past a pool of brackish water full of trash. Animated silhouettes rustled along the edges as enormous rats scurried, and feral dogs skulked in the shadows. The first dog let out a quick bark.

Thomp! Thomp!

The dog yelped and went silent. The bullets from the compact MP5 with a silencer sounded like little more than compressed air blown through a tube. Another feral dog, swollen with a disease from wading in the excrement-filled water to keep cool, stood and prowled toward them.

Thomp!

Through the binocular night vision goggles, Stu smiled as he dropped another dog. The MP5 looked like a toy cap gun in Stu's freakishly large hands.

Since the war started, thousands of abandoned dogs settled in the streets. Most haunted alleys and scavenged trash heaps for food. Their hair, matted and disgusting, hid infections, and some dogs had missing limbs. Others had littered so many puppies their nipples dragged on the ground from their spent udders.

In neighborhoods like this one, they were early warning networks for anyone living nearby. The moment they started barking, Iraqi families sleeping on their roofs would wake up. For a platoon hunting murderers and insurgents, that wouldn't do. The best solution was a silent, 35 cent 9mm bullet.

A switch flipped in Voodoo's mind. A switch that had no time for the abandoned dogs waiting for starvation to kill them, a switch that had no time for emotions or being subjective. He needed to be decisive, especially when they had a terrorist who tortured children in their crosshairs.

They pressed on until Voodoo slowed in front of a small compound. Three-meter-high walls surrounded an expansive one-story home with a wide gate that faced the street. Another pool of black water blocked the right side of the building. Voodoo focused on the tone in his ears; he changed position several times before making the call. He pointed his infrared laser mounted on his rifle and lassoed the gate. Done. Target acquired. Mild relief washed over him. Now came the assault.

"Batter up," Frisco called out on the radio. Stu transitioned from the short MP5 to his long-barreled M4 and stood on the opposite side of the gate from Frisco. Voodoo fell back across the street with Heath and Bobby to hold security. Within seconds, the rest of the platoon set assault positions, covering all sides of the compound, being careful to avoid the risk of fratricide. Frisco and Stu focused on the gate while Voodoo watched their six, facing the opposite direction toward the buildings adjacent to the target compound so no one could sneak up from the rooftops nearby.

Pop! Pop!

Subsonic 9mm rounds from a handgun broke the silence.

Dap! Dap! Dap!

The supersonic hollow point 5.56 bullets of an M4 fired in response. Voodoo turned back as a man in a white dishdasha appeared holding a handgun at the gate. Frisco and Stu lit him up with rounds from their rifle.

Dap! Dap! Dap! ... Dap! Dap! Dap! Dap! Dap!

Voodoo moved to take cover behind a parked car on the opposite side of the street. He took a controlled breath. Years of training calmed his nerves and sharpened his resolve as his adrenaline spiked. He tightened the grip on his rifle.

A pregnant pause swelled before the real gunfire erupted. From behind the platoon, the Iraqi forces, in their hand-me-down blue camouflage and AK-47s, fired recklessly in all directions. Their rounds ricocheted off the surrounding buildings. Iraqi families sleeping on the roofs of the neighboring homes scurried away from the gunfire.

Shooters focused on the entryway where a man had emerged. Voodoo crouched deeper beside the car and traced the roof across the building behind him with the crosshairs of his weapon. The Iraqi soldiers continued spraying and praying. Voodoo couldn't find the threat.

Dap! Dap! Dap! Dap! Dap!

Multiple weapons fired. None of them belonged to Voodoo or his platoon.

• • •

Voodoo twitched. His eyes moved rapidly behind his eyelids. Sweat droplets beaded and fell. Quiet whispers and hollow grunts slipped from his lips.

Voodoo never really dreamt, he just closed his eyes and waited for the nightmares—nightmares disguised as memories. Sometimes they were joyful. Those hurt the most.

Occasionally, there was a voice—a voice from his past, a visitor, a prophecy in the form of poetry. And tonight, that familiar visitor sat waiting, and it would change his life forever.

CHAPTER 4
The Little Hawk

I t was still dark outside when Taka-chan awoke. The dizziness had subsided. The memory of Dr. Ichikawa and his delirium remained. But now, a cryptic message, delivered by a familiar voice in a dream she just had, repeated in her mind.

A flurry of emotions blew through her—frustration, anger, disappointment, excitement. Endorphins pumped into her supercharged brain.

She wiped the drool from her chin and checked the clock. It had been only an hour since Dr. Ichikawa left. Perhaps she still had time to find answers or find Dr. Ichikawa before something terrible happened.

Not that he doesn't deserve it, Dr. Hawkins thought before an immediate pang of guilt struck her chest. Dr. Ichikawa had been like a father to her. Regardless of his mistakes, he didn't deserve to have something bad happen to him. And she wasn't perfectly innocent herself. *I should have known...*

Her mouth smacked chalky and dry. She went to the kitchen for water and checked her equilibrium as she stood. She cupped the water, splashed her face, and slurped straight out of the faucet before shutting it off with a squeak.

She retrieved her phone, but calls went straight to her mentor's voice mail. Text messages floated in the ethereal realm of zeroes and ones with no response. *He must be at the lab. Where else would he go at this hour?* Taka-chan crammed her laptop in a bag and rushed out the front door.

Fifteen minutes later, Dr. Hawkins rummaged through her colleague's office at RCAST, the Research Center for Advanced Science and Technology at the University of Tokyo, hoping for any indicator as to what happened to him. Nothing topped his desk but a sleeping computer and two photos, one of himself, Dr. Hawkins, and their other team member, Dr. Naomi Shimoda. Dr. Hawkins replayed that moment in her head. The other picture was of two little girls and a boy playing at a park. She remembered that day too.

Doctors had diagnosed her with hyperthymesia—the ability to recall events with perfect clarity. Anything she experienced presented in her mind like a digital video library. As a result, some called her a savant, though she didn't use the term. Yet she was a genius. She graduated high school at fourteen, double-major undergrad at seventeen. She studied computer science at Caltech for grad school, then moved on to Carnegie Mellon for postgraduate work.

Upon graduation, every major tech company approached her with lucrative job opportunities. But an invitation to work on a project with Dr. Kenzo Ichikawa, a renowned optogeneticist at the University of Tokyo, piqued her interest. The use of light to control genetically modified neurons had far-reaching implications. Also, she knew his work well. They had a history. Besides, it was the least she could do for him.

"*Go-en ga aru n desu ne.*" That's what Dr. Ichikawa said when she first arrived. *It seems we have fate, does it not?*

Go-en ga aru. Though it was a common Japanese expression, Taka-chan didn't believe in fate. Neither did Dr. Ichikawa, as she later learned. The hypocrisy of his statement was scintillating. He speculated that if we opened enough of the human mind to access our intuitive prediction of the world, we would grasp our future reality, something others considered to be an unknowable fate. He needed her to help identify the link between human intuition, natural human instincts, and machine learning.

Capitalizing on Dr. Hawkins's expertise in artificial intelligence, they pioneered new frontiers in scientific development. While Dr. Naomi Shimoda and Dr. Ichikawa focused on accessing and manipulating the human brain, Dr. Hawkins developed algorithms that would mimic the brain's activity and enhance it.

Being the youngest PhD in the lab who would spend most of her time off playing video games, her colleagues translated her family name, Hawkins, to "*taka*," Japanese for "hawk." From then on, everyone called her Taka-chan—"Little Hawk."

Now I'm even more lost, she thought as she sat at her desk, revisiting the many decisions that led her there. She surveyed memories through her mind like a Google image search, hoping to find any evidence as to what happened to him.

Male Japanese voices derailed her train of thought. Instinctively, she disconnected the computer monitor to kill the feed. She grabbed her laptop from her bag, pulled an Ethernet cable from another computer, and connected it to her desktop tower before hiding inside a closet.

"It happened less than an hour ago, so we need to get as much information as we can now before anyone starts looking. Some of the guys are taking care of the body," a man's voice said. "Dragon told us to grab hard drives from the computers and anything in the lab that looks important."

Taka-chan's hands went to her mouth. *Body?* She envisioned the weathered face of Dr. Ichikawa, heard his final words to her. She blinked back tears; she couldn't let his sacrifice—all their efforts—be for nothing. She quietly slipped the other RJ-45 adaptor of the Ethernet cable into her laptop, bridging the two computers. She logged into a cloud storage location and began extracting files.

Inside the closet, Taka-chan could see only the glow of her computer screen, her palms sweating as she relegated her life's work to a progress bar and dumped all her data onto the cloud. At the same time, she couldn't help but fixate on the sounds of strange hands tearing through her office.

Taka-chan cracked the closet door. She could barely make out black figures wearing hoods, faces distorted, eyes dark. They carried a bag with something round in it.

They rummaged through the lab like meth fiends jonesing for a fix.

"It's not here. Did we find the other two members of his team yet?"

"Doesn't look like it. They'll show up, though. If they file a missing person's report, the police will let us know. Let's grab all the hard drives."

Dr. Hawkins's laptop pushed years of data and algorithms to the cloud at an excruciatingly slow pace. Her fingers drummed erratically as she considered her options.

They said the police would let them know if we go to them. Are they the police?

She had to warn Naomi. She crouched into a fetal position facing the door with her feet on the ground. Making as little noise as possible, she pecked at her phone while the thieves invaded her workspace and tore apart her team's work.

A shadow stepped in front of the closet. She stopped breathing. Her heart jumped into her throat. Without finishing her thought, she sent her text message. The figure paused, bent over, grabbed the Ethernet cable running under the door, and pulled.

The data transfer progress bar pegged 100 percent right as the closet door was flung open.

"*Yatta!*" one of the men said.

Taka-chan slammed the laptop shut and leaped up. She smashed the computer into the flesh of the man's face with a sickening crunch. His head snapped back as he fell onto her desk. She used the momentum to bulldoze the man and sprinted for the main exit her would-be assailant left open.

The second man pursued. Dr. Hawkins had an advantage: Junior Olympic track and years of marathon running. She tucked her laptop under her arm and sprinted down the hall to the stairwell and bounded three flights to the ground floor. Taka-chan punched out the doors of the Experimental Research building onto the courtyard of the University of Tokyo.

As long as she was out in the open, she stood a chance. She just needed to move. No time to breathe, she ran, her hair whipping behind her in the rain. Raijin pounded his taiko drum, and the skies thundered.

She approached the main road, cut left, and headed down the thoroughfare. As she turned, her foot caught a slick piece of concrete, and she lost her footing.

She glided, then she crashed.

Her elbow cracked against the concrete as it took the brunt of her body weight.

Pain, incapacitating pain, shot from her elbow through her entire body.

Get up!

Nausea sent burning acid to the back of her throat. She gulped it down in defiance.

Get up!

She rolled to her knees and attempted to stand. Her rain-soaked hair tangled and obscured her vision, but there was no denying what she saw next. The tip of a long sword flashed beyond the hair over her face; a shadowy figure emerged behind the blade.

Her body went rigid.

Before she had time to respond, an electric shock bit her between the shoulders. Her body locked and jolted. A hand reached around her and smothered her mouth and nose with a cloth.

Her vision blurred.

In her mind, the familiar voice from her recent dream spoke again:

The crane's blood flows in your veins. Dark eyes are watching. Fast feet will fail a midnight flight. A steady mind in the darkness will find the light. When the blind warriors emerge, lie down and say your name.

Images flashed across her mind—of faceless men and rain, then isolation and darkness, and finally, angelic light. She knew what would happen next. More importantly, she knew some-one *else* would come.

CHAPTER 5

The Witch Doctor

"It's an Iraqi Death Blossom!" Heath yelled. A body lay in the entryway. Heath motioned to the platoon chief on the left side of the building to focus on the Iraqis. The chief gave the cease-fire signal to the Iraqi commander. The intermittent fire continued until the fervor wore itself out. A dog yelped.

At least they're consistent, *Voodoo thought.*

In addition to discipline, Iraqi soldiers lacked any semblance of common sense when excited. Death Blossom was a term the chief liked to use, and it caught on. It was in reference to the '80s movie The Last Starfighter. *The main character flew a spaceship with a button called the "Death Blossom," which caused the ship to spin and fire in every direction recklessly as a last resort. A lot of the younger shooters weren't even born when the movie came out, but it was the perfect metaphor for their partner force's behavior in firefights—they were out of control. In this case, the only thing they took out was another disgusting dog.*

The platoon chief motioned for the partner forces to commence the assault. Stu and Frisco stepped back as the Iraqis clumsily stepped over the cadaver in the white man-jams and flooded the house.

Despite a few random screams, the assault appeared to go smoothly. After several minutes, the Iraqis pushed the "all clear" signal over the net. They started turning on the lights in the house as they commenced battlefield forensics.

"Voodoo, get in here!" the chief called out. Voodoo stepped around the body. A postmortem erection had already formed, creating a man-jam tent in the body's midsection. Voodoo had seen worse.

He jogged through the courtyard and walked into the house entryway. Iraqi soldiers searched the home.

BAM!

Everyone crouched as the sound of a flashbang went off somewhere near the rear of the house. The Iraqi commander, dressed like a Middle Eastern G.I. Joe with a bushy mustache, ran out of the back bathroom, waving his hands.

"No bomb! No bomb! Drop flashbang!"

A young Jordanian woman, working as an interpreter wearing Army digital camouflage and an oversize gray helmet, stood beside the Iraqi commander. She translated an incoming barrage of Arabic.

"Apparently, one of his men threw a flashbang into the bathroom to clear it out even though nothing was in there," she said.

"After you passed 'all clear'?" one of the shooters yelled out. "Bunch of damn idiots!" The Iraqi commander bowed his head in apology, then spat at his men in Arabic.

Voodoo walked through a hallway. Bobby, the EOD guy, had a big smile on his face as he pulled a brand-new 105mm rocket out of a closet; any time an EOD guy found explosives, they got giddy. Other shooters tossed the house, slipping important items into plastic bags.

Soldiers escorted two veiled Iraqi women outside as a baby slept motionless on a dusty rug. The mother chose to leave it be. It was very apparent these women were seasoned veterans of military raids. They felt no need to disturb the baby's sleep with such a minor trifle as a platoon of special operators in their living room and a dead man on their doorstep.

Voodoo made his way to a large open room. It smelled of livestock and Mediterranean spices mixed with sweat. Four Iraqi men knelt on the ground with zip ties around their wrists, hands behind their backs, and hoods on their heads. Three shooters followed behind Voodoo including Frisco and Stu, who had to dip his head to get through the doorway.

"You know why we call him Voodoo?" Frisco asked the other shooter. The new guy gestured that he didn't. "You're about to find out."

Voodoo walked the room and concentrated on his equipment. His tingling fingers steadied as he realized which man they were after. He pointed to the second man from the right. Everyone nodded in agreement but stood still.

Voodoo stepped back and motioned for the shooters to get behind the captives. He pulled a black balaclava up from around his neck. Almost on cue, Frisco and Stu removed the hoods.

As the four men squinted to adapt to the light, Voodoo stood motionless in front of them. He strategically placed the black cloth of the balaclava to cover his mouth and nose, obscuring most of his face, and the military helmet with the night vision goggles flipped up shadowed his oval, light eyes. He pierced them with his gaze, his eyes naturally angled up a bit and intense. Voodoo reached into his cargo pants pocket and pulled out a purple velvet bag. He loosened the leather band that cinched it shut and crouched down. He wiped the ground on the floor between the Iraqi men and him to make it presentable.

Voodoo looked each one in the eye. The prisoners ranged in age and size, but the second from the right, a man in his twenties, held up his head to look tough. His trembling body betrayed him.

Voodoo turned the bag upside down. Chicken bones spilled all over the floor. Voodoo stared at the bones and mumbled incoherent gibberish as he waved his hands in fluid motions. His eyelids fluttered. The Iraqi men leered at Voodoo in confusion and fear.

Then, Voodoo stopped moving.

With a damning glance, Voodoo shot his eyes at the bones, then the second man from the right, and pointed at him. Voodoo's index finger extended like a death sentence. Frisco immediately snapped a bag back over the man's head and dragged him out of sight. The other Iraqi men screamed in terror at the display of witchcraft. Stu and the other shooters thrust bags over the remaining men's heads and dragged them out as well. A trail of urine snaked behind.

The room fell silent.

As soon as the captives were out of earshot, the room erupted with laughter.

"That never gets old!" Frisco said as he walked back into the room. The new guy buckled over and shook, completely cracking up.

The Jordanian translator caught the spectacle from the hallway. "Don't you think it's wrong to mess with them like that?"

As if I care, Voodoo thought.

Voodoo gave the translator a cold glance. "These men used cordless drills to force drill bits through little boys' hands to punish their parents."

The interpreter swallowed and averted her eyes.

Voodoo never did his little performances to mock the people they were after, though. He protected his real "voodoo" however possible and pretending to be a witch doctor just happened to be an easy way to do that.

"Home run," the chief pushed over the radio. Brevity codes usually followed themes and related to pertinent points in the mission. Everyone now knew they had captured their primary target. Military personnel throughout the house continued their search. AK-47 assault rifles, rocket-propelled grenades, documents, and electronics all worked their way into bags for documentation.

Just then, a voice broke the silence on the radio.

"Uh, Chief, we just found a dude chained to a pole in the backyard." Frisco and Voodoo made their way to the back door, where a huge Iraqi man wildly waved his arms and jumped up and down. He was chained to a stake in the ground next to a stable with a bull in it.

"Just relax, dude, we'll set you loose," the new guy said. One of the Iraqi soldiers mumbled something, but the interpreter wasn't around to translate. Voodoo and Frisco arrived just as the new guy dislodged the stake from the ground that held the chains in place. The unchained man went crazy, attempting to hug everyone nearby—a frothing mess of overwhelming body odor. Mud and feces stained his man-jams.

The Iraqi soldier became frantic and tried to restrain him. The unchained man discarded the soldier with a wave. The interpreter emerged, and the soldier released a stream of Arabic.

"Um, apparently this man has 'special needs.' They most likely had him chained because they couldn't control him."

"Like the Iraqi version of Sloth from Goonies!" Frisco called out with a little too much excitement. "He just needs a Baby Ruth and some friends." One of the new guys didn't seem to understand the reference.

The chief came around the corner. "We can't have this guy running around the compound wildly. Someone is gonna shoot him."

"We can't chain him up again either," the interpreter said.

"Let's do the next best thing," Frisco offered. "Let's give him a bump helmet with a chem light and tell everyone not to shoot the guy with the chem light on his head." He was half joking.

The chief thought for a moment. "Why the hell not? We're almost done here anyway. Get Stu and strap the helmet to the guy's head, so we don't accidentally kill him."

By this time, the vehicles had pulled up to the front of the compound; forensic analysis of the target was nearly complete. Voodoo jumped into an RG-33 and dug around for a bump helmet. Unlike regular military headgear, a bump helmet was similar to headgear worn when riding a bike or rock climbing. It had no ballistic properties yet was perfect for accident prevention. He found one under a seat, along with a zip tie and a green chem light, which he strapped to the helmet. By the time he returned, Stu appeared to be Greco Roman wrestling the unchained man.

"Retard strength is a thing!" Stu called out, laughing. Voodoo cracked the chem light to activate the illumination and handed the helmet to Frisco.

"Everybody clear out the yard. The second we get the helmet on, we're gonna set Happy Pants over here loose," Frisco advised. Voodoo put the word out over the radio to not shoot the man with the green chem light on his head. Sporadic laughter responded.

Frisco jumped on the unchained man's back like a bull rider and struggled to get the helmet on his elongated head. Stu hooked one of his legs with his right arm and drove the unchained man into the wall, pinning Frisco between them. Frisco let out a grunt as the air expelled from his lungs. He was half laughing as the unchained man crushed him. Voodoo ran up to the side and grabbed the strap to the helmet and clipped it shut.

"Got it!"

The three men let go. As the unchained man paused to admire the headgear, the shooters made their way into the house and closed the door behind them; the newly liberated man flittered around the yard like a big goofy firefly.

"What do we do about him now?" one of the new guys asked.

"What're we, social workers? Not our problem. He's not a terrorist, so he's free, I guess to run around and be...free?" Stu said, himself unsure what to do and not really caring at the same time. This wasn't the first time they had come across something like this—the last mission they found a man chained to a toilet. Most people never think about what happens to people with disabilities in third world countries, but these men had seen it first-hand.

A few moments later, the platoon completed forensics collection.

"Dugout," the chief pushed out over the radio. The assaulters worked their way back to their vehicles for a final headcount to return to base. The Iraqi soldiers called a local police element to come to handle the body, and some remained for their arrival. Voodoo climbed into the back of the RG-33 and reached into his backpack. He pulled out a long, frozen sock shaped like a cylinder with four cold low-budget brand citrus-flavored soda cans inside. Coolers didn't fit in the vehicle, and this option guaranteed the drinks stayed cool. He handed one to Frisco, who was sitting in the front seat.

"Thanks, bro-migo! They always taste the best at the end of an op!" Frisco said with a smile. "Not a bad one tonight. Shwacked a dude, found the objective, freed a disabled guy chained to the ground. You know, the usual." The two laughed.

Radio checks passed over the net until finally, the chief pushed a full headcount to the ground force commander.

"Home Base." The vehicles rumbled, and Frisco gave the first navigation order. "All forward. Right turn fifty meters."

Voodoo relaxed. As the convoy rolled out, a green chem light happily bobbed around in the darkness. Frantic Iraqi soldiers and a reinforcement of police scampered about chasing the green glow.

The bellow of a bull echoed as a crash reverberated through the streets. A silhouette of horns broke free from the yard and chased the bobbing chem light and the flailing police into the black water beside the compound. Voodoo smiled to himself and sipped his soda.

All at once, the memory imploded with a vacuous hush. The RG-33, Frisco, the citrus soda, everything blinked out of existence. Silence.

Nothingness.

The sharp images and emotions of the mission in Iraq had surrendered to something else—an interloper, a hijacker armed with darkness, and magazines filled with words.

At first, in an empty void, Voodoo heard what he thought to be distant breaths, then the sibilance of whispers marching closer—a phrase repeating. It was soft at first, swishing in his ears.

With the rhythm of a drum, no, a heartbeat, the words drew closer, thumping into Voodoo's mind. They rapped away, forming impressions—encouragement, warning—until they articulated with clarity.

In three days, an old friend will be lost, an old friend regained. When the light of Amaterasu protects you, rise and face the eastern threat.

Snap! *Voodoo returned to the RG-33. The engines rumbled, the magazine locked into his rifle dug into his thigh, and the laces of his boots were tightly cinched around his feet.*

An overwhelming sense of dread poured over him. He wanted to shout, Not again! *when—*

BOOM!

*The blast tossed the RG-33 into the air and shock waves pulsed through them. The V-shaped hull deflected the impact, pitching the vehicle to the left. For an instant Voodoo floated, then—*Crack! *Voodoo's helmet slammed against the roof. The* *flailing body of the shooter across from him plunged into Voodoo as the earth punched back.* Crunch! *Voodoo's right arm snapped beneath the shooter's weight.*

• • •

Voodoo's eyes shot open. He inhaled sharply and sat bolt upright. Burning nerve endings lit up his arm. He rolled to pull free.

He panted.

Visions of fire blocked his eyes, citrus and gunpowder filled his nose, and electric spiders crawled over his skin. He blinked. He blinked again. Light filtered into the room through the shutters.

He swallowed.

A gray West Elm comforter. White organic cotton sheets. A pile of laundry next to a dusty acoustic guitar.

Like the moment before a car crash, his body and mind activated every fight or flight response only to awaken to nothing. His hand reached out to his left in his king-size bed, to where his wife once slept, to the spot that now remained empty—no comforting hand to squeeze back.

He slid his hand back and forth across the empty sheets anyway.

Just think of her. His breaths calmed; his pounding heartbeat slowed.

Just like every other night, Voodoo didn't choose his memories or his dreams; they chose him. And he always found the explosion. Always disturbing. Yet tonight something disturbed him even more: the voice.

Inside his mind, the mechanical arms of a clock engaged. *Tick, tick, tick, tick...* Voodoo didn't know what it all meant;

he didn't know where to start searching for answers. The voice mentioned Amaterasu, the Japanese sun goddess, but he was in San Diego. He knew only that he had three days to decipher his dreams, to follow the call of the night's siren.

He would soon learn he wasn't alone.

CHAPTER 6

Skull Rapid

WESTWATER CANYON
SOUTHERN UTAH, USA

The townspeople of Westwater once believed the rapids of Hades Canyon, as they called it, were so violent they would smash fish against the walls and dash their brains on the rocks. The infamous Skull Rapid, midway down the canyon, forces the river to the right before careening left. The dramatic detour creates an unforgiving hydraulic churn. It feeds into a violent whirlpool called the Room of Doom and an enormous rock wall upon which water erupts thirty feet into the air called the Rock of Shock.

Gavin stood beside the river. Ancient rock layers of black Vishnu Schist and red Wingate Sandstone towered above, split in half by the eroding waters of the silty brown Colorado River flowing beside him. It was day two of the trip, the day when every decision mattered as he and his fellow guides prepared to usher fifteen customers on three rafts through the whitewater rush of Hades Canyon. Gavin knew the dangers. Joel and Ally had taught him how to anticipate the flow of the river, how to read the rapids. It was a rite of passage in Gavin's family, and since the events of 9/11 a few years earlier, this would be his only real chance to prove himself knowing that a very different life waited for him at the end of the summer. Before he went to sleep last night, he was confident everything would go along without a hitch. Until he dreamt...

Something about today is off, Gavin thought. And it had everything to do with the dream he had the night before.

He knew the water behind Skull Rapid was eighty feet deep. The river passed over a flat boulder, and the sharp change in elevation created a stationary wave that faced upstream in a formation called a "hole." Frowning holes held the water in, whereas smiling holes pushed it out. Debris trapped in the rapid would get thrust into the depths.

Victims of Skull's frowning hole submerged so quickly the deep water burst their sinuses. Their limbs locked up in the frigid temperatures. Trapped in unexpected, suspended animation, few survive. For this reason, rafting companies only trusted experienced river guides with customers in the canyon. Today would be Gavin's first shot—with customers that is. At nineteen, his youthful confidence coupled with his training usually held off concerns. Not so much today.

Don't worry about it. It's not like dreams can tell the future.

Gavin tightened his black Chaco sandals. The early morning light on the edge of the cliffs painted the western canyon in gold, and Gavin adjusted his Vagabond River Expeditions blue hat to shade his eyes. He tossed some dry bags into his raft and headed back to help pack the other rafts.

After breaking camp, they would push through Dolores Canyon rapids, then Marble Canyon, Staircase, Big Hummer,

Funnel Falls, Surprise, then eddy out into an open space called Cocaine Cove to catch a breath and make ready for Skull. From there, they would set a safe distance between the boats. They wouldn't stay too long, though.

"If you're looking long, you're looking wrong," the guides would always say. Observe the path of the water, determine the best route through the obstacles, and then make it happen. Guides that spend too long fixating on the rapid would trip up. It's easy to be overwhelmed by the power of the more severe rapids. This group had no intention of making that mistake.

"How're you feelin', Gavin?" Ally asked as she packed up her gear, her frizzy brown hair mashed underneath her blue Vagabond hat, her lips pursing when she smiled like she was sucking on something sour.

"Good, I guess. Could be better."

"That's not the answer I was expecting," Ally said.

"Sorry. You know how sometimes you have a dream that sorta sticks with you? I mean, most dreams you forget right away while others just—"

"I once spent an entire day angry at my ex-boyfriend for something he did in my dream. Does that count?" she asked.

He grinned. "That totally counts. And for the record, if I ever make you angry in your dreams, I apologize."

Ally smiled. "You can't apologize for something you won't do."

"Not even for something your subconscious hasn't made up yet?"

The two laughed.

"How's your head feeling? Do you have a headache again today?" Ally asked.

"Come to think of it, no. I feel pretty good."

"Good. You're gonna need to stay focused today runnin' the canyon for the first time with your own boat."

Joel, Gavin, and Ally worked for a company based out of Moab, Utah, called Vagabond River Expeditions. The river companies in Moab were like small high school cliques. Rich, snooty kids, preppy kids, jocks, and outcasts. That's where Vagabond fit in: the misfits of the hierarchy. The owner, Rob, had an adjacent property where an abandoned steakhouse called The Outpost once operated. Now, the open steak pit and dining room porch served as a makeshift housing area for semi-homeless river guides.

Gavin and some of the other guides slept in tents there between trips to save money. The furniture from the dump, the water they stole from the motel next door through a hose, and semireliable electricity from who-knows-where made for a cozy little home. Adding to the ambiance was an old kegerator full of alcohol and a blow-up adult doll somebody found on the side of the highway.

Gavin hadn't been quite sure how things were going to work out when he first came to work for Vagabond. Two other companies, the preppies and the jocks, turned him down despite him being related to one of the owners.

None of that mattered now. Gavin was happy to have a job working in the canyon, and even happier to call Vagabond home, at least for the time being. *At the end of this summer, though...*

"Be sure to rig for flip, not rig for trip, Gavin," Joel told him. Gavin knew that mild float days, with no whitewater, didn't require the boat's gear to be secured as tightly so customers could access the cooler for snacks.

This wasn't one of those days. A recent heatwave in Colorado sent melted water from the remaining snowpack cascading into the canyon in the form of high water, fueling the anger of Hades Canyon.

"Everyone gather around," Joel called out. The fifteen guests sat on the ground, ready for their instructions. "We need to go over a few things before we get on the river. First of all, today we are going to hit some pretty big rapids. This is what you all came here for and what we love doing. However, I must remind you of all the risks.

"We are fifty miles from civilization of any kind. There is no way out of this canyon except through those rapids. The walls of the canyon are too steep to climb, and the water is too fast to try to fight. So, on that note, let's talk about what to do in case you fall out of the boat.

"The rocks in this river don't stick out because the water is shallow, they stick out because they are massive. The water is really deep. So, if you fall out, grab your life jacket and tuck in a ball. The flotation will bring you to the surface. Try to put your feet in front of you and face downstream. If the water pushes you into the rocks, use your feet to bounce off them. Don't try to stand up if you aren't extremely sure of your footing. If you try to stand on the rocks and your foot gets stuck, the water may push you over and pin you down.

"Floating with your feet in front of you in a semitucked position should prevent this 'foot entrapment.' If your butt gets stuck in between two rocks, well, that's called a 'butt entrapment.' That's never happened before, so we'll be sure to pull out one of those fancy new digital cameras, take your picture, and make you famous." Joel winked. The guests let out a nervous laugh.

Joel continued for another ten minutes and reassured the guests they were in good hands. He mentioned the throw ropes near the guides. He helped them rehearse catching the rope, then pulling it over their shoulders and facing downstream; facing upstream meant all the water would be rushing in their face making it difficult to breathe and hold on. He also discussed how to pull someone out by their life jacket with their back to the raft.

"Don't ever pull on their arm. The force of the water will dislocate their shoulder." A few wide eyes and fidgeting followed that statement. "Here's the plan for today. The river is broken into two sections: everything before Skull and everything after Skull. The rapids will gradually get more intense as we go along."

The customers blinked.

"I don't need you to remember all the names of the rapids even though they're cool. The only thing I want you to remember is this: After a rapid called Surprise, there's a cove on the right side of the river called Cocaine Cove. Before you ask, yes, it was called that because people used to do coke there. No, I don't have any coke."

Nervous laughter relieved a bit of tension. One guy sighed and said, "Bummer."

"We'll most likely stop the boats at Cocaine Cove to regroup before dropping into Skull. Cocaine Cove is something called an 'eddy.' Stones in the river divert water behind them and force the current to move upstream. The line where the water moves in two different directions is called an 'eddy fence.'

"Eddies can be a safe place but can be dangerous as well. The deep water in the canyon may cause the eddy water to bubble or boil up at random times. These are called 'explosive eddies.' Skull is the very next rapid after Surprise, and it's only a few hundred yards downstream from there. At high water, it comes quickly, so stopping in the cove helps us keep a proper distance. That way, we don't run into each other yet stay close enough to help each other out. If anything happens, listen to the guide and remember what we just taught you."

Ally instructed the customers to submerge their orange flotation devices in the river before putting them on. "This will allow us to strap them down tighter. The river has a nasty habit of ripping people out of loose life jackets," Ally said rather matter-of-factly. A heavyset man wiped the sweat from his forehead; he looked pale.

Everyone seemed ready. The customers gave each other fist bumps, jumped up and down, and slapped each other on the back to motivate. The river guides slipped on their slick vest-like kayak life jackets, each adorned with a fixed-blade knife in the event of entanglement.

"No, I'd rather hold on to it myself," a male voice said behind Gavin. He turned around to see an older man clutching a dry bag tightly against his chest. A thick coat of SPF 50 zinc sunscreen covered his face. His Columbia shirt and pants, Teva sandals, and wide-brimmed hat appeared fresh off the shelf. He stood next to an attractive middle-aged blonde woman.

She leaned close to him. "Did you do it last night?"

The man nodded.

She patted him on the shoulder. "I'm so sorry. We're here for you," she said. "Come on, girls."

Two teenagers followed her over to the rafts. One gave Gavin a warm smile, looped her loose hair behind her ear, then turned to get onto Joel's boat.

Gavin zipped up his life jacket and helped a customer onto his rig. In the corner of his eye, he caught the older man stealing glances at him, and it wasn't the first time.

Gavin stepped back to where Joel and Ally happened to be close together. Gavin leaned in and spoke with a hushed voice.

"Hey, I think there's something off with one of the portable bags of water," Gavin said, using an old nickname guides gave passengers who only offer dead weight in the boat.

Joel looked over his shoulder.

"Which one?"

"The Asian guy in Ally's raft. He's...I dunno, gripping his dry bag like his life depends on it. I keep catching him leering at me. It started yesterday."

Ally chortled and gave a dismissive hand gesture. "Remember those guys with the dry bag we thought were transporting drugs and they turned out to be carrying their father's ashes? People are weird. I wouldn't worry about it. I mean, look at him, he looks like some scientist or something. He's probably scared out of his mind."

Joel and Gavin stole a glance, then chuckled.

"You're right. It's probably nothing," Gavin said.

"Are you good otherwise?" Joel asked one last time before they set out, his signature crooked smile looking especially crooked. "Just follow my lead, and we'll be fine. The water's looking a bit higher today, so be ready. It feels like we're around 17,000 cubic feet per second. Skull's gonna be rockin'."

"How deep is that?" a French man asked with a slight accent as he hopped into the conversation.

"A cubic foot is about the size of a basketball. Seventeen thousand cubic feet per second means that roughly 17,000 basketballs are floating past us every second." The French man's eyes widened.

"But the river is so narrow! How can so much water be passing by so quickly?"

"I told you it was deep." Joel smiled. "This canyon plays for keeps." A young couple preparing to board Ally's boat gave each other a goofy grin with anxious excitement.

Joel, Gavin, and Ally lined the three blue boats in that order. The most experienced guide would find the best line in each rapid, and the others would follow. The least qualified boat would ride in the middle with the other two to buffer on each end in case of a lost passenger or overturned raft. Unlike other rivers, dumping the boat in this canyon meant everyone might have to swim all the way to the last rapid before rescue. It was a sobering thought.

The passengers loaded onto each boat, and the respective guides were the last to enter as Joel embarked, followed by Gavin, then Ally. An egret searching the mud in the delta took flight at the sound of the rafts scraping off the beach.

At the sight of it, Gavin's thoughts wandered, images appeared, and words from his dream whispered in his mind.

The crane's blood is in your veins. A plan drawn, a plan revised. Hades will reach for Persephone. No coins for Charon, you shall not pass.

He shook the words from his head and the unsettling images that came with them. He needed to stay focused. He had five people's lives in his hands and Skull Rapid waiting in the belly of Hades Canyon.

Don't worry about it, he told himself. *It's not like dreams can tell the future...right?*

CHAPTER 7
Gaining Acceptance

"I'll be at the Directorate building," Voodoo said into the phone. "Just enter the grinder and let somebody know you're looking for me."

"I knew that I could rely on you, Voodoo," Frisco said. "See you soon, bro."

Voodoo pressed the red button to end the call.

His eyes burned. They always burned. He hated waking up as much as he hated going to sleep. But he always wanted both those things at the same time.

He blinked and thought about the call.

Frisco. Stu. Even though his nightmares projected crisp images from his past, it had been years since Voodoo last saw Stu and Frisco in real life. And they wanted to meet with him.

Voodoo placed his feet on the carpet. The soft white pile compressed under his toes. He wiped away the strain of the last night's "rest" from his head with the back of his hand.

The voice, Voodoo thought. *It's back. And now Frisco wants to see me.*

Voodoo pictured Frisco in the RG-33, the smell of citrus and gunpowder fresh in his nostrils. He saw Stu's massive figure that night in Iraq, giving him a nod.

A nod from Stu—the simple gesture epitomized everything Stu had ever given Voodoo. Acceptance. *Not every part of my dreams is bad.*

His mind wandered to the time he first met Stu and Frisco.

• • •

"We've got a new tech with us on this training trip," one of the shooters said.

"I think the new term is 'enabler,'" the platoon chief clarified.

I hate that term. It makes me sound like the help.

"Tell me why we need these guys again?"

"They find the targets. Without them, we don't get any ops once we're down range. If you have a problem with this guy, send him back to me. We had to fire the last 'enabler.' I don't suspect this guy will be any different," the chief said, as if Voodoo was deaf or no more than a disposable tool.

It was a cold February afternoon as they stood at 7,000 feet of elevation in the Wasatch Mountains, Utah. A line of shooters, in their gray layered Patagonia winter wear, shuffled into a long line. Their snowshoes held them aloft above the fresh powder, rucksacks anchored them to the earth.

Just stick your head down, put in the work, *Voodoo thought.* They'll come around. They always come around.

The snow crunched under Stu's and Frisco's feet as they made their way over to Voodoo.

"Listen, I don't want you here," Stu said. "You're not special. You're not a shooter. We fought for years to get here. Broke our backs to become special operators and you just stroll up."

Not special. I'll remember that.

"Relax, Stu. Very few ops nowadays are done without guys like...what's your name?"

"Voodoo. Everyone just calls me Voodoo."

"Is there a story behind that, or do you just think you're cool?" Frisco asked.

"Definitely a story behind it. That's what my last platoon called me. And the one before that. And the one before that."

"Holy... How many pumps have you done? I didn't realize dudes like you have been around that long," Frisco said. Flurries of snow blew between them as the wind picked up.

Stu jumped in. "I don't care what you've done. You're with us now. Our last enabler fell out on this evolution, couldn't cut it. Said his 'calves hurt' or some other bull crap." The giant of a man felt it necessary to intimidate Voodoo. They were a bunch of kids on the playground sizing each other up. Compared to these guys, at five-eight, 165 pounds, and half-Japanese, Voodoo didn't size up too well. He'd prove them wrong.

Voodoo knew what would happen. They would ignore him like an annoying little brother, make snide comments, peck at him.

Be patient. Keep your head down.

"Button it up, ladies! The slopes are now closed to the public. We're going to hike up this Black Diamond to 9,000 feet where we'll camp for the night. Move out," the chief ordered.

The peak drew Voodoo's eyes upward. The clouds split just briefly enough to reveal the 12,000-foot mountain looming over them, a sharp Black Diamond ski course writhing up the slope. Voodoo cinched his rifle tight against his chest, gripped the hiking poles in his hands, dug the points of the poles into the snow, and confronted the mountain.

It wasn't a brisk pace, but relentless. Pills of Diamox kept acute mountain sickness at bay, but everyone needed to stay vigilant and watch out for headaches—the first sign of the sickness, which could escalate to high altitude cerebral edema. Voodoo rucked behind Frisco, keeping the space between them tight. Their squad ran point; they were the first up the mountain.

Several hours later, they made camp. They shoved Voodoo with a new guy into a tiny two-man tent. They heated up water with a Jetboil, put it into a Nalgene bottle, and shoved it into the foot of their sleeping bags to keep warm. Temperatures dropped well below zero degrees Fahrenheit.

At 2:30 a.m., a finger flicked Voodoo in the forehead.

"Be ready to move out in ten minutes," Stu said. Voodoo couldn't see his face in the darkness; the cold air from outside the tent pricked Voodoo's skin like daggers.

Ten minutes? That means I have five.

In moments, Voodoo had packed his ruck, packed the tent, put on his kit, and stood ready in the dark before predawn. One of the new guys struggled. Voodoo stabbed his poles in the ground and gave the new guy a hand. Alpha Squad, the point element, stood ready well before anyone else in the rest of the troop.

"We were able to coordinate with a private landowner out here and we've got a little surprise for you," one of the training cadre said. "We're gonna conduct a little stress test to get you all warmed up."

Voodoo knew what that meant—shoot, move, and communicate.

I wonder if they'll even let me play...

The training cadre walked up to each shooter, wrote their name on a piece of tape, and stuck it to the back of their bump helmets. Everyone rucked to a crest, fresh snow made for slow going as they reached a flattened area, away from the ski slopes, hidden in the darkness of the mild blizzard. At 50, 100, and 150 meters, target silhouettes spread out in front of them, barely within sight even with night vision. The intermittent reflection of the crescent moon on the snow helped.

"Individually, you all have one minute to move tactically through the snow and engage the targets in the right order. Move quickly; the longer we take to get this done, the longer everyone freezes. As soon as you're done, we need to summit before the slopes open."

One by the one, shooters attacked the challenge, stumbling through the snow, taking out the targets. Some were better than others. Voodoo already knew this. Despite their reputation as multifaceted killers, no one person was good at all of them.

A member of the training cadre turned to Voodoo. "You're up," he said. "Just like any other situation, if you get confused, do something. It doesn't matter what, just do something."

Voodoo exhaled sharply and got after it. One target, two targets, three, four, five, then six. Plink! Plink! Plink! Plink! Plink! Plink! Done.

Voodoo stepped back into the formation of trembling warfighters, fighting to keep warm in their puffy jackets.

"That's everyone. We'll post your times when we get up top. New guys, pick up the brass and clean up the silhouettes."

The new guys looked at each other as the others headed out. "How the hell are we supposed to find all the spent brass in a blizzard?"

"You don't," Voodoo said quietly as he walked over to them. "So, we'll get what we can."

Voodoo looked like anyone else in the darkness, any other new guy picking up the brass. New guys have to prove themselves. Voodoo was far from a new guy. He'd already been on over a *hundred combat operations downrange. Nobody here knew that. Nobody here cared.*

Be patient. Keep your head down.

Voodoo dug through the snow, demoralized and frustrated by the stinging pain in his fingers and feet. Frozen toes. There is nothing worse for morale than frozen toes.

Staying to clean up brass put them behind, so they had to sprint up the mountain to catch up. Voodoo's muscles screamed as he stomped up the slope, conquering his way to the top.

It didn't take long before he found his spot right behind Frisco. Stu bounded up the mountain with his massive legs just ahead.

"Whoa! You got up here quick," Frisco said. "You don't have to walk so close, by the way." Voodoo could feel Frisco smiling under his cold weather gear.

"Yeah," Voodoo replied. "I do."

Frisco's hidden smile grew wider. "Hey man, you like Bob Ross?"

The question threw Voodoo completely off guard. He laughed out loud. "The painter guy?"

"Yeah, I've got the whole platoon way into him. We call it the 'moment of zen.' Everyone shuts up once a week and just watches the dude paint. When we get back, you should join us."

The frigid wind howled as Voodoo adjusted his balaclava.

"Sounds good, man," Voodoo replied and chuckled to himself. Every platoon had a weird quirk. Voodoo had just found it. Voodoo later learned that Frisco, unlike anyone else, saw people for what they really were. He was smart, a good leader, and open-minded. Voodoo wished everyone were like Frisco.

They soon arrived at the ski lift at 12,000 feet. It was still dark but one of the ski lift operators had left the door open for everyone to get warm. Two platoons of shooters, nearly forty guys, packed into the room, dropped their gear, and removed their outer layers.

The training cadre found a whiteboard near the office and started writing down the results from the stress test: a name, a time, and a score. The list labeled everyone equally. Voodoo slipped over when he had the chance and made a startling discovery. Voodoo shot in the top 25 percent. He outshot thirty of the forty elite warriors standing around him.

Not special.

The platoon chief walked up behind Voodoo. The chief slid his finger across the whiteboard, removing Voodoo's name from the rankings, making sure Voodoo got a good look as he did it.

"These are shooters' scores," he said to Voodoo.

Voodoo thought of several snarky comebacks, mouthy phrases that he would have spit at anyone else growing up. But he couldn't upset the wolf pack behind him, especially not when the alpha stood challenging him. Voodoo had a second-degree black belt. He could hold his own. But years of patience taught him that manipulating people slowly is always the better path. Gain their trust. Wear them down.

"Roger that, Chief," Voodoo replied, but not before realizing the chief's scores fell well below his.

"Voodoo!" Stu's voice boomed from behind him. Voodoo turned to see Stu holding a bag of spent brass one of the new guys handed him. What now? *The new guy looked over at Voodoo as well, the fear clear on his face: Had they picked up enough? Or was this something else? The rest of the room looked at Stu first then snapped their head over to Voodoo.*

Blood rushed to Voodoo's face. His body temperature spiked as the room became a hundred degrees hotter. Voodoo prepared for the worst.

"You may not have known what you were getting yourself into...but you put out like a shooter."

The new guy smiled at Voodoo. Frisco pumped his eyebrows. Stu gave him a nod.

And just like that, and just like every platoon Voodoo had ever worked with, Voodoo was in.

• • •

Voodoo's mind shifted from the snowy mountains back to the present, to his feet resting on the white carpet beneath him.

The timing of the call from Frisco would have shocked Voodoo had it not been for the voice in his dream. Even more than Stu, Voodoo always saw Frisco as his brother.

And now Frisco needed his help.

Voodoo got up, showered, threw on his uniform, and grabbed an energy drink from the fridge. He left his dreams from the night before in the sweat-soaked sheets of his empty bed. The same bed that he once shared with his wife.

Amid the many decisions he made in life, he never once regretted loving her. Not a day went by, though, that Voodoo didn't regret failing her. And with the specter of his many mistakes, and a prophetic voice echoing the words from his nightmare, he prepared to meet his fate.

Voodoo grabbed his keys and headed out the door. He had questions, the clock was ticking, and apparently, Frisco and Stu had the answers.

CHAPTER 8

The Directorate

Through an open passageway inside the Directorate building, Voodoo noticed Frisco and Stu swipe their badges at a metal door on the opposite side of the open asphalt lot called the "grinder."

People always said Stu looked like "The Mountain" from *Game of Thrones*. But, walking together, the two reminded Voodoo of Ivan Drago and Rocky Balboa. Except Stu had considerably more blond hair all over his body. And Frisco looked like a less muscular version of the Italian Stallion.

As a failed professional BMX star and a former lineman for the University of Nebraska, Frisco and Stu seemed an unlikely pairing. Their love for their country and the pride that came from working with the best combat operators in the business brought them together. The strength of their brotherhood and the personnel in Naval Special Warfare kept them there.

Three junior personnel in uniform loaded black cases through a sizeable open door on the back of a twenty-five-foot-long white trailer parked outside the warehouse. They traded insults as a form of humor as Stu and Frisco approached.

A grunt lugging equipment noticed Frisco and put down the black Pelican case he was carrying.

"Hey, I'm looking for the Directorate. Any idea if I'm in the right place?" Frisco asked.

"You must be the guys looking for Voodoo. Let me show you. My name is Freddie, but everyone calls me Sparks." He extended his freckled and muscular hand. Freddie "Sparks" Davidson's thick red hair matched his personality—constantly fired up.

"Eric Francisco. But everyone calls me Frisco. This is Stu Slater."

The giant and Sparks clasped hands.

"Yeah, Voodoo said you'd be coming by. Let me show you our new digs!" Sparks nearly skipped across the grinder at the opportunity to play tour guide. They entered the warehouse. More chain-link separated the open space and a high ceiling into discrete sections.

The ceiling stretched forty feet high. Large shelves packed with equipment lined the left and right sides. The far wall had several forty-eight-inch TV screens gripped to the cinder block, and workbenches sat stationed in the middle of the room. The calypso beat of reggae music played from a Bluetooth speaker.

Voodoo tracked the gaze of his old friends, taking in the broken drone arms and motors that lay in a boneyard of carbon fiber. Radio-controlled cars and other ground robots were in another section beside solar panels and batteries. A female technician conducted surgery on a robot dog with no head in the middle of the room.

Sparks rambled about photogrammetry, training AI drones in virtual reality, and the future of drone warfare. Stu's face went blank. It was apparent little of what Sparks said remained in Stu's head. Voodoo grinned.

"What's in those big cases?" Frisco asked.

Sparks proceeded to explain the pride and joy of the Directorate. Leveraging commercial technology from Silicon Valley, including tech from flying car research, their most recent prototype involved combining a variety of these technologies into one deployable kit they called the "Business-in-a-Box," or BIB.

The BIB was a system of systems, with a fixed-wing electric unmanned vertical takeoff and landing (eVTOL) aircraft with a sixteen-foot wingspan at its foundation. It broke down into two cases, each shaped like a coffin.

Mounted on the bottom of the aircraft was an electro-optical and infrared camera, four mounting bays for artificially intelligent drones, an entire self-sustained cellular network, and an Iridium satellite link. It was literally a flying cell tower. Also, within the kit, tactically secure cell phones connected to augmented reality glasses and contact lenses.

"Overwhelmed" didn't begin to explain Stu's and Frisco's faces. Stu looked like a lost child at a science museum.

The men and women of the Directorate were a different breed. They were technicians—in telecommunications, artificial intelligence, robotics, augmented and virtual reality—who solved problems with techniques the average shooter never dreamed of. Each member was hand-selected by their chief, who finally decided to make his presence known.

"Hey, Voodoo, you've got visitors," Sparks said.

A huge smile beamed across Voodoo's face as he walked over and put out his right hand. Frisco's and Voodoo's hands clasped before they embraced in the typical bro hug, slapping each other's backs like heterosexual exclamation points.

"Did we just stumble into the land of the good idea fairies? I mean, holy crap, bro," Frisco started.

"Yeah, we got a lot going on for sure," Voodoo said, lifting one eyebrow and perusing the room with his eyes. "It's good to see you. What've you been up to?"

"I decided to put in for a commission after our last deployment together. I'm the officer in charge of my own platoon now on the East Coast with Omega. Stu here is the platoon chief."

"What's up, Stu?" Voodoo said.

Stu answered Voodoo with a nod.

"I can't imagine a better person to be an OIC, Frisco. Team guys need someone like you. I'm confident you're an amazing leader," Voodoo said, genuinely happy for his friend.

"Thanks, bro-migo. It's been a challenge."

Voodoo knew challenges. "We were lucky on our last pump together with good leaders, but I've had some dudes that... I just mean some people are better than others at this kind of thing." Sparks still stood nearby, his eyes taking in the easy familiarity of these three comrades. "You just need to know how to communicate with the shooters. Like you," Voodoo said, nodding to Stu. "Most of the time I used stick figures and dip."

Stu shrugged and then agreed, "You're not wrong."

"Except for you, Frisco, you just need cold Rip Its in a frozen sock."

"Hell yeah. Best thing ever. But only after an op." The two laughed.

"You know what sounds amazing?" Sparks jumped in. "A burrito. You guys wanna grab a burrito?" He was half squatting, giving finger guns, and looking for takers. Stu glared at him. Voodoo remembered being on the receiving end of that look.

"It's 10:30, which means you haven't eaten in an hour, Sparks. Of course you want a burrito," the female technician vivisecting the robot dog pointed out.

"Growin' boy's gotta eat. Who's in?" Sparks waited. Stu examined Sparks like a booger stuck to his finger.

"Sparks, sometimes I wonder if I should chain you to a stake in the ground...or at least put you in a bump helmet with a chem light attached to it," Voodoo replied. Frisco and Stu laughed. Sparks looked on confused, obviously missing the inside joke.

"So, your call sounded urgent. What's up?" Voodoo asked. On the surface he appeared calm. Deep down, Voodoo braced himself. *Tick, tick, tick, tick.*

"Do you have somewhere we can talk?" Frisco gestured with his thumb toward the exit.

"Follow me." Voodoo snagged a cold Red Bull from a fridge and the three walked out of the warehouse and into the main building.

"Let me know when you want to get a burrito!" Sparks yelled after them.

Upstairs, they closed the door, huddled around Voodoo's desk, and took seats. Stu's body swallowed a folding chair.

Voodoo reached into his pocket for a small Visine bottle and placed some drops in his eyes.

"I hate to say it but you're looking a bit rough," Frisco started.

Voodoo blinked hard. "You need to work on your icebreakers, Frisco." Voodoo took a swig from his Red Bull. "I'm good, man. Just got a few things keeping me up recently."

Like a voice from the darkness.

Frisco merely nodded. "Getting straight to the point, there are a couple of reasons I'm here, but the main one is that I've been asked to lead an HRT Task Force in Japan."

There it is. Japan. The voice's mention of Amaterasu echoed in his mind. And HRT stood for "Hostage Rescue Team."

I know where this is going. "Are the hostages in Japan, or are you staging there for somewhere else?" Voodoo asked.

"Not exactly sure at this point." Then came the first question Voodoo expected. "I know that you're half-Japanese, but do you speak it at all?"

"A bit. My mother was Japanese, so I grew up with it."

"Does that mean you can order food or carry on a conversation?"

"The latter."

"Okay, good. I've been asked to liaise with our Japanese counterparts, so having a native speaker will be clutch." If there was a formal invitation hiding in that statement, Voodoo missed it. "We have to leave tonight for Japan but, before we do, I have to go meet with some AI company here in town."

"It's not Xiphos AI, is it?"

Frisco blinked. "Are you familiar with them?"

"I do prototype work with startups and Xiphos is one of the better companies in town. What do you need to do there?"

"From what I've been told, a couple of scientists are missing, including an American. It appears they were taken, and the authorities have no idea who did it. A colleague of the victims is supposed to meet us there," Frisco said, his face serious.

Voodoo rubbed his chin. "Normally things like this are the jurisdiction of the FBI. You've got the State Department in the mix as well. Japan is one of the safest countries on earth. Why would they send some Task Force guys over as opposed to letting local authorities figure it out?"

Voodoo had a valid question, it seemed, because Frisco sat there for a moment searching Voodoo's desk with his brown eyes for answers and then shrugged.

"Honestly, I only know two things. An American is missing, and the government is worried about something called the 'God Algorithm.' Does that mean anything to you?"

Voodoo shook his head. "Do you think this will become some kind of KFR?"

"Kidnap for ransom? No clue. I just know that this whole thing took place within the last day, and they are throwing everything they have at it. I've never heard of a response to a missing person escalate this quickly. Usually, the chief of station and the FBI do their thing for a long while before anyone else gets called. This time it feels like they just decided to call everyone in from the get-go."

"What do you want me to do?"

"I want you to come with me, bro-chacho. My commanding officer told me that I could build my own team and request personnel from any command to help with this mission. Stu's on board. And I want you...and your toys."

Voodoo laughed. "Ah, so it's my toys you want. Typical shooter. That's what the acronym stands for, right? Steal Everything And Leave?" Voodoo put his hands behind his head, looked out the window of his office, and leaned back in his chair.

"You know what I mean." Frisco almost sounded wounded. "Is there anything going on at home keeping you from heading out there with me?"

Voodoo's smile drifted away. He chewed on his cheek as he stared out the window.

"I know we haven't spoken in a long time, and I'm not all that big on social media, but...you haven't heard?"

"Heard what?" Frisco asked. Voodoo didn't want to say it out loud, but he knew he had to. He brought his hands down to his lap and looked back at Frisco.

"There's no one at home... My wife died of cancer about a year ago."

Voodoo always tried to emotionally disassociate the words from the pain as they left his mouth, but this time the sting in his chest hurt more than usual. He knew that Frisco felt the same by the sunken expression on his face.

The more time someone spends in the military, the more one learns that home life keeps you sane. It gives you purpose. Those without proper support, and even those with support, have a hard time dealing with the difficulty of being a warfighter let alone posttraumatic stress disorder (PTSD), traumatic brain injury (TBI), the loss of your friends, or that catchall diagnosis referred to as "operator syndrome." The military created dozens of programs to help people adapt, but many still self-medicated or, worse, took matters into their own hands...

Voodoo treated his loss and PTSD with a borderline destructive obsession with his job. He supplemented his fixation with CrossFit, distance runs, and consuming more energy drinks than a Korean *StarCraft* eSports team. *I know my triggers*, he would tell himself. *Just keep busy. Push through. You'll get over it.*

From the outside, his naturally positive disposition and lack of traditional substance abuse appeared healthy but, deep down, Voodoo knew his insomnia and attempts at perpetual distraction were unsustainable. Were it not for a hatred of alcohol stemming from the loss of a friend when he was a kid, Voodoo would most likely be in a far worse state.

Voodoo extended and rubbed his right arm. His mind flashed briefly to his dream. *Tick, tick, tick, tick.*

Frisco finally broke the silence. "I'm sorry, man. I can't imagine doing this job without my wife or my daughters for that matter." There was a quiet pause. "What kind of cancer was it?"

"Pancreatic. We didn't discover it until really late. There were other symptoms and indicators early on, but the doctors just weren't tracking it. Once they did, though...she only had months left."

The playful witch doctor that fought in Iraq was now a weary warrior of life.

"That was part of the reason I stayed here at the Directorate for so long. Even if I wanted to go on another deployment, my wife was getting sick, and... One minute, you know what to expect each day you live; you know what to expect when you come home at night. The next... Long story short, no, nothing is keeping me at home. The Directorate is my life, and I work for the warfighter. You want my help, and I'm there." Voodoo snapped back from the cloud in his mind that was forming. "I have one ask."

"Name it."

"I want to bring Sparks with me."

Frisco chuckled. "The burrito guy? Why him?"

"I know that he comes across like an obnoxious ball of energy, but he's sharp and really tough. He's good with tech like me, but he's strong like Stu."

Stu, who had remained silent throughout the conversation, squinted as if to tell Voodoo no such man existed.

"I'll need his help with some of the gear I want to bring. Also, you may want to take someone with you onto the objective, and Sparks is your guy."

"You're my guy, Voodoo. I mean...you know what I mean." The two laughed.

"Glad you clarified that last part. You almost sounded sincere."

"I don't see why Sparks can't come along," Frisco said.

Stu shook his head and folded his arms. Voodoo wondered if Sparks would ever see a nod from the man.

"Good. I'll let Sparks know that he needs to prep the BIB for transit. I'll have him coordinate with Stu as to where he needs to be with the gear. In the meantime, when do we need to get over to Xiphos?"

"Right now."

CHAPTER 9
The Visitor

DOWNTOWN SAN DIEGO, CALIFORNIA, USA

Dr. Naomi Shimoda exited the elevator on the sixteenth floor of 501 West Broadway in downtown San Diego. She quickly checked herself in the reflection of the opposing elevator doors and straightened her pencil skirt, black blazer, and crisp pink button-down. Naomi ran her hand along her black hair, still fastidiously tight in a high black ponytail. She was a slight woman of no more than one hundred pounds with a round, regal, and youthful face that hid her actual age. Her straight nose and sharp eyes gave her an elegant intensity.

She towed a small rolling bag and a designer hobo. Behind her business exterior, she hid decades of research in her laptop and carried the weight of her friends' lives on her shoulders.

As Naomi entered the headquarters of Xiphos AI, she took in the atmosphere. Art made of faux grass and moss decorated the walls. Computer scientists and software engineers loitered in various stages of development, ranging from coding binges to complete distraction. Some wore Bose headphones with computer monitors rotated vertically to view long streams of code while others struggled to manage little more than a laptop. Hipsters stacked tape cassettes on their desks next to piles of energy drinks. LaCroix sparkling water cans filled the kitchen on the opposite side of the room; cold brew coffee was on tap.

Taka-chan would love it here, Naomi thought.

The receptionist motioned her to a glass conference room, and she made her way over. Six men and a woman stood as she walked in. She exchanged pleasantries first with the CEO, a fit, thirtysomething, Korean American named Janet Han. She then greeted Devon Lim, the CFO, then Andy Smith, the CTO, who seemed like average guys.

Then there were the next four.

Naomi felt she was looking at the human embodiment of testosterone. One of them was so big Naomi wondered if he could be classified as a human.

"I'm Frisco," the first one said. Naomi's eyes widened as she took in the massive figure beside Frisco that also rose to his feet. "Don't be alarmed at Stu's size," Frisco started. "He's a big teddy bear. You know what? Feel free to call him Stu-Bear."

"No, I'd prefer you didn't." The giant put out his hand and swallowed hers with his grip. "I'm Stu."

Naomi then shook Frisco's hand as well.

"And these two gentlemen are Sparks and—"

"Voodoo. Everyone just calls me Voodoo."

Naomi took a seat. Outside the Xiphos AI conference room window, the bright sunlight shimmered on the water of San Diego Harbor as a large Navy destroyer passed under the bridge in the distance. Sailboats tacked across the bay.

In just five hours since landing in Los Angeles and receiving the news of her friends' disappearances, Naomi's life had become an emotional blur. She hoped this random meeting would shed some light on her predicament and her nightmare would end. She collected her thoughts and her emotions to remain focused.

Andy, the CTO, verbally stepped over himself as he tried to convene the meeting. Andy was tall, almost as tall as the Stu-Bear, but extremely thin with scarecrow-like mannerisms. He was a white man with the air of Ivy League education about him.

"Last month, our board members set us up with the opportunity to brief the SECDEF," Andy said.

"Hang on, what?" Frisco was not expecting that apparently.

"Yes. Two of our board members are friends with the secretary of defense from when he was still in the military. He was in town promoting some senior flag officers at Miramar. They set up a meeting for us and we briefed him on what we can do. He said he'd be in touch. We just didn't expect it to be so soon, or under such dire circumstances."

"And what is it that your company does?" Naomi asked. She interlaced her fingers and rested them on the table with her back straight.

Janet jumped in. "Crowd-sourced data processing. We also do a lot of work with machine learning models and advanced algorithm development."

"What do you mean by algorithms and models? Stu-Bear here has a short attention span," Frisco said. Voodoo chuckled. Stu-Bear did not.

Janet continued, "Of course. Machine learning is a fancy way of saying how a computer understands things." Janet went on to explain it as a field of study concerned with the design and development of algorithms and techniques that allow computers to learn, what many associated with artificial intelligence.

"So, think of it this way, a computer sees everything in zeroes and ones. The easiest example is computer vision.

"Imagine you take a picture. You can look at that picture and tell the computer which pixels in an image represent a person. The computer will convert the pixels to zeroes and ones. The computer will then remember that picture and use it as a reference. Then, you show it another picture and tell it that picture also represents a person. The computer will compare the two, determine what pixels are consistent using statistics, and use that to create a model for reference. The more pictures you give it, the better the model. This is sometimes called a 'neural network,' but the math used to make this model is referred to as an 'algorithm.'"

"Seems simple enough," Frisco said as he followed along. "But doesn't that take a lot of processing power?"

"We have two parts to our company—the part we present to the public and the part we are offering to the government. The public version will involve people signing up to offer their computers like an Airbnb. During certain times of the day, people can rent out processing capacity from their gaming consoles or computers. People or companies from all over the world will log into our service and request a certain amount of processing power.

"The incentive to people renting out their computers will be credit to buy new gaming consoles or they can cash out. Companies processing massive amounts of data and machine learning get processing power on the cheap. Companies who use this service are not allowed to know which computers are processing their data and vice versa. We can then scale out the processing across a secure network and continually increase the amount of capacity."

Everyone in the room nodded. From her work with Dr. Hawkins, Naomi was very familiar with machine learning but had never heard of anything like what they were doing at Xiphos AI.

"What is the part you are offering to the government?" Naomi asked.

"Now, the government variant of this is significantly more aggressive *and* sensitive in nature. What we've created is the ability to process information using as much or as little of the internet as we like. Most computers use weak security settings. Instead of targeting specific computers, we can target every computer with weak security in an idle state and then momentarily slave them to our network.

"Imagine if you could use 2 percent of every computer on earth for whatever you wanted. It wouldn't be a constant process and it wouldn't last very long. It would present itself as a short blip on most computers and the processing would be done. But, technically, we can use that same process for slaving the computers to our network for pulling small amounts of select data."

"The internet would become a supercomputer, but you'd be stealing the real estate. Is that correct?" Voodoo said.

Andy stepped in to respond. "Exactly, but only temporarily. And we wouldn't be leaving malware or any evidence we were there." He shook his hands in front of his body as if the gesture absolved him of any wrongdoing.

"Why would it be necessary to steal the real estate, though? Would the legal implications not vastly outweigh the benefits?" Naomi asked.

Andy continued, "Of course. We see this capability as a nuclear option of sorts. We look at it this way: Data is only useful if you can process it effectively. The US doesn't demand data from civilians. Other countries, like China, have the ability to demand data of every one of their users whenever they want it. Every company in China is either subsidized or contractually liable to support the government whenever asked. AI needs both processing power and data to grow and China has both from a billion people available whenever they want it. That puts the Western world at a significant disadvantage."

"So, what you are saying is that you have the ability to process data or an algorithm at a massive scale. Bigger than any other supercomputer, technically?" Naomi asked.

"Indeed. If you have the right algorithm," Andy said.

"Do you run algorithms yourself?" Naomi asked.

"Some. Mostly convolution neural networks for computer vision or natural language processing," Andy replied. "Are you familiar with that?"

"Extremely. I'm an optogeneticist from the University of Tokyo and my work with Dr. Ichikawa and Taka, I mean, Dr. Hawkins focused on computer science and predictive algorithms."

Naomi noticed Devon's and Stu's eyes ping-pong back and forth in the technical jargon—laced information exchange.

"And they're the ones that are missing, correct?" Janet asked carefully from the head of the table.

Naomi nodded her head.

"When you say optogenetics, are you talking about... Okay, I have no idea what that is," Devon, the CFO and least technical person in the room, admitted. He was a short man with a receding hairline, a double-breasted suit, and a rainbow flag lapel pin. His gold tie tack and potbelly fighting the buttons of his white dress shirt seemed out of place with the fresh startup atmosphere.

"Dr. Ichikawa is a neurologist who helped pioneer a new field of study that is now known as optogenetics. He experimented with ways to see how the nerves in the brain communicate, and he wanted to help repair them for people with diseases like Parkinson's. Most recently, he was interested in seeing if he could manipulate the brain using different wavelengths of light and see the results without invasively accessing the human brain. Specifically, he did not want to poke sensors into people to get information."

"Which I'm sure they appreciated," Devon jested. Everyone gave him a polite partial smile then looked back at Naomi. Any other time she would have laughed, but, at this moment, with her friends' lives on the line, it wasn't in her.

Naomi remained the consummate professional people knew her to be.

"Through this study, he focused heavily on machine learning to synthesize data and determine the best processes for conducting this research. We had found a way to use algal proteins to excite neurons in the brain. These proteins could be stimulated by light to let ions in and activate nerves.

"Well, to make this happen, we needed to find a way to deliver the proteins to the brain. We used machine learning to help us find the right type of protein. Once we found it, we needed to activate it through the bloodstream by hitting it with light."

Devon's face reminded Naomi of one of her grad school students who was about to drop her class. Stu-Bear and Sparks looked like they needed an energy drink.

"I want to say I understand how algae helped you get into the brain, but I'm not following," Devon said.

"Not algae...algal proteins. Just proteins. We have lots of different types of proteins in our body and we manipulated them to push a change to the neurons in the brain. That is it. The only catch is that to cause the desired effect through the bloodstream, we needed to deliver them through a virus."

The seven sat silent.

"So, let me get this straight, your project involved nerves, algae, viruses, light, and AI to fix people's brains?" Devon stated, half excited and half shocked.

"Basically, yes."

"Let me guess...you created zombies!" His head nodded as if he had cracked a great code and he smiled, letting everyone know he was pleased with himself.

Naomi finally allowed herself the slightest grin.

Idiots are delightful, she thought.

"Not hardly. Viruses are not *always* bad. There are over ten million viruses in a drop of seawater. Using them as a vehicle, we created new neural pathways. We created new ways for the brain to communicate. We had found, for some, a potential cure to life-threatening diseases."

"How many people have you been able to help with this technology?" Voodoo asked.

"Nobody as of yet. We have not been authorized to test on humans. Most of our studies have been on mice."

Andy offered, as he stroked his chin, "Indeed. That sort of thing can take time. Do you think your work has something to do with why they went missing? The work sounds pretty benign, basically."

"I think it is time I showed you all something." Naomi pulled out her phone. "After presenting the results of some of our research at MIT, I caught a flight back to Japan through LA. I got the news about their disappearance after Taka-chan failed to appear at work the next morning. It all happened while I was on my flight. As soon as I landed in LA, my phone blew up and that is when the government asked me to remain in LA before I was finally asked to come down here. Listen to this."

She thumbed her iPhone and her text messages glided across the screen. Everyone leaned forward to listen.

Naomi read the last text message she received from her friend.

"'Kenzo's in trouble. Injected something into my arm. *Kami no Enzantejun*, in my Dropbox. Keep safe. They're coming. Find out everything you can about someone named "Drag"—'

"The message stopped there. It was sent less than twelve hours ago. I cannot get a hold of any of them. The police in Japan cannot find them, and for some reason, the US government desperately wants to know where they went...as do I."

CHAPTER 10

The Coalition

Naomi's facade cracked. An unprofessional weakness bubbled to the surface, and she became emotional.

"Excuse me..."

Naomi stood, grabbed her handbag, and stepped out of the conference room. She exited Xiphos into the hallway near the elevators. Unaware of how to find the restroom, she stopped. Her feet rooted to the ground. She frantically rummaged through her purse. The tissue packet she carried everywhere was missing in action.

It took several moments before she realized her hand was wet from tears dropping from her eyes. Then it hit her. *My friends and colleagues may be dead, and my trip to the US may be the only thing that saved my life.*

An eruption of terror and mourning welled up inside her. She couldn't remember the last time she ever cried, let alone cried in public.

I am not *this person*, she thought.

Voodoo stepped out the main office doors of Xiphos holding a box of tissues. He reached out his arm and offered them without looking at her directly. She tried to hide her fragile state by keeping her back to him and immediately realized the futility. She took several and thanked him.

"Take your time. We'll be waiting inside."

"No." She sniffled. "I am fine," she lied. Naomi sobbed. She did what she could to keep her mascara from running. There were too many emotions to control.

The elevator door opened, and two Xiphos employees stepped out. They halted as they saw Naomi.

"Her dog, Puddles, just got neutered. She's taking it as well as can be expected," Voodoo said.

Who would say such a stupid thing? Then she realized how silly this probably looked. Here she stood as a grown woman in her early forties bawling in the hallway like some overdramatic, stereotypical vision of weakness. The egalitarian feminist in Naomi wanted to slap herself.

She decided to play along instead.

"Poor Puddles," Naomi said between sniffles. The Xiphos employees nodded, slightly confused, and shuffled into the office.

Naomi let out a laugh and dabbed tissues under her eyes, the levity lifting her spirit. The mischievous grin on Voodoo's face reminded Naomi of her hapa-Japanese friends back in Hawaii.

She took a deep breath and allowed herself to relax for a moment. She wiped her eyes and nose again several times as she regained her composure. She pulled out her compact and quickly fixed her makeup.

"I think I am alright now. Let's get back inside."

Voodoo nodded and gave an assuring smile. He opened the door for her, and the two reentered the conference room and took their seats at the table. Frisco visually conferred Voodoo, who gave a confirming nod for things to continue.

"I hate to just dive back into things—"

"Please, that is why we are here," she replied a little more adamantly than she intended. She lifted her chin as a display of composure.

"Of course," Frisco said. He nodded his head a few times. "Any idea why the government is so urgent to find them?" Frisco asked.

"It could have something to do with our funding."

"Who were your investors?" Voodoo asked.

"Kenzo handled most of it directly. I do know that academic institutions and private companies both invested in the research."

Frisco walked over to the SMART Board on the wall of the conference room.

"Okay, let's go through what we know. Dr. Ichikawa and Dr. Hawkins are missing. We may presume the worst, but we have no idea one way or the other. Ichikawa injected something into Hawkins according to the text." Frisco stopped and spun around. "Hang on, what the heck is that about?"

Everyone's eyes shifted to Naomi, who sat silent.

"Was it a sedative? It sounds like he gave her a sedative to, I dunno, keep her out of trouble?" Sparks considered, his red hair glowing.

"What're your ideas?" Voodoo asked Naomi directly.

"I am not sure exactly. I've had hours to consider it. Dr. Ichikawa believes that finding cures with new neural pathways was just the beginning. He felt the human mind is a model for how we should be creating algorithms.

"He kept saying it would answer so many questions, but it was something way too powerful to control, so he needed to take his time and get it right. Even though there was pressure...I mean...we felt like we needed to move quickly."

Janet leaned forward. "That sounds...ominous. What do you mean it's too powerful for someone to control?"

"There are a couple of examples I can give. First, you know how sometimes you get a feeling something is going to happen before it happens? Or animals can sense something and immediately know what it means because their lives depend on it?"

"Yeah," all seven said simultaneously before exchanging uncomfortable glances.

"Dr. Ichikawa felt that...instinct, for lack of a better word, is an example of our brains doing subconscious predictive analysis. Our brain takes in everything we see around us, processes it, and then sends the information to our sympathetic and parasympathetic nervous systems. These predictions affect fight or flight.

"Second, it is a pretty common saying that humans do not use the bulk of the processing capacity in their brains. As a neurologist, I can tell you that is nonsense, but we do have enormous capacity. Imagine if we could tap into the way that animals understand their environment and can predict things based on that information and...amplify it. He felt there is a link between how our brain's intuition and artificial intelligence both function."

Andy said, "That's absurd. People have messed around with that concept for years, but neural activity and chemical reactions in the body are not the same as zeroes and ones."

"Dr. Ichikawa genuinely believed they are. One thing that always concerned me is that I always felt like he...like he already knew how to do it, and he was not ready to share it with us. I could tell by how he already had a name for it."

"What did he call it?" Devon asked.

She leaned forward, took a deep breath, and continued in a quiet tone, "He called it '*Kami no Enzantejun.*'"

"Dr. Hawkins used that wording in the text message," Frisco said. Voodoo nodded as if he already understood.

The others looked at each other, confused.

"What does that mean?" Janet asked, looking at Frisco then back at Naomi.

"The God Algorithm."

"So, there's this team of doctors working on something called the God Algorithm, and two of them have gone missing. The SECDEF wants the remaining member to work with us to track them down, and he's mobilized a bunch of Special Operations guys to go to Japan and figure things out," Sparks summarized.

"Actually, yeah. Thanks, Sparks. That brings me back to the beginning." Frisco turned back to the SMART Board and started writing. "God Algorithm. Missing doctors. Including somebody named 'Drag.'" He stepped back and studied the words.

"I think that may be short for 'dragon,'" Naomi guessed. "I am unsure, though."

Frisco turned to the room. "I think we have a good idea of where we need to go with all this information. Dr. Shimoda, if you're willing, I'd like you to come with us to help track down who did this. I've been told I need to escort you to the Japanese National Police Agency after we stop by the US embassy. Are you alright with that?"

Naomi nodded. "Of course."

Voodoo suddenly started giving directions. "Janet, we don't have a whole lot of time before we have to get on our flight. I want you to sit down with Naomi and go over all the algorithms she has in the Dropbox and see how you can apply them.

If you're okay with that?" Voodoo gestured toward Naomi, requesting approval.

She nodded.

"Also, can you get access to any relevant data? Like video feeds or something like that?"

Naomi said, "The Tokyo authorities gave us access to some CCTV feeds near the school to help us with our research. I may be able to pull some other information through our accounts, but this is not my specialty."

Janet nodded. "Give us what you have, and I'm sure we'll figure it out," Janet said, glancing over at Andy then back at Frisco. "I just need to know what is legal and what isn't."

"Leave that up to me," Sparks said. "I'll work with Andy to figure out what we have access to, and I'll get some of our analysts looking into what legal authority we have to investigate."

Voodoo continued, "Perfect. We need that done before we leave here in the next hour or so." He then gestured toward Janet and Andy. "Use every possible resource, so we have plenty of leads before we land in Tokyo. We're losing half of a day just traveling over there. We can't lose any more." He paused to think for a moment.

"It doesn't make sense for us to leave without someone to stay behind," Voodoo said as he paced the back wall.

Sparks raised his hand. "I need to get the BIB ready anyway. I'll head back to the office and change my flight. I'll grab a couple of intel analysts from the support center, contact Delta Zulu, and get them specifically assigned to this task here. I'll meet you guys in Japan in a day. Plus, it gives me a chance to pack protein for the flight. You know what I'm sayin'?"

"What is Delta Zulu?" Naomi asked, confused.

"You know how movies always have some random guy in a house somewhere living in his mom's basement, hacking the world's computers?"

Everyone in the room nodded.

"Delta Zulu is the cool version of that guy. He's our break-glass-in-case-of-emergency guy," Voodoo said.

"How will he be able to help?"

"He's a professional penetration tester for major corporations who also operates as a cybermercenary doing side gigs. He's been chomping at the bit to help with something like this."

The energized room of competent and willing supporters overwhelmed Naomi. Any doubt that followed her into the room crumbled. The combination of technical, scientific, and military expertise inspired her.

Naomi looked out the window of the conference room. Between the two towers of the Hyatt hotel she could see the Spanish-influenced red tile roofs on Coronado Island. As much as she wanted to feel comforted by the room full of people rallying behind her, a pit grew in Naomi's stomach. *Everyone will soon discover the truth about the God Algorithm.* And it was only a matter of time before they revealed the source of their funding. She prayed that she made the right decision hiding it from them for now. She knew the truth—this secret—was the reason her friends were missing...or dead.

CHAPTER 11
The Anmoku-Dan

TOKYO, JAPAN

odies flowed in and out of the spacious pathways and tightly packed businesses of the *shotengai* like blood through an aorta. A high glass ceiling overhead protected pedestrians and shoppers from the rain while the wide tiled road was large enough for vehicles and trucks to drive through the Japanese mall.

Hundreds of people walked along the path. Children in school uniforms mingled in whispering cliques. Elderly ladies, hunched over from years of working in the fields, pushed wheeled walkers stuffed with bargains from the "hundred yen" store.

High school girls rolled their plaid skirts at the waist to make them shorter, undid several buttons on their white dress shirts, caked on makeup, and wore the stereotypical ubiquitous "loose socks"—long, bunched-up, thick white socks that they adhered to their legs with glue sticks to keep them from falling.

Even while keeping uniform standards, this was an attempt at Japanese teenage defiance and prestige.

A large monitor covering the side of a building played sumo wrestling matches as an audience gathered to watch. Lines of bicycles called *mamachari* filled sections on the edge of the pathway. Foreign missionaries handed out pamphlets for free English lessons at the local church while businessmen sat at a sushi bar. The smell of Japanese curry filled the air.

Bosozoku mingled around the entrance, half sitting on their souped-up street bikes. Unlike American biker gangs, *bosozoku* rode racing motorcycles with open mufflers to amplify the sound of their motors and made extensive efforts to show dominance through noise and literal physical obstruction. They entertained themselves by ignoring traffic and annoying the police. They were pathetic children playing at real games of crime. They were nothing compared to the yakuza. And they were nothing compared to Ryu.

Ryu penetrated the arched entryway of the *shotengai* with a dark swagger; a cigarette burned in his mouth. Ryu was like the living embodiment of smoke—poisonous, dark, and insidious. He wore a tailored black suit and a white dress shirt. His obsidian-black hair was disheveled and contradicted his exquisite clothes but defined his look, defined his persona. Beneath his suit hid a six-foot-tall body of lean, dense muscle mass covered in traditional tattoos of serpents and ancient demons indicative of someone in his line of work.

One of the shop owners recognized him. The owner averted his eyes and bowed slightly at his neck. Another shop owner on the opposite side of the *shotengai* noticed and gave the same response.

A young *bosozoku* leaning against his Honda CBR500 whispered to his friend, "*Anmoku-dan.*"

Ryu looked at the boys and raised his index finger to his mouth, his cold eyes demanding their silence. They bowed and scampered off. As they looked back to catch one more glance at Ryu, he pursed his lips and whistled an eerie note. They turned and ran, hastened by the Japanese superstition that comes with whistling—it invites the dead.

Ryu passed a *koban*. On nearly every corner in the city, police posted at least one officer in small stations. Many visiting the country accredited the safety and peace of the island nation to the constant police presence, and the trust people have for them. Ryu peered into the *koban* and waited to make eye contact with the officer. Ryu paused, rested a hand in his pocket, and took a drag from his cigarette.

The young officer looked up and noticed him, averted his eyes, and lowered his head. Ryu stared at him a moment longer and exhaled smoke from his nose. Appeased by the act of subtle submission, Ryu continued along the path to his destination.

The peace in Japan wasn't a balance between the good citizens and the diligent police as most thought. Minor crime was kept in check through an informal agreement between organized crime and the police. As long as law enforcement stayed out of their way, the balance would remain intact. The more commonly known gang of ultraright Japanese, called the yakuza, dominated drugs and human trafficking. This area was very different, however, until Ryu showed up.

Ryu arrived at the pachinko parlor and approached the front entrance.

"*O kaeri nasai, Tanigawa sama!*" the doorman said as he opened the door. Ryu did not attempt to greet the man, acknowledge his welcome or even existence as he entered the building.

Sounds of tiny metal balls dropping and plinking filled the air. J-pop music blared from speakers. The Japanese version of casinos, pachinko parlors are filled with smoking gamblers hoping to strike it rich. Addicts in this parlor focused on machines that dropped metal balls vertically down pegs in the hope that they fall into holes in a drum. The drum rotates, and if the symbols match when it ends, the player wins.

When players won, more balls fell out the bottom. Neon lights and images based on anime and historical characters themed the devices. Most systems were digitally randomized. Any mathematician will tell you, though, there's no such thing as digital randomization. Everything is a code. Ryu could tell you the same thing.

Ryu walked through the crowded, smoke-filled gaming floor and worked his way to the back. He passed dozens of middle-aged men in motionless fixation. A woman sat with her baby as her other child ran around the parlor. A security guard noticed Ryu and used his right arm to clear away a curtain for him to enter a hallway leading to a back room where five men sat around a table. They were shirtless and covered in tattoos. Kirin beer bottles and sake covered the table where they played a game with *oicho-kabu* cards.

Four of them popped to their feet as soon as he arrived.

"Taro is bringing the delivery to the safe house. I need three of you to meet him," Ryu said.

"*Hai, Fuku-Honbucho san!*" Their quick response was reflective of his position as a senior lieutenant in the Tokugawa-Kai, the Tokyo yakuza syndicate. Ryu had earned his position. And had more ambitions.

In the early 2000s, the Japanese police implemented several anti-racketeering measures to stop the yakuza. The Tokugawa-Kai of the Tokyo region fell into decline. Significant leaders in the family were arrested. Ryu used this as an opportunity to prove himself.

No one knew where Ryu came from or how he got his connections, but, amid the crackdown, crystal methamphetamines, or "*shabu*," crept through the streets of major cities among the young *bosozoku* motorcycle gangs. The increase in activity was strategic and deliberate, meeting demand but not drawing too much attention. Just like the mysterious arrival of his shabu, Ryu also began laundering money through connections at a local pachinko parlor. He eventually "convinced" the owner of the establishment to sell it to him. Ryu's legend spread.

He eventually caught the attention of the *kumicho*, or head, of the Tokugawa-Kai. Ryu proposed an aggressive plan; he wanted to buy stock in a large corporation and establish himself in a process the yakuza use to publicly humiliate a company's management, a form of blackmail, called "*sokaiya*." As a minor stockholder in a major corporation, he had the right to attend board meetings...and influence board members. The *kumicho* promoted him to the rank of fuku-honbucho, a leader of his region of the city.

The neighborhood also noticed an increase in "companions," or drinking girls, in the pachinko parlor and some of the adjacent clubs. These girls came from the Philippines and had a high turnover rate. It seemed every few weeks a new group of them came through. The actions of his men and the way they appeared to navigate gray lines in ethical darkness skillfully earned them their nickname, the "*Anmoku-dan*," or "dark eyes clan."

Beside the card table, one man remained standing.

"Have the other packages arrived?"

The man answered, "They are in the hotel upstairs, sir."

"How do they look?"

"I think it best you decide for yourself." The yakuza threw on a shirt, and the two meandered through a tunnel to a separate building. After climbing several flights of stairs, they stepped into a large open room. The floor was traditional tatami, with rice paper sliding shoji doors. A small table low to the ground sat in the middle with pillows around it for sitting. Several other doorways led to more private rooms.

On the far wall, seven Filipino girls and a boy stood in a line with their heads down. They ranged in ages between fifteen and eighteen. They all wore dresses or clothes too young for their age. One girl wore the same uniform as the girls in the *shotengai* outside with loose socks. The youngest dressed as an anime character.

"What do you think, sir?" the man asked. Ryu inspected them carefully.

"They're a little older than what our guests normally prefer," Ryu said dryly.

"Would you like me to request new packages?"

"No, there isn't any time. We'll make things more interesting with the older girl. When our guests arrive later on tonight, put her in the back room with some rope. They'll get creative on their own."

CHAPTER 12
Go-En ga Aru

Hands gripped Voodoo's throat. No, not hands. A strap. Smoke. Voodoo squinted. Smoke filled the armored vehicle. The retention strap to his M4 pulled across his neck, strangling him. The shooter, sitting across from Voodoo before the explosion, now lay crumpled beside him. Voodoo's right arm, trapped under the shooter and broken across a metal bar, hinged unnaturally, snapped at the joint. A ringing hummed from the very center of his skull. Spilled soda, sticky and wet, clung to his skin. The citrus scent underscored the invasive gases in the air.

Men screamed, injured and shaken. Inside his head, the voices of Voodoo's tactical instructors yelled, Do something! It doesn't matter what, just DO something!

Voodoo pulled a small fixed-blade knife from his belt with his functional arm and sawed at his gun strap until it popped loose. He inhaled deeply and immediately gagged on the smoke that filled his lungs.

He screamed in agony as he pushed the shooter off his arm enough to wrench it free. The toxic concoction of smoke and misery blurred his focus. With weak stabbing motions, he sheathed *the blade. He reached for the handle on the rear exit door of the RG-33 and pulled hard, but his awkward angle gave him no leverage. Nothing happened. He groped along the edge of the door until he found the hydraulic release and pushed. The door cracked open. His mind flooded with momentary relief.*

As soon as enough space opened, he extended his left arm to crawl out when a stinging barrage of gunfire deflected off the back of the vehicle. With a snap, his arm instinctively retracted. Other shooters behind him, stacked on top of each other, barked at Voodoo to go through.

Do they burn alive in the vehicle or crawl to their deaths in a hail of bullets? Voodoo didn't have a choice. He grabbed his rifle in his left hand and began to crawl as bullets plinked off the metal. He committed, scrambling forward with only one functional arm.

The dream shifted to silence and darkness. The voice, once again, spoke to Voodoo from oblivion.

In two days, an old friend will be lost, an old friend regained. When the light of Amaterasu protects you, rise and face the eastern threat.

Snap! *Voodoo's dream returned to the burning vehicle in a burst of oranges, reds, and browns. He cleared his legs from the door, shifted to a crouching position, and presented his M4. His right arm hung useless, the joint hyperextended, angled in the opposite direction. His knees wobbled; heartbeat raced; he grew light-headed as his body went into shock. Each breath sounded like a hollow echo in his head. He held the gun in his weak arm and found his cheek well with the butt of the weapon. He scanned the horizon, seeking safety, maneuvering tactical vectors in his mind.*

GA! GA! GA! GA! GA! GA! GA!

The .50-caliber machine gun mounted on top of the vehicle behind the destroyed RG-33 blasted hot lead. The shooter inside controlled the weapon via the CROWS and fired at the building beside it. The operator laid waste to a potential threat from the third floor. Chunks of cinder block and dirt rained down from the building; the acrid smell of gunpowder mixed with the deadly fire of the RG-33. Hot spent brass bounced off the metal armor of the vehicle.

Was this another Iraqi Death Blossom? Voodoo couldn't tell. Dirt leaped around his feet. He looked down, baffled by the unnatural occurrence, and lifted his feet one at a time, doubting his observed reality.

"Voodoo, get to cover! They're shooting at YOU!" a voice yelled. More lead whizzed by his head.

A shooter behind him clawed at the dirt to escape the dead RG-33. If Voodoo ran, the shooter would be completely exposed. Voodoo placed himself in a blocking position directly in front of the open RG-33 door. He fired a flurry of rounds toward the building in a desperate attempt to suppress the threat.

A silhouette appeared in the window on the first floor of a structure to his left. Voodoo shifted the barrel of his rifle and aimed. Through the dust, the shadow appeared to be holding a weapon. Voodoo pulled the trigger.

Dap!

The glass shattered.

Dap! Dap!

He hurled two more rounds from his rifle. The dust cleared just enough for Voodoo to see the face of his target.

The eyes of a boy, probably no older than seven, looked back at him, the spark of life extinguished.

He went limp, then fell out of sight.

•••

37.518774, 151.487253

SOMEWHERE EAST OF JAPAN

"Sir! ... Sir! Are you alright, sir?"

Voodoo gasped for air and yelled out. His hands instinctively grasped whatever was in reach. His right hand strangled the airplane armrest, and his left clenched Naomi's arm.

Naomi flinched with a fright. "Ah!" she yelled.

The pinpricks of a thousand adrenaline arachnids hatched from eggs traveled throughout Voodoo's body. He had avoided the car crash but held on to the face of the person he last saw in his dream, his memory underscored by the scent of citrus and gunpowder.

Passengers in the seats around him popped their heads up in curiosity. A baby cried, and an exasperated mother glared at Voodoo.

Voodoo was still processing his surroundings. It was dark, but he could tell he was on a plane. He was no longer in danger. Someone was comforting him. Was it...? No, she's gone. But he didn't let go all the same.

He forced himself to take a deep breath.

"Sir, are you okay?" a concerned male flight attendant asked.

Voodoo forced another deep breath and addressed the flight attendant. "Yes...sorry. I fell asleep and seem to have had a bit of a nightmare. I'm sorry if I scared anyone."

The flight attendant nodded, observed Naomi's hand holding Voodoo, and gave a reassuring smile before moving to the aft section of the cabin.

"What was that about?" Naomi asked. Surprise and concern spread across her face, enhanced by her perfect makeup.

"Nothing. I have bad dreams sometimes."

"Dreams of what?"

"I... It's hard to explain... It's like you're driving a car, and you're about to have an accident and adrenaline surges through your whole body, but then, nothing happens, and your body is...activated."

"Your sympathetic nervous system is turned on. I understand what is happening to you. What was the dream, though?" Naomi's attempt to be supportive by describing a biological response was endearing.

Voodoo's right arm ached. *I hate talking about my dreams.* After his last deployment, he started seeing a therapist, and they prescribed medication—prazosin and Zoloft. Voodoo always felt weird about the treatment, though. It was as if not being a shooter meant he didn't deserve the right to therapy. He stopped going. Stopped the meds too.

Even though he knew better, he felt treatment implied he wasn't strong enough. Or he was still the pathetic person bullied in his childhood, for being small, for missing his mother; the awkward kid, the hyper kid, the weak kid he spent every day of his life trying to erase. Despite everything he accomplished, he always felt he wasn't enough. This desire to fill a void pushed him to achieve incredible things. It also prevented him from finding satisfaction; it sequestered him from peace, buried him in chaos.

"Well, what was the dream?" Naomi persisted.

Voodoo took a breath. "It's a memory. I was with my platoon, and we hit an IED. The explosion always goes off, and I wake up."

"I am sorry. That must be difficult." The way she spoke and the way it felt to have her hand touching his was definitely... welcome. *Maybe I can trust her...*

"Recently, there's been a bit more to the dreams, though."

"Like what?"

Like I'm losing my mind...

Voodoo's mouth opened and closed several times before he finally committed. "Mixed in my older memories, the dream I always seem to have, I get this voice telling me a prophetic riddle."

Voodoo felt her stiffen, almost shiver, as if the hairs of Naomi's entire body stood on end. He immediately regretted telling her.

"I'm sorry. I seem to have upset you—"

"No, not at all." Naomi cupped her forehead with her hand, her eyes wide. She turned to Voodoo. "*Go-en ga aru.*" *There is fate*, she said in Japanese. "I had no idea more people were having these dreams."

"You mean I'm not alone?"

CHAPTER 13
The Video Feed

TOKYO, JAPAN

Ryu leaned back in his chair with his right leg crossed over the left, studying the scene on the monitors in the security room of the pachinko parlor. A wall of ten different screens displayed varying video angles throughout the gaming floor. A pan-tilt camera automatically zoomed in and out on different individuals as a computer vision model processed facial recognition software and categorized the gamblers. Boxes appeared around each person and profiled them by color based on the amount of time and money they spent in the parlor. Customers were also black-listed or white-listed, including some persons categorized into a BOLO—be on the lookout—list.

Taro entered the room; Ryu gestured to the security guard to step out. He pressed a button under the main computer and the security feeds of the pachinko floor switched to four different rooms in the hotel across the street.

On the screens, five men dressed in suits and ties entered the room. They took off their coats, loosened their neckties, and sat around the small table on the tatami floor. One man, who appeared to be the most junior, poured everyone shots of whiskey as the group joked. The same facial recognition software used in the pachinko parlor presented blue boxes superimposed over the men's faces. Names appeared under the boxes alongside their rank and position as officers in the National Police Agency.

They beckoned the girls over. Some were hesitant, but Ryu staged several men dressed as hotel employees to remain as handlers in the room to ensure the "packages" were compliant. In the monitor, yellow boxes appeared around the girls with package numbers and their cities of origin under their faces.

The teenagers sat next to the men or on their laps as they drank. Over the space of an hour, Ryu watched as they increased in varying levels of inebriation and took the girls into the back rooms. Ryu communicated via radio to one of his handlers at the hotel who wore communications devices in one ear. Ryu told him to present the girl with the rope in one of the rooms. Two men entered. Ryu documented the entire event.

Traps like this were not new to Ryu. He had been playing games of blackmail and manipulation his entire life even before his training. The yakuza happened to help him become a master at it.

During the Tokugawa shogunate of Japan, the last of the feudal military governments that ended in the late 1800s, there were four main castes: the samurai, the peasants, the craftsmen, and the merchants. Below these touchable classes existed the *burakumin*, the "untouchables." These individuals were tanners, butchers, and all others that worked with the dead.

Out of the outcasts and underlings, beggars and dissidents, rose the yakuza, which established themselves in groups and cohorts, organized and strategized. They eventually became large enough to manipulate the merchant infrastructure, influence trade, and secure power. Among the *burakumin*, many arrived from overseas to do the menial tasks of the upper castes. These foreigners eventually found their way into the yakuza. And that was how Ryu came into power.

"Record these videos and make sure we make several copies. Just like last time."

"*Hai.*"

"Have you had any luck with the laptop?" Ryu asked.

"I was able to get in. Let me know when you would like to send the message," Taro replied. The scar on his upper lip where a cleft palate once cursed his face twisted as he spoke.

Ryu nodded. "So, we have everything then?"

"I'll have to work through the code, but I should be able to apply it once we get the access we need. The trap is set."

"Notify the chairman as soon as you have access."

Taro nodded. "Oh, you should also know that our sources tell us they may be bringing Xiphos AI into this."

"The company the chairman's been after?"

"Yes, apparently one of their connections monitoring senior military correspondence tipped him off. And, should we gain access, we may be able to bring our tools online in real time," Taro said.

Ryu's lips curved up at the edges. He had gambled years ago in a deal with the chairman of Xin Jishu International, Mr. Hwang Li-Liang, uncertain of the outcome at the time.

"This partnership is paying off. I hate to see it end."

The two watched the video feed for another half hour before Ryu and Taro stood up and left the security room.

They walked through the tunnel and up to the room with the "packages." The malingering officers mucked about in various stages of drunken debauchery and salacious recreational activities.

Taro slid open the shoji door, and Ryu entered. He stood at the entryway and whistled a low, melancholy tune. The men, annoyed at the interruption, glared at the intruder.

"Who the hell are you?" one of them said.

The yakuza handlers dressed as attendants stationed in the room locked their eyes onto Ryu. He moved his head to the side and back. The men immediately understood the signal.

"*Dete ike!*" *Get the hell out!* they yelled at the youngsters. The Filipino packages scooped their garments in their arms in shame. As if *they* were to blame for their appearance. One girl didn't move because she couldn't.

Ryu walked over to the package that was bound, gagged, and kneeling on the floor. Her body trembled.

Ryu knelt, removed a pocketknife, and cut her loose. As soon as Ryu slipped the gag from her mouth, she wailed. She bled from where the rope burned into her skin.

Ryu nudged her with the back of his hand and pointed to the door. The girl fought to stand; her legs numb. She crawled to her clothes and whimpered as she struggled to the exit. Taro, with an air of frustration, stepped into the room and grabbed her by the arm. She winced at his contact then bit her tongue, realizing who touched her, fearful of the repercussions. The shoji door shut behind them.

The police officers seethed.

"Do you have any idea who we are?" one of them said, stepping forward, his dress shirt unbuttoned and his fly open.

"The facial recognition software on my cameras told me exactly who you are the moment you walked in." Ryu gestured at the cameras hidden in the corners of the room.

Their red drunken faces went flush.

A tall man in his midfifties with an upturned nose, heavy-lidded eyes, and piglike features stepped forward. He seemed to understand the weight of the situation through his drunken haze.

"You want something from us. What is it?"

"Ah, Inspector Yoshimoto, thank you for asking. Last night, two important scientists went missing from the University of Tokyo. Are you working on that case?"

The men looked at each other sheepishly. "We're supposed to be."

"I am going to help you get back to work. And to do that, you will give me access to all of the CCTV feeds across the city."

"You want us to do what?!" one of the men blurted out. "No one here has that kind of authority. We certainly can't just *give* it to *you.*"

"I don't care how you do it. You *will* give it to *me.*" Ryu lit a cigarette, took a long drag, and exhaled with his lips in a tight circle as he lowered his arm holding the cigarette. Ryu stared at the last man who spoke and gave a cold stare, underscored by silent tension. The man lowered his head, defeated, broken.

"I also need the flight manifests for every commercial aircraft coming into Japan from the United States in the next twenty-four hours." He took another drag of his cigarette. "You have until tomorrow at 7 a.m. to get me everything I demand; otherwise, everyone on the internet will know who you are and what you did here."

Ryu flicked the lit cigarette in the mouthy officer's face. The man flinched but didn't move, refusing to lift his head.

And with that, Ryu planted the seed of extortion. The silence in the room, the fear of their actions going public, and the insidious evil of the man standing before them nurtured the spiteful and decrepit plant. All Ryu had to do now was wait for it to bear fruit.

CHAPTER 14

The Daughter and the Cure

33.956304, 142.000100
SOMEWHERE EAST OF JAPAN

"What exactly does that mean?" Voodoo asked, replacing his hand on his lap.

"I think there may be others who are having dreams like the one you describe."

"I seriously doubt they're like the ones *I'm* having. Whatever the voices say in my dreams always turns out to come true."

"That is what I mean."

Voodoo's dark eyebrows furrowed, amplifying his intense demeanor.

"What aren't you telling me?"

Everything. "Nothing," she said defensively. "I mean—" Naomi had a nervous habit of biting the inside of her lower lip, slightly distorting the shape of her mouth. It got worse when she was lying. She caught herself doing it now. She sighed.

"Dr. Ichikawa had a daughter who died about twenty years ago. She had a rare neurological disease that he tried everything he could imagine to cure. At the time, he was already a well-respected neurologist and geneticist, so the fact that he could not find a cure for his daughter was heartbreaking. Her body began to degrade as her mind fell apart. He became desperate. He decided to implement an aggressive protein therapy on his daughter to try to normalize the neurological activity in her brain. He used viruses to deliver the proteins.

"According to Kenzo, his daughter regained her cognitive skills; she started speaking again. She seemed to have turned a corner. But then, she started speaking nonsense. She mentioned something about a river and a lost hawk. She died later that day."

Voodoo tapped his knee with his finger.

"What does that have to do with my dreams?"

"Her dreams were specific. And I cannot help but wonder..."

"There's no way her dreams have anything to do with mine," Voodoo said dismissively.

"How long have you had these dreams? I mean, prophetic ones that come true."

Voodoo's fingertips chattered on his knee.

"It's hard to say. I've always been one of those people who have vivid dreams, so I don't have a clue."

"Do they sound like a poem? Like a clear, distinct voice from someone you trust?"

"That's...exactly what they sound like."

"Are they mixed with images of events that come true?" she asked.

"Now you're freaking me out." Voodoo's tapping stopped.

"So, they *are* the same," Naomi said. "What else can you tell me about them?"

"I hear this voice and then see these images that would coincide with them. They sorta told me what was going to happen, and then I knew what to do next. Most of the time, I would listen, and they turned out exactly as they said."

"What do you mean 'most of the time'?" Naomi pressed him.

"There was one instance in which these dreams felt more like a curse than a blessing." Voodoo looked out the window at the condensed air passing over a light on the wing of the Boeing 787 Dreamliner.

Naomi waited for him to continue, knowing now was the moment to remain silent. She examined his face, cauliflower ears most likely caused by years of wrestling, his bloodshot hazel eyes, and the puffiness inherent with sleep deprivation or carrying the weight of a burden too heavy for the spirit. Likely both.

"I had a dream that my wife was going to die...and then she did."

No... Of all the things she thought Voodoo was about to say, that was not it. Her mouth sat agape.

"I had a dream that she would be diagnosed with a disease and that no one would find it until it was too late."

Naomi's eyes started to well up. "What do you mean?"

"I mean, I dreamt she would get sick. She knew what these dreams meant. So, she went with me to see the doctor even though she showed no symptoms. I had no idea what sickness she had, so they didn't know what tests to run. The dreams, which were normally really specific, were frustratingly vague. They just kept saying to cherish the time with her. By the time they discovered she had pancreatic cancer, it had already spread to her lymph nodes and throughout her body."

A tear rolled down Naomi's cheek. "I am so sorry."

"Imagine being the only person who knows how to save someone, and nobody listens. Then you get to watch—"

Voodoo looked back out the window, still. He froze at that moment between emotional chaos and control.

Naomi understood that place well. Her dire circumstance had trapped her in that same limbo the moment she received the call about her friends going missing.

Naomi reached out to hold his hand, seeking the connection and consolation that only human contact can bring. She retreated and interlaced her fingers on her lap instead.

She tried to think of some witty thing to say the way he did for her earlier when she was distraught. Nothing came to mind.

Voodoo took a deep breath and looked at Naomi. His emotional IQ seemed to recognize the weight of the conversation and the tear on Naomi's cheek.

"Poor Puddles," he said.

She let out a laugh. "He's such a trooper." She wiped the sympathetic tear from her eye with an upward motion of her finger to keep her mascara from running. "Do you have any children?"

Voodoo picked a piece of lint off his pants and rolled it between his fingers.

"No. She wanted kids. I did too until... I just didn't feel right bringing a kid into the world after what I'd done, I mean, with my job and everything. Timing didn't work out. You know, the usual reasons you regret later."

I definitely know my regrets. She waited a moment and finally asked, "How long ago did she die?"

"It was a little over a year ago. I hadn't had another of those voice dreams until last night and then again just now."

"Last night? You mean when Taka-chan and Kenzo went missing?"

"Apparently."

"What did the voice say?" she said anxiously.

"In two days, an old friend will be lost, an old friend regained. When the light of Amaterasu protects you, rise and face the eastern threat."

Naomi pursed her lips as she thought. "Any idea what all of that means?"

"I have some images, but they're all mixed with my other memories. It's as if the trauma of combat and losing my wife are too much. It's made my brain and emotions all jumbled."

Kenzo never told me who he designated for Project Kawa. Is Voodoo the subject?

Naomi measured her words.

"Perhaps there is something I should tell you. There is a lot more to the God Algorithm than what we discussed. I am going to need to get you to my lab, take a blood sample, and run some tests. I may want to monitor the neural activity in your brain," Naomi said.

"Hard pass. Sorry. We don't have time for something like that."

A flurry of frustration and excitement whirred in Naomi's chest.

"But it may give us a much better idea as to what is going on, and it may clear up some of the images in your dreams."

The captain's voice came over the loudspeaker. They were making their final descent into Tokyo.

"This conversation is gonna have to wait," Voodoo said. "After we land, I'm gonna need to split off from the group."

"What?" This wasn't something they had discussed earlier.

Voodoo leaned closer to Naomi and kept his voice low. "You'll have to discuss that with Frisco. If I had my way, we wouldn't have been on the same flight in the first place, but we didn't have much choice. We need to disassociate ourselves from each other."

"Why?"

"Naomi, your friends are missing. That means *you're* also in danger." In all the commotion regarding her friends' disappearances, and after linking up with this team effort, Naomi had forgotten to consider her welfare. Another layer of fear compacted on her.

"So, what are *you* going to do if you are not with us?"

"I need to gather intelligence on my own as you all work with the authorities."

"Are you sure that is wise?" Naomi felt safe with Voodoo. She didn't like the idea of him leaving her.

"This is what I do, Naomi."

"Gather intelligence on missing persons?"

"Sometimes. People bring me in when they can't find someone. Usually, these are people that don't want anyone to find them."

"So, you will be looking for the people who did this? Like an investigator?"

"More like a hunter."

Naomi looked at the man sitting beside her and remembered the other members of Frisco's team. She raised her head to view over the seats and catch the silhouettes of other passengers. The massive outline of Stu swelled several rows in front, and Frisco across from him, with more nearby: muscular and intense, like every moment of their lives was the moment before a fight. Voodoo's team was all around her.

In any other circumstance, she would hate the way that made her feel. Naomi abhorred violence. Growing up in Hawaii, she avoided people in the military because of it. Naomi never wanted anything to do with the bravado and idiocy that came with uniformed personnel who couldn't do anything better with their lives, so they enlisted like lemmings.

At least that's how she'd felt when her friends' lives weren't on the line.

The government didn't just choose the average Marine grunt or Navy squid to protect her, they sent the best they could offer. They sent Voodoo and his team. And she was grateful.

"If we separate, I can be watching from a distance and collecting information. Who I am *with* you is not nearly as powerful as who I can be *for* you. Trust me."

To Naomi's surprise, she did. What she didn't trust was the growing sense of dread billowing up inside her. If Voodoo was really having these dreams, there may be more people that she doesn't know about. If so, who are they? And how did it happen?

CHAPTER 15
The Rapids

WESTWATER CANYON
SOUTHERN UTAH, USA

"Fish's brains are scattered on the walls of this canyon!" Ally shouted at the customers in her boat, referencing the old tales from the town of Westwater. "Keep a lookout for any Colorado pikeminnows with a headache!" Ally got a kick out of her joke as she giggled. Her passengers politely grinned, half believing her.

Joel rose to his feet and addressed the two other guides with a snappy salute accented by his signature crooked smile. Gavin nodded in understanding. Joel always saluted, referencing the AC/DC song "For Those About to Rock," just before dropping into the rapids. Gavin immediately caught the reference, extended his pinky and thumb, and replied with a shaka. Ally always saluted back like a dork. Growing up with diplomats as parents meant she missed out on a lot of pop culture references including an AC/DC song, even the ones that were now twenty years old.

Before the waters got rough, Gavin took one last opportunity to consider his rig. On each boat, a square-shaped metal frame was strapped down in the middle of an oval-shaped raft. On each side, a D-shaped ring, or D ring, secured the oars to the frame. Unlike its title, D rings had a break in the ring for sliding the oars in and out. Oars without a D ring were virtually useless.

In the center of the boat, guides used coolers as makeshift benches as they rowed. Guides sat in the very center of the rig facing the bow, or front as opposed to the back, the stern. Customers sat on the tube that created the boat's outline. They would hold on to a rope called the "chicken line" along the edge and lean toward the middle of the boat to avoid falling out. Guides would use their legs to press against the oar frame to increase leverage as they rowed. Everything came down to leverage with these boats.

Gavin picked up his metal ammunition, or ammo, can. Since the end of the Vietnam War, river guides used old foot-long metal ammo cans or much larger rocket boxes on the river. They were very durable and easy to strap down. Each customer got an ammo can to stash important items like their wallet or their black, clamshell 2G cell phones that seemed to be so popular these days. Guides would paint and decorate their own to make it easily identifiable.

Rocket boxes were another story. There weren't any bathrooms or toilets on the river. The speed and depth of the Colorado River meant people couldn't wade out and use it to relieve themselves. The canyon was a national park, so rafting groups couldn't use the beach and bury the excrement, so they did the next best thing and packed it out.

This is where the old rocket boxes came in handy. Guests and guides would sit on the rocket box when they needed to do their business. When they would stand, the rocket box would leave grooves in their buttocks and thighs. From then on, rocket boxes used as port-a-potties became known as "groovers." Even though modern rafting companies carried metal boxes with mountable toilet seats, guides still called them groovers nonetheless.

Weight on the boat is also an important factor. Sometimes, when guides didn't have enough passengers to balance the boat or make it heavy enough in the water for stability, they would carry large bags of drinking water. It eventually became a joke to call passengers "portable bags of water." Customers didn't care for that nickname, especially after signing documents to waive legal liability in the event they get maimed or dismembered.

Gavin stared at his ammo can. He had thought carefully about the best place to strap it down when he'd geared up. He needed room to balance five customers with three in the front and two in the back. As a first-year boater, he also had to carry the groover, which always went in the back. He had felt compelled to strap it down along the edge of the boat, where the cooler met the raft with the oar right above it. To balance it out, he'd placed one of the customer's ammo cans on the other side.

The waves picked up and the rafts entered their first hurdle. The trio smoothly navigated through the rapids one by one. Dolores Canyon, followed by Marble Canyon, then Staircase, were all straight shots down the middle of the river. The boats crashed and jostled in the waves. Near deafening liquid thunder echoed throughout the canyon. The portable bags of water cheered. Gavin was stoked. Ally's passengers kept looking for fish on the canyon walls.

A mild lull before hitting the bigger rapids allowed everyone to recognize the power of the murky brown water rushing them through the metamorphic rock. Millions of years of erosion created fluting on the cliffs. Like a hundred ice cream scoopers had dug into the rock, divots and holes appeared all over the black Vishnu Schist.

"Why does the rock look like it's wet?" a tall, muscular woman asked.

"That's called desert varnish. The high metal content in the sandstone oxidizes and creates that dark and aged look on the rock," Gavin replied.

"Why is some of the rock red and some of it black?" a different person asked.

"This canyon is part of something called the 'Great Unconformity.' The red rock is sedimentary, which means layers of sediment created it. Long ago, this was a giant ocean, and the sediment settled at the bottom. Over time, layers and layers created rock. The rock below it is the exciting stuff. That's not sedimentary rock; it's metamorphic. Metamorphic rock is made through pressure. It's usually the oldest rock because it's made by being subjected to pressure over millions of years.

"Now, here's the cool part. The black rock is called 'Schist.' Schist in the canyons is named after Hindu gods. This type of rock is called 'Vishnu Schist.' It's about 1.2 billion years old. So, there's the rock that's over a billion years old and sedimentary rock 200–300 million years old right on top of it. There are nearly a billion years of rock missing, and no one knows why."

The muscular woman furrowed her brow. "No one has any idea how that happened? Is there something special about this area?"

"This area is part of a larger formation called the 'Uncompahgre Plateau.' That's a native Ute word that means 'dirty water' or 'rocks that make water red.' We're right in the middle of that plateau, and it's something called a 'geographic uplift.' Have you ever baked a cake and had it crack in the middle?"

The guests nodded.

"That's what the ground is doing all around us. It's rising, but at the same time, the river is running right with that crack. The sandstone is just hardened sand, so it crumbles easily and makes the water brown. This river is 40 percent silt. That means that almost half of the water is sand moving really quickly. It's slicing the rock in half. That's what created this area, the Grand Canyon as well, and exposed that ancient rock. Schist is the oldest naturally exposed rock on earth. Outside of the Colorado, the only place you'll see rock like this is on the Zambezi River in Africa."

The guests looked around as though a great mystery of the universe had been unlocked. Then a growing rumble brought them back to reality—they were entering the bowels of Hades Canyon.

Big Hummer, named for a massive rock in the middle of the river, created an enormous hole that gave the customers their first taste of the power of the river as they slammed through. Funnel Falls required setting the boat sideways and allowing the flow of the water to drop the raft in bow first. To the uninitiated, this specific maneuver looked particularly smooth.

Up ahead, Joel expertly navigated through Funnel and into Surprise. The steep descent of these rapids blocked Gavin's view, so he couldn't see what happened to Joel as his boat dropped down below.

Gavin focused on the next obstacle. The customers whiteknuckled the chicken line. Gavin nudged the boat, bumped a large rock, and entered Surprise at a slightly crooked angle.

A white egret glided over Gavin's boat and drew his attention to river right. It was then that he saw it.

As Joel paddled into Cocaine Cove, an immense boil erupted from beneath his raft at the eddy fence. The counter flow of the eddy jerked each end of the boat in different directions. The raft violently spun 180 degrees. One of the teenage girls from earlier ejected from the bow and somersaulted backward into the cold, brown explosive eddy. The customers fell on top of each other, initially unaware of their lost cargo.

With a stubborn thud, a curling wave smashed the front of Gavin's raft, soaking everyone on board. The customers, who hadn't seen Joel's boat, shouted with excitement. Gavin's focus sharpened. His grip tightened on the wooden knobs of his oars.

His blue raft, slightly askew, pushed on through the rapid. Gavin could do nothing until he cleared the hydraulic churn of Surprise Rapid. As soon as he was able, Gavin spun the boat so it was perpendicular to the flow of the river with the stern facing Joel and aggressively rowed toward Cocaine Cove, to stick to the plan and save the swimmer if possible. The river shoved Gavin's raft. It was moving much faster than he expected. Veins protruded from his arms. The water was urgent, angry, like the river had its own intentions.

And they weren't good.

Gavin's heartbeat raced. He looked up at Ally's boat entering Surprise as Joel's passengers screamed for the missing girl.

He had to get over to Joel. He couldn't run into Ally. He couldn't get swept away right into Skull Rapid. Like an acrophobic on a ledge, he was afraid to look down—or downstream in this case. He especially couldn't look at the looming terror known as Skull now within eyesight to his right.

Gavin rowed as hard as he could. Both legs pressed against the frame of the rig, his back arched. The blades of his oars stabbed into the choppy river over and over. Suddenly, his arm lost its tension. Gavin's head snapped to the left as the D ring disconnected from the rig. It levitated downward along the length of the oar with a high-pitched metallic sound. Time seemed to slow as he stared at the D ring drawn toward the river. Gavin could do nothing to stop it. There wasn't even a splash as the waves reached up like silty brown claws and snatched the D ring off the oar.

Gavin had lost his leverage. His left oar was useless. Seventeen thousand basketballs of water rushed by each second through black metamorphic rock, and Hades Canyon roared with anger. Like Charon waiting to ferry the dead to the underworld across the river Styx, Skull Rapid opened its jaws downstream.

CHAPTER 16

The Digital Ghost

AKIHABARA
TOKYO, JAPAN

Voodoo stepped out of the train station at Akihabara and gazed at a very alien world. Five- to fifteen-story buildings covered in twenty-foot-tall anime characters lined the street. Neon lights and advertisements overwhelmed the senses. Girls in high school uniforms and Gen Z Japanese posted in front of stores dressed as maids, chickens, and famous anime characters distributing pamphlets. Roman characters mixed with Japanese katakana and kanji on vertical signs as beacons, beckoning the would-be shoppers. A strong smell of ramen with its pork and soy broth tempted his nostrils. Hundreds of people filled the streets.

Formerly known as a place to buy electrical hardware and black-market items after World War II, Akihabara Station once had the nickname "Electric Town." During the 1980s, this area of Tokyo shifted away from general electronics like washing machines and televisions to computers. It eventually became a focal point for Japanese anime, manga, video games, and something called "otaku" culture.

Voodoo had never been to Akihabara. He had only been to Japan once when he was younger. The unique modern architecture reminded Voodoo of a video game.

I'm pretty sure I've played this level.

The concept of Voodoo being in a game was not far from the truth. Predators surrounded Voodoo. At least that's how he prepared. Seasoned veterans of combat operations like Voodoo saw the world differently than anyone else. Japan was now an operational environment as far as he was concerned.

And the threats were real.

Voodoo remained on edge to help protect the real person at risk. Naomi was a target, and he needed to use her knowledge and vulnerability to his advantage. Akihabara offered the perfect opportunity to gather the hardware he needed to blend into his new environment and take control of the hunt.

Akihabara bustled less than two kilometers from the University of Tokyo. The large tourist and local population offered him the opportunity to hide as a person with *konketsu* as they called it in Japanese, or mixed blood. Slim-fitting jeans, a button-down dress shirt, a zip-up hoodie, and gelled hair mimicking local youth helped Voodoo blend into the environment. In a black canvas messenger bag slung over his shoulder, Voodoo hid the amenities he would need for the next two days. These included a gaming laptop, a FLIR thermal camera adapter, a Yagi antenna, a software-defined radio, a ceramic microwave oven power amplifier, and a pair of augmented reality contact lenses Voodoo snuck out of the BIB.

Akihabara also offered him access to a wide variety of local electronics intended for pleasure, but to Voodoo, these were more important for fighting than anything else. The black messenger bag over his shoulder would soon become home to an arsenal of stylized cyberweapons unique to his mission. Instead of a magazine of bullets, Voodoo would carry a box of phones.

It was just past noon on a Thursday in June as Voodoo walked among the various stores and entered into a small mobile phone retailer. Voodoo identified several of the most common handsets on the market. He purchased SIM cards from every one of the telecommunications companies and stepped out of the store and found a *kisaten*, or coffee shop, with free Wi-Fi.

Voodoo sat and executed a choreographed sleight of hand routine. He pulled a storage data (SD) card from his pocket and loaded specialized software onto each phone one at a time under the table. He opened a box, removed the phone, and loaded the software before rotating to the next and discarding the box into the shopping bag. When it was all said and done, Voodoo had six phones with perfectly matching software configurations. He only kept one cord for charging and discarded the rest.

In his time in the military, exposure to private companies, national research laboratories, open-source literature, dark web hackers, and hours of YouTube videos, Voodoo established a wide breadth of technical knowledge regarding computers and telecommunications. If an object emitted radio waves, Voodoo knew how to exploit it. Most importantly, he understood how to mask his signature in these environments and hide in plain sight.

Unlike other temporal beings, bound to earth with strong electronic footprints, Instagram feeds, Facebook posts, TikTok videos, or tweets, Voodoo was a digital ghost. He danced between the physical and ephemeral realms of cyberexistence. Avoiding a digital footprint was not just how he lived, it was how he hunted. Japan was now his hunting ground, and he just needed to find his prey.

Voodoo pulled up an encrypted group chat application designed and hosted on a secure server by Delta Zulu. He pinged the group.

THURSDAY 12:13 P.M.

Vudu: I'm up. Comms check.
DZ: Loud and clear.
Sparks: Lima Charlie.
Janet: I'm here.

Like everything else on this mission, Voodoo and Frisco decided to take an unorthodox approach to finding answers. After going through customs at Tokyo Airport, Naomi, Frisco, Stu, and the rest of the shooters in his platoon made their way down to the US embassy to meet with Frisco's commanding officer. He was coordinating with local military leaders, the Japanese National Police Agency, the chief of station, and the US ambassador. They felt that was the best place to keep Naomi safe and tease out more relevant information.

Voodoo also manipulated military bureaucracy to help in this effort. Military movement is complicated. Orders need to be approved, and mobility needs to be verified. That is unless you're in a country like Japan. By submitting his requests from a separate command, Voodoo didn't need to check in with Frisco's leadership. As far as they were concerned, he was a free agent to do whatever he wanted. More importantly, anyone else tracking the deployment of Frisco's team wouldn't see Voodoo hiding out in the open.

Voodoo arrived in the country as any other American service member traveling for temporary duty to Japan. No one asked where he was going, and his travel orders authorized him to stay in Tokyo. His goal was to piggyback on any interactions Naomi had with local police to gather the fastest intel on the ground and skirt any bureaucracy that may hinder their actions.

Voodoo and Frisco also had another idea. Whether they liked it or not, somebody was going to come after Naomi. The only question was whether Frisco and his team intended to hide her as long as possible. Or do they use her as bait to find Dr. Hawkins? Time was of the essence.

THURSDAY 12:15 P.M.

Vudu: Give me an update.

Janet: There were a lot of files in the Dropbox account. Dr. Hawkins had some pretty robust computer vision tools, and we put those to work. We ran them against the video feeds from the area around the University of Tokyo.

DZ: I piggybacked the CCTV feeds and followed the origin of those feeds to identify critical network nodes to start mapping out their IT network.

Sparks: I ate the best California burrito!

Vudu: @Janet, give me what you found.

Janet: The tools tracked the night they disappeared. I'm sure the police are checking their homes. We only had the university CCTV, but that was enough to get us started. I created a cut of what I found. Pay attention to their faces.

Voodoo clicked on a link to a video. A street-level view showed rain pouring on a dark street. Several streetlights lit up a broad road where no cars traveled. It was night, and the heavy rain seemed to be the only activity.

From the left side of the screen, a woman entered at a dead sprint. She made a sharp left turn, slipped, and flew sideways through the air at least two meters before colliding with the concrete. She struggled to regain her composure. She awkwardly wobbled in place until she found her way to her knees.

Then the shadows from the wall in the background rearranged and shifted. A man in a trench coat materialized from nothing. He moved his arm from behind his back and presented a curved blade and held it under her face.

Two more men dressed in black came running from the left, and one man placed his hand on her back. Her body shook while another man put his hand around her face. She collapsed on the ground. They picked up her body like a sack and carried her to an unmarked white truck.

THURSDAY 12:22 P.M.

Janet: I got a close-up of these guys' faces. Look carefully.

Several thumbnails appeared in chat. Each image that Voodoo viewed had faces with less and less distinguishable features.

Vudu: What happened to their faces?
Janet: I'm not sure. The facial recognition software doesn't even recognize these as faces.
Vudu: Interesting. What happens next?

Janet: Our CCTV feeds were limited, so we couldn't see where they went. That's when I used one of Dr. Hawkins's tools to see what it would do. Things got exciting, but I think DZ should explain that.

DZ: I got us access to the rest of the videos we needed.

Vudu: How much is the "rest"?

DZ: All of Tokyo. They all go into one principal server repository. So I...did what I do.

Sparks: Nice.

Vudu: @**Janet**, did you run the algorithm based on that information?

Janet: Yes. I've done as much as I've been able to understand up until now. We tracked the vehicle to one central location. Starlight Pachinko Parlor.

Voodoo pulled up a search engine and typed in "pachinko." A variety of links popped up describing how the game works, its history in Japan, and its controversy. During World War II, Koreans were brought to Japan to work as laborers. After the war, many remained. When the Korean peninsula split in two, the loyalties of the ethnic Koreans in Japan split as well. It was common knowledge that some pachinko parlor owners were not just Korean, but North Korean sympathizers known to send money and support back to the Democratic People's Republic of Korea.

THURSDAY 12:36 P.M.

Vudu: Pachinko parlors may be associated with North Korea as per the quick search I just did. Did you find anything about that place in particular? Did the CV tool give us any...predictions?

Janet: I've only been messing with it a little while. I've been running sections separate from each other because Dr. Hawkins was mixing a lot of different types of code. It's gonna take me a while to figure it out.

Vudu: Keep at it. @**DZ** did you find anything else after we go to the pachinko parlor?

DZ: I need more info. Get me MAC addresses.

Vudu: What about the university? I need to know more about Ichikawa's past. Naomi was vague about who was funding their project.

DZ: On it.

Vudu: I'll get you the MAC addresses. @**Sparks** status on support and the BIB.

Sparks: Ready to ship. I can put it on the next flight out.

Vudu: Hold off. Let me gather more intel on the ground and get an update from Frisco. I'll head to the pachinko parlor and then to Ichikawa's house if possible. @**DZ** I need to know as much as you can learn about Ichikawa's finances as well. Something about what Naomi said about not knowing where the money came from has me curious. @**Janet** Get with your CFO and try to make sense of whatever DZ finds.

Janet: Got it.

DZ: Ditto.

Voodoo pulled up his map application and searched for the Starlight Pachinko Parlor. Based on Delta Zulu's chat message, he needed to get into the building and identify the MAC address of the access points in the building. MAC addresses, or media access control addresses, are unique identifiers that differentiate electronics that use Wi-Fi. Home routers and cell phones all have MAC addresses. Delta Zulu needed the Wi-Fi routers from inside the pachinko parlor to know which computers to go after. To find this, someone would have to go into the building and use a phone or similar hardware to sniff out the Wi-Fi in the air.

Voodoo pushed aside the coffee he'd let go cold, ready to gather up his things to leave the coffee shop. A group of people gathering around a massive media wall playing the news grabbed his attention. On the screen, talking heads mouthed as video played of a crime scene at a park. The video didn't have any audio, only captions, and his ability to read Japanese was virtually nonexistent.

"*Shintai wa atama ga nai no?*" he heard a woman ask her friend.

The body does not have a head? Voodoo translated.

Voodoo would have to research this as he made his way to the first objective. He had something more important to focus on: Voodoo needed to find a way inside the Starlight Pachinko Parlor.

CHAPTER 17
The AI War

US EMBASSY
TOKYO, JAPAN

"We're in the middle of a what?" Frisco found the statement incredible. Naomi could scarcely believe the words herself. Twenty-four hours earlier, Naomi Shimoda mingled at the Bush Room at MIT, presenting a discourse on optogenetics and machine learning. Now she sat in the crowded office of the US ambassador to Japan, surrounded by white walls with crown molding, a mahogany desk, and hardwood floors. The room felt presidential, stiff, unyielding. And this is where she learned that her friends' lives hung in the balance as part of some artificial intelligence arms race.

"What does that mean?" Frisco asked.

"It means this is bigger than you realize. It's the entire reason we brought you here. We're adamant about finding out what happened to Dr. Hawkins and in protectin' Dr. Shimoda," the chief of station said.

Naomi's stomach twisted; nausea threatened. "What happened to Dr. Ichikawa?" she asked. She already knew the answer but wanted the confirmation. She wanted closure.

The US ambassador to Japan, Yumiko Kurosawa, positioned herself across from Frisco and Naomi at her office at the US embassy in Tokyo. Beside her sat the chief of station, Miles Johnson, and Frisco's commanding officer, Commander John "Buck" Buchanan. Also in the room were the National Police Agency Superintendent General and Captain Hiroyuki Tanaka of the Special Assault Team, the Japanese equivalent of SWAT. Between the two men sat a Japanese translator and a representative from the FBI. Stu quietly filled a chair in the back of the room.

"I'm sorry to have to tell you this, but the body of Kenzo Ichikawa was discovered earlier. He was found in a pond in the Koishikawa Korakuen Gardens just before it opened to the public," the ambassador said.

"Why did you not tell me when I was in LA?" Naomi asked, still processing the finality of the ambassador's words.

"We...didn't know the specifics just yet and wanted to tell you in person." The ambassador held her head down as she spoke. "We were able to coordinate early with the police to keep the word from getting out to the press, even though we had identified the body by his fingerprints."

Naomi glanced over at the superintendent general and the captain beside him.

"*O ki no doku sama deshita*," he said. He and the captain bowed. The phrase literally translated to "honorable one of the poisoned life force." It's a fixed phrase to offer condolences during times of loss. Naomi gave a compulsory bow in return. Her life force felt poisoned indeed. "We have our best investigators searching for answers."

The ambassador continued, "I'm sorry to say, however, it won't be long before the press finds out because...we haven't found...all of him."

"What does that mean?" A desire to retch continued to build in her gut.

"His head is missing," Buck Buchanan stated bluntly then released a compact mouthful of tobacco spit into a plastic bottle. He was a tall, muscular man with a slight hunch. Buck wore a white dress shirt and slacks instead of the service khaki uniform typical of a military officer not coordinating a clandestine mission. He looked like he spent years with weight on his back and probably did. His white head was bald, and his forehead must have spent the better part of two decades browbeating everyone around him. No one seemed to appreciate his acerbic personality.

Naomi clenched her teeth and breathed deliberately through her nose. "Do you have any idea who did it?" she asked, her eyes glazing over. She focused on the corner of the desk right in front of her; she couldn't move.

"We're working on it," Captain Tanaka said. "But we don't have many clues other than how he died."

"From what they gleaned from the body, it appeared to be some form of seppuku," the chief of station said.

The words ripped Naomi out of her fugue.

"Ritual suicide? Like, he stabbed himself, and then someone else cut his head off?" Naomi walked her thoughts through the action.

"So it seems," said the ambassador.

Anger slipped past Naomi's grief. "That makes even less sense than anything else in this whole situation. I mean, why on earth would he kill himself? This goes well beyond the fact that you cannot commit seppuku without someone there to finish the act. Kenzo was not a traditional person. This feels more like he was murdered as some form of symbolism," Naomi said.

"That may be. Police are investigating the scene, but we have no camera feeds tracking any activity around the park that night," the chief of station said.

"So, Dr. Hawkins is another casualty in this 'war' you mentioned? How do you know that this was not some random act?" Naomi said. "Also, I am not comfortable with the fact that you knew so much about what we were doing, and you just let this happen. Can you explain to me how long you have been monitoring us?"

Miles Johnson was a thin man. He had dark skin and a slight Southern accent that came and went. Like the other occidentals in the room, he seemed very out of place. Japan's homogeneous population had that effect on foreigners.

"Dr. Shimoda, do you know where all of your money comes from? Dr. Ichikawa may have been in over his head somewhere."

"Are you saying one of the investors did this?" Naomi asked.

"That's what we'd like to figure out." The chief of station leaned forward in his chair, placing his elbows on his knees. He looked Naomi and Frisco in the eyes.

"Similar to generations before us fightin' for nuclear weapons, we're on the dawn of a new age. We're in an artificial intelligence arms race that is escalatin' into a hot war. And Dr. Kenzo Ichikawa is the first casualty. We're concerned that Dr. Hawkins may be next."

"But we were treating neurons to help with Parkinson's disease and mapping out camera feeds with machine learning. What does that have to do with some AI war?" She folded her arms to contain herself.

"You're well aware that's not *all* you were doin'. You were workin' on things that are very different than the way that everyone else is tryin' to solve this problem. First of all, is the— what do you call it? The God Algorithm?" Miles asked.

"Yes," Naomi replied with a nod. The speed of her gesture exuded a get-on-with-it vibe.

"As I said before, we're afraid Dr. Ichikawa's death is part of an international arms race for artificial intelligence. As much as the United States and the West would like to slow the weaponization of AI, nothin' is stoppin' Russia and China from doin' it. Both of those countries are willin' to compromise the privacy of their people to accomplish this task. For example, has Dr. Hawkins ever run this algorithm at scale?"

"So that is why you had me stop by Xiphos. You want to run the God Algorithm on their network." Naomi's sharp eyes narrowed. *Is the US government behind this? To get the God Algorithm for themselves? Did the government kill my friends to justify escalation, to get access to both our algorithm and the Xiphos network?* Naomi thought. *Good thing they do not have all of it.*

Miles asked, "Any idea what would happen if you did?"

"The goal of the God Algorithm is to mimic human instincts and magnify them. So, putting the God Algorithm at scale would allow you to create a competent predictive model of the future."

"How capable?" Frisco asked.

Naomi's bottom lip slipped between her teeth, and she bit down lightly before releasing it to speak.

"Imagine you could identify the most likely outcome to a particular plan of action. You could create an extremely accurate model of how to achieve any result you wanted."

"Like you could see the future?" the ambassador asked.

That's precisely what it can do. "It cannot predict chaos theory, but it can be quite powerful with the right data source," Naomi diverted.

"Wait," Frisco jumped in, "I thought artificial intelligence had to do with creating thinking robots? Like, you know, the Turing test and all that stuff—creating robots that act like people." He shifted the angle of his body toward Naomi.

But it was Miles Johnson who answered. "That's usually referred to as 'general AI.' We won't see true humanlike AI before we see overpopulation on Mars. It's not just the processing power, it's the sophisticated layers of software and machine learning to make it work. Think of that as a separate part of the war. The part we will see in the near future, during this initial growth of AI, will be specialized machine learning for specific tasks to amplify human capacity, automate and autonomize processes." The chief of station's words unnerved Naomi. She didn't like this new world in which she lived.

He went on. "The world's powers are aggressively chasin' AI solutions. They aren't afraid to do tests on people either. Just look at Russia's blood dopin'. China is workin' on buildin' supersoldiers who don't need to sleep even though this shortens their soldiers' lifespans. They have 1.3 billion people to experiment on, so why should they care?

"To further prove my point, Dr. Shimoda, tell us about Dr. Ichikawa's daughter."

Regardless of how critical to the current situation, to suddenly splay Kenzo's whole life out in the open for analysis felt invasive.

"I...I am not sure...what I can say, really..." Naomi said. *I know what I can say...I just refuse.* As this conversation progressed, she trusted certain parties less and less.

Buck decided to become relevant. "Everything you know would be a good start," he said, his voice grating.

"How does this prove your point again?" Naomi snapped.

"We know that Dr. Ichikawa's daughter died of a rare disease. That disease motivated the work you were doing on the algorithm," the chief of station said.

"There you have it then. What else do you want?"

"We're trying to find your colleagues. You owe us some cooperation." Buck ejected more tobacco spit into the bottle.

"Cooperation? I owe you nothing!" Naomi shot to her feet and pointed angrily at Buck and the chief of station. "I have just lost my mentor and my best friend, and here you are telling me that my life's work had something to do with some international arms race. You are also telling me that you have been watching us, but you were too *inept* at recognizing that our lives were in danger this entire time!"

Buck snarled. Miles remained composed. The other people in the room stiffened, and she suddenly remembered the size of the audience.

"Naomi, we're just trying to help," the ambassador said calmly. "We understand how hard this must be for you."

Naomi paced the room with her arms folded in an attempt to isolate the myriad of emotions welling up inside.

Frisco rotated in his chair to face her.

"Naomi, you know we have a team here to support you. We're gonna find the answers."

That's what I'm afraid of. She wanted to find the killer, save Taka-chan and herself, but...

Frisco continued, "Luckily, we have the algorithm already, thanks to Dr. Hawkins's quick thinking. Is there something else we should be concerned about?"

Naomi took several deep breaths as she paced, then answered Frisco directly, almost as a slight to everyone else in the room.

"The algorithm has two parts. The part that Dr. Hawkins sent at the last minute and another part we call the 'key.'"

"Where is it now?" Buck said. The way his upper lip curled made him look like he was constantly smelling something unpleasant, his upper lip most likely.

Naomi saw people as binary figures—zeroes and ones, good people or wasted energy.

Buck was officially a zero.

Frisco repeated the question. "Naomi, please, any idea where the key might be?"

"In my lab."

Miles and Buck glanced at each other, frowns implying a problem. Naomi read the room.

"Did something happen to my lab?"

"It was torn to pieces," the superintendent general stated.

"I want to go see it right away. I need to stop by my apartment on the way."

"Before you go, there's something I'd like to show you, Dr. Shimoda." Miles Johnson opened a laptop on the ambassador's desk. As he rotated the monitor to allow Naomi to see, she immediately recognized the scene to be from inside her own lab.

"What is this?" Naomi asked, her skin tingling.

Miles Johnson nodded to the SAT captain, who handed him something out of Naomi's sight. Miles Johnson then held up a Samsung cell phone in a plastic evidence bag. "We found this cell phone pinned under some toppled equipment in the lab. Do you recognize it?"

Project Kawa.

"I am not sure. It probably belonged to Kenzo."

"All call history on the phone has been erased. We *were* able to retrieve a video recording from this phone that took place the day that Dr. Hawkins disappeared and, apparently, the day Dr. Ichikawa was murdered. Listen carefully."

The phone must have been lying on a counter or some other horizontal surface because only the ceiling could be seen.

"I walked in an hour ago and found you like this," a woman's voice said.

Taka-chan.

"You weren't supposed to be in until later. I thought I had time," Dr. Ichikawa replied.

"This is too much, Kenzo. Why on earth would you keep all this a secret? Don't you think we could have worked better together if I knew what you were doing?"

"I thought you would quit."

"Well, you got that right." Heavy footsteps pounded out of the room. "I quit!"

The video stopped.

Miles Johnson's eyes focused on Naomi. "Any idea what that was all about?"

Naomi shook her head, genuinely at a loss as to what they had been fighting about.

"I do not have a clue. Perhaps if I can go to the lab, I can help you find the answers."

The SAT captain nodded. "We'll have someone escort you to your apartment first and then to the lab."

"We have one more important question, though. Do you know where the key you mentioned may have been stored? Was it somewhere safe?" the ambassador asked.

"Dr. Ichikawa locked it in a secure location in the lab that only he could get into. It was accessible only through a retinal scan."

"Did you say a retinal scan?" Frisco asked, his eyes askance.

"Yes."

That was when it dawned on her too. Parts of Dr. Ichikawa were still missing.

CHAPTER 18

The Corporate Merger

TOKYO, JAPAN

His phone rang. The businessman, or "salaryman," as is the term in Japan, ignored it and downed another shot of sake. The sumo matches on the media wall across the street from the sushi bar held his gaze as he finished another slice of sashimi. He couldn't remember how long he'd been there or how much he had to drink. The off-site business lunch in town got canceled, so he'd decided to call it a day. The more he drank, the more he defaulted to muscle memory—get off work, drink sake, eat dinner, drink sake, play pachinko.

His phone rang again. It was the wife. He did what any salaryman would do getting a call from the mother of his children during work hours.

He ignored it.

He had a substantial buzz, and his cheeks were flushed. He paid his bill then placed both hands on the table to stabilize himself as he stood up and headed out. He ambled down the *shotengai* and lackadaisically glanced once more at the sumo wrestlers on the screen. A woman passed him with a short skirt and his eyes wandered, lingering uncomfortably longer than they should.

He found the entrance to the pachinko parlor and made his way over. The security guard looked at him and made eye contact. The guard gave a courteous bow in acknowledgment of the returning customer.

About ten meters from the entrance, the salaryman collided with a large mass, another pedestrian.

"*Sumimasen! Gomen nasai!*" the pedestrian said incessantly.

"*Ii yo. Daijobu,*" the salaryman replied, accepting the man's apology, but considering how drunk he felt, he just assumed *he* was the one not paying attention.

He made his way into the pachinko parlor and looked for his lucky machine—first row on the left, third machine down. He wanted the one with a cartoon version of the ancient Japanese goddess Amaterasu. He liked to let his imagination wander as he played the game, which always involved elaborate ways of figuring out what she was hiding.

He sat down and let routine take the helm. He knew tonight was going to be a long one.

• • •

People have relationships with their cell phones. What they don't realize is that phones, as they are designed, are extremely needy—constantly reminding you they are low on power and desperate for network coverage. If you leave them alone for too long, they start pinging and buzzing, turning you into a codependent.

Voodoo always felt that mobile phones are like an insecure girlfriend constantly searching for reassurance in a lousy relationship. Cell phones are the "Stage Five Clinger" you pick up at the bar at 2 a.m. who won't leave you alone because they feel there's a "connection." To a cell phone, love is four bars, and they'll desperately seek out coverage wherever they can get it. As long as they are on, phones will search for reception until they die.

Also, like a controlling boyfriend, cell phones can become stalkers.

They're always watching; they're high-maintenance partners who remember everywhere you've been. Even when you think the phone is in airplane mode, something is running in the background, gathering information to push off to a third party, or post on the internet. They stalk your every move, pretending it's in your best interest, when they're really just in it for themselves.

Voodoo was already leaving the *shotengai* by the time he pulled out one of his needy girlfriends. Identifying his mark was much more straightforward than he thought it would be. The pocket of the salaryman's suit jacket was the perfect place for Voodoo to "accidentally" lose a piece of hardware; the salaryman now had a stalker in his coat and thus unwittingly smuggled radio surveillance hardware into the pachinko parlor. Voodoo digitally slaved the phone he dropped in the man's pocket to his and all the information it collected streamed to Voodoo in real time. Voodoo's four other girlfriends remained in the bag with their power off.

As long as the salaryman's phone sat in the pachinko parlor, every device inside would be detected including the Wi-Fi MAC address DZ wanted. It required only a few minutes to get what they needed, and the elaborate encryption and self-destructive software installed on the phone meant no one would ever know what the phone could do.

Just like the engineers at Xiphos or Dr. Hawkins, Voodoo had some machine learning tricks of his own. Every device that Voodoo carried could continuously collect, process, and analyze information. His tools then used k-means algorithms to search for anomalies and outliers. Wherever Voodoo went, he created patterns, which fed models, which trained neural networks, which output results. Results that later tipped Voodoo to whether someone was following him or could help him find his prey.

In such an event, Voodoo could then set his phone to detect the strength of the signal from a target device that person uses. He could then know the values of that device's RSSI, or received signal strength indicator, which popped up as numbers on Voodoo's phone or on the augmented reality contact lenses he snuck out of the Directorate.

It was nearing 5 p.m. when Voodoo made his way out of the *shotengai* and down into the subway. He beeped a prepaid card, walked through the turnstile and boarded the next train.

As it moved, Voodoo stood, holding on to a pole on a tightly packed train, hustling along to its schedule with impeccable precision. A salaryman stared out the window, searching the world flying by for his life's purpose. Elementary school students, with their black Prussian empire–like uniforms, shoved and giggled.

Voodoo turned on one of his phones and felt a haptic buzz. He opened the secure chat application, and messages populated the screen.

DZ: I got into Ichikawa's emails, used that to figure out how he was tracking and reporting his project funding. I pushed the financial stuff to Xiphos.

Janet: Interesting stuff. Apparently, they had funding from two major donors. They had millions for the computer vision work from a company called Orasi Technologies, and other funding came from a different source. The project had a couple different internal names that hid the exact nature of the work. I kept finding it referenced by either a serial number or the names "Project Tsuru" and "Project Kawa."

Vudu: Did you find any white papers or statements of work defining the projects?

DZ: Not yet. I can keep looking.

Janet: What do Tsuru and Kawa mean?

Vudu: "Crane." Like the bird. And "river." Tell me about the other investor.

Janet: The other investment company is called Toyotomi Industries. They are a conglomerate that used to be a big deal but are much smaller than they once were.

Vudu: Anything good?

Janet: They focus on tech investment but do some stuff in pharmaceuticals and biosciences. They also have a dying logistics division. There is one thing that you should be aware of. Toyotomi just had a merger about six months ago with XJI, the Chinese tech VC group.

Voodoo mulled this new information over as the subway train zoomed through the city. A large Chinese company called Xin Jishu International, or better known as XJI, had recently merged with a Japanese conglomerate and invested in academic research in artificial intelligence. At first glance, that information seemed harmless enough. Voodoo knew otherwise.

THURSDAY 5:20 P.M.

Vudu: Is it possible that Xin Jishu knew about Dr. Ichikawa's work?

Janet: No idea. If they did, you could assume who else knows.

Vudu: China.

Sparks: I found out some information for you about North Korea.

Vudu: Send it.

Sparks: Apparently, they've been picking up their kidnapping activities out of Japan as of late. Back in the '90s, it was big for them to sneak up to the shore of Japan's west coast and snag random people to teach their military personnel Japanese. This is how their spies became good at infiltrating other countries.

Vudu: Any idea if there is a link to what we've got going on here?

Sparks: Not sure yet. Kinda weird that reports are coming out about that after twenty years of inactivity. Apparently, these guys have never heard of Rosetta Stone.

Vudu: Check. Have the analysts at the support center keep digging. I'm still interested in the person Hawkins mentioned called Dragon. Also, I should have asked for this earlier, but see if we can get call histories from Ichikawa's and Hawkins's cell phones.

Sparks: On it.

Janet: @**Vudu**, you should also know that I found something weird with the other company I mentioned.

Vudu: Go ahead.

Janet: They do a lot of work with machine learning but, the more I dug into them, the less legit they felt.

Vudu: How do you mean?

Janet: Ever heard of a shell company?

Vudu: Yeah, an inactive or fake company used for financial maneuvers. Do you think that someone is pushing money to Ichikawa secretly?

Janet: It's hard to say. Either way, this all seems weird.

Vudu: Let me know if you find anything else.

Voodoo knew that, as part of policy, every Chinese company ultimately answered to the Chinese government. If the government asked for information on investments or private customers, the company handed it over, no questions asked. Unlike the United States where warrants and court orders protected the rights of citizens, there was no such thing as private information as far as China was concerned.

So, anything XJI invested in ultimately became knowledge or property of the Chinese government. By purchasing Toyotomi, everything the Japanese conglomerate did now funneled straight to the Chinese government.

This included the God Algorithm. It started to make sense to Voodoo why the US government brought Special Operations into things.

As Voodoo's train neared the next station, he remembered the news he saw earlier and did a search.

"Parts of the body of prominent optogeneticist Dr. Kenzo Ichikawa found at Koishikawa Korakuen Gardens," the story read.

I need to meet up with Frisco and get an update, Voodoo thought.

Voodoo set a strategic chessboard in his mind and considered the new data. Two investment groups with questionable interests and shady backgrounds invested in Dr. Ichikawa's research, and now he's dead. The Chinese may be tracking the God Algorithm, and North Korea has increased its kidnapping activities.

Hopefully, the pachinko parlor yields some results.

Voodoo's train came to a stop and exhaled a steady stream of passengers. Another train arrived as Voodoo navigated the human obstacles bumping across the platform. He pulled the SIM card from his phone and snapped it in half. He then took his phone and threw it onto the tracks just as the train swooshed past. The wheels of the subway car disintegrated the Stage Five Clinger he bought only a few hours earlier.

Voodoo had officially broken up with his first Japanese girlfriend—his issues with commitment ran a little too deep.

The action was subtle enough that no one noticed. No matter how many phones Voodoo used as he connected to the internet, he couldn't hold on to a digital device for too long.

He couldn't have any stalkers.

He frequently alternated his clothes and hoodie to confuse any peering cameras on any mission, including changing his gait. His physical husk and digital soul shifted and adapted continuously. He had to perpetually evolve in his hunting grounds, gaining strength against his adversaries. He hid in plain sight. He moved one step closer to his enemies with every radio wave he intercepted.

Voodoo vanished out of the subway like a digital specter vaporizing from the physical world. And, like a ghost, he existed only to haunt the living.

CHAPTER 19

The Swimmer

WESTWATER CANYON
SOUTHERN UTAH, USA

The cold water shocked the air out of her lungs; her body went rigid. Disembodied liquid hands thrashed her about as blasting jets of water filled her ears. She tucked into a fetal position and compacted her fists, driving her nails into her palms.

Her back bounced off a rock wall with a dull thud as she submerged. She smashed her eyes shut and clenched her teeth.

Each horrifying second stretched and slowed the longer she remained underwater. The scream of the current and darkness of the brown, silty Colorado River disoriented and blinded her. She held tighter.

Fear set in. Her pulse spiked as she became hypoxic, her lungs grew hot, and her nose burned from inhaling water. The sound grew quieter, and cold surrounded her, but she knew she was moving, ushered through the eroded metamorphic rock, into the void of Hades Canyon.

The guides told her what dangers hid within the depths, how it all flowed to the gnarling teeth of something called Skull Rapid. Kerry imagined herself swallowed whole—lost like flotsam beside the bloated carcass of a beaver, dead-eyed and vacant like a fish with its brains bashed on the Vishnu Schist.

Suddenly the sound of the current vanished as the roar of the river assaulted her ears. Her body drew a dramatic and deep breath with a high-pitched gasp. She opened her eyes and splashes of water slapped her face.

"Kerry!" She could hear her sister's scream, but from where? The rock walls blurred past her.

"Kerry, look over here! Kerry! Look over here!" It was a man's voice and much closer. She turned her head downstream and opened her eyes enough to recognize a blue blurry object. One of the rafts was downstream. "Kerry, look at me!" She regained her sight and her breath just long enough. A guide stood in the middle of the boat. "Kerry, put one of your hands up!"

Kerry shot her right hand in the air. A small red bag flew toward her, and yellow rope paid out. It sailed over her head, and the line landed on her face. She frantically clawed at the rope until her fingers recognized a grip. Her knuckles tightened, and she tucked into a ball. She shifted back to the boat and fixated on the guide. The Vishnu Schist towered black and ominous. The rope snapped taut.

"Just don't let go. When you get close to the raft, let us turn you around so we can pull you in." She wanted to feel relieved but the turbulent water was still yanking at her feet. She knew the darkness of the water. She knew the cold—infinite and torturous. Skull was just ahead, and the last place she wanted to be was in the water.

"Get up and help me pull her out! I have to get this oar working," the guide yelled to a muscular woman sitting behind him. The guide spun Kerry around with her back to the raft. The muscular woman reached for Kerry's shoulder to help the guide. Kerry felt two sets of hands grab her lifejacket at her shoulders as she popped out of the water and landed in the back of the boat. The air was warm and shocking. Her legs were numb. She rolled on her side and coughed violently before turning onto her back again. She didn't want to move as she stared at the blue sky.

She glanced over to see the guide wave his arms in some signal to the lead boat. Then he manipulated a blue strap, and she noticed only one oar was attached to the boat. The left oar lay parallel to the side of the raft, and the guide held it in place with his left hand. He shimmied it through an ammo can handle and secured it with another strap.

Kerry shifted to a sitting position on the floor of the raft, pinned between a middle-aged man, a tall, muscular woman, and the groover. The raft seemed to be rotating to the right, and the rapids grew louder.

The raft increased in speed.

Kerry finally recognized the guide. It was Gavin and not Joel. Where was her sister?

Upstream, Joel fought the river with his oars. Ally's raft crashed into the bottom of Surprise. Her customers, oblivious to the recent rescue, hooted and cheered. Joel would have to wait for Ally's boat to pass before dropping back into the main current, or they would collide.

"Push through to Skull! Skip the cove! Just push through!" Joel yelled to Ally. The river muffled the exchange as the guides communicated upstream. Skull drew closer. The entire river appeared to be pushing right.

Spray from the Rock of Shock rose into the air like perpetual fireworks. A standing wave of water waited only one hundred yards away. They were dangerously close to the right side of the river as Gavin used the right oar to spin the boat clockwise until the bow faced upstream. At the same time, he pulled hard on a strap, cinching down the left oar, using the ammo can handle as a makeshift D ring.

Gavin snapped his head up. A large formation of rock in the shape of an arrow pointed down at them. Gavin exhaled sharply, put his head down, dug the blades into the water, and rowed.

As the river increased in speed, the rapid came into view. The standing wave was on the opposite side of an enormous hole in the river. The angry hydraulic was easily fifteen feet deep, and it appeared as though the entire river fed right into it.

Being near the stern of the boat as it faced downstream, Kerry finally saw the jaws of Skull Rapid. Just beyond, the canyon created the rectangular-shaped Room of Doom. Water in the room spun in circles. Trees and dead animals floated and submerged in the frothy brown water like a whirlpool to the underworld.

Beside the Room of Doom, water crawled dozens of feet up the canyon wall and stretched to the sky. Kerry hugged the groover and grit her teeth.

Gavin didn't pull for long before they met a big wave on the left side of the river. A mild splash hit their boat, and Kerry flinched. Then, abruptly, Gavin stopped rowing.

He pulled the blades of the oars out of the water.

The Rock of Shock passed to their left.

They cleared Skull.

The current pulled them downstream. The jaws of Skull remained agape, empty, and disappointed as their boat drifted away.

Gavin turned around and looked at Kerry with a big smile. His attempt at a goatee underscored his youth.

"Nice work, guys! That was awesome!" The passengers all cheered. "Skull can be the most horrifying rapid or the most boring, depending on how you run it. If you run it right, you skirt the whole rapid like we just did. We have three rapids to go, but these last ones are a party!"

Part of Kerry cringed at the invitation to Gavin's "party"; it was the part that still felt purgatory groping at her heels, but Kerry's chest tingled for a different reason. The adrenaline sparked by fear had converted to exhilaration. On the backside of danger, she saw the reflection of a stronger woman inside herself; a woman who didn't care about how she never looked right in low-rise jeans; a woman who wasn't afraid of her own potential; a young woman who would have done more for a dying friend...a friend who was now gone.

She gazed at the canyon around her and marveled at its power. Kerry had faced a gauntlet of unforgiving natural realities and come out the other side. She had been reborn.

Gavin reached out his hand in the shape of a fist. "You good?" he asked Kerry, already seeming to know the answer.

Kerry gave a grin. "Never better," she replied as she made a fist and bumped his.

Gavin beamed. "Fate is a river. We just have to make it through the rapids. I'll have to tell you specifically what this means later, but last night someone told me where to find you." His glance grew sincere and warm. "I'm glad I did what she told me."

CHAPTER 20
The Guys in Masks

TOKYO, JAPAN

I t's easy to pick out a shooter roaming about the civilian population on a clandestine operation—just look for a muscular guy wearing a flannel shirt, jeans, black wraparound Gatorz sunglasses, a Garmin watch, and a someone's-gonna-die look on their face.

The humid summer air hit Frisco and Stu as they stepped out of the embassy. They flanked Naomi in their civilian shooter attire, ready to "blend" into the Japanese population after their less than productive meeting with the brass.

To say Naomi was not encouraged by the way things went at the embassy would be a dramatic understatement. Kenzo was dead, the missing Taka-chan may be dead as well, and apparently, Naomi was on the front lines of an artificial intelligence cold war being manipulated like a pawn on a chessboard by inept government officials. The only solace she seemed to find came from the personal security detail beside her as she walked out of the embassy to the waiting police escort.

She needed to find out what happened to her lab. But first, she needed to stop by her apartment.

"So, Naomi," Frisco started.

She braced herself for some snarky comment as they stepped into the police car. The door shut with Naomi in the front, Frisco and Stu in the back like a couple of perps.

"Just between us, word on the street has it that Buck is filing a hostile work environment complaint against you. I think you hurt his feelings."

Naomi smiled politely.

"In all seriousness, though, I've never seen anyone speak to him like that," Frisco said. "That was awesome."

The giant gave an awkward smile and nodded his head in agreement.

"I probably could have handled that better," she considered.

"Nah," Frisco said. "We just got a lot of heavy information dumped in our laps. Not being emotional would've been weird. I'll be the first to admit that my CO's delivery sucks."

"He seems like...a hard man to deal with."

"'Hard' is a generous word," Frisco replied thoughtfully.

Stu explained, "Buck comes from a hard time. In our community, there is nothing but hard dudes who all claim they are willing to make hard decisions. And then there are guys like Buck who are hard-headed and make it hard for everyone else."

"We need to buy you a thesaurus, Stu, but I agree with the sentiment."

Naomi let out a chuckle. She was growing fond of the way Stu and Frisco pecked at each other.

It was midafternoon in the metropolis and the streets were filled with heavy traffic. As they arrived, blue uniformed police held security while Frisco and Stu walked Naomi to her apartment.

"Take your shoes off at the genkan, please."

"What's a genkan?" Stu asked.

"That little area behind the door where you take off your shoes," she replied. Westerners, particularly men, go to elaborate lengths to keep shoes on their feet, so asking for their removal always made men look vulnerable. In a country like Japan, where it is custom to remove shoes, routine simplifies the process. The way Stu and Frisco tightly cinched their black Salomons on their feet wasn't doing them any favors.

Naomi lived in an apartment with a typical Tokyo layout. A narrow pathway that also served as the kitchen opened to a living area. A small bathroom sat behind the kitchen.

Stu looked like a giant trapped in a cage. He cocked his head to keep it from hitting the ceiling and walked sideways to fit inside.

"I feel like I'm visiting the home of a hobbit," Stu said.

Naomi let out a chortle.

"Are you sure you don't want us to wait outside while you freshen up?" Frisco asked. Naomi realized the tight quarters didn't require her security detail to remain in the room itself.

"You are right. Perhaps you should wait outside with the police officers for a few minutes. Do you mind?"

"Of course not," Frisco said. Stu grumbled.

Naomi watched as Stu and Frisco awkwardly moved back to the genkan, Stu wobbling like a penguin. They took turns putting on their shoes in the tiny space. Frisco smashed himself in the corner while Stu bobbled on one foot, jamming the other into a shoe like a giant toddler.

"I feel like we're getting dressed in a closet," Frisco said. "I'm sure you're kicking us out so quickly just to mess with us."

Naomi chuckled again.

"Hey, the police escorts aren't here anymore," Frisco said as he opened the door. "I'm gonna go check down the hall and see where they went. Stu, stay outside the door just in case."

The door closed behind Stu; Naomi gave her apartment a once-over. Her drawers, futons, and clothes all seemed to be just as she left them. Then came the moment of truth.

Please tell me it's still here.

She took a deep breath and opened her refrigerator. Nestled within an egg carton in a plastic bag, a black terabyte hard drive hibernated in the chill. She retrieved the cell phone–sized item and slipped it into her purse, finally allowing herself to exhale.

Thank God.

She snatched a Yakult yogurt drink, popped off the aluminum seal, and downed it in celebration as she leaned against the wall, allowing the refrigerator door to squeeze itself shut.

Her pink futon resting in the corner drew her eye. The sight made her sluggish. International travel, uncomfortable airplane seats, and Voodoo's nightmares were taking their toll. That and the secrets. She shook herself awake to remain focused. The thought of Voodoo's dreams reminded her of their brief conversation.

Naomi had questions.

She also had answers she wasn't sharing—some of which rested in the terabyte drive she had just rescued from the egg carton in her refrigerator. She always wondered why Kenzo told her to keep a spare somewhere safe. Now she knew why.

She needed to come clean eventually, especially considering the new facts. Voodoo's dreams certainly changed the dynamic. Naomi wanted to say she knew everything Dr. Ichikawa was up to, but that just wasn't true. Voodoo's dreams proved that.

Naomi's mind raced.

Kenzo created the proteins that he put into his daughter's bloodstream to try to cure her disease. Those same proteins eventually created predictive dreams. Those dreams appeared prophetic to him and led Dr. Ichikawa down a dark path toward an algorithm that, in essence, could tell the future. None of *that* explains Voodoo's experiences unless he had the very same protein in his system as well.

But how did it get there? Naomi wondered. *How many others have it in their bloodstream? Was the virus used to deliver the protein somehow spreading? If so, how did it get out of the lab? Perhaps the protein itself mutated into a prion virus like mad cow disease? Or a combination of the two like a coronavirus?*

There was only one way to find out. She would need a sample of Voodoo's blood and access to a lab. She could make a genetic and chemical comparison between his blood and the blood of Dr. Ichikawa's daughter, since she now had all that data in her purse. She just needed to get Voodoo to meet them at the university. That was assuming all her equipment still worked.

Naomi grabbed a fresh pair of pants, a shirt, and some underwear and turned toward the bathroom.

The door was closed.

She froze. Naomi lived alone. She never closed the door.

Suddenly, the door whipped open, and a blur of a man lunged at her. A calloused hand cupped her mouth, and another wrapped around her head. A dense mass shoved her back. The force of the assailant's body drove her to the tatami floor.

Naomi opened her mouth to scream, but flesh intruded into her mouth before smashing her jaw shut. Her free arms punched pathetically at his sides. Her 103-pound frame was no match for her assailant. He maneuvered to his knees and sat back to position his weight on her pelvis. He squeezed his elbows and held tight against his sides while he held her mouth. He crushed her head in his grasp.

His face was a mere inch from hers, obscured by a mask. An angry fire burned behind his dark eyes. His breath reeked of halitosis, the type someone gets when they haven't eaten in a long time. His body odor a bath of garlic. His weight compressed her internal organs.

Her eyes bulged as she searched her room for something to help fight back.

I can't breathe!

She wiggled her chin low enough to retract her lips as she tussled. Her mouth opened just wide enough to get the skin on his palm to slide between her incisors. She clamped down with her teeth and thrashed side to side.

The man pulled back his hand just long enough for her to yell. "STU! STU! HELP ME!"

The man swung back, slapped Naomi hard across the face, caught her ear with his open hand. A high-pitched ring assaulted her head. Her face stung, eyes watered. The man reached back, grabbed something, covered her mouth again, now with a cloth pungent with chemicals. He rolled to his feet, her head engulfed between his hands, ready to stand with her dangling like a rag doll.

His strength horrified her.

She swung her arms and legs frantically and squeezed her eyes shut to clear her vision. Her eyes blinked open just in time to see it.

The towering shadow of a man filled the room. Stu grabbed the assailant from behind in a rear-naked choke with his right arm and yanked back hard. The assailant instantly released Naomi, who collapsed to the ground gasping for air.

She rolled onto all fours coughing.

Stu's arms swallowed the man's head. He stepped back hard to pull the man off balance. The assailant flailed and kicked for only a moment before his arms dropped to his sides, listless. Stu's arms squeezed his neck in a "sleeper hold," cutting off blood to the carotid arteries, the victim blacking out in seconds. Stu held on a little longer, then he let go. The man dropped to the tatami floor in a heap. A gentle snore croaked from his nose.

"You okay?" Stu asked.

Naomi nodded, crawling away in retreat.

Naomi wet herself from shock during the attack. She felt it ironic considering all of the times that she mentioned what happens to the body's sympathetic nervous system during a fight or flight scenario. The most common outcome to extreme fear is people soil themselves as the body transfers energy from digestion and sphincter dilation to breathing and adrenaline release. She was happy it was only urine, but she had no intention of informing Stu; she only hoped the smell wouldn't give her away. Thankfully, enough sweat and testosterone infused the air as well, masking it.

"What's up with his face?" Stu asked.

"I think it is a mask."

"Let's find out." Stu grabbed the flesh of the man's face and pulled. At first, it didn't budge. Then, it did. The layer of skin on the assailant's face sloughed off and ripped, revealing a normal Japanese man underneath. Tattoos decorated the lower part of his neck, leading her to assume they covered his whole body.

"Why not just wear a normal mask? This doesn't make sense," Stu said.

"They still look kind of normal, I suppose. I'm not sure." Naomi looked up at the door and realized the police hadn't followed Stu in. "Where's Frisco?"

"He went to see where the police went."

The assailant snored.

"We need to tie this dude up. Got some zip ties?"

Naomi canted her head sideways and half squinted.

"Why on earth would I have zip ties?"

Stu shrugged. He reminded Naomi of a caveman next to a deer carcass.

"I'll see what I have. We may be able to take some of my clothes and tie up his hands with those." Naomi searched her drawers and presented some thick string. "Will this work?"

Stu took the coarse white string, rolled the snoring attacker onto his stomach, and put his knee on his back to tie his hands. Stu's back was to the entryway as he pinned the man down. Naomi stood in front of him in the middle of the small living space.

Naomi picked up her phone to dial for the police when the door of her apartment opened, and two officers stepped in.

Frisco must have found them.

But as they got closer, she realized their faces were the same as her assailant's: featureless.

"Stu, turn around!" Naomi called out. The men in police uniforms reached to their belts and pulled out some type of a baton.

The first officer shoved the business end of his baton into Stu and leaned in hard. Ten thousand volts bit Stu in his lower back. He lurched forward over the sleeping body on the ground and nearly crushed Naomi, who jumped back against the wall.

The other officer met his partner, and the two men stood side by side with the prior assailant on the ground. Stu rose to his feet, seething like a demon. His body looked like it filled one-third the width of the room as he stood between the masked men and Naomi. One officer held out his baton as a warning to keep back.

The other, taller of the two officers squatted down and unwrapped the hands of the assailant.

"*Nani ga hoshii desu ka?*" Naomi asked. She already knew what they wanted, but she needed to stall them. The men didn't answer. The tall officer slapped the face of the assailant on the ground to wake him. The look on Stu's face danced between confusion and anger.

Naomi thought, *Are these the same officers as before, but they put masks on, or did something happen to those officers? Where's Frisco?*

The assailant on the ground stirred and the shorter officer glanced down at him.

Instantly, Stu took one step forward and leaned in hard with a haymaker to the shorter officer.

The man weaved under Stu's punch but shoved the baton into Stu's armpit.

Stu flinched, and his arm tucked tightly into his chest as he flew sideways and crushed Naomi's tiny desk.

Both officers lunged forward, shocking Stu with the batons.

"I'm gonna kill you!" Stu yelled between gritted teeth.

With every attempt to move, they struck again. No matter how strong, 10,000 volts debilitate the strongest of animals, and the Stu-Bear collapsed into a fetal position. Even when he tried to make himself small, Stu was enormous.

The short man stood over Stu with occasional prods to make sure he didn't move while the taller man angled toward Naomi. The assailant in black rose to his feet like flesh reanimated.

"Please...no!"

Naomi filled with dread as the men grabbed her by the arms and covered her mouth with the cloth.

Frisco, where are you?

CHAPTER 21

The Breach

" These files are a lot more complicated than I expected them to be," Andy said as he stared at his computer. Reading code without context is hard enough; reading code and trying to implement it without the author felt insurmountable.

"Well, the person that wrote them did make something called the God Algorithm. Are we sure that we downloaded everything from the Dropbox account?" Janet Han asked, looking over Andy's bony shoulder as she manned her own laptop.

They sat in Andy's office at Xiphos AI. It was 7 a.m. Working through the night, they were able to implement some of the easier computer vision algorithms quickly, but the more advanced variations remained elusive. They had been working nonstop with the codes they received nearly twenty-four hours earlier. They hadn't changed clothes, and the bingeing reminded Andy of their younger days building software for their first company.

"I'm surprised that Naomi didn't put up more of an argument when we described what our company is capable of," Janet said, releasing her ponytail and running her fingers through her hair. A slight beard shaded Andy's face in splotchy sections as it grew from the last time he shaved thirty hours earlier.

"What do you mean?" Andy asked.

"You know, same ol' thing. We're a private company trying to offer the government the ability to access numerous computers in the world for massive processing. I'm just surprised she didn't freak out about it is all."

"Well, I would like to think that fear for her friend's life superseded all other concerns at the time," Andy said. His long fingers nimbly piloted the keyboard.

It was a source of significant debate within their company. Many of the members of the team didn't even know the capability existed. Xiphos marketed itself as the company that enables the little guy to benefit from the data growth boom.

Since 2015, data was now more valuable than oil. Data manipulated elections, controlled and confirmed purchases, dominated marketing strategies, and the future required both machine learning and significant processing capacity. Andy and Janet hated the idea of the tech giants dominating and lording over the average Joes of the world. Xiphos AI was a chance to take that back and let the public use their hardware and resources to their advantage.

Despite the villainous undertones, Xiphos Gov developed by accident. During the creation of their system, they realized they could unintentionally take control of an unwitting person's computer and use it to process data. The mistake initially alarmed them.

Then, it inspired them.

It was a much simpler process than they expected. Xiphos AI sought out a large group of willing people to help them experiment. Suddenly they had the ability to probe and identify latent computers—from unsuspecting people—to be assimilated into a massive processing hive.

"It's the same old argument: China and Russia aren't going to play by the rules, why should we? At least this way we can help ourselves by helping the government. China is going to steal from its citizens regardless. We've seen the writing on the wall. If we don't step up to help fight this war, no one will. Large defense contractors, with their entrenched mindsets, don't see the value and, with the way things are moving so quickly, can't draw the right talent. The average citizen doesn't even know this is going on," Janet said. "It's like how they also don't know their information is harvested daily. They're too busy checking their 'gram feeds for followers, not realizing they are feeding a machine that is sucking away their money."

The average citizen is grossly unaware of how much money their daily interactions on the internet are really worth. Private companies capitalize on this ignorance and exploit the average user. Maintaining a social presence costs time, time spent creating personas to draw attention, attention that creates followers, followers that watch ads, advertisements that hide the real metrics. Every time a user touches their account, they develop metrics that feed statistics and algorithms. And this data can be manipulated.

This same data is available to governments who aren't afraid to exploit it. When they successfully discovered how to usurp excess processing power from unsuspecting users, they discovered a side effect: they could also harvest that user's data at the same time.

Democratic countries do not approve of this type of manipulation. In many cases, Western governments don't even know
how to access it. Janet and Andy knew this because their interactions with Voodoo helped them learn about the flaws in how
the government acquires and uses new technology.

The entire defense research and acquisition process was
designed in the 1960s by the secretary of defense. The idea
being that milestone-based checks and balances would allow the
government to develop new technology at a pace that wouldn't
escalate the arms race with the Soviet Union. At the time, it
was a good idea. Nobody wanted the economic escalation and
danger of nuclear weapons development to run out of control.

However, everything changed in the year 2000. Up until
then, government laboratories exceeded private industry in
technology development. Suddenly, technology boomed, with
supercomputers, processing chips, the internet, and cellular
technology, which dramatically increased the private world's
ability to grow exponentially. Giant defense contractors like the
companies building ships and jets, bogged down in their own
bureaucracy, had a hard time finding talent and fell behind. This
sudden boom left the defense ecosystem of the United States in
the dust. As the research and acquisition process failed to adapt,
aggressive warfighters began seeking answers elsewhere.

Startups became that answer. Andy and Janet pounced.

As they attended undergraduate and graduate schools like
MIT and Carnegie Mellon, Andy and Janet realized that almost
all the students were from foreign countries, and many of them
were from China. As students, Janet and Andy didn't see this as
that big of an issue. When they entered the industry, however,
they realized the ramifications of sharing information through
manufacturing with other countries. Theft of intellectual

property proved rampant, and China now had more PhDs in engineering than the US had graduate students total.

Andy and Janet stared at the screen as Andy typed.

"So, I told Voodoo about XJI. I'm sure he's already putting the pieces together," Janet said.

Six months earlier, XJI gave Xiphos AI a very aggressive pitch for investment. Janet and Andy decided to talk to Voodoo about it. Voodoo warned them about Chinese investment in companies hoping to work with the government. It was a very overt tactic on their part. If Chinese companies own a piece of the intellectual property of startups hoping to work with the US government, the startup immediately lost their eligibility, and the Chinese gained access to the intellectual property before it went to the US government.

Rob, replicate, and replace—that's the Chinese strategy. Voodoo also warned them that the usual outcome of refusing an investment from a Chinese company resulted in dramatic increases in cyberattacks.

Xiphos was not an exception.

They denied the offer and faced a deluge of penetration attempts on their network. Fortunately, before they sent the official refusal to XJI, Voodoo helped them prepare for the onslaught of hacking attempts.

"Good thing our cybersecurity is on point—"

Andy stopped just as he noticed something strange. He replayed the video he had sent over to Voodoo of the capture of Dr. Hawkins. He watched her fall, try to get up, and then get tased by her assailants.

He stopped.

"Um, Janet...watch."

The same video played again.

"There." Andy pointed at the monitor. On the paused screen, two men carried Dr. Hawkins off-screen as the third picked something up off the ground.

"Does that look like a computer to you?" Andy asked. The angle of the camera feed obscured what the third man picked up, but the corner of something silver was evident once he pointed it out.

"So, the guys that grabbed her have her computer."

"We can only assume they were able to get into it." They looked at each other and blood rushed to their heads.

"Pull up Dropbox again," Janet said. Andy clicked on the browser tab for the Dropbox account, logged in using the information that Naomi gave him, and navigated to the God Algorithm's file.

Janet's and Andy's jaws went slack.

All the files were gone.

Janet ran out of the room and sprinted across the open architecture office to the back section where their lead IT guy sat. Andy could see Janet through the glass walls as she frantically communicated with the IT lead via exaggerated facial expressions, her hand on one hip while the other rubbed the top of her head over and over.

Andy pulled the plug out of his computer and disconnected the Ethernet cable.

Please don't tell me they got into our network.

CHAPTER 22
The Reinforcement

"Sir!" The young female officer saluted as an inspector approached the parked patrol cars beneath Naomi's apartment building. "Dr. Shimoda is upstairs with the Americans and two other officers."

Above them, the ten-story building stood on pillars creating a space underneath for a parking garage. The peculiar engineering of the complex didn't include stairs spiraling down at each end of the building as would be expected. Instead, three sets of stairs attached to the front, ascending diagonally from left to right as if the builders had added them last.

"Very well," he replied. "Radio to the other men to get down here. I want to get a quick update."

"Yes, sir. I'll have two other men relieve them."

"That won't be necessary. I have some men already heading up," he replied. The young officer couldn't help but fixate on the inspector's piglike facial features. The officer averted her gaze. Chatter squawked on the radio, and a reply echoed back.

"My squad is going to take over from here. I know that Dr. Shimoda will be leaving here soon, so go ahead and meet us at the university," the inspector said.

The young officer frowned. But they had just arrived, and they were explicitly directed by their sergeant to remain and escort Dr. Shimoda to the university. As a young officer recently promoted to the rank of senior police officer, this was the type of detail that could make or break her career. The murder of Dr. Kenzo Ichikawa had already garnered national attention. The last thing she wanted to do was to make a mistake. Now an inspector, who outranked her sergeant, told her to leave the premises. Yet her sergeant was her immediate supervisor.

"Inspector, Sergeant Ooda ordered me to remain with Dr. Shimoda no matter what. Perhaps we can remain with your men and travel to the university with you from here." She motioned to key up the radio when the inspector leaned forward and grabbed her hand.

"My squad is taking over. I will notify Sergeant Ooda myself. Now leave!"

"Yes, sir!" She spun around as the two men from her security detail near Naomi's apartment arrived. "The inspector has ordered us to move on to set up security at the university." She was in no position to question the orders, no matter if out of sequence. They jumped into their vehicles and drove off, leaving the inspector and two patrol cars behind.

• • •

Frisco stepped out of the apartment and swiveled his head from left to right. Aside from the tiny Japanese washing machines or raccoon-like ceramic *tanuki* on some doorsteps, the concrete walkway in front of the apartment doors remained empty in both directions. He headed down a passageway and looked over the railing. In the parking lot below, officers climbed into patrol cars and mounted motorcycles.

"Where are you going?" he yelled, leaning over the rails and waving his arms.

He hustled down the stairwell. In the parking lot below, he made an unexpected discovery.

What the hell is wrong with these guys? he thought as he drew closer.

Two Japanese patrol cars sat at the bottom, with two policemen standing alongside. The faces of the officers appeared to be featureless, a blank canvas of flesh. They were neutral palettes with the outline of a nose and a mouth, emotionless and empty. They motioned for Frisco to come toward them. His quick descent came to a halt at the end of the stairs.

Frisco held his position with both hands on the rails, staring at them.

"*Oi, gaijin! Koi!*" one of the officers barked. Frisco didn't have a clue what they were saying, but he got the gist.

The threat Frisco's team expected to face in Japan had just arrived.

He took a slow step backward, his eyes fixed on the pair of goblins in front of him. He snapped his body around to sprint up the stairs.

With a jolt, a hand clutched his leg at the ankle and electricity surged through his body. He leaped sideways and slammed into the railing.

"*Tsukande yare!*" they yelled. Two officers flanked him under the stairwell. They grabbed his legs and dragged him toward one of the patrol cars, their constricting grip punctuated by isolated electric stabs.

Frisco kicked frantically and, with a connection to the groin of one, managed to break free, twisted, popped up, and sprinted toward an alley.

He made it only fifty meters before another bite of electricity brought him skidding to his knees. Repeated strikes forced him into a fetal position. He covered his head as the attackers softened him with kicks to the abdomen. Handcuffs clicked open.

Surrounded by four assaulters, between flinches and kicks, Frisco saw a man in a hoodie sprinting toward him down the alley, then slowing to become one with the shadows.

Voodoo shifted to a crouch, rolling his feet, heel to toe, as he crept closer.

Then, like an apparition trying to steal the body of the living, he attacked.

Voodoo grabbed the first goblin's shirt and pulled hard as he kicked the back of the man's knee. The masked officer's legs buckled; asphalt met tailbone as his hands spread to brace his weight. Voodoo struck him on the side of the neck with the blade edge of his hand. The isolated blow to the brachial plexus nerve overloaded the signals to the man's brain. He blacked out instantly.

Voodoo discarded him.

The three other men turned to engage Voodoo. One thrust with a baton. Voodoo parried, grabbed his baton-wielding limb, and rotated hard, manipulating the man's weight and momentum against him. The officer flipped through the air and slammed against the asphalt. Air expelled from his lungs with a grunt upon impact.

Voodoo ripped the baton from his hand and thrust the business end into the man's chest.

Voodoo quickly snapped his attention to the remaining officers.

Another bite immobilized Frisco.

He shut his eyes and bit down.

Scuffles met with yelling, then feet running off.

When he opened his eyes, Voodoo was standing over him. Frisco looked around to see three of the assailants jumping into a patrol car, leaving the fourth to fend for himself on the ground where Voodoo took him out.

"Where the hell did you come from?" Frisco asked. He touched his lip and looked to see blood on his fingers.

"I was across the street, watching for an opportunity to meet up with you. I was trying to keep anyone from seeing me after I heard the news about Dr. Ichikawa." Voodoo sifted through the downed man's clothes as he spoke. "Then I saw you run out and get attacked. Right before that, I saw some plainclothes officer come up. He gave instructions, and the initial security detail took off, leaving the freaks with masks to take their place. I'm not sure what was going on there."

Voodoo pulled a cell phone from the officer's pocket. Then he grabbed the sleeping man's face and pulled. The skin-like material ripped off, revealing an average-looking man underneath. Voodoo used the facial recognition feature on the phone to unlock it. He then slipped a small black card into the phone.

"What're you doing?" Frisco asked.

"I'm planting a bug on his phone."

"Aren't you worried he'll find it?"

"It runs as supplemental software in the background, and it's encrypted. It's set to delete itself after a few days regardless."

Voodoo tapped on the phone with unnatural calm for a long moment then placed it back in the officer's pocket. Frisco swiveled his head, checking the perimeter.

"What's up with his buddies just ditching him like that?" Frisco asked.

"No clue." Voodoo looked up from the alley toward the apartment complex. "We haven't seen anything happen up at Naomi's apartment, and I can't see Stu. We should check."

"On it," Frisco replied as he struggled to get to his feet. Voodoo took an arm and helped him.

"Are you sure?" Voodoo asked.

"I'm good, man. Check the patrol car that's still here. I'll see what's up with Stu." Frisco immediately regretted his zeal. It was hard to move; he felt the way he would two days after a heavy squat day at the gym. Those guys had worked him over more than Frisco realized.

He fought through the pain and got up the stairs. As he reached the fourth floor, he noticed two more men dragging Naomi to the stairwell on the opposite side of the building.

"Voodoo! They're taking Naomi!" he warned, leaning over the railing to the parking lot below.

Voodoo cut the kidnappers off at the parking garage, electric baton in hand.

A man in black turned to confront Voodoo, remnants of a torn mask still stuck to his face. The other dragged Naomi behind his partner.

The man in black presented a baton of his own.

Voodoo and his opponent squared off.

Voodoo feigned a lunge as the man in black stepped deep to the left and out of the way.

Frisco reached the bottom of the stairs, sweat dripping from his face, and paused to watch the encounter. *I know that look.* It was the look he got whenever Voodoo practiced witchcraft in Iraq; the look right before he started messing with someone's head.

Voodoo treated everything like a chess match. Everyone was a pawn for him to maneuver. The man in black was about to discover what it's like to have Voodoo manipulate him like a marionette.

Voodoo stared at the man's center mass. Gross motor movement always starts with the middle of the body. Unlike the gibberish taught in movies, you never watch an opponent's eyes. You watch their hips.

Voodoo's body mirrored every movement. The man in black was light on his feet. Every time he switched his stance, so did Voodoo, a mirror image.

Then Voodoo lunged.

His opponent stepped sideways again.

This time Voodoo was ready. Voodoo swung hard with a round kick inside the man's knee, buckling the joint.

Voodoo followed up with two quick strikes, one to his opponent's throat with his left hand and an electric stab with the baton from the other.

The man flew backward onto the asphalt, grabbed his throat, and coughed. Voodoo menacingly pointed the baton at the remaining officer, who immediately dropped Naomi and ran.

The man in black scrambled up and raced behind him to their car.

"Naomi, are you alright?" Frisco asked as he ran to her. She was nonresponsive. "Voodoo, pick her up and get her out of here! I need to check on Stu."

Just as he spoke, a series of bangs and thuds sounded as a man dressed in a police uniform tumbled down the stairs and flopped to the bottom like a rag doll. Frisco looked up to see Stu. His chest heaved. His massive muscles were vascular and jacked. Stu's attacker lay in a crumpled mass.

"Looks like Stu's okay," Frisco reported.

The patrol car whipped around. Voodoo's victim from the alley, alive and well, it seemed, screeched to a stop and the other two pretend cops quickly snatched the uniformed ball of flesh at the bottom of the stairs and shoved him in the patrol car. The four men sped off.

"What the hell was that?" Frisco blurted. Stu came running down the stairs. Naomi's voice croaked as she woke up.

"I wonder how deep their connections are in the real police," Voodoo said.

"It makes me wonder who we can trust. Naomi, are you alright?" Frisco asked. Naomi was still wearing the black skirt and pink button-down shirt from the day before. Her hair was tousled, her makeup smeared, and her face flushed where the assailant struck her.

"I'll be okay." She put her hand on her head. "I don't feel safe here anymore. We need to leave," she said, fighting to regain her bearings.

Voodoo asked Frisco, "What happened up there?"

Frisco bit his lip, then answered, "We didn't clear her place properly before we stepped back out. Dropped checking the bathroom. Such a damned small place that..." He broke off from his excuse. He knew there was none. "Bro-fessor Voodoo, what do you think we do now?"

"We're being watched," Voodoo said, looking up from his position next to Naomi in the shadows. "Anything we do is gonna be tracked visually from here on out unless we take precautions."

"What're you thinkin'?"

"Naomi comes with me. You two head back to the embassy. Two goofy American dudes running around in Japan sticks out too much and may lead the assailants straight to her. I have an idea where I can take her."

CHAPTER 23
The Love Hotel

KABUKICHO

TOKYO, JAPAN

"*Shinjuku eki onegaishimasu,*" Voodoo said as Naomi slid into the taxi beside him.

"No, we need to get to the university," Naomi said as she placed her hand on Voodoo's arm.

"I'm not sure we can trust the police. Whoever those guys are, they're most likely anticipating our every move," Voodoo said.

"What is in Shinjuku, then?"

"The busiest train station on the planet. Obfuscation. I'll find us a place to hide out for a bit. We have some work to do."

With no other valid argument, Naomi acquiesced. She preferred to be in control of her situations, made a point to do that normally. But the last several minutes had proven how little control she had. And if Voodoo hadn't shown up...

The taxi stumbled its way through Tokyo traffic as Voodoo and Naomi sat in the back seat. Naomi hugged her rolling bag with her feet as Voodoo held his bag on his lap.

"Is that all you have?" she asked.

"I travel as light as possible. I can always buy clothes, and Sparks is bringing stuff for me in the BIB anyway."

"How much time do you think we have?" Naomi asked.

"The dream told me we only have two days before this whole thing is over."

"Are your dreams usually that specific?"

"They tend to be...relatively specific, but I know I'm missing a lot. Instead of images associated with the dream, I just have my memories of—"

Voodoo cut himself off. Slipping in "how I murdered a child on a combat mission," that he's relived that moment every night in his nightmares, wasn't exactly something you do easily. That's why Voodoo never had. "I have memories of the explosion and a firefight," Voodoo finished.

"Is there any way to see past it, or do you think it is hidden in the vision somewhere?"

"No, it's like two separate voices are trying to speak to me: the memory in my subconscious and the voice in the darkness."

"Interesting," Naomi said as she glanced at Voodoo then did a double take. "Voodoo, is something different about your eyes? They look darker."

Voodoo reached up and pushed his eyelids open, brought his index finger up, then removed a contact lens. His eyes shifted from dark brown back to hazel.

"You're just full of surprises. Is that part of a disguise?"

"You can say that. These are augmented reality contact lenses. Inside the center of the lens is a 500-micron femto projector just smaller than the head of a pin." He lifted his wrist to show her a rectangular box that looked like a rudimentary digital watch. "The contact lenses are connected via electro-neurography to the nerves in my hand. I can control a menu of options to display text messages or video feeds from my phone in the contact lens."

Naomi stared at it. "I have heard of that sort of thing, but I have never seen one in real life. I had no idea you were wearing it."

"That's kinda the point. The cool thing is that I can see the video from my phone or anything on the network with my eyes open or shut. It displays like a little TV screen in the corner of my eye."

"When this whole thing is said and done, I want some. Imagine what you can do to the dreaming mind if you can send someone images while their eyes are closed."

"I'd never thought of that. Then again, up until yesterday, I'd never heard of optogenetics either."

"It is good we met then," Naomi said, her perfect eyebrows raised as her lips curved in a smile. "How long have you been wearing the lenses?"

"I put them in right before I headed to your apartment. I needed to get some equipment in place first before they would be effective." Voodoo slipped the contact back in his eye.

"I've been wondering, we haven't spoken much about Dr. Hawkins other than her work. What's she like?" Voodoo asked.

Naomi took a slow breath and a smile crept across her face. "Hilarious, stubborn, childish, brilliant. She reminds me of you, to be honest. She has the same energy—obsessive and passionate. She is not perfect, but perfectly so."

Voodoo looked out the window and slowly nodded his head.

"Her father is Japanese and grew up here, but she moved back to the States after high school. She is also very private. I know that she plays a lot of computer games, but sometimes, it is like she has a different life online. Like there is much more to her than I know."

"Well, perhaps we can figure it out when we find her. What about you? Do you have a family?"

Naomi's lip curved up slightly, then a mild sadness filled her face.

"Taka-chan and Kenzo are the closest thing I have to family. I say that because I have always been obsessed with my career, becoming known for accomplishing amazing things in my field. With them, I felt like I had found kindred spirits, a unified goal in accomplishing the impossible, changing the world. I never thought it would turn out like this..."

"We'll get her back. I promise." Voodoo gave a reassuring smile and the taxi came to a halt.

Less than an hour after the attempted assault on Naomi's life, they found themselves in a sea of people pouring out of the train station and filling the streets. Naomi wore a blue hoodie that Voodoo gave her. She'd ditched the designer handbag from earlier for a messenger bag, changed into some fresh clothes, and now dragged her small rolling suitcase behind with the few items she'd gathered quickly at her apartment.

They scurried along the busy streets flooded with activity. Voodoo relied on the waves of people to hide their path. His training in surveillance detection taught him to use natural opportunities to check his six. An alert would also tip him of any anomalies detected by his "girlfriends" straight into his contact lens.

"I hate to tell you this," Voodoo started. They were walking down a major thoroughfare in Kabukicho. During World War II, this area of Tokyo was heavily bombed, and the residential area predominantly destroyed. Reconstruction plans called for a large kabuki theater. That never happened, but the name remained. Now, Kabukicho is famous as Tokyo's red-light district. "We need to find a love hotel."

"Um, excuse me?"

"A love hotel. I'm sure you know what that is?"

"Of course I know what that is." Naomi glared at him before she softened. "I want to think you are joking, but I am following your line of thinking. They will not ask for your passport; we can pay with cash...I understand."

"Good. We need to regroup. I'm glad you're cool with this."

"I never said that. I just understand why we are doing it," Naomi stated.

Voodoo chuckled. "Trust me. This is very out of character for me."

"Which part, hunting kidnappers or dragging women through busy streets to prostitution dens?"

"The latter. I hunt people all the time." Voodoo winked. "I have some people gathering intel for us, and I need some time to find out if they've made any progress."

Naomi and Voodoo rambled through the busy streets as Voodoo thumbed the screen of his phone.

"I got one. And it's only a few hundred meters from here." Voodoo and Naomi came around the corner. A flood of bodies surrounded them. On the sides of the river of people, vending machines with everything from bags of rice and coffee to underwear and ramen lined the street. They walked up to an entryway with a neon sign that read The Passion Love Hotel.

Voodoo laughed out loud. "I'm so sorry, but this is hilarious."

Naomi rolled her eyes.

Voodoo used cash on hand to reserve the room for the night. The hotel offered the option of a "stay" or a "visit." Love hotels are a uniquely Japanese invention. In addition to the apparent association with prostitution, love hotels also offer privacy for intimacy. Whether they live in small apartments or with their parents, love hotels offer space and amenities for couples to be alone.

They checked into their room. The walls had pleated white curtains all around with LED lights behind them, creating a rainbow motif that flowed around the room. The floor lit up with pastels to match the undulating color on the walls, and a faux cowhide rug lay on the ground under a small couch next to a large banister bed. An elaborate picture of Hello Kitty nearly covered the entire ceiling.

"This is too Japanese even for me," Naomi said.

"I can feel 'the passion' already," Voodoo said, immediately regretting it.

To his relief, Naomi laughed. "You can feel however you like, just do it out here. I need to take a shower." She headed for the bathroom and instinctively stopped, like an animal recognizing a one-time trap. Voodoo saw her hesitation, stepped past her, checked out the small room, and gave her a thumbs-up. She smiled, carried her bag into the bathroom, and closed the door.

Voodoo opted to cozy up with his "girlfriend" in the meantime. He activated the chat application. Messages from Janet populated his screen.

THURSDAY 6:02 P.M.

> **Janet:** @**Vudu**, we've got a severe problem. The Dropbox with the God Algorithm is empty, and we're pretty sure someone has hijacked the Xiphos network.

THURSDAY 6:08 P.M.

Janet: @**Vudu**, where the hell are you?

Vudu: I'm here. Tell me what's going on.

Janet: Some of the algorithms weren't working, so we checked the Dropbox account. Everything was gone. Our network started acting weird and then shut off. We're in the middle of trying to figure out what happened.

Vudu: Dammit.

DZ: I'd track it down, but I've been busy with the collection on the pachinko parlor. I've found something you may need to see.

Vudu: Gimme something good.

DZ: I've been able to gain access to almost every computer in the pachinko parlor, but there is a separate network there that has some insane security.

Vudu: What's significant about that?

DZ: I'm used to people using VPNs and whatnot, but they are running security that I usually see on highly classified government systems.

Vudu: What're you saying then?

DZ: If you can penetrate the network, I think it'll open several doors for us. I've tracked the communication to some hubs outside of Japan...in China.

Voodoo knew what Delta Zulu was asking. He needed to get into the pachinko parlor, find the actual computer, and slip a thumb drive inside to gain access while active. Voodoo didn't like this idea.

> **Vudu:** I'm not super excited about needing to go in there. Do we know anything else about that place?
>
> **DZ:** The good news is that the network I need you to access is separate from the rest of the pachinko parlor. Remember the time I got hired to do some white hat hacking of that cruise ship?
>
> **Vudu:** Haha. Yeah.

Voodoo recalled it well. In between jobs, Delta Zulu took work as a contract cybermercenary doing white hat hacking for companies. They would hire him to test their networks operating as an average hacker trying to get in. In one instance, a trendy cruise line hired him to conduct penetration testing. Delta Zulu was able to take control of the entire ship at sea. He liked to refer to himself as "Captain" over the next few months.

> **DZ:** I hope that gives you some ideas. I'm standing by. I've already gained access to the pachinko parlor itself.
>
> **Vudu:** What about the traffic into China? Do you think it's China itself?
>
> **DZ:** This could be Division 121.
>
> **Vudu:** Who's that?
>
> **DZ:** North Korea's hacking division—which operates from outside the country itself.

Voodoo considered the proposition for a moment. Voodoo needed to know that what he was about to do would get them the required access. With luck, it may even help with Xiphos AI.

> **Vudu:** @**Janet**, were you able to shut the network down?

Janet: Our primary Xiphos network is offline right now, but we aren't sure the extent of the damage or what they were able to do. The good news is the Xiphos Gov operates on a completely different network for security reasons just like this. That is still safe.

Vudu: That's a relief. Do you feel comfortable using it if we need to?

Janet: I'll have to look into it, and I'll need some help. @**DZ** let me know when you've got time.

Sparks: @**Vudu** I have some information for you about Ichikawa's and Hawkins's cell phone records: there aren't any.

Vudu: What do you mean?

Sparks: They've been deleted. No records at all. Someone with network access to the service provider must have removed all of them.

Vudu: @**DZ** Think this could be Division 121?

DZ: Anything is possible at this point.

CHAPTER 24
Coming Clean

Voodoo sifted through apps and pulled up a tracking application to check on the status of the other phones connected to his network. The drunk salaryman remained inside the pachinko parlor in the same spot he had been several hours earlier when Voodoo bumped into him. The stalker was doing its job.

Two new cell phones appeared on the application. Just before Voodoo and Naomi snuck off, Frisco and Voodoo gave each other an update on the events at the embassy, the AI cold war, Voodoo's dreams potentially being linked, and the key required to unlock the algorithm that may be able to predict events in the future. Frisco and Stu then took a separate route back to the embassy to report to their CO. Frisco took one of Voodoo's phones with him.

If cell phones are like needy significant others, the phone Voodoo infected with a bug was a one-night stand. The relationship would be short, and then Voodoo would ghost it. The phone he'd bugged from the officer in the alley showed the man now moving through the city in the vicinity of the university.

Naomi exited the bathroom. She wore a T-shirt and jeans and rubbed her hair with a towel. Voodoo could see redness on her face where her assailant struck her.

"I see the ambiance is still...visually invasive. This is quite the place," Naomi said.

"Nothing but the best for scientists on the lam."

Voodoo spent the next few minutes updating Naomi on the chat messages and the severity of the situation.

"Here's the gist. We can go to the pachinko parlor to try to get answers there or go to the university like we originally planned. I'm not sure we'll be able to use the God Algorithm unless we can get a hold of the key you mentioned to Frisco at the embassy. We also need to figure out the North Koreans' and the Chinese investment company's roles in this whole mess."

"That is a lot, Voodoo. I cannot help but think our first option is to go to the pachinko parlor," she said.

"I'm not gonna lie, I'm really dreading that. I have no idea what's inside there. Usually, we stake out a place for a long time before trying to get in."

Naomi listened on the edge of the bed, sitting on her hands.

"The pachinko parlor probably comes first, but I have to ask, is the university the only place where you kept the key? There must be some other way to decrypt the God Algorithm. Having a tool that can help us predict the future would be clutch right about now."

Naomi stood up and paced the room. She bit her lip. Voodoo watched the gears turn in her head.

"I need to tell you something..."

"What is it?"

"I can already decrypt the algorithm."

Voodoo stood up. "What do you mean?"

Naomi averted her eyes and kept pacing. "I stored a hidden copy of our historic files in my apartment. That's why I needed to go back there." Naomi pulled the hard drive from her bag as evidence. "But I didn't have the most recent version of the algorithm itself." Naomi paused, mustering more courage. "The moment I got the text from Taka-chan, I downloaded *her* copy of the algorithm so I would have everything once I retrieved my drive. I then loaded one of the old versions from my laptop that had issues onto the Dropbox account. I was not sure what was going to happen to it."

Voodoo didn't move.

"Why did you do that?"

Everything about her body language screamed internal conflict as she paced, picked at her fingers, and chewed her lip.

"Naomi, what're you hiding?"

On the other side of the room, her tiny body trembled.

"If we want to save your friend, I need to know the truth. Whatever it is, I'm sure we can figure it out." Voodoo's words seemed to be too much. Naomi dropped onto the edge of the bed and buried her face into her hands. She started bawling.

Voodoo moved near her and knelt. Rainbow lights flowed around him in the bizarre hotel room.

"I did not lie directly. The God Algorithm does not work on its own," she said, wiping her face with the bathroom towel. "You need...you need the proteins from Tsuru's blood."

"Who's Tsuru?"

"Dr. Ichikawa's daughter."

Project Tsuru.

"Before his daughter's death, Kenzo drew several vials of her blood and extracted the enzymes for study. That is what he had locked up in the lab. To this day, we were using that same enzyme to try to replicate, or at least fully understand, what changed with the proteins and the virus that entered her body and created the...result."

"Why didn't you just say that in the beginning? What's wrong with that?"

"Remember how I said that we were doing optogenetics testing on mice?"

"Yeah."

"We were not just testing on mice. We were testing on people. More specifically, one person."

"Was Tsuru the test subject? Were you using her as a guinea pig?"

"No, no, no." Naomi shook her head adamantly. "Tsuru died twenty years ago. We were testing...on Dr. Ichikawa himself. He injected the proteins into his bloodstream."

"Did you hide this because these tests were illegal? Or is there some other reason?"

Naomi wiped more tears from her eyes.

"They were most assuredly illegal. He was not the only one, we later learned. There was another. So, to push forward, we needed to get funding elsewhere."

"So, where did he get it?"

"A shareholder at Toyotomi Industries. That is all I know. We all knew it was not the right way to do things. We were just so close...."

"I see." Voodoo stood and walked the room. "How exactly does it work?"

"We use light to access the proteins while the patient is sleeping and then connect an EEG to monitor brain activity.

The readings feed into the algorithm, which processes them, learns from them, and then pushes data back into the brain through the light. This creates a loop. The more processing power the God Algorithm gets, the more effectively it learns and pushes information into the brain. The patient then sees the results as they sleep. The proteins are the key. Without them, there's no way for the light to communicate with the neurons in the brain. And only Tsuru's proteins work with the God Algorithm."

"So, it then builds predictive algorithms based on our instincts? Where our brain interprets them in a way we understand, projecting them in...our dreams?"

"Exactly."

"Do you think I have this protein in my blood?"

"We have to get you into the lab to find out."

Voodoo wanted to be horrified. He wanted to feel something other than the numb response in his chest.

"Even if I do have this protein in my system, how am I able to have these dreams without being connected to the network?" Voodoo asked.

"That may have been because of another test we were doing."

"Project Kawa," Voodoo said.

"How did you know that?"

"Did some digging. What is it?"

Naomi took a deep breath. "We started working with a theory of Kenzo's he came up with a long time ago—the idea of being able to remotely trigger the God Algorithm proteins in patients."

"Wait, don't you need a bunch of lab equipment to do that?"

"On the back end, yes. But not for the response. You just need an object that can emit light in the near-infrared spectrum.

We were focusing on cell phones. Ever heard of something called a 'Type 0 SMS'?"

"Yeah. That's a hidden text message. Engineers use them to test network connectivity to phones quietly without people knowing it."

"Taka-chan programmed a phone sitting beside Ichikawa's head in that same way, a conduit of connectivity between him and the God Algorithm. The God Algorithm just sends a series of code to the phone via a Type 0 SMS, it emits light outside the visible spectrum to activate the protein and the brain does the rest, at a very basic level."

"Define 'basic level.'" The numbness in Voodoo's chest dissolved and reformed in a flurry of anxiety.

"The God Algorithm operator can input information and transmit it. But it is a one-way conversation. Human intuition is very powerful on its own. A lot of times our subconscious is already predicting outcomes for us. Plenty of people have semiprophetic dreams all the time. We just make it so that the information is condensed.

"The ultimate goal of Project Kawa was to create a 'river of information,' as Kenzo put it. The intent was to make someone on the system able to push their predictions to someone else on the system, allowing the recipient to make a subconscious prediction from the intuition of two people."

"Who the hell thinks of this crap?" Voodoo threw his hands up, completely incredulous. "I work with some weird technology, but this is insane! Normally I would be wildly excited but... holy crap, Naomi! You're telling me a guy I've never met may have been jamming code into my head through my cell phone!"

Naomi's face crumpled and a new eruption of tears streamed down her face.

Voodoo thought of the years he spent manipulating technology, the targets he hunted, his ability to find anyone using radio waves. *How could I have been so careless?* He lived his life off the grid and not only was someone able to find him, they were able to hack their way into his own mind, drawing out his greatest fears, making them reality. Voodoo's blood flowed hot, burning like magma fueled by anger, tempered by embarrassment. Voodoo clenched his teeth, nostrils flaring as he stared at Naomi. More specifically, he stared at the part in Naomi's hair as she buried her face in her hands.

This isn't her fault, he told himself. *Calm down. Just find a way to get through this. Don't get triggered. You've got work to do. Focus on the work.*

He paced the room instead, took deep breaths, and shook out the tension in his hands.

It took a few minutes, minutes filled with Naomi's tears and Voodoo's anger, but he was able to regain control—or give the impression that he had.

Voodoo sat down beside Naomi, doing what he normally would do in this situation—suppress his feelings and focus on something else. Anything would be better than the real desire in his heart: tear the room apart in an existential rage, run for his life. But Voodoo knew there was nowhere to go, nowhere to run. He would just carry the panic with him like a mocking demon on his shoulder. Eventually, the hatred would just dissolve, and Voodoo would be reminded of his past, his own mistakes, and how, no matter what he did, everything was always *his* fault. *I deserve this, whatever "this" is.*

If he had work, if he had purpose, he could make it through. *Focus on the work.*

He put his arm around Naomi and rubbed her shoulder. It felt like the right thing to do even though she should have been comforting *him*. After all, he didn't know when or how, but he may be the subject of some crazy experiment. And had been for years.

Naomi sniffled, as if she were trying to suck her shame into her puffy eyes.

"So...I may have this protein in my system."

Naomi nodded.

Voodoo let go of Naomi and placed his hands on his lap and looked up. Hello Kitty's eyes stared back at him from the ceiling. She wasn't going to be any help. Then it struck him.

"This may be a good thing."

Naomi swallowed and looked at him through bloodshot eyes.

"How?"

"If we can get me to a lab and I have the protein in my system, do you think we can run the algorithm? Do you have everything you need?"

"Yes. If you have the protein, I can use the algorithm on my computer and connect to Xiphos Gov. I just need the right medical equipment."

"At your lab..."

"There may be another option...but I do *not* like it."

Voodoo waited.

"The head of neuroscience at Waseda University is constantly hitting on me on behalf of his superweird son."

"Now I'm interested," Voodoo replied, cracking a slight grin. Naomi took a defeated breath.

"The boy is in his late twenties, way too young for me, and creepy, but if I promise to go out with him, he will let me into their facility for sure."

"Think he'll do it after hours?"

"I am positive he will."

"Sounds like we know what we need to do. I'll start making plans for the pachinko parlor, and you can swipe right on whatever creepy scientist dating app you're using. The good news is that we already have a room at The Passion Love Hotel," Voodoo offered with a double-pump of his eyebrows and a Vanna White–esque gesture with his arm.

Naomi tried to glare at Voodoo and keep a straight face then started laughing in spite of herself. He could see the weight visibly sloughing off Naomi's shoulders, albeit a small amount of weight.

Voodoo felt the haptic buzz of his cell phone.

THURSDAY 6:35 P.M.

> **Frisco:** @**Vudu**, you need to check the local news. We thought things were going to get weird. They just did.

Voodoo pointed the remote control at the TV in the hotel and clicked until he found a news channel.

"The popular Korean pop, or K-pop, band 4UBaby landed at Chofu Airport today at 4 p.m. to exuberant fanfare. The band, which consists of over twenty different female vocalists, arrived at the smaller, lesser-known airport just outside of Tokyo in three private jets. It is estimated that over 10,000 people assembled along the gates of the airport as the planes arrived. Authorities struggled to control the crowd," the male news anchor said.

"The band will begin a national tour of Japan beginning tomorrow night at the Budokan."

"In other news," a female anchor chimed in, "CCTV video of an altercation between two American military personnel and municipal police has gone viral this evening. The video depicts two men striking several police officers. At one point, an officer is seen getting tossed down some stairs by a tall, muscular white male. NHK News reached out to the superintendent general of the Japanese National Police Agency for comment. He stated that an investigation is ongoing.

"It is speculated that this incident is related to the recent murder of renowned neurologist and optogeneticist Dr. Kenzo Ichikawa, whose body was discovered earlier at Koishikawa Korakuen Gardens. The altercation between police and foreign military personnel happened at the residence of a colleague of Dr. Ichikawa, Dr. Naomi Shimoda, who is also sought for questioning.

"Civil response to the incident, and the potential relation to Dr. Ichikawa's murder, has resulted in protests at military installations around the country as well as the US embassy in Tokyo. The National Police Agency urged public patience as they work to identify the officers and question the American military personnel involved."

Voodoo and Naomi watched in shock.

"Now I am a fugitive," Naomi commented. "Not how I expected to start the morning."

"I'm not sure what good the National Police Agency are going to be from here on out. I'm sure Frisco and Stu's CO and the embassy won't be too keen on allowing them to do anything else either."

Naomi folded her arms and stared at the screen. "I have met their CO. He is not going to be happy about this..."

CHAPTER 25
The Deepfake

Commander Buck Buchanan was not happy. Frisco and Stu didn't see the Japanese media report until after they arrived back at the US embassy, where their CO waited for them.

Frisco recounted the events, the disappearance of the original officers, and the attack.

"That does *not* explain what I see right here. Watch this video. Tell me why this looks like my OIC and chief are beating the hell out of some police officers." Stu and Frisco watched as the event at Naomi's apartment played out from two different CCTV feeds captured from across the street and from an adjacent building.

"As I said, sir, we were attacked, but the guys that did it were wearing masks and carried cattle prods or Tasers of some type." Frisco looked more carefully at the video on the television screen. The men Frisco and Stu fought were all dressed as officers and even had regular Japanese faces. The video was choppy. He pointed to the screen. "That's not what happened. This video doesn't make any sense," Frisco said.

Buck looked at Stu.

"Sir, I wouldn't chuck a dude down a stairwell unless he deserved it. That prick deserved it. They attacked Naomi after hiding in the bathroom. They set us up," Stu said. Buck glared at Stu and Frisco.

"Speaking of Dr. Shimoda, where is she?" Buck asked, his brow clearly warming up for an aggressive browbeating.

"With Voodoo," Frisco said.

"Who's Voodoo?"

Frisco fought an exasperated sigh. "The guy from the Directorate I told you about, sir. I told you he's on orders from headquarters to support. He's been our intel lead out in the field this whole time reporting to me."

"That's where you messed up, Frisco. Everyone on this operation reports to *me*. I want them here. Now!" Buck's judgmental brow furrowed and cracked. He pulled out a can of tobacco and tapped it against his knuckle before opening the lid. He grabbed a pinch and then packed it inside his lower lip.

"With all due respect, sir, guys dressed like the police just attacked us, and they only did so because the police knew where she was. Voodoo and she are off the police's radar, but I can get a hold of them anytime we want. They're searching for a safe place to hole up as we speak," Frisco said.

"I don't think you heard me. I want them here now. Let the police figure things out from here. You just created an international incident less than three hours after arriving in the country."

You're not wrong there, Buck. In the short time since arriving, Frisco and Stu had already created an enormous mess. News across the country showed a massive white man and a Hispanic male beating up police officers. The incident metastasized like a media cancer spreading fury toward the Americans. They would be sequestered to the embassy for the rest of their stay until they solved the mystery of how the images were doctored or became persona non grata, never to return to Japan.

"Sir, when you asked me to find the best support for this mission, I immediately sought out Voodoo because of what he brings to the fight. He's the best signals guy I've ever worked with. We did two pumps together in Iraq and Afghanistan, and I promise you he'll figure out who doctored those videos if we give him some time."

"You trust a damned enabler, one dude, to protect the most important asset during a hostage crisis?" Buck scowled at Frisco, his disbelief tangible.

"Voodoo is part of our team, sir. I wouldn't bring him in if I didn't trust him. What you didn't see in that video was Voodoo helping us fight off those guys dressed like officers. With all due respect, if he hadn't shown up, your asset, as you call her, would be long gone."

Buck appeared to be mulling it over. Frisco grew distraught. He couldn't figure out how this could be happening. Not only was the video doctored, but it was also as if they were changing the video in real time.

"Get a hold of this enabler, find out what intel he has, find out where Dr. Shimoda is holed up, then give me an update," Buck conceded.

Frisco was surprised. Buck didn't back down, but he *did* seem to be open to the idea of using Voodoo.

"Yes, sir," Frisco said. He ran his hand through his thick dark brown hair and sighed with relief, grateful the interaction with Buck ended relatively smoothly. Frisco had experienced worse, so he chalked that one up as a win.

The blond, hairy giant and the Italian Stallion found an open office in the embassy and closed the door. Frisco pulled out the phone that Voodoo gave him and tapped on the chat application. He pinged Voodoo and gave him the news.

THURSDAY 6:35 P.M.

>   **Frisco:** @**Vudu**, you need to check the local news. We thought things were going to get weird. They just did.

THURSDAY 6:40 P.M.

>   **Vudu:** That's not good. Where are you?
>   **Frisco:** Back at the embassy. I took a taxi over after we split up. You?
>   **Vudu:** Safe. I'll get you a grid when the time comes. Did you just turn on the app? Did you see the above chat messages about what happened at Xiphos?

Frisco scrolled up on the chat application. He read about the potential Xiphos hack and Delta Zulu discovering the peculiar computer security at the pachinko parlor.

>   **Frisco:** Not good about Xiphos. @**Janet** Think it's the Chinese?
>   **Janet:** I don't think so, but it's hard to say. I watched the video footage we captured again, and it looks like the kidnappers have Dr. Hawkins's computer. They probably just got into her account that way.
>   **Frisco:** So, whoever took Dr. Hawkins is the same group that now has the algorithm. All they're missing is the key, which is why they're after Dr. Shimoda. The only

real lead we have right now is the pachinko parlor then. What do we do?

Vudu: We need to get into the computer at the pachinko parlor. We also may have a lead if Dr. Hawkins's laptop is still turned on. They probably used it to log into Dropbox.

DZ: I'm way ahead of you. I'll track it down and follow the trail where it leads. Hopefully, we can find out who hacked Xiphos.

Frisco: Now, what about the pachinko parlor? What do you propose we do there?

Vudu: Do you have anyone there at the embassy we might be able to trust? On the Japanese side of the house.

Frisco tipped his head back and took a deep breath. Stu had been reading the conversation alongside Frisco. Frisco looked over at the giant beside him.

"Any ideas, Stu?"

"What about the SAT guy? What was his name, Captain... Suzuki or something like that?"

Frisco laughed. "We haven't met a single person named Suzuki. You just made that up."

Stu shrugged.

"You're thinking about Captain"—Frisco snapped his fingers to try to jog his memory—"Tanaka, I think, was his name. Their SWAT guy, or SAT as they call it here, when we met with the ambassador. Why are you thinking him?"

"I think that maybe we can slip him some intel on the down-low and see if maybe he can do a raid on the pachinko parlor or something like that. Stir some things up."

Frisco: @**Vudu**, what if we can get the SAT guys here to do a raid on the pachinko parlor?

Vudu: Risky. What if they're holding Dr. Hawkins and they decide to kill her, or we burn our only lead?

Frisco: What else do we have?

Voodoo took a while to respond. He knew they had to find a way to make the raid on the pachinko parlor seem to be Captain Tanaka's idea.

Vudu: SAT could inform their superiors we gave them the info and the moles in their ranks are onto us.

Frisco: Okay. We'll need to tip the Japanese that the pachinko parlor is a potential lead without it coming from us.

Vudu: @**DZ** I have an idea. If Frisco can get the SAT team to do a raid on the pachinko parlor, do you think we can coordinate a distraction?

DZ: You know I can.

Vudu: Perfect. I'll send the details via direct message. @**Frisco** let's do it. I'll have Naomi send the police an anonymous tip from a Japanese account about the pachinko parlor directly to the SAT captain. I just need his email address. I'll mention North Koreans kidnapping Japanese citizens and how something big is going to happen at 3 a.m. That should do it. @**DZ** can you be ready by then?

DZ: You know I can.

Frisco: Won't that tip the regular police, though?

Vudu: By tipping them that North Koreans are kidnapping Japanese, it becomes a strictly domestic issue, not related to the American hostage situation. Any moles wouldn't connect it. You should still get back in his good graces and see if he'll share intel with you, though.

Frisco: I'll give it a try. They all still think we beat up a bunch of random Japanese officers. Any idea what's going on there?

Janet: I have an idea. Deepfake.

Frisco thought for a moment and then it clicked. Deepfake is the general term for using machine learning to manipulate images and voices to make it seem like someone is saying something that never happened. Recent technology made deepfakes particularly accurate and invasive—celebrities saying things they never said or superimposing faces on nude photos and stuff like that.

Janet: The hard part is that it takes a lot of information and time to process the images. If you had the right imagery models and processing power, you could do it...

Vudu: Like the Xiphos network and a facial recognition library?

Janet: Exactly.

Vudu: This isn't good. They're most likely searching for us across the city's CCTV feeds and then creating deepfakes on their operatives to manipulate video feeds to get the public against us.

Frisco put the phone down and buried his face in his hands. "We're done," he said to Stu.

"I don't get it. How are we done?" Stu asked.

"They most likely have access to all the videos across the city."

Stu shrugged.

"Well, the CCTV feeds all around the city are watching our every move. We're foreigners in Japan. It's not hard to find us, especially you, bro-zilla. Take that and add that they most likely have a mole in the National Police Agency, and we don't have a chance of finding Dr. Hawkins, let alone hunting down Ichikawa's killers."

"We're still not done," Stu said. Frisco turned to Stu. He squinted at the obstinate giant sitting beside him and wondered if he was listening.

"You're not listening, Stu—"

"No. You're not listening. We're not done. Those videos show us, not Voodoo. I'll bet money they aren't trackin' *him*."

Frisco looked at Stu and realized he was right. Voodoo was a specter. He observed from the shadows and only made himself known when necessary—all the more reason for Buck to keep Voodoo out in the field.

Frisco: @**Vudu** you're point on this now, brother. We have one problem, though. My CO wants you to bring Naomi back to the embassy immediately. I'm trying to hold him off, but I don't know how long I can keep you out there.

Vudu: I know Buck, and I know how he thinks, so here is what we do:

Frisco: Wait, Buck acted like he doesn't know you.

Vudu: Of course he did. We did a deployment together when he was still a junior officer. He's arrogant, dumb, and career hungry. Admitting he knows an enabler, well... Anyway, he likes control. But a part of him just doesn't want anything to go wrong because it'll hurt his chances for promotion. Here's what we do: we need to tell him about the deepfakes, the situation with Xiphos, and how it all points to the pachinko parlor. Ask Janet about the Chinese investors and Sparks about the potential North Korean involvement. Let your CO know that information came to light because he, the CO, authorized you to find the right team to solve this problem.

Make the CO feel like he's in control, he's getting credit, and that we have a plan. He's freaking out because he doesn't feel like he has a handle on the situation. If he still doesn't understand, draw him some stick figures and offer him some chewing tobacco. That should do it.

Frisco: It's disturbing the way you understand how to manipulate shooters, Voodoo, especially officers.

Vudu: Not my first rodeo. Now let's crush these guys, sir, unless you need me to draw you some stick figures.

Frisco: Haha. Where are you anyway?

Vudu: At a love hotel...

Frisco: A what?!

Vudu: :)

Frisco grinned at Stu. "I'm glad Voodoo's on our side."

"I'm gonna tell you something, and I'll kill you if you ever repeat it."

Frisco's smile faded. "What is it?"

"Voodoo scares the hell out of me. Children shouldn't be afraid of the boogeyman, they should be afraid of Voodoo—creepy little guy hiding in the shadows stealing people's Wi-Fi. He's like a demon who visits you in the night and gives you cyberherpes."

Frisco burst out laughing. His body shook as his face turned red and tears formed in his eyes. It took him a moment until he could respond. "You've put a lot of thought into this," he said. And considering it was Stu, that was saying something.

Frisco's response didn't faze Stu. "I'm just sayin', bro. I'd rather fight a guy with a gun than some dude like Voodoo. At least I know my right and left limits on the battlefield. I'm not sure where guys like me fit in the wars of the future if everything is fought with radio waves and computer stuff," Stu said.

Frisco thought about what Stu said, and for the second time in this conversation, Stu made a surprisingly astute observation.

"Good point. If Voodoo had his way, he would rather have drones and artificial intelligence fighting the battles than his buddies. I know that operation we did in Iraq years ago when we hit that IED messed him up. We took some damage that night."

"We lost Bobby too. After we took that building and called in air support, it got crazy," Stu replied.

"Voodoo was a little different after that op. Part of me wonders if he blames himself for some of those civilians we found in the building."

"That's war, bro. Every good operator loves combat, only a crazy person would love war. And this AI crap is something different," Stu said.

Frisco pointed out, "But imagine if we lose this AI arms race. Imagine rogue nations predicting the future, feeding computers to fight wars based on their desires, manipulating markets. They won't care about ethical issues the way we do. Mathematically, we'll never catch up. Eventually, computers, not humans, will be targeting shooters on the battlefield. Damn computers would be ruthless. If we allow some rogue state to get ahead, we'll all get slaughtered."

Stu nodded. "Like I said, Voodoo scares the hell out of me."

Frisco didn't laugh the second time he said it. For the first time, Voodoo, and the future he represented, scared Frisco too.

CHAPTER 26

The Kanda River

KABUKICHO
TOKYO, JAPAN

Naomi slept under the basking glow of the face of Hello Kitty mounted to the ceiling. The undulating rainbow lights dimmed to set the mood for postcoital slumber though no such activity took place here tonight.

Shortly before she fell asleep, Voodoo and Naomi took the risk of reaching out in confidence to her colleague at Waseda University just north of their location. He agreed to give her access to the university EEG, or electroencephalography machine, after hours. He and his son would have to be there in person, of course, to give them access. Naomi was not excited about that part of the deal but figured it would ensure their secrecy in the matter.

Voodoo and Naomi would have to wait until midnight before they could head out to the university love connection. Naomi subsequently walked over to the bed and passed out.

Voodoo took the opportunity to slip out of the hotel room and step out into the evening glow of neon in search of sustenance. They had a long night ahead of them.

He exited the hotel and was surprised to see the street still heavy with foot traffic. A dramatic shift in pedestrian personalities caught Voodoo's attention—the sidewalks and pedestrian roads that once ushered families now catered to men prowling the pavement. Women occupied apartment entryways. Their hands delicately gripped fans that waved up and down. Their eyes empty, ambivalently beckoning any would-be john.

A man in a cheap suit, a loose tie, and an inebriated stagger meandered over to one of the women. She took him by the arm and led him in. Another woman quickly took her place with similar apathetic enthusiasm.

Voodoo found his way down the street and into a 7-Eleven less than a block from their hotel. Unlike the questionable food in their Western counterparts, Japanese convenience stores, or "*conbini*," offer a wide variety of meals and are the staple for most single men and women on the way home after a long day at work. Voodoo grabbed a small Styrofoam plate of yakisoba, several servings of teriyaki chicken, as well as water and a few Red Bulls.

As he stepped out of the *conbini*, Voodoo noticed an electronics store where a small toy quadcopter buzzed around entertaining bored employees. A twentysomething male cashier bowed as Voodoo entered.

Like a fine connoisseur, Voodoo perused the merchandise before discovering a variety of LiPo batteries, felt their weight in his hands, and assessed the voltage adapters. Voodoo found some 6S 40C LiPo batteries made by a brand whose reputation was dubious at best. LiPo is an abbreviation of lithium polymer, the little brother of lithium ion, which are some of the most widely used batteries on earth and are found in cell phones. Unlike their commercial counterparts, LiPo batteries used for drones are notorious for being volatile when misused. Accidents involve an event called "thermal runaway," wherein the batteries overheat, expand, and explode.

Perfect.

Voodoo made the expensive purchase along with some tools and set off back to the hotel. Back in the room, Naomi still zonked out, Voodoo sat on the floor and picked the dark, burnt carcinogens off the sweet meat skewered on a stick with his teeth. He pulled out his laptop and established a secure connection via a virtual private network.

Through his computer, Voodoo accessed the "one-night stand"—the phone he infected on the fake police officer at Naomi's apartment. All phones that use open-source software push information back to their geek overlords for maintenance. Unbeknownst to most users, this data is either continuously updated to software developers or stored on the phone.

Voodoo intercepted both.

Voodoo analyzed the activity of the one-night stand on a geo-rectified map. Analyzing the behavior saved on the phone from the past month, Voodoo watched where the phone went, when it became active, and how it was used. The one-night stand divulged every little secret to Voodoo.

The phone consistently moved along a waterway that Voodoo identified as the Kanda River. Several rivers and their tributaries fed into Tokyo Harbor. The Kanda is one of those minor tributaries of the largest river in that part of Tokyo, the Sumida River. The phone seemed to be most active where the Kanda met the Sumida. Voodoo followed the river and noticed an interesting coincidence. The Kanda River flowed less than a hundred meters south of the Tokyo Dome and the Koishikawa Korakuen Gardens, where Dr. Ichikawa was murdered.

That was when he saw it.

The Starlight Pachinko Parlor was also right along the Kanda River by less than half a mile and a similar distance from the University of Tokyo. Direct access to the water offered many opportunities, but it was extremely overt. They must be piggybacking on a cargo boat or something that transits that area not to draw attention.

Voodoo pulled up his chat application.

THURSDAY 9:25 P.M.

Vudu: @**Sparks** You there?

Voodoo continued to look at the map of the city while he waited for a response. He considered how this new information might be relevant. Perhaps this was a clue as to what happened to Dr. Hawkins. If they took her on the river right away, she could be anywhere. It had been almost two days since her disappearance.

His view of the map was interrupted by a new message.

THURSDAY 9:30 P.M.

Sparks: I'm here. What's up?
Vudu: I need you to look into activity on the Kanda River in Tokyo. Find anything regarding frequent transit for barges or supply routes. The guys that attacked us are using it for something. Find me whatever you can.
Sparks: I'll have the guys here check it out. What about me? I'm ready with the BIB. Where do you want me?

Vudu: I have a strong impression I'll know in the next six or seven hours. Be ready for anything.

Sparks: I've got my bump helmet on. I'll crack the chem light when I get there. (Still not sure what that means.)

Vudu: Haha. Atta boy!

Even in text messages Voodoo could hear Sparks's enthusiasm—the manic desire to be useful. Voodoo took Sparks under his wing during a deployment they did together in Afghanistan. It was there that Voodoo learned how Sparks had been diagnosed with overactive adrenal glands.

Doctors ran him through a battery of tests but didn't find any sign of androgenic steroids, cortisol, or epinephrine typical of an imbalance in the endocrine system. Instead, he just had adrenaline constantly coursing through his veins, dilated pupils, and more energy than a team of Alaskan huskies prepping for the Iditarod. Mix that with an abusive childhood and Voodoo quickly realized Sparks needed strong mentorship and room to run free. They had been crushing the technology game at the Directorate ever since—two messed-up sled dogs with no musher holding them back.

Returning to the task at hand, Voodoo reached for his girlfriend and activated the microphone on the false officer's phone remotely through an app. He pulled out some headphones and listened.

As the familiar scratching of static filled his ear with white noise, Voodoo pulled out the 6S battery and the other equipment he purchased. A dull pressure behind his eyes warned of a headache. He glanced over at Naomi sleeping and envied her ability to rest. His opportunity to find solace would come soon enough.

For now, he needed to get ready.

He had only a day left to figure this whole thing out. One day to avoid a compromised police force in a foreign country and stop a ticking clock in an international AI cold war. Most people in this situation would buckle from the stress. Most people would surrender to higher authorities seeking answers and let them deal with the problem.

Voodoo wasn't most people. He promised to see this thing through. He looked over at Naomi sleeping under a massive Hello Kitty picture and saw only an opportunity at redemption. This was his chance to set things right, to fix his mistakes. An innocent life was on the line. He'd stolen one; he needed to save this one. He didn't need any more motivation than that.

He nursed a Red Bull, hoping the caffeine and taurine, whatever the hell that does, would deal with the growing pain in his head. He slipped some Visine drops in his eyes. Compared to some of the headaches he used to get when he was younger, the dull ache in his head from insomnia and caffeine abuse was nothing.

Voodoo went to work MacGyvering a makeshift weapon for a surprise he planned for the pachinko parlor later that night.

While he worked, stripping and soldering leads, he could hear only rustling and music as his target's phone slid around in the man's pocket.

Smoke floated up from the coffee table as Voodoo soldered the equipment until cogent voices slipped through the slop.

"Ryu...Americans are trapped in the embassy...public anger will just escalate...according to plan," he heard one man say.

"...we still don't know who attacked you...tell Ryu," another voice said.

"...Division 121 searching...her face...if it's on the internet."

J-pop music overpowered the microphone. Voodoo checked the location. They were inside the pachinko parlor.

There wasn't much to go on, but they seemed to be confirming what he already knew. A name did pop out, though.

Ryu.

Voodoo thought of an old video game with that name that Americans always butchered when they pronounced it.

Voodoo considered the way Ryu could be written. Japanese names are always written in Chinese characters called kanji. Parents take liberty with the characters when naming children and can use any style that matches the pronunciation. When Japanese meet, they often explain to each other what kanji they use for their names by writing them on the palm of their hands with their finger.

Voodoo wished his kanji skills were up to par, but he knew that it didn't matter this time. There was only one real way to write Ryu, and Voodoo knew it.

Dragon.

CHAPTER 27

The Past Is Prologue

KABUKICHO

TOKYO, JAPAN

Voodoo consolidated his equipment into his bag and cleaned up the makeshift workspace he created while Naomi slept. It was getting close to midnight, and Voodoo wanted to use the last few minutes reviewing intel before they set off for the lab.

As he studied a digital map of Tokyo, a new message arrived from Delta Zulu.

THURSDAY 11:23 P.M.

DZ: @Vudu I was doing some digging in Ichikawa's email and discovered a unique IP address. He has a cloud server where he kept pertinent information. There's a ton of stuff in there, but most of it appears to be personal logs. I found something you need to see.

Thumbnails appeared in chat with links to two video files. Voodoo pressed the first icon.

The video was a bit grainy. It appeared to be before HD video, using early 2000s or late '90s technology. A girl lay on a hospital bed, and a younger version of Kenzo Ichikawa sat in front of the video, recording his actions for a log.

"I've tried everything," he said. He pointed to a wand in the corner with a figure eight–shaped object attached to the front. "That represents my first failure—transcranial magnetic stimulation, which uses a noninvasive means of altering the magnetic field in the brain. No change. I've also tried genetically encoded calcium indicators, but that technology is still too nascent."

Dr. Ichikawa stopped speaking. He stood and walked over to Tsuru as she rested and held her hand. Tsuru lay on the hospital bed in front of him, twitching. She slid her legs along the sheets, trying to kick the torment from her body. Every time she cried out from the pain in her skull, it looked like part of Dr. Ichikawa died inside.

"The headaches started a year ago," he said from across the room. "Steadily getting worse until she degraded to a state of pure agony." He stared at the face of his lovely daughter. "Tsuru is such a hopeful girl. She dreams of becoming an artist, traveling the world. I worry that the only thing she can do now is die in tremendous pain. She last spoke two weeks ago. Now she speaks in little more than grunts and screams between oxycodone injections. I have one last option."

He slipped a syringe into the catheter on her arm and injected the contents.

"I have theorized that some proteins delivered into lipids via a virus can affect neural activity when light stimulates the brain. It's called optogenetics. It's an advanced, noninvasive method. I do not have time for trials to determine the appropriate proteins, so I am taking a lot of risks. I don't know what will happen, but I don't know what else to do." He connected a machine near her head as the injection of lab-designed proteins entered her bloodstream through a virus. Within moments, she fell quiet, the twitching stopped, and she rested. A tear of relief etched Kenzo's cheek.

Voodoo fast-forwarded the video. Over the space of an hour, technicians came and went, monitoring vitals, computers hummed, and diagnostic software processed.

Kenzo Ichikawa rested his head on his daughter's hand. Before long, he nodded off. Voodoo fast-forwarded the video until he saw Ichikawa's head pop up. He pressed play again.

Voodoo's whole body tingled as Tsuru's eyes opened. She lifted her hand and placed it on her father's head.

"*Otosan...*" she said. "*Otosan...sugoi yume wo mita.*"

Dr. Ichikawa looked at her, and his daughter, Tsuru, smiled at him. The muscles on his face contracted then relaxed as tears poured down his cheeks.

"Tsuru-chan..." he said, staring intensely into her eyes. He exhaled a stuttered breath from his lungs.

"*Otosan, sugoi yume wo mita,*" she said again. *Father, I had a wonderful dream.*

"What kind of dream, my dear?" He wiped his cheeks.

"I heard a beautiful tanka. I need you to listen to it."

"Of course," he said, a smile lighting up his face.

Arai kawa
michibiku tsuru ga
sora ni iku.
Mayowareta taka
su ni kaeru michi.

On the rough river, the crane that will guide, will go to the sky. The hawk that was lost, is the path to return to the nest.

Voodoo paused the video and replayed the poem. A tingling sensation grew into warm hands squeezing his heart. Again and again he listened to the words, trying to find their meaning. *Lost hawk... Dr. Hawkins? But how would she...*

He needed time to think. He decided to click on the second thumbnail.

In a separate video, Dr. Ichikawa sat beside the hospital bed. The camera angle tilted to the right, most likely recording when he thought he had turned it off. The bed was empty, new sheets and a blanket lay flat where Tsuru rested before, speaking to her father for the last time.

Ichikawa slumped in the chair, a husk of a man who was no longer a father—just a scientist. A large-bellied man entered the room, pulled up another chair, and sat down. The angle of the camera made it hard to see his face.

"*O ki no doku sama,*" the man said. *I'm sorry for your loss.*

Kenzo merely nodded.

"What's next?" the man asked.

"I have an idea. I just don't know if it's possible."

"Tell me."

"This is going to sound crazy, but I think Tsuru's dream gave her a glimpse of the future through an algorithm I designed. I believe the protein can be magnified by computer logic. I have been dabbling with game theory, and this new technology called machine learning. Listen, I need some time, to gather some of my money—"

"Speaking of money," the large man said. "My investors have pulled their cash. I will no longer be able to support you now that Tsuru is dead. And you need to refund whatever is left."

Kenzo's face went slack. "What...what do you mean?"

"I mean, the bottom line is the bottom line. I've never pretended to be anything other than what I am—a businessman. You've been a friend, you really have. But I need a return on my investment."

Kenzo stood. His face shook from side to side in utter disbelief. "You're going to do this now? Pull all my funding when I've lost everything. Tsuru's mother left me years ago—"

"Mother? She was a lost girl who left a baby at your doorstep. Don't pretend she was anything else."

"Even so, I have never pretended to be a perfect man. I've made my mistakes. Tsuru was my chance to change all that. I can't stop now."

"Then don't. You still owe me money. I heard you've paid out of pocket for some of these experiments you've been doing, some of which aren't even legal yet. And now you're broke. Maybe you can find something promising out of this mess. Maybe not. Perhaps there's a way to replicate this project. But this time, don't get close to the subject, observe from a distance."

"I'd have to find someone with similar genetic markers and potentially the same disease," Dr. Ichikawa said, thinking out loud.

"I don't care what you do. Get me my money."

"I'll get the money, but I never want to see *you* again."

Voodoo stopped the video.

This led to Project Tsuru and Project Kawa, Voodoo thought. *Who was the man in the video? Most importantly, who became the new subject? Or was it subjects?*

Voodoo would find out soon enough.

CHAPTER 28

No Coins for Charon

WESTWATER CANYON

SOUTHERN UTAH, USA

"Nice work, Gavin!" Ally yelled out more like an uncontrolled spectator than an encouraging senior guide. The whole event transpired in less than a minute—the throw bag, the rescue, fixing the oar, the narrow escape. The passengers on Ally's boat let out an enormous sigh of relief before drinking in the sight of Skull Rapid ahead. Gratitude for the deliverance of the swimmer from the other raft immediately shifted to their own welfare as they gripped the chicken line.

Ally's young face carried a stern resolve as she balanced her attention between the rapids ahead and the cliff in front of her. She rested one foot on the metal frame as she sat on the cooler in the middle of the boat. Each purchase of her blades sponsored the safety of the passengers, but only if done correctly, only at the right time. Upstream, Joel's raft exited Cocaine Cove like a taxiing aircraft entering a runway.

The raft passed Marker Rock—the point of no return. Nothing but laser focus shot from Ally's eyes. She put her head down, leaned forward, and executed. Her blades dug deep, devoid of aerated slop near the water's surface. She arched her back and pulled, then feathered her oars.

Two pulls followed by a third, and the raft hit a wave. The mild, anticlimactic splash contradicted the raging torrent only ten meters away. The water smashing into the Rock of Shock and the Room of Doom screamed like a frustrated Scylla and Charybdis. The raft floated with the current. Ally's countenance shifted back to a lighthearted, warm exuberance.

"Nice work, guys!" she let out as if the portable bags of water did anything other than offer ballast. The passengers hooted.

Ally rotated the boat with the bow forward in preparation for the next hurdle before speaking. "Well, I tell this to every group that runs the river, Skull is either the most horrifying rapid you've ever seen because it's about to eat you alive or it's the biggest letdown. From the show Gavin just put on, I think you guys just got a little of both."

The young couple shared a glance and looked a bit shaken by the drama. "I'll take a letdown any day. That rapid looked like no joke," the man admitted.

"I'm so glad the other customers are okay," his wife said, clasping her husband's hand. He nodded in agreement as she let out a deep breath and shook her head quickly to dislodge her nervous energy.

"This is a wild place, and it's not over yet. We have three more rapids ahead. Bowling Alley, Sock-It-to-Me, and Last Chance." Ally pointed. "Looks like Gavin, once again, is showing us how to get it done."

Gavin's boat entered as the river created a series of large successive waves that climaxed to a triangular point like heading markers pointing down the river. The bulky raft flexed to the shape of the rapid. The passengers gasped as the cold water hit them.

Ally's boat followed suit. The man looked upstream to see that Joel's raft had also avoided catastrophe at Skull.

The guides worked their way downstream through the ensuing rapids. Like Funnel Falls, the rafts started perpendicular to the flow of the river and straightened with one push of the right oar to enter Sock-It-to-Me bow first. They blasted through a huge hole and avoided a feature the guides called the Magnetic Wall. Finally, they rolled the dice with Last Chance. With a flurry of spectacular crashes and reckless abandon, the guides hit the rapid with the rafts in random orientations. The customers whooped and pointed as each boat ignored every rule they thought they had learned about rafting—the guides hit the rapid sideways, almost dumping the passengers out.

The river rescinded its anger, and the water calmed. The rafts and the passengers floated among the black rock as an egret stoically observed from above.

"That crane looks like it's been following us," the woman said to her husband.

"That's an egret. Legends say that the egret flies these canyons to escort boats to safety. It looks like the legend is correct. You made it through, guys!" Ally tended to sound like a kindergarten teacher, but instead of condescension, the customers felt genuinely encouraged and proud of their achievement. They applauded, and Ally gave them all high fives.

Gavin, Ally, and Joel slowed their respective boats to bring them close together. The customers recounted the events, sharing their perspectives with exaggerated flair.

"Kerry, are you okay?" her sister yelled out.

Her mother ranted, "Hunny, I was so afraid. I thought you were going to die...then I thought I was going to die...then your sister thought I was going to die. For some reason, you falling out of the boat meant we were all going to die!"

Kerry giggled and brushed it off.

Passengers in all three boats chuckled and grinned at each other. They were the only people for dozens, if not a hundred miles. They were on another planet, isolated and alone, but together—a band of travelers returning from the underworld.

"There aren't any rapids from here on out," Joel said. "We have a good hour of floating ahead of us. Would anyone like to go swimming?"

Several customers looked at the guides with hesitation, then, one by one, started taking him up on the offer. The three rafts floated like giant planets with orbiting satellites of orange life jackets bobbing in the water. Only the guides, Kerry, and the elderly Asian man remained on board. The guides looked to each other, ready to finally have a conversation about the swimmer. Before Gavin had the chance to speak, Kerry took the liberty of sitting beside him on his cooler.

"How did you know where to find me?" Kerry said, putting her hands flat under her thighs as she sat. She slightly shifted her weight and bumped her shoulder against his. Gavin grinned at her.

The others on the boats all turned to hear his answer.

"That's kind of a weird story. I've only been a guide for, like, a month. Being a river guide is like a rite of passage in my family, so I've always wanted to do it. This was the first time I've ever run with my own raft, well, with customers, that is. Every other time another guide was in the boat with me just in case. Last night I felt pretty good about what was supposed to happen today, but then I had a dream. The dream was kinda like a vision but different. It was poetic."

"What do you mean?" Kerry asked, cocking her head.

"Like it came in the form of a poem. I distinctly remember what it said though:

'The crane's blood is in your veins. A plan drawn, a plan revised. Hades will reach for Persephone. No coins for Charon, you shall not pass.' That's what the dream said, and I recognized my mother's voice. Which is weird because she died ten years ago."

"Do those words have special meaning to you?" Kerry asked, her eyes drifting across the raft to the man on Ally's boat, who looked intently at Gavin, apparently absorbing every word.

"When I dreamt, I also saw images of our three boats floating in the same order they were supposed to be in, but there was a big X across them right at Surprise Rapid. The image showed my broken D ring, and me using an ammo can instead. It also showed me throwing rope to help someone just upstream from my boat. So, I rearranged my raft before we set out."

"What do those lines mean? They sound different from the images," Kerry said, tying her long brown hair into a ponytail. Small wisps slipped out and curved around her face.

"I'm not sure about the crane part. I can't help but assume they were talking about the egrets that fly through the canyon. 'A plan drawn, a plan revised' obviously refers to how we had to change our plans. I'm not sure about the next part," Gavin said.

Ally spoke up, "The next line said something about Hades and Persephone, right? Persephone was a beautiful mortal that Hades kidnapped and took to the underworld. That one seems pretty obvious to me. The poem is referring to when you fell out of the boat, and the river tried to take you."

Kerry narrowed her eyes, retreating into her thoughts.

"And Charon?" Gavin asked.

Ally was the only person who paid attention in high school English it seemed. "Charon is the boatman that escorts the dead across the river Styx, but you need two coins. That's why the Greeks placed coins on the dead so that Charon could escort them safely to the underworld. I think Skull is Charon in this case." Gavin nodded in agreement, and his eyebrows rose.

"So, 'no coins for Charon' meant it wasn't our time to go to the underworld, and we made it through the rapids," Gavin said.

"Why didn't you tell me about this when we were talking this morning?" Ally asked. If Ally was capable of sounding annoyed, she hinted at it. Joel listened as their rafts rubbed alongside. "I'm pretty sure a premonition of doom in the canyon merits some kind of conversation."

"I was too busy apologizing for what I haven't done yet in your dreams if you remember correctly," Gavin said. "Besides, it's not exactly the best show of confidence to the senior guides if you're having dreams about failing on your first solo out."

Joel said, "That's fair, I suppose. Either way, it's a good thing you had that dream. There's no frickin' way you would have made it through Skull with one oar. Premonition or not, you made the right move."

"And who knows where I'd be," Kerry said with an appreciative smile.

Ally leaned forward. "I get the impression that, even without our help, you're the type of person who can tough things out on their own, Kerry."

Kerry smiled back, pride swelling inside her.

Those still in the boats fell silent as each absorbed the gravity of what they'd faced. Ally saw the man taking in the widening canyon downstream, his face finally serene, his shoulders relaxed.

Then his eyes lifted, and he scanned the sky. Ally followed his gaze to the egret.

When he said nothing, the surprisingly wise, frizzy-haired river guide spoke. "The egret guides us on a journey down the river and helps keep us safe, but we still have to make it through the rough rapids on our own." Ally gave a pursed grin. "Just keep ready for the next canyon."

Dr. Kenzo Ichikawa, the man, cast his eyes downstream. "I hope to be..."

CHAPTER 29
The Honeypot

"How bad is it? What do you think happened?" Janet folded her arms and shook her head.

She set down her cold brew coffee; it didn't taste the same at Xiphos AI now. The faux grass on the wall seemed tacky. Even the warm San Diego sun shimmering through the windows felt tainted from the cyberattack, the complete loss of their proprietary network, and the very foundation of their company.

"It's tough to say, honestly. It looks like they were able to get into our network," the IT guy said.

"But hasn't it been running this entire time?" Andy asked. His hand rubbed the scraggly growth of hair on his chin as he leaned against the wall. Xiphos employees spied from their workstations, trying to figure out what was happening.

"It has." The IT guy filtered through several screens monitoring internal network traffic and security protocols. Then he stopped, slack-jawed.

"I hate to say this, but it looks like they have full access to the primary Xiphos network. And...they've been running their own code."

"What do you mean?" Janet asked, her head inches away from the IT guy's face as she leaned into the monitor.

"Look for yourself. You built the thing," he replied, trying to clear the way for his boss to see the display.

Andy and Janet filtered through the data until they realized what he meant. In between customer-driven events on the network, random administrative codes using a massive amount of information sporadically spiked in the system.

"I originally thought these were the surges you were doing for that government project you have going on in the back room. But now that I look at it, I realize this is someone else entirely that's been using our network to process data."

The irony didn't escape Andy. Their entire Xiphos Gov network revolved around gaining access to the root of other people's computers, placing a secure shell on it, and then using its power to supply the processing needs as a service. The difference was that the Xiphos primary network comprised of witting people who volunteered the processing power on their gaming systems at home for Xiphos to use at the company's discretion. Any time the network was used it cost money. But now someone *else* was stealing Xiphos's processing power. If Janet shut down the network to fix this, it meant cutting off all their paying customers from their services as well.

But there was only one solution, and Janet knew it. She *had* to shut it all off.

Janet pulled out her laptop, connected to the internet via a personal hotspot on her cell phone to keep clear of the Xiphos network, and contacted Delta Zulu.

Janet: @**DZ** we need your help. It looks like somebody rooted our network. I know that I asked you earlier to keep an eye on our system for us. Did you see anything?

While she waited, Janet considered the financial ramifications. Xiphos would need to disclose to customers about the breach in case their data were compromised. The jury was still out on that one, however. Andy took heart in knowing that at least the Xiphos Gov capability operated on an air-gapped computer that only accesses the network when it is time to run. The only way for someone to root that would be to insert a thumb drive into that particular server physically, and that was nearly impossible. Fifteen minutes later, Delta Zulu responded.

DZ: I've got good news and bad news.
Janet: Lay it on me.
DZ: I accessed the Dropbox account and checked to determine when files were loaded and removed. I found some things that may need explanation. We'll start with everything after Dr. Hawkins first loaded it up. A few hours later, someone accessed the account and switched things out. Based on what I can tell, Naomi logged into the account before you did. Under the "events" option, you can see when files moved. From what I can tell, Naomi accessed it; then you did to pull the files...then I did.
Janet: What? Why did you log into it?
DZ: I put something in place to give us an advantage. I figured that Dr. Hawkins's computer would be compromised at some point, so I put a honeypot in the files.

Janet grew a devilish grin.

A honeypot is a widely used term that is synonymous with being a trap. In espionage, a honeypot is usually a beautiful woman sent to elicit information from an unsuspecting man. In the cyberworld, a honeypot is a file or server that draws a hacker's attention but leads cyberforensics personnel or authorities straight back to the hacker. Delta Zulu now had a mole on the network of whoever stole the God Algorithm.

Janet: I want to say that I'm mad, but that was an excellent idea. But I am concerned that Naomi got into it before all of us. Do you think she had some kind of malicious intent?

DZ: I've been tracking her this whole time. If she has been doing something sketchy, I'm not seeing it, and I'm pretty sure Voodoo would pick up on it too.

Janet: Okay. So, do you know who stole our files?

DZ: They first pulled the information back to Dr. Hawkins's computer. Then I saw it appear on a computer in Tokyo before going straight to China.

Janet: Is it at XJI?

DZ: Yes...and no. It went to XJI but also into a different location. I'm very excited about this. It went straight into, what I think, is Division 121.

Janet: What's that?

DZ: North Korea's cyberwarfare agency.

Janet: Is there a chance they honeypot us at the same time? I mean, we downloaded the files first before they deleted them.

DZ: I considered that. That's why I'm going to help you. Most likely, they've been using your network to run the deepfakes. Your network is exactly what someone would need to process imagery and run computer vision in real time at that speed. I'm going to give your IT guys a few tips, then I'm going to go after the guys that stole it. But I need you to keep the network up. We need more time to gather intel on whoever is doing this before we take it down, which would tip them off that we know.

Janet took a deep breath. She knew this was going to hurt, especially in their pocketbook. Janet also remembered this whole operation was a request of the SECDEF. She could always make the government pay for it.

Janet: We'll keep the network going. We need to stand by for when Voodoo needs Xiphos Gov anyway. Thank you. I'm legitimately impressed you're able to do so much just being one guy.

There was a long pause before the next message arrived.

DZ: Who said I'm a guy? And who said Delta Zulu is one person?

CHAPTER 30

The Lab

WASEDA UNIVERSITY
TOKYO, JAPAN

"Please tell me that's the guy," Voodoo said to Naomi as they entered the medical research facility at Waseda University. In front of them stood two gawky men at the door, their faces beaming. Yoshi Saito and his son Toshi were more than elated to see the legendary Naomi Shimoda walking up to them. Legendary, not just for her accomplishments as a neurologist, but for her seemingly ageless beauty and lack of a husband.

Shortly before midnight, Voodoo had awakened Naomi. He instructed her to leave her luggage behind as they had rented the room for more than one night. They traveled light, carrying only bags slung over their shoulders, and varied their travel between taxis and walking to mitigate detection.

Voodoo didn't have time to show Naomi the videos, only telling her about them as they rushed along. Kenzo never spoke of an early investor, or any debt, according Naomi. They needed more information on that. The answers would have to wait until after they finished at the hospital. Things were about to start moving faster than either of them realized.

It was just past midnight when they arrived and met the men who would facilitate the crucial next part of their operation. The two men barely broke five-one, and acne scars covered Yoshi's face, a trait Toshi unfortunately inherited. Their thin frames made Naomi look bulky next to them. Naomi elbowed Voodoo as he chuckled.

"You told them no pictures, right? No posting anything on social media," Voodoo confirmed.

"Of course. Yoshi said his son would be disappointed, but he understood."

As they walked closer, Naomi inhaled deeply in an apparent attempt to muster the courage to face something painful.

"I want to say that Taka-chan owes me when this whole thing is over, but that would be ungrateful. I will do anything to get my friend back," she said.

"Well said. Now let's make a love connection," Voodoo said. She elbowed him again.

Yoshi and Toshi greeted Naomi and Voodoo with incessant bows. When one person bent over, the other was up and vice versa. Yoshi then Toshi then Yoshi. They reminded Voodoo of skinny Weeble Wobbles. Their merry faces looked painted onto their tiny bodies.

The display went on awkwardly longer than necessary before Naomi's patience wore thin and she shut it off. "Enough! Let's go." They made their way into the building and into a lab where they set up various machines including the EEG.

Naomi pulled out her computer and set up an Ethernet connection between her laptop and the EEG.

"Did you bring the supplies I asked for?" she asked Yoshi.

"Yes, of course." He stepped out into the hallway and motioned for a technician to enter the room. "This is the phlebotomist you asked for. She will take the blood sample as requested. You can trust her."

"Thank you," Naomi replied. "What about the sedative?"

The technician handed her a syringe.

The phlebotomist drew two vials of blood from Voodoo's arm as he sat on a reclining seat, before leaving the room.

"The initial tests you requested should be done in the next hour," the technician said. Naomi nodded in a slight bow as a show of gratitude.

"Gentlemen, I would appreciate it if you would wait outside," Naomi ordered dismissively.

"Of course, of course," Yoshi and Toshi said as they incessantly bowed, walking backward out the door.

"Voodoo, it will take a few moments for me to prepare. While I do this, I am going to explain what is going to happen." She held up a small device with several lights on it. "This is called a Light Plate Apparatus or LPA. This will emit some lights toward your head. The frequency of the lights will interact with the enzymes that we assume are already in your bloodstream to manipulate the neural activity in your brain."

"And what if they're not?" Voodoo asked.

"Then this will do absolutely nothing. The neurons need the protein to react to the light, otherwise there is no way to communicate directly with your brain. Long before the bloodwork comes back, I'll know if this is working. In the meantime, you will get a nice nap."

"That doesn't sound terrible."

Naomi smiled. She reached over and grabbed another object. She held a cap connected to dozens of cables and electrical connections.

"That looks like Frankenstein's shower cap." Voodoo didn't want to admit it, but he was nervous. Bad jokes tended to be a side effect.

"This is an electroencephalogram or EEG. This cap goes on your head and outputs graph-like detail to a computer. I am going to put this on your head, make sure everything is working, then I will give you a mild sedative. Once you fall asleep, the EEG will feed data to my laptop running Taka-chan's code.

"Basically, there will be a loop of data going from your head to the computer, and then the computer is going to push code to the LPA, which will stimulate your brain. Sound simple?"

"As simple as hacking a person's brain can sound, I suppose."

"Good. All of these lights and graphs will help me stimulate specific sections of your brain. I am going to help you pull out memories and motivate your brain to control the emotional response so you can focus on the right images. Then we will amplify it to make them clearer. As we do this, the God Algorithm will use machine learning to make your visions stronger and more accurate. At the right time, I will notify Janet from your phone—since you've given me access—and she will let me access the Xiphos Gov network."

"Tell me again how you know this will work," Voodoo said.

"We used Kenzo's mind to create the God Algorithm. We have hours upon hours of evidence showing this works. This process also refined the algorithm itself. The combination of a human's innate perceptions coupled with artificial intelligence processing through the God Algorithm can provide a glimpse of future events. It is the only way we may be able to find Taka-chan and remove the threat of Kenzo's killer. This technology also made Kenzo obsessed, though. It forced him to make rash decisions..." Naomi's countenance changed as she said it.

"Okay. Is there anything else I should be aware of before we do this? You're not gonna melt my brain, are you?" Voodoo's joke intimated more of his real concern, and Naomi picked up on it.

"I am not going to lie; this is not without risk. This could damage part of your psyche if we are not careful."

"Then *be* careful. I don't see any other way out at this point. Perhaps we have a safe word. If I scream 'banana' pull me out."

Naomi laughed out loud. Voodoo smiled.

"Okay. Let's do this then."

Naomi placed the cap on Voodoo's head and turned on the EEG. Over the space of fifteen minutes, she conducted a variety of tests and asked a series of control questions to establish a baseline for his brain activity.

"I think we are ready," she said. She injected a sedative into Voodoo's arm to help him sleep. Voodoo didn't want to admit it, but his body yearned for the rest. It had been more than twenty-four hours since he last slept, years since he'd slept peacefully. He gave a feeble attempt to relax his mind and his anxiety. Being under a sedative meant that Naomi and he would be vulnerable if anyone were to find them.

He had to let go of that now. This test was the best chance of finding Taka-chan. They needed to understand the voice in his dreams. He needed to embrace the mental vivisection waiting in his nightmares.

Voodoo's eyelids grew heavy. Naomi reached out and touched Voodoo's arm. Her calming touch anchored Voodoo to reality like a synaptic bridge. He closed his eyes as he felt the warmth of her skin and the gentle pressure of her fingertips. His body calmed. His heartbeat slowed. A solitary tear formed and rolled down his cheek as he felt his mind release.

Voodoo drifted off.

Worse than living through the tragedies of his life, nothing scared Voodoo more than having to relive them through his nightmares. And here he was, standing on the precipice of darkness, willingly jumping into the abyss. Voodoo knew the battle waiting for him; he knew the demons lurking in the recesses of his memory. Yet, as he faded from reality, Voodoo strapped on his mental armor and descended into the hell of his mind.

CHAPTER 31
The Kuroshio Maru

38.484065, 142.865456
SOMEWHERE EAST OF JAPAN

An unseasonably early typhoon pushed north over the Korean Peninsula and into the Sea of Japan, where most events disintegrate into tropical storms. However, Typhoon Nabi seemed to have no intention of standing down. The captain of the *Kuroshio Maru*, the smallest of the once-thriving fleet of cargo ships from Toyotomi Industries, added this to his many concerns as his ship ripped through the ocean at seventeen knots, steaming north on the far western waters of the Pacific Ocean. The aged ship, which fell into the mini bulker category, had a deadweight of 8,000 tons and a length of 122.5 meters. Tonight, the ship powered north on its namesake current, the Kuroshio.

Named after the dark water that travels north along the edge of the Pacific Ocean, the Kuroshio, or "black current," pushes the warm water from the tropics north toward the Kamchatka Peninsula. The area is known for creating extremely nutrient-rich waters teeming with fish. It is also an area known for another natural phenomenon known as the North Wall Effect where the current of the Kuroshio meets the Oyashio, and a thermal effect compounds into massive multidirectional waves.

To make things worse, since the merger between Toyotomi Industries and Xin Jishu International, the captain of the *Kuroshio Maru* found himself in new company. His entire crew was now Chinese and many of them seemed inexperienced in the world of the merchant marine. His ship was once part of a vast armada of cargo vessels supporting the mighty Japanese conglomerate. The *Kuroshio Maru* was now one of only two ships that remained in the aging fleet.

Footsteps approached the bridge. The ship's crew bristled. The quartermaster manning the helm stiffened and swallowed. They knew who was coming.

"Report," Ryu said behind him.

It wasn't the tattoos or the curt way that he spoke; it was the cloud that seemed to hover over the man in black, the darkness in his eyes, the eerie whistling in the passageway.

"We will be steaming north for the better part of a day before we reach our destination. We should arrive a few hours ahead of schedule." The captain turned to address Ryu. "Is there anything else the chairman asked of us?"

Ryu shook his head.

"You received the new coordinates, correct?"

"West side of Kunashir Island, yes, sir."

Ryu stood motionless, watching the vast emptiness of the dark sea under the night sky. The captain had grown accustomed to being kept in the dark with Ryu and his mysterious shipments. He knew not to ask specifics about anything below deck, or the random stops in the middle of the ocean.

Something about *this* trip felt different.

Ryu's presence, the unorthodox destination, and weather reports of the typhoon set his superstitious sailing intuition on edge. Nothing about this situation felt right. The weather reports indicated the storm hitting Korea would directly cross their path. The chairman requested they arrive by late Friday evening and head back immediately. At the rate the storm traveled, they would make it there and back on time. The numbers all added up.

Only Ryu's story didn't.

CHAPTER 32

The Stairwell

V oices broke the squelch of radio static and screamed in Voodoo's ear.

"Vick One is down hard! Push Vick Two in a blocking position to provide cover!"

"Negative! Vicks Two and Three are trapped! Iraqi vicks are down hard! Convoy is pinned!"

Voodoo stared at the broken window.

The image of two lifeless eyes stared back at him.

His heartbeat thumped in his eardrums, his mind swimming in denial. Pain receptors lit up his arm, electrifying his entire body. His jaw tingled, his mouth salivated, and bile crawled up his throat. He ejected the viscous, bloody spit from his mouth.

Shooters moved behind him, and he felt a squeeze on his shoulder.

"Push up to the entryway of that building. I'll cover these guys," a voice said as Heath stood behind Voodoo, covering the hatch of the RG-33 that now lay on its side. A human shape waved him on. Voodoo ran to meet it.

"Cover this door. We need to get the guys out of Vick One. Get ready for a hasty assault," the shooter said. The damaged vehicle lay on its side like a dead beast. The driver's-side door opened vertically, and the driver pushed his way out, followed by Frisco.

"This way!" Voodoo yelled.

GA! GA! GA! GA! GA! GA! GA!

The CROWS fired a barrage in an orange blaze married with the tinkling of expended brass. Voodoo scanned the area. Dust and smoke hindered his peripheral vision. Random flashes of light sparked all around him.

Voodoo focused his rifle on the doorway. He stood to the side and away from the fatal funnel of the entryway should the door open. His right arm was useless; his nondominant arm struggled to keep the rifle parallel to the ground. His legs trembled, and the muzzle oscillated faintly in unintentional figure eights as he fought to keep it steady. His mental faculties dissolved with each wave of excruciating pain.

He leaned against the wall to steady himself. Two shooters, then three, then six stacked up behind Voodoo.

"Alpha Squad, headcount," he heard the chief yell. Shooters tapped their helmets and gave a thumbs-up, one by one until they got to Voodoo. He pointed his barrel skyward and rolled around the man behind him, a subliminal message to the next shooter to take point. Voodoo worked his way to the back of the train where his injury and subsequent tactical limitations would not put others at risk.

Eight men started in the downed vehicle. Two were missing. Voodoo caught sight of Stu as he dragged someone out of the RG-33. Stu hefted the injured shooter on his back in a fireman carry and ran to meet the line of warfighters at the door.

"Alpha Squad is up, Chief." The injured shooter on Stu's back groaned as Stu held him in place with one arm while still carrying his M4 at the ready in the other.

"We're gonna take the roof, set security, then call in Close Air Support," the chief ordered. Frisco moved up to the number two position in the stack. The point man grabbed the handle of the door. Locked. He stepped in front and unleashed a donkey kick. The door flew open.

Frisco punched his barrel through the door, followed by the breacher scanning the corners. They cleared the open entryways, using angles to sweep the boxy hallways of what appeared to have once been a municipal building.

A long hallway led to several offices on the right and a large stairwell in the middle climbing upward. Frisco ran point with Stu and Voodoo in the rear. They flowed through the building as an armed snake, their footsteps silent as they rolled their boots from heel to toe to keep their heads level and focus sharp.

As he headed for the stairwell, Voodoo avoided a glance at the first room on the right on the ground floor. He knew who waited for him on the other side of the door, below the broken window; he pressed forward.

They pushed up the stairs to the fourth floor, where the stairway met the roof. Heath, also the squad sniper, found a corner to use as overwatch, unsheathed his .300 Win Mag, and scanned the horizon. The platoon joint terminal attack controller, or JTAC, took a knee in the center of the roof and keyed his UHF radio. Communication waves reached out to the hot open sky in search of nearby air support. He began speaking in a language of his own as he communicated with pilots and Air Weapons Stations. He knelt like a spartan negotiating with Ares to smite his enemies.

"You see anyone engaging our vehicles, or anyone with a rifle on the rooftops, drop 'em!" the chief yelled.

BAA!

The .300 Win Mag rifle detonated a .338 Lapua round, and the kinetic pressure cracked the night air. Without the usual *suppressor, the sound of the sniper rifle, more than any other weapon, meant surgical precision, a death sentence from the grim reaper.*

"Chief, we've got a green on blue on our hands," Heath called out. *The partner forces had turned on Voodoo's platoon.* "The Iraqi police, or someone dressed like police, are shooting at us. They appear to be shooting at the Iraqi military guys too."

Dap! Dap! Dap! ... Dap! Dap! Dap! Dap! Dap!

Green tip 5.56 rounds hurled from the shooters' rifles. Voodoo took cover at the far end of the roof and laid down his weapon. He reached into a pocket on his body armor and pulled out some thick zip ties. He wrapped one around the wrist of his broken arm, another through part of his body armor, then cinched the two together, pinning his injured arm against his body in a makeshift sling. He winced, grit his teeth, and swore incessantly in his little world of isolated anguish.

The shooter Stu hauled up to the roof lay on his back, nonresponsive. It was Bobby, the EOD guy. The platoon chief and Stu knelt on either side of him. They ran their hands along his legs and arms and squeezed, searching for holes in his flesh, pausing incrementally to sniff their fingers. In the dark and confusion, the only way to know that someone is bleeding is to smell the blood, the metallic scent directing them to the appropriate limb in need of the wrenching pain of a tourniquet.

"Do something! It doesn't matter what, just DO something!" *the voice of Voodoo's tactical instructors yelled in his thoughts.*

Voodoo picked up his rifle and maneuvered to the ledge of the building to gain situational awareness. Gunpowder, dust, and blood filled his nostrils. On the roof of a nearby building, he could barely make out shadows moving, the outline of weapons in hands. A green chem light floated motionless in the brackish water below.

Voodoo turned to the JTAC. "We've got military-aged males moving tactically on the building to the south, 150 meters from our position."

BAA!

The sniper fired another round. A shadow dropped out of sight as several others protruded as curved bulges on the roof.

Voodoo weighed his options. Heath covered one corner, Stu and the chief worked on the downed shooter, the JTAC sought out Close Air Support, and Frisco manned a separate part of the building with another squad member. That meant all eight personnel were actively engaged.

Who was covering the stairs?

Who was watching their six?

Voodoo made his way over to the stairwell and pointed his barrel down into the emptiness. He took a knee and held his position, protecting the shooters behind him as they engaged the enemy.

"Roger that, Warhammer," the JTAC called out over the radio. "We've got fast movers inbound from the west! Stand by!"

Ares was listening.

Up in the sky, a quick flash of light and a direct line of bullets beamed like a molten laser before Voodoo heard it.

The .30 caliber rounds of the A-10 Warthog blasted from spinning barrels mounted to the front of the aircraft at 4,200 rounds per minute. The orange barrage perforated the building 150 meters to the south of their location, utterly decimating the men on the rooftop in a cloud of pink powder and severed limbs.

BWWWWAAAAAAAAAAAAAA!

The jet engines scorched the sky at low altitude with a sharp Doppler shift as the aircraft completed its strafing run.

Shooters yelled.

Dap! Dap! Dap!

"Contact fifty meters! Two men out in the open!"

Dap! Dap! Dap! ... Dap! Dap! Dap! Dap! Dap!

"Changing mags!"

Dap! Dap!

"I can't stop the bleeding! We're gonna lose Bobby!"

Amid the violence and mayhem, Voodoo fixated on the stairwell.

His mind drifted.

Two empty eyes stared at him.

Did I really kill a kid?

Unanswered questions pulled Voodoo's feet down the stairs. A step. Then another...and another.

Did I murder an innocent child?

The answer waited below.

Voodoo descended the staircase. The boy was in this building. Voodoo had to know. He had to be sure. He should have checked earlier. He most certainly should not *break line of sight with his squad, but they were engaged in a fierce battle. His field of fire lay below. It lay within. His threat was dead already, though. And separating yourself from your unit in the firefight is how soldiers go missing.*

He pressed on.

This is how people die.

This is how soldiers disappear and get their heads cut off as part of some propaganda video.

Before he knew it, Voodoo was standing outside the door of the room to the right of the main entryway four floors below his teammates. He stood outside the room with the window that he shattered with a well-directed bullet, the room where he took the life of an innocent child.

He pushed the door open with his gun barrel.

Bedding lay on the dusty tile floor. A rug lay in the center of the room, a semblance of comfort. Through the broken glass, a war raged on outside. But for Voodoo, here in this room, the finality of impulsive decisions lay delicately on the floor.

The boy's body must have rolled after he hit the ground. He lay on his back, his head tilted to his left side, and eyes wide open.

Two lifeless pupils stared blankly.

Voodoo stopped breathing.

The boy's mouth cracked open, and a whisper, breathy and haunting, escaped his lips as he spoke.

"Voodoo..." the boy said. "This is all your fault."

CHAPTER 33

The Lab Results

WASEDA UNIVERSITY
TOKYO, JAPAN

The protein is in his blood!

Copious streams of data poured in from Voodoo's brain, setting Naomi's scientific mind alight with fascination only for a wave of guilt to douse the excitement.

It had been nearly ninety minutes since Voodoo began his test. The signals on her screen monitoring his biorhythm and neural activity indicated that Voodoo had finally reached REM sleep. Naomi carefully weighed her options as her clinical mind methodically organized and processed each step. Before her, the LPA frantically emitted lights toward Voodoo's hypothalamus to elicit activity in his memories.

Naomi had a theory. There are many side effects from traumatic experiences, each requiring tailored treatment. There are incidences of some veterans with PTSD suffering psychotic schizophrenia, which may be "unlocked" by traumatic events like some genetic time bomb. Other studies showed that PTSD could elicit physiological changes as well. In the case of military veterans, it often caused the hypothalamus to shrink. If this were the case with Voodoo, perhaps this physiological change caused his prophetic dreams to become lost within the noise of his trauma. She hoped the God Algorithm would be able to guide Voodoo through his memories and clear out the emotional blockage to make room for more accurate information.

A lead weight in Naomi's stomach anchored her to reality. *How will I know if Voodoo is losing his mind? How can I be sure this event alone won't unlock dormant triggers in his genetics?*

Well into uncharted territory, Naomi knew her only hope lay in the Xiphos Gov network having the power to process the trillion or so neurons firing in Voodoo's brain.

This whole concept is problematic, she thought. *Just have faith.*

The work with Dr. Ichikawa helped create a deep learning neural network capable of anticipating and adapting to the patient. Naomi needed that ability now more than ever.

As Naomi prepared to move the position of the LPA to create a different effect on Voodoo's dreams, a message arrived on Voodoo's phone.

FRIDAY 1:38 A.M.

Janet: Xiphos Gov is up. Ready to initiate processing.

Vudu: This is Naomi. Voodoo is on the machine. I am almost ready.

Janet: The network is at your disposal. Let us know if you need anything else.

Based on the work they did in the lab with Dr. Ichikawa, Naomi knew that the algorithm was most effective at the end of

REM sleep. During that time, the brain is the most active, as the human mind is working the hardest to process the random neurons firing and present them as lucid dreams. According to the readings on her system, she had another thirty minutes before Voodoo would be ready. At that time, the Xiphos Gov network would allow Voodoo the ability to process data at a level never seen before.

What is this really *going to do to his mind?*

For the next thirty minutes, there was nothing she could do but wait.

• • •

Voodoo's dream reset. He found himself at the top of the staircase, staring into the darkness. Voodoo descended.

Before he knew it, Voodoo was standing outside the door of the room to the right of the main entryway four floors below his teammates. It didn't feel like déjà vu, but rather a new experience, a unique event yet still one where he knew the outcome. He stood outside the room with the window that he shattered with a well-directed bullet, the place where Voodoo took the life of a young boy...or so he thought.

He pushed the door open with his gun barrel.

As the door opened, the white fluorescent light, tile floor, and sterility of a hospital room lay in front of him. Sunlight shone through a window onto a patient on a bed. Tulips, daffodils, cards, balloons, and other tokens of well-wishing cradled the patient. An empty chair faced the mechanical bed where the woman lay, weak, worn down by the disease ravaging her body. She wore a bandana on her head, yet thin strands of once healthy, amber-colored hair snuck out, weak and deathly.

She was the most beautiful woman Voodoo had ever known.

Voodoo's rifle dropped from his hand onto the ground. He disconnected the buckle to the chinstrap and discarded his helmet. He slowly moved toward her, disbelief fading with each step.

She opened her eyes and immediately smiled, the way she always did when she looked at him. The smile that always kept her harnessed to his heart, the smile that kept him sane.

He sat beside her and took her hand. The hand he always reached for when he awoke from his nightmares. The dreams he always ran from. The very same dreams that now allowed him to be with his love one last time.

He looked her in the eyes and began to weep.

"I'm sorry I couldn't save you," he sobbed. "I knew what was happening, and nobody listened!" he pleaded with her.

Her eyebrows rose slightly; her eyes searched his face. "I know. We've been through this. It's not your fault."

"Of course it's my fault. I knew you were sick and couldn't stop it." Voodoo held her hand with his good one. He kissed it, then buried his face as he knelt beside her.

She reached out and rubbed her other hand through his thick brown hair, ignoring the sweat and the stench of war.

"Knowing the end gave us hope to enjoy the present."

"I...still need you. I can't do this alone," Voodoo said.

She smiled. The same smile Voodoo had known for half his life.

"You're not alone. You've just never allowed yourself to see it."

She gazed at Voodoo with her deep green eyes. He always felt they were too wise and kind to be wasted on someone like him. She caressed his cheek, and his entire body warmed.

Then her smile began to fade. Her brow furrowed.

"You'll never be alone. But more importantly, someone that is alone needs you. Time is running out."

Voodoo raised his head, taken aback by the words coming from her mouth.

"She needs you. Save her!"

• • •

The door to the lab opened, and the phlebotomist from earlier walked into the room carrying a manila folder.

"Here are the lab results you asked for. I printed out those other readings you mentioned to simplify your comparative analysis. I posted them next to each other for your convenience," the technician said.

"Thank you."

Naomi watched as the sensors recording Voodoo's mind reached optimal levels. It had been nearly thirty minutes. She changed the position of the LPA to Voodoo's temporal lobe, to help Voodoo process information through the Xiphos network. She picked up the phone to send a message.

FRIDAY 2:15 A.M.

Vudu: We are ready. I am activating the algorithm now.
Janet: Good luck.

Naomi pressed several keys on the engineering graphic user interface and pressed enter. She expected some huge humming sound or dramatic explosion of light, but little changed on her computer. She knew, in the end, Voodoo's mind was in the driver's seat. As soon as his subconscious was ready, he would chew through the emotional blockage and dig his way down to the information he needed. At least that's what she hoped would happen. There was also a good chance nothing was happening. There was also a chance that Voodoo's brain was collapsing in on itself.

She opened the folder the technician gave her and thumbed through the results. When she got to the comparison chart, she paused.

"How is this possible?" she said out loud. "Then that means—"

Voodoo's phone pinged. She picked it up.

FRIDAY 2:17 A.M.

DZ: Naomi, is anyone else there with you? This is urgent.

Vudu: Just a couple of other scientists. Why?

DZ: I found your picture on social media. You weren't tagged by name, but I know that it's your face. If I was able to see you, at this place now, that means others will be able to find you too.

Vudu: Like the police?

DZ: I wouldn't be worried about the police. You need to leave. NOW!

Naomi looked up at her screen. Her jaw dropped. The gentle wavy lines from earlier now spiked beyond the range of the screen and she scrambled to reset the parameters high enough to capture the rates as they skyrocketed. Leave now and Voodoo's mind would implode. Or...maybe it already had.

• • •

Again, Voodoo stood at the top of the stairwell. The darkness of the descent beckoned, calling out to him to search for answers to questions he no longer needed to ask.

Fires and explosions lit his eyes. The gunpowder, blood, and sweat filled his nostrils. War raged all around him. It raged inside him.

He sought silence in the cacophony. He descended, away from the battle his mind never left, from the fight that, in reality, ended nearly a decade earlier.

With a rush, images flashed across Voodoo's mind—storms and oceans, raging rivers, explosions, and bright lights. His mother smiled upon him, young and happy, then weak and dying.

Thousands of cranes circled the skies in a mesh of clarity and mass confusion. He stood amid computer language itself, passing between dimensions of comprehension until, finally, he had a clear vision of a river.

A half-moon illuminated a beach in a large dark canyon. A man knelt beside a wide river as the flow of the water sparkled under the moonlight. The torrent of rapids echoed down the canyon in the distance. The man held a small metal cylinder in his hands. He wept the tears that only someone who has lost a loved one understands.

The man stood and unscrewed the cap to the cylinder and turned it over. A powderlike substance spread across the air. A gust of wind carried the particles into the dark night sky, while the rest fell to the lapping water on the beach and vanished in the silt. He shuddered and cried. When the contents fell no more, the man stood, staring for several moments before screwing the lid back on.

He walked over to a bag, stowed the cylinder, and retrieved an object. He stood and walked toward one of the rafts on the beach, brandishing a syringe and a dry bag.

The images shifted.

Voodoo saw Tokyo. The same man stepped into an elevator; his body trembled. A dark figure stared at him. Even in the dream, Voodoo could sense the presence of the foreboding shadow. A faint whistle haunted the air.

Voodoo's dreams followed the man to a lab, where he frantically sifted through items on a shelf. The man, a scientist it appeared, reached into a safe and pulled out two vials and extracted the contents of one into a syringe. He replaced the bottles in the safe with blood from a separate project.

The scene changed to a small cargo ship on the ocean. The words Toyotomi Industries were written on the side. The vessel pitched and rolled in a light sea.

Suddenly Voodoo was back at the bottom of the stairs in his original dream, preparing to open the door to where the young boy lay. He pushed the door open with his weapon. A body lay on the ground staring back at him. He stepped closer.

Frisco lay dead on the ground. The face blurred. Then it was Stu. It blurred again and became his own.

Scenes flashed across Voodoo's mind, as though controlled by a restless child with a remote.

Men in black sprinted down a dimly lit road.

A clash of swords clanged; bloodied bodies filled a white hallway.

A sniper fired rounds down an alley as metal balls poured all over the ground.

A building exploded on a Japanese street in the middle of the night.

More visions whirred across his mind at breakneck speeds. Story lines began and ended then started over with entirely different outcomes. He contemplated the eventuality of what felt like an infinite number of possibilities. He watched chaos theory play out in his mind.

That was when it came, the interloping voice, the voice of his mother.

Old gods and new will battle on contested lands. In one day, an old friend will be lost, an old friend regained. When the light of Amaterasu protects you, close your eyes to see through the light. Then, rise and face the eastern threat.

Unlike before, when Voodoo's memory overpowered the image, the dream became clear. There was an island, isolated. It had dense vegetation and was sparsely populated. He saw a beached ship and armies wearing four different colors merging in battle. In the sky above, ancient gods clashed.

Then, just as it all began, everything went dark.

Silence.

He was aware but listening only to his conscience. He could not hear his heartbeat or his thoughts. He could hear only his very existence.

For the first time in his entire life, Voodoo felt complete and utter peace. He felt whole. He didn't think that his history or problems had been erased. He felt only solitude. He felt open.

A single pin of light slowly appeared in front of him. He focused his attention.

It expanded.

The dot grew brighter and brighter.

He couldn't feel his body but knew he was traveling faster than he'd ever moved.

His consciousness flew through the void until, just as his momentary transcendence began, it all stopped.

Voodoo stood beside his wife once again. Rays of morning light crept through the white wooden shudders of their bedroom as his wife stood in the sun, fit and young. Her comforter. Her blue dress. Her perfume.

Just as he loved to remember her.

He reached out and held her hand, and she looked at him. Her grip was healthy and intense.

"The time has come," she said. "You must go."

He nodded. Voodoo's wife took both his hands and pulled them toward her chest.

"She needs you."

His wife gripped tighter. Her intensity was focused, desperate yet with resolve. He felt nothing but passion as she implored.

"Listen to me. You need to hurry! Only you know the truth. You have to make them listen!"

The urgency of her message shook him. The danger was visceral and profound. Her resolution passed through her hands and filled his body as she cried out.

"Gavin." His name echoed. "Gavin, you must hurry! She needs you!"

She looked over his shoulder at something beyond. Her eyes widened.

"They've found you, Gavin! Run!"

CHAPTER 34

The Dream Is Over

MOAB, UTAH, USA

Nestled within a valley of Navajo sandstone, in the shadow of the white-capped La Sal Mountains, Moab teemed with summer life along the two lanes of US Route 191. Sunburnt tourists and tanned tour guides walked along the road to catch a bite at the local brewery, lounged near the ice cream shop, or perused the shops for overpriced souvenirs bearing the image of the hunched, flute-playing god, Kokopelli.

A white bus jostled and bounced along the highway and, despite the concerning bangs and backfires, managed to find its way home to Vagabond River Expeditions. It towed a trailer with three rafts strapped on top and came to a stop in the dirt parking lot beside the cabin-like front office. Weary customers and river guides stepped off the bus into the late afternoon heat.

"Come on, Kerry," her sister said as she stared out the window. Customers stepped off the bus, some excited to head to their next adventure while others lingered to drink in the experience a little longer. *I don't want this journey to end.* She didn't want to return to the life waiting for her outside of the canyon. She longed to stay in this moment, remain in the world where she still knew the clutches of hell at her heels, the warmth of heaven kissing her skin.

Outside the window she saw the guides, and a strong feeling flooded her. She was only seventeen but mature enough to recognize the emotion growing inside.

Jealousy.

She wanted to stay with the guides who pulled her from the water. She wished to remain in the dichotomy of ancient mysteries hiding within millions of years of lost rock layers. She wanted to feel the guidance of the egret flying over her head as she traversed life's journeys. Kerry wanted to help people. She wanted to pay forward the second chance the canyon gave her.

Kerry reluctantly gathered herself and reached down to grab her bag when she heard voices on the bus behind her.

"Everyone has their reason why they come on the river and sometimes they are similar. I'm glad I was able to be here for yours...whatever it may have been," a woman said.

Kerry looked back to see Ally and Kenzo Ichikawa.

He nodded his head and gave a bow. There was sadness in the man's eyes but not depression. It looked more like longing. The kind of sadness you feel when something magical has come to an end, the feeling your life has changed, and you'll never feel this raw and enlightened ever again.

Kerry understood the feeling completely.

"Perhaps we'll see each other again someday," Ally said.

"*Go-en ga attara,*" he replied.

"What does that mean?"

"If there is fate." He smiled at her and turned quickly toward the front of the bus where he made eye contact with Kerry. She smiled back before sliding from her seat and off the bus.

As her foot made contact with the dirt parking lot, she saw Gavin, stepped sideways, and leaned against the white metal of the Vagabond River Expeditions shuttle.

Gavin stood next to Joel and a barrel-chested older man with a bow to his legs.

"Joel had a yard sale today, Steve! Swimmers everywhere!" Ally blurted out from inside the bus, her voice sailing over Kerry's head. Joel gave Ally a look of annoyance as she stepped off the bus, not noticing Kerry standing to the side.

Joel hung his head low. "We hit a boil in Cocaine Cove, and I lost one"—he raised his index finger at Ally—"just *one* off the bow," Joel said. The large man put his hand on Joel's shoulder and leaned forward to keep his voice down.

"You know the eddies are dangerous over 14,000 cubic feet. Why would you risk using the cove? It doesn't gain you much, considering. You're lucky you were able to get the swimmer into the raft in time," Steve said.

"He didn't get them back in the boat," Ally said as she arrived. "Gavin did. And with quite the dramatic flair, I must say."

Gavin tried not to look proud of himself, but he certainly was. Kerry couldn't help but feel proud of him too.

"Really? The first-year guide did it?" Steve looked genuinely impressed. "We'll make a guide out of you yet, Gavin!" he said, slapping Gavin hard on the back.

Gavin coughed at the sudden impact, and Kerry giggled. Gavin gave a big smile as he turned and noticed Kerry standing beside the bus.

"Hey," Gavin said, walking over as Joel, Steve, and Ally continued talking. "It's the swimmer!"

"Hey," she said, giving an awkward glance to the ground and shuffling her feet, realizing for the first time she was considerably taller than him. She looked toward the highway and saw her mother and sister walking toward the main road, most likely headed to their hotel down the strip, but Kerry wanted one last moment to speak with Gavin.

The corner of Gavin's mouth cracked with a slight smile. Kerry was hoping their life-changing adventure would somehow last, that she could spend more time getting to know Gavin and the other guides.

She knew otherwise. The guides had another trip in the morning.

Like the setting sun in the west, the day ebbed, and reality flowed in with the twilight. The fantasy was fading.

Dr. Kenzo Ichikawa clutched his dry bag as he too stepped up to Gavin.

Kenzo cleared his throat and coughed into his fist as he prepared to speak.

Kenzo glanced at Kerry. Her eyes jumped back and forth between Gavin and Kenzo.

"I want you to know that...well, I think your family would be proud of what you did today." Kenzo Ichikawa paused, rubbing his dry bag with his left hand. "I have a feeling what happened on this river changed a lot of lives today," he said.

Gavin returned a quizzical glance. "Um, yeah...I'm glad to hear it. Hopefully, you can come back and see us sometime," Gavin said, sounding more like a business rep for Vagabond rather than a river guide.

"*Go-en ga attara*," Dr. Ichikawa said before shouldering his bag and heading off down the road, his head bowed. He carried himself away like a down-trodden warrior at the end of a journey, stepping off toward a war that would never end.

Kerry's mother and sister waved her on in the distance.

"Perhaps someday I'll come back and see you too," Kerry said, ignoring her family.

Gavin looked over his shoulder briefly, then took Kerry by the elbow and led her toward the road.

"I... Nobody here knows this yet, but at the end of this summer, I won't be going to school or coming back to be a guide," Gavin said. "I've enlisted in the military. I go to boot camp at the end of the summer."

Kerry's jaw dropped. "Do you think they'll send you to Afghanistan?" she said, horrified at the idea. Once again, though, her chest filled with pride.

"Most likely. That's kinda the point," Gavin said. "It hasn't been long since 9/11. The real war is just starting."

Kerry nodded, unsure what to say next.

"Hey, looks like you've got some people waiting for you."

She looked to her right, where her mother and sister waved at her again to move along. Behind them walked Kenzo Ichikawa. She gave Gavin one last grateful look and a farewell before shuffling off down the road, the orange glow of the sun dropping onto the edges of the red rocks to the west. She would never see the world the same ever again. She had her canyons to explore and rapids to survive. As for Gavin, his days of pulling people from the clutches of hell had just begun.

CHAPTER 35
The New Murder

"Explain to us again why you left your post."

"As I said, I was ordered to, sir, by Inspector Yoshimoto. I told him that Sergeant Ooda specifically told me not to leave, but the chain of command states that I must obey the orders of the most senior officer on the scene. In that case, it was Inspector Yoshimoto." The senior police officer sweat profusely through her blue uniform under the interrogation room lights.

"Inspector Yoshimoto was not on the CCTV feeds. The only thing we saw was your vehicle leaving and two remaining," the interrogator stated.

Captain Tanaka watched through the one-directional mirror, observing the interrogator questioning the young officer. After the incident at Naomi Shimoda's apartment, her subsequent disappearance, and the video that leaked to the press, the police force retreated into crisis control. Instead of seeking answers for the death of Dr. Ichikawa, they were managing an international incident in which American military personnel assigned to liaise with the Japanese police were now suspects in an assault case.

As Captain Tanaka watched, he noted that nothing about the officer's body language or diction indicated deception. The senior police officer appeared to be speaking the truth, which confounded Captain Tanaka further. To add to the turbulence, they couldn't find the assaulted officers.

"That's impossible," the senior police officer argued. "Inspector Yoshimoto ordered me to leave. The other men in my squad can account for it. If it were my men, then show me which ones got assaulted!"

"Either one of two things is taking place here: You're telling the truth, and Inspector Yoshimoto relieved your men and somehow doctored the video and men impersonating officers got into an altercation with the Americans, or you're the one who's in on it. You're the one who facilitated the whole thing."

Inspector Yoshimoto had an alibi. His phone records and his men confirmed his whereabouts on the other side of the city where they were pounding the pavement, chasing leads.

But still, none of this made any sense.

"What did the Americans say about the attack? Did you ask them?"

"This isn't the time for you to deflect. Just tell us what happened," the interrogator demanded.

The door to the observation room opened, and one of Captain Tanaka's men from the Special Assault Team entered.

"Sir, there's been a development."

"Go ahead," Captain Tanaka said without removing his eyes from the interrogation.

"The CEO of Toyotomi Industries was just found dead in his apartment."

"Cause of death?" Captain Tanaka asked completely out of instinct. His mind defaulted to emotionless, objective information gathering.

"Seppuku."

"How long ago?"

"Forensics claims it must have been over a day."

"Who found him?" Captain Tanaka pivoted to face his teammate.

"His assistant. He requested to have all of his meetings cleared for the day. She went to check on him this evening, and that is when they discovered the body."

"Interesting. Any correlation to Ichikawa's death?"

"When they found his body, he still had a blade in his stomach."

"Which would make sense if he committed seppuku. He would use his blade. Unlike the situation with Dr. Ichikawa, where they didn't find any murder weapon."

"That's just it, sir. The blade they found had other blood on it. They're testing it now to confirm. Also, the weird thing is that it's not a Japanese tanto. It appears to be a Korean jingum."

"Are you saying that he was killed with a Korean weapon in a traditional Japanese fashion?" Captain Tanaka asked.

"Yes, sir."

"Have they checked the security feeds? Have they found any immediate leads?"

"Video outside the building shows nothing. It's like all activity of the CEO has been erased out of existence."

Probably because it has, Captain Tanaka thought.

He looked back toward the interrogation room where the young senior police officer sat sweating under the interrogation lights. His phone shook with its familiar vibration, and Captain Tanaka answered. He listened to the voice on the other end before responding.

"Tell the Americans I'm on my way back to the embassy. We have a lot to discuss."

• • •

Large armored vehicles are rare in Japan. Tight streets and heavy traffic make motorcycles and light trucks the transportation of choice for police trying to move with agility through the city. None of this applies at nearly 3 a.m. With the streets cleared, the heavily armored SAT vehicle rumbled down the narrow streets of Tokyo toward the target location.

A tip regarding human trafficking potentially associated with North Korean operatives piqued Captain Tanaka's interest. The superintendent general placed anything regarding kidnapping as his highest priority, and the Special Assault Team led the charge.

It had been a strange evening at best. Since the discovery of Dr. Kenzo Ichikawa's body, Captain Tanaka and his team had been scouring the city for clues. The CCTV feed leaked to the press regarding the Americans attacking the Japanese didn't help the situation in the slightest. The death of Toyotomi Industries' CEO compounded his dilemma.

Their destination, the Starlight Pachinko Parlor, had been under investigation before. Captain Tanaka didn't know how deep the corruption associated with the pachinko parlor ran, but he knew the time had come for more aggressive tactics.

Tonight, they intended to gather intelligence and conduct surveillance for evidence of illegal activity. The superintendent didn't want any more negative attention. A paid informant had entered the facility less than an hour earlier to pre-stage as a customer. The tip said something big would happen at 3 a.m. They just didn't know what.

Captain Tanaka's instincts told him to be ready for anything. If that meant conducting a hasty assault to save some hostages, so be it.

At 2:30, the armored car pulled to a stop several blocks away from the pachinko parlor. Captain Tanaka rotated in his position in the front seat and looked at his men. Eight bodies sat behind him in black military uniforms, black balaclavas, clear eye protection, and helmets. It took a great deal of effort to find a uniform large enough to fit one of the men.

"*Tsuyaku shite kure,*" he said to one of his men behind him.

"*Hai,*" the officer replied. "He wants me to translate for him," he said.

Captain Tanaka began speaking through the translator sitting beside the two Americans, Frisco and Stu.

"He wants you to shut off your phones. You are to remain in the vehicle no matter what happens. Obviously, as per Japanese law, as Americans, you're not allowed to have weapons outside of the military installations, so don't get any ideas. You're here to advise and get intel. That's it. He's taking a big risk by allowing you to come with us," the translator said.

"We understand, and we appreciate your faith in this matter. Let us know if there is anything we can do," Frisco replied. He pulled out his phone, shut it off, then slipped it back into his pocket. Stu did the same.

"You need to understand, we came here to help with this investigation, but those men were after Dr. Shimoda. They were armed. If we hadn't fought back, they would have taken her," Frisco said.

Tanaka nodded.

From the time he left the interrogation room at the police station until he arrived at the embassy, Captain Tanaka had already started putting things together. The death of a prominent scientist, the murder of a Japanese conglomerate CEO with a Korean weapon, and the orchestrated manipulation of the city's CCTV feeds in real time meant none of this was a coincidence. These events were nothing short of a call to war; someone wanted these men to suffer; someone wanted Japan to bleed. Whoever they were, they wanted everyone to know Korea was behind it.

In light of the many possible actors in this AI war, Captain Tanaka was suspicious of all of them except Frisco.

Before working with the Japanese National Police Agency, Captain Tanaka enlisted in the Japanese Ground Self-Defense Force as part of the 1st Special Forces Group. Captain Tanaka was a shooter.

He had trained with Americans like Frisco in the military. He vividly remembered conducting fast-rope training from a helicopter with the Task Force in Southern California when one of their men fell. Task Force shooters helped save the Japanese soldier's life. Captain Tanaka felt honored to work with them again. It took little effort to convince him there was something very off about the videos.

Five hours earlier, Frisco reached out to Captain Tanaka. They both felt it was time to fix their mess.

"I don't think they expected us to believe those videos were real," Captain Tanaka had told Frisco through a translator. "They intended to sow discord with the public, and they accomplished it. If we come out and say that the videos were doctored, and Americans were not attacking police but random Japanese who set them up, it sounds like a cover-up. We lose either way."

"They wanted us sidelined so we couldn't protect Dr. Shimoda," Frisco replied.

"Exactly. The whole purpose of the deepfake is to slow us down, create chaos while they follow through with whatever it is they are really up to. Do you know where Dr. Shimoda is now? Is she safe?" Captain Tanaka asked.

"The last I heard, she found a place to hide while we figure things out. She's been contacting us through a go-between," Frisco said.

Captain Tanaka knew that Frisco was holding back. Trust was still weak between the two for a good reason. The police leak led to her potential kidnapping. The entire altercation sullied the reputation of his department. It was a black mark on the honor of his unit; he intended to rectify that personally.

"We're already questioning the officers that were supposed to be protecting her. In the meantime, I just received a tip that I need to look into," Captain Tanaka said.

"While you're at it, we've received some intel on a couple of locations, and maybe you can look into it for us."

"Certainly. What is it?" Captain Tanaka asked.

"Have you ever heard of a place called the Starlight Pachinko Parlor?"

"How do you know that name?" Captain Tanaka asked suspiciously.

"Dr. Shimoda gave us access to some CCTV feeds from the night of Dr. Hawkins's disappearance, and we were able to track a small truck back to that building. We've been following some other leads, but that one seems to be the most credible," Frisco said.

"How come you didn't mention this earlier?"

"We just found out about it. We're pretty far behind, we don't have the resources you do."

Captain Tanaka thought about it. The only way that he could gain Frisco's trust was to show faith himself.

"I'll tell you what, come with me tonight. We just found out that the CEO of Toyotomi Industries has been murdered in a similar way to Dr. Kenzo Ichikawa. He was found with a Korean weapon in his stomach. This murder and our mutual investigation may be related. I'll need you to change clothes, though."

Now it was close to 3 a.m. Captain Tanaka sat in the armored car waiting for the event that the anonymous email said would take place.

Monitors presented CCTV feeds in the armored car. One from the front of the pachinko parlor, and the other from the alley behind the main building. In Captain Tanaka's ear, the sound of J-pop blared, and pachinko balls clinked as their agent in the pachinko parlor streamed audio.

"Is there anything you guys know about this facility? Like who owns it or their criminal history?" Frisco asked.

"The official owner is a Korean named Han Hyonu, but we know he's not the one pushing the money here. There is a pretty heavy yakuza presence tied to the Tokyo syndicate. The local shop owners call them the '*Anmoku-dan*' or the 'dark eyes clan.' We've heard reports of people seeing them wearing strange masks that hide their faces."

"Like the guys that attacked us? They were wearing these rubbery masks that made their faces look like a blank canvas. Now that I think about it, the masks made their eyes look dark," Frisco said.

"The video didn't show anyone wearing masks."

"We think it was a deepfake."

Captain Tanaka nodded. He thought of the video feeds near the CEO's apartment. Then it hit him.

"The leader of the *Anmoku-dan* is a guy named Ryu Tanigawa. He runs with some big money. He may even be tied to Toyotomi Industries."

"Why would he be working with Koreans?" Frisco asked.

"Yakuza take anyone loyal, and there are different types of yakuza as well. Ultranationalists are purists, while others are just criminals. There are Chinese and Korean yakuza. As long as they toe the line, the leadership will take them. They want desperate and dangerous people. Using foreigners is a pretty common tactic."

"Is there any chance these guys are tied to the Chinese government as well?"

"Anything is possible. Pachinko parlors have been on the decline in the past couple of decades. My sources tell me the Starlight is doing just fine, though."

"Any ideas how?" Frisco asked.

"It's hard to say with organized crime. The parlor may have excellent return customers, they could be laundering money for the syndicate, shaking down the local shops, or they could be selling drugs. Hopefully, by the end of tonight, we'll have a better idea."

Stu finally piped in, "The only thing I know is that kinetic energy is the best energy. It always feels better to be on the offensive. I don't do well waiting for the intel to develop."

Unfortunately for Frisco, Stu, Captain Tanaka, and his men, for the next thirty minutes, that was all they *could* do.

CHAPTER 36

Escape and Evasion

WASEDA UNIVERSITY
TOKYO, JAPAN

"They found us!"

In that nearly tangible moment, when the waking world rips the veil between dreams and reality, Voodoo could still hear the voice of his wife. Her pleas and prayers penetrated deep into his soul.

"Voodoo! We need to run! They have found us, Voodoo!" Naomi implored, her voice drowning out the dreams floating on the surface of his memory. Through his closed eyes, numbers appeared on the augmented reality display of his contact lenses. He opened his eyes and saw Naomi disconnecting wires from the EEG then shoving her computer and a manila folder into her bag.

"Voodoo, please! Wake up!" she implored again. Voodoo shook his head to bring himself back to reality. The sedative and the shock of the network ripped away mixed into a debilitating cocktail. He blinked hard and forced his eyes open; the bright light of the hospital room stung.

It took a moment for Voodoo to realize what he was looking at. In the corner of his eye, a number appeared, reading "-102." Signal strength measurements working backward from detection indicated energy proximity. Someone was close.

I forgot to take out the contact lenses, Voodoo thought.

"Voodoo! I think they've almost found us!" Naomi shouted in a breathy whisper. She was panicked.

"They already have."

-90

They're getting closer.

Voodoo's limbs were concrete, his muscles tight. He struggled to work his way out of the chair. Naomi grabbed him by the upper arm to help him to his feet.

"Where are Yoshi and Toshi?" Voodoo asked.

"There is a lobby just down the hallway; I assume they just stayed there while we conducted the experiment." With heavy steps, Voodoo walked toward the door leading to the hallway.

-82

Voodoo grabbed his bag off the table and plucked out his current girlfriend. He held the phone close to his body and placed his other hand flat above it with about six inches of separation.

-80

He then moved his hand below the phone at the same distance.

-101

"They're on the floor below us," he declared. Naomi stared at him.

"How can you tell?"

"Antennas on phones detect Wi-Fi signals. My hand between the signal and the antenna interferes with the reception. They're below us on the first floor."

They had come up by elevator, but Voodoo knew the stairs he'd seen to the right would be the solution in the end. Yet his tired feet and a premonition leaned toward the elevators first. It would be better to help Yoshi and Toshi.

"Lobby. Let's move." Voodoo and Naomi exited the lab and cut left toward the lobby. The hallway felt longer than Voodoo remembered as he willed his body to move faster.

"Are you okay? What did the dreams tell you?"

"I need therapy," Voodoo replied, his body waking with each step. Stress propelled him; now was not the time for physical weakness.

They reached the lobby where Yoshi and Toshi sat waiting. They were asleep with their heads resting on each other.

-70

Voodoo moved his hands above and below his phone. The signal was below him but closer.

They're near the elevator. Dammit!

"Quick! We need to get to the stairs!" Voodoo ordered.

Voodoo jogged over as best as his body would allow and slapped them both over the head.

"*Ikou!*"

"*Ara!*"

"*Itai!*"

The two men popped their little heads up in surprise. They immediately noticed Naomi and gave the same goofy grin.

"*Oi! Ikou tta!*" Voodoo grabbed Yoshi by the arm. Naomi grabbed Toshi and the four scurried down the hallway.

-50

The elevator doors opened.

-35

Voodoo looked back and saw four men dressed in black suits, white dress shirts, and black ties. They were wearing the same masks as the other men but instead of batons...they carried swords.

"Come on!" Voodoo urged as the four increased speed toward the stairwell at the end of the hallway. Voodoo's adrenaline broke through the chemical blockage and surged him awake.

They were halfway to the stairwell when the doors swung open.

Two more yakuza burst through the threshold with their weapons at the ready.

They were pinned.

Voodoo opened the first door he could find and shoved Naomi, Yoshi, and Toshi inside, jumping in behind them. They slammed the door shut just as the squad of thugs converged on their location.

-25

Angry voices yelled from outside the door as Voodoo locked it just in time.

"Yoshi, call hospital security!" Naomi ordered.

Yoshi fumbled for his phone, frantic and sweating. He dropped it on the ground, cracking the screen. Yoshi picked it up and mumbled to himself about the damage as he dusted it off. He caught a glance from Naomi, whose angry scowl motivated him to move faster. He clumsily slid his fingers and pecked at the screen.

Naomi rolled her eyes and turned to Voodoo.

"What now?" she asked. They were in a storage locker, which support staff also used as a break room. Cleaning supplies, brooms, mops, a small refrigerator, and a microwave sat in the corner beside some chairs.

"Our best chance is security, but it depends on how serious these guys are," Voodoo said.

Yoshi held the phone to his ear.

"*Moshi moshi?*" He proceeded to speak to someone about needing security on the second floor because yakuza, with katanas, were trying to kill him.

"Real subtle," Voodoo mumbled sarcastically. "Tell security there are men with weapons in the hospital on the second floor, and that's it." He turned to Naomi with an exasperated look on his face. "I'm regretting forcing you to use these guys."

"I regretted it the moment I thought of it."

"How did you know they were coming?"

"DZ sent me a message. He said he found me on social media, and others probably did too."

Inside Voodoo's mind, in blinks and flashes, images from his dream ran through his head. He fought to make sense of the copious streams of data fading from his conscious mind, with only the strongest lingering in his short-term memory. He knew the thoughts weren't lost; he just had to find a way to retrieve them. First, he needed to figure out what to do right now.

The pounding at the door stopped. Footsteps sprinted away.

-50

-60

"They're running off. I wonder what that means?" Naomi asked.

"They said security has just arrived. We should stay here," Yoshi said.

"Hey, what did your dream say? I was worried I was going to kill you when I hooked you up to the Xiphos network and the data went off the charts."

Streams of data flew across Voodoo's mind with a flurry of relevance. Voodoo pulled out his phone from the bag and began typing.

"Hang on..."

FRIDAY 2:51 A.M.

> **Vudu**: @**Sparks**, get on the next flight to a city called Nakashibetsu. NOW!
>
> **Vudu**: @**Frisco** Dr. Hawkins is not in Tokyo. Pachinko parlor assault is gonna be a trap!
>
> **Sparks**: @**Vudu** Moving. It's gonna be tricky, but I think I can make it.
>
> **Vudu**: We've got less than 24 hours. Move!
>
> **DZ**: Should I still commence the trigger? What do you know?
>
> **Vudu**: Not enough. If we don't hear from Frisco, commence the trigger. We need to give the SAT team the best chance possible.
>
> **DZ**: Best chance at what?
>
> **Vudu**: Stopping an atrocity.

Frisco wasn't responding, and the assault was moments away. Voodoo had only pieces. He was trying to process the scenes that passed through his mind; only sections remained cogent and usable. The most crucial part of the puzzle was almost twenty-four hours away. He just needed to figure out precisely where. Most importantly, he needed to get everyone out of the hospital.

Naomi nudged him.

"So? What happened?"

"I'll tell you later. But my brain still works, and I think we have the answers we need."

-55

Screaming filled the hallway as male voices clashed and clanging metal resonated. Voodoo grabbed a fire extinguisher, held the nozzle at the ready, and cracked the door.

A hand shoved through, and Voodoo flung the door open to see two remaining yakuza. He slammed the butt of the extinguisher into the first yakuza, breaking his nose. The yakuza cupped his face in an eruption of blood. Voodoo pointed the nozzle at the other man at the door and released a spray of potassium bicarbonate in a cloud of white. Voodoo followed through, striking the man with the butt of the fire extinguisher in his temple, knocking him out instantly.

Voodoo motioned at Naomi and her dainty suitors to run. Down the hall near the elevator, a cluster of black suits and security guards fought. One lay bleeding on the floor.

Voodoo waved the others on and pointed toward the stairs before ditching the extinguisher.

They made a run for it.

Naomi led the escape as Voodoo pulled up the rear with Yoshi and Toshi between them. They opened the door just as voices screamed behind them.

"*Tomare!*" the yakuza bellowed, commanding them to stop.

"Run!" Voodoo yelled. The four sprinted down the hallway, yanked the door to the stairwell, and headed down, the door closing behind.

They punched out the first floor and ran toward the exit and headed to the busiest street they could find. They needed to get to cover. CCTVs would be staring at them from numerous street devices while their assailants pounded right on their heels. Shinmejiro-Dori, a major thoroughfare to the north, offered a potential escape. Voodoo wondered what to do with Naomi's groupies.

"Yoshi, Toshi, it's time we split up. They're after Naomi and me and not you. We'll run to Shinmejiro Dori, and you break off at an alley nearby and duck into one of the buildings. I'll make a lot of noise to draw them away from you," Voodoo said as they ran.

"No, they'll catch us!" Toshi pleaded, only reminding Voodoo how civilians are liabilities in combat. He was ready to vault into a dead sprint and leave the leprechaun men behind out of spite.

Voodoo swiveled his head back. Several of the yakuza gained on them.

True to his form, Toshi tripped and fell to the ground hard. Yoshi stopped to help him.

"Get up! Come on!" Naomi pleaded.

It was too late. The yakuza were upon them.

The three men dressed in black suits and armed with razor-sharp weapons stopped five meters from Voodoo, Naomi, Yoshi, and Toshi. Voodoo stepped forward, drawing a metaphorical line on the asphalt. The center figure raised a katana above his head, and the long silvery blade shimmered in the streetlights. Voodoo studied his opponent.

With swords at the ready, the other two dispersed to surround them.

Flank, isolate, and kill. That's what's coming.

Multiple scenarios played out in his mind at lightning speed. His opponents had three feet of range with their weapons. The curved blade of the katana meant the advantage lay in slashing motions and not direct stabs. Circular movement would be their avenue of attack. Voodoo would have to bait them in and take a sword if he stood a chance. His only option—speed, surprise, and violence of action.

Voodoo's hands tingled.

Voodoo hooked his arm through his canvas messenger bag as a shield, then moved on the man in the middle.

The yakuza sliced the katana at Voodoo's head.

Voodoo weaved and deflected the blade. Now at close range, Voodoo stabbed his index finger into the man's eye. It slid into the socket and Voodoo felt a pop. The jellylike liquid aqueous humor of the man's eye poured out of his face as Voodoo retracted his strike. In an instant, Voodoo took control of the man's sword-wielding hand.

The man shrieked then instinctively pulled his arm up to resist Voodoo's grasp. Voodoo used the momentum against him, pulled the blade toward the man's head, and slit his throat.

The yakuza collapsed. Arterial spray erupted. Coughs of blood sputtered and gurgled out of his mouth.

Voodoo dropped his messenger bag, now holding a bloodied katana.

The two other yakuza flanked Yoshi, Toshi, and Naomi, who huddled together in the middle of the alley. Wasting no time, Voodoo chose the man on his right and lunged toward him.

Voodoo raised his sword high in preparation for a strike at the yakuza's head. As the man telegraphed a block in response, Voodoo shifted. He swung the blade low and horizontal to the ground, slicing the man's kneecap.

The yakuza wailed as the blade severed his patellar tendon. The tendon snapped back over his kneecap, his leg failed, and he crumbled in a heap.

Voodoo leaped to engage the final attacker.

The remaining yakuza raised his sword to strike Naomi. Voodoo leaped just as the man initiated his swing.

Voodoo blocked the strike.

His opponent parried.

Voodoo feinted high just as he did to cut the other man's tendon. The yakuza anticipated and dropped his blade to block an incoming low strike.

He fell for the trap.

Voodoo followed through and sliced his opponent's shoulder. The man winced and froze. Voodoo shifted and brought his blade down hard in a vertical strike, severing his opponent's hand.

The yakuza released a blood-curdling scream as he stared at the wet meat where his hand once connected to his arm.

"Go!" Voodoo ordered as he grabbed his bag. "We gotta get out of here!" Yoshi, Toshi, and Naomi stared at Voodoo, bewildered and afraid. Voodoo realized the closest Yoshi or Toshi had ever been to combat had been a graphic novel or anime. Until today.

Voodoo wasn't sure how to process those events himself. There is a concept in Japanese martial arts called "*mushin*," a term that translates to "no mind." It is the goal of the martial artist to repetitively train fine and gross motor functions over and over until the mind no longer needs to think to take action. The body merely reacts. Heightened by prophetic dreams, supplemented by infinite outcomes, Voodoo felt his mind and body achieving *mushin* in a way he never thought imaginable.

-50

He felt powerful and omniscient...and it frightened him. He had accessed the God Algorithm as it was truly intended. What would happen if someone were to weaponize this power?

No one should have this kind of advantage, Voodoo thought. And suddenly Voodoo, too, felt bewildered and afraid.

-85

Voodoo grabbed Yoshi and Toshi by the arm and pulled them up. They sprinted toward the primary street just south of the Kanda River. Voodoo discarded his blade in a dumpster as they ran.

A taxi happened to be passing by on the major thoroughfare as they arrived. Voodoo waved it down.

"This is where we part ways, gentlemen. It's been a pleasure!"

"But we—"

Voodoo stuffed them inside the taxi.

-103

Naomi's eyes remained fixed on Voodoo, her chest heaving.

-115

"Do not tell me we are headed back to the love hotel," Naomi said.

"No, we need to keep a pachinko parlor from blowing up."

Signal Lost.

CHAPTER 37

No Way Out

STARLIGHT PACHINKO PARLOR
TOKYO, JAPAN

*A*materasu is a stingy wench.

At least that's what the salaryman thought as he pressed the button and watched the pachinko balls drop from the shimmering image of the goddess on the screen. His successes and failures undulated in fits and starts, perpetuating the concept that most people who play slot machines fail to accept—the sunk money principle. There is an underlying idea that because you have spent a lot of cash, the payoff will be equally lucrative. That's the trap. The microendorphin rushes that trick the mind into clinging on to hope insist otherwise.

The salaryman was a firm believer in sunk money eventually paying off. The salaryman was also in a tremendous amount of debt. The salaryman was also a drunk.

He sat in front of the machine where Amaterasu stood, brilliant and exuberant, hiding her secrets from the salaryman, who desperately sought to discover them. He pressed the button, and more pachinko balls dropped with no success. It was nearly 3 a.m.; he felt he had been there way too long, even for him.

The sobering reality of a buzz wearing off made him feel useless. He had work in the morning, and an angry wife waiting for him at home. At least, he thought she was waiting for him.

He never answered the phone.

He decided that he would give Amaterasu one last try, one last press to leave with a little bit of dignity. The salaryman pressed the button on the pachinko machine again. His brain failed to process what happened next.

The machine lit up and screamed, blaring lights and music blasted across the gaming floor. The salaryman rose to his feet.

"I won!" he yelled out. He jumped up and down. Hundreds of pachinko balls poured out of the machine. He pulled out a bucket to collect the winnings, but there were too many. He turned to find another bucket and realized that Amaterasu was not the only god sharing her bounty.

All around the parlor, pachinko balls poured out of every machine. He was one of only a few addicted diehards remaining on the floor, so balls just fell everywhere, blanketing the concrete.

He scrambled to find buckets and set them under machines. He had at least five filled before he picked up his phone and dialed his wife.

"I finally won! We're rich!"

He fought to make out her groggy words against the insanity around him. "What? What..." He slipped onto the ground as he stepped on the balls.

Then he understood her.

"What do you mean you want a divorce?"

• • •

Cyberwarfare is like fighting a poltergeist—when an anomaly appears, it comes as a disembodied entity flipping switches, disabling functionality, and raising hell. If the only role of a ghost is to afflict the living, the pachinko parlor had just become a haunted house. With a keystroke and open-source penetration tools, Delta Zulu infected the network with binary demonic precision. The pachinko machines lit up all at once and evacuated their mechanical bowels, spilling tens of thousands of small metal balls all over the pachinko parlor gaming floor.

Captain Tanaka studied the video feeds of the front of the pachinko parlor and the back alley. The gaming floor soundtrack thumped in his ear as it streamed from his civilian agent inside. Suddenly the music on the floor became nothing more than a cacophony of bells, alarms, and people screaming.

"What's going on?" Captain Tanaka asked. Garbled words and shouts replied.

He looked at the video feed. He could see lights and music blaring from inside. Two homeless men, lying in makeshift beds in the *shotengai*, leaped to their feet and sprinted through the casino entrance, barreling past the security guard, who failed to stop them.

An entirely different scenario played out in the back alley.

A door opened, a young girl, dressed in a tight miniskirt, darted out the door. Immediately following her, a man emerged in pursuit. Her ponytail bobbed and whipped as she swiveled her head to look behind her. The pursuer stretched out his arm and grabbed the girl by her long black hair.

He yanked back, clotheslining her, sending her head back and feet forward. Her body slammed to the ground. She recoiled from the impact and rolled onto her side. Her pursuer slapped her across the face then yanked on her hair again, motivating her to move. She resisted. He pulled a knife and held it to the girl's throat. With the blade below her chin and his hand gripping her hair, he forced her back into the pachinko parlor. The door closed behind him.

Captain Tanaka had seen enough. The video alone was probable cause to engage. Nothing else mattered now. At least one life was in danger.

"Delta Squad, dismount and prepare to make entry!" he yelled out over the radio. He turned to the two Americans sitting behind him. "*Suwatte matte kure!*" he said to them.

The translator chimed in, "Sit and wait."

They nodded in compliance.

Captain Tanaka and his team assembled in formation and set off, sprinting down the empty streets, their black uniforms moving along the walls like living shadows.

"Kosuke, we're making assault. Can you hear me?" he said over the radio to the agent inside. No response, only machines blaring.

Captain Tanaka and his team moved with a purpose. They were nearing the front of the target location when they heard the first gunshots.

Pop! Pop!

The subsonic rounds of a 9mm handgun penetrated the discord.

Captain Tanaka's squad moved through the side alley like a dark serpent, the butt of their MP5s tight to their cheek wells, their eyes focused. The point man reached the back door and tried the handle. Locked.

He pivoted toward the men behind him and made a fist with his left hand, then patted it against his helmet. A breacher moved into position with a small strip of C-4. He removed a plastic lining on some gel attached to the explosives then slapped it on the door.

The squad fell back behind cover.

"Breaching! Breaching! Breaching!"

BAM!

The door blew open.

Piercing through the smoke, Captain Tanaka's black serpent of a team slithered through the entryway.

• • •

Frisco and Stu sat with the driver of the armored car and monitored the CCTV video feeds. The radios squawked in Japanese as they listened to the SAT team navigate into position. They watched as Captain Tanaka's squad prepared to make entry. Then, just as quickly as the men in black arrived, they simply vanished.

The video displayed an empty alley.

Frisco leaned back out of sight of the officer in the front seat. He held down the power button on his cell phone and turned it facedown to hide the LED illumination and waited. Something was off. He needed to check his messages.

Even in a foreign language, Frisco and Stu could make out the gist of the radio traffic. The squad was preparing to make entry. Then, echoing through the canyon of buildings, came the sound of a concussive explosion from a breaching charge. Frisco and Stu knew it all too well.

The video still showed an empty alley. Nothing indicated activity of any kind. A blank canvas. The other video feed of the front of the pachinko parlor was the same story.

"Where'd the security guard go? He was just there," Frisco asked out loud.

"I bet they're doing the deepfake thing again," Stu said. A leaden feeling grew in Frisco's stomach.

Did they know we were coming? he wondered.

The phone buzzed over and over, indicative of a missed conversation. He carefully opened the phone. A flood of messages filled his screen, but one line in particular captured his attention.

Vudu: @**Frisco** Dr. Hawkins is not in Tokyo. Pachinko parlor assault is gonna be a trap!

Frisco showed the screen to Stu, who gave Frisco a nod. The two burst out the armored truck onto the asphalt and sped off, the driver of the armored car screaming behind them.

"*Tomare!*"

Stu's and Frisco's bodies instinctively took over in a dramatic example of *mushin*. They didn't have weapons. They didn't have body armor. They knew only one thing—they weren't trained to sit idly by while other men fought their battles or walked into their traps.

• • •

Captain Tanaka's men flooded the room. A table with beer bottles and *oicho-kabu* cards sat in the center, and a hallway led to the gaming floor where the sound of the tiny metal balls intermixed with alarms and J-pop. Patrons scuffled as security guards shoved them aside, including Captain Tanaka's agent. One guard pulled out a baton and started beating a homeless man.

They dispersed to cover entryways. Two individual team members broke off like breadcrumbs to cover uncleared doorways in preparation for the next maneuver. A door to the left led in the opposite direction from the gaming floor, while a set of stairs leading up caught Captain Tanaka's attention.

Pop! Pop! Pop!

A handgun fired upstairs. Captain Tanaka's men remained unfazed, the barrels of their MP5s focused on their respective fields of fire; two men held their eyes on the stairs.

Captain Tanaka weighed his options. If the girl was in danger, they needed to move quickly.

In that moment of indecision, fate decided for him.

Pop! Pop!

Thumping sounds descended the stairs following the gunshots. The body of the girl in a miniskirt collapsed in a puddle of flesh. Her empty eyes stared blankly as blood from her head wound pooled behind her.

Captain Tanaka's eyes narrowed. With a knife-hand gesture, he motioned for his team to advance. They flung a flashbang up the stairs.

BAM!

Five men, including Captain Tanaka, sprinted up. In front of them lay a passageway that extended the length of the gaming floor below. There were doors on each side, all of them closed.

Captain Tanaka motioned for his men to search each room.

They pushed forward in pairs to the first set of doors. They tried the handles. Unlocked. They flung open the doors and swept the corners with their MP5s.

Empty.

Not even storage supplies.

They continued forward.

Two more rooms.

Unlocked.

They punched inside.

Empty.

No furniture. No futons. No fighters. The rooms were completely vacant.

Captain Tanaka's hairs stood on end.

"Fall back!" he yelled out.

Da! Da! Da! Da! Da! Da! Da! Da! Da!

Gunfire erupted downstairs.

Guttural screams, breaking bottles mixed with the J-pop and pachinko alarms blared.

In one direction, a hallway led to more rooms. In the other, the stairwell led down to a firefight.

"Hardpoint in this room!" he ordered.

Movement down the hall.

Faceless men in suits darted out, guns at the ready.

Captain Tanaka pulled his trigger.

• • •

Frisco and Stu tore through the *shotengai*, their arms pumping, weaponless. They stopped right along the alley's edge.

"Are we seriously about to jump into a gunfight without any weapons?" Frisco said.

Stu-Bear shrugged his massive traps.

They peeped around the corner and scanned the alley. The back door still smoked where the breaching charge blast created a hole. From the front of the pachinko parlor, pandemonium erupted.

The path in front of them remained empty. More gunfire cracked from inside the building.

"Follow me," Frisco said. Experience taught Frisco that he needed to find a way to use the current insanity to his advantage.

Frisco and Stu headed straight to the gaming floor instead of the back alley. The sound of machines, J-pop music, and screaming patrons was deafening. They shuffled their feet, keeping their soles flat to not lose their footing on the steel balls. They skirted the walls around the side of the pachinko parlor, rounded the perimeter, and made their way to a curtain heading to where they assumed they could reach the back room.

BAM!

The familiar crash of a flashbang instigated more gunfire.

"*Oi! Gaijin! Nani shitein no yo?*" a security guard yelled. He reached for Frisco, failing to notice the hulking monster in black just behind him. Stu grabbed the security guard by the back of his black blazer and lifted him off the ground like a feeble kitten.

"*Hanashite kure!*" he shrieked. Stu launched him across the gaming floor. He hit the ground and slid, rolling on the spilled balls.

Frisco craned his neck around the corner through the curtain. Stu squeezed him on his shoulder, signaling he was ready to move. They stalked forward in a half crouch, smoothly stepping heel to toe to keep their heads level.

Straight ahead, a table lay on its side. Sporadic gunfire and shouts erupted. With a loud thud, the back of a head full of dark hair hit the ground. Blood pooled beside the body and filled the path in front of Frisco.

He paused, took a breath, and pressed on.

• • •

Captain Tanaka engaged the threats. They fired back. Snaps and whirs buzzed by as the faceless men disappeared into rooms on the far end.

"Ichiro is down!" one of his men yelled. Captain Tanaka felt a hand on his shoulder, giving him the nonverbal cue to switch out.

A spray of bullets fired up at them from downstairs.

Captain Tanaka's head swiveled. They were in a channelized entrance that just went hot. To make matters worse, they were pinned between whoever was shooting at them from downstairs and the faceless men in the hallway. He had at least one man down.

"Get into that room!" he ordered as they dragged the casualty. The rest of his men collapsed their formation inside.

"Bravo Squad. This is Captain Tanaka. Come in," his voice squawked over the radio. No response.

"Bravo Squad. Come in!" he repeated. He pulled out his phone, and the call failed. He checked the cellular service icon. No bars.

Something was jamming their signals.

• • •

Frisco recognized the man on the ground as one of Captain Tanaka's teammates, lying on his back bleeding. He made eye contact with Frisco. The officer blinked. Frisco squatted down. The officer blinked again and then guided Frisco with his eyes along his arm to his hand. His index finger extended out, pointing. Just out of his reach, Frisco saw the officer's gun.

Frisco nodded. He reached for the weapon using the wall to conceal himself. He picked up the gun. The familiar knurling on the grip of the MP5 set off an immediate physical reaction in Frisco. Weaponized. Operational. For the first time since coming to Japan, Frisco felt whole again. His shooter instincts kicked in; time to get to work—eliminate the threat.

He brought the weapon to the ready, took a breath, then angled around the corner.

Two men—only targets to Frisco's mind now—in black suits fired intermittent rounds up the stairs while the other stood on the far end of the room, covering another doorway.

Da! Da!

In one fluid motion, Frisco fired, downed the first target then—

Da! Da!

The second dropped.

Frisco snapped to the third.

Da! Da! ... Da!

Two rounds hit the chest, and the third drove through the target's eye. Years of training ingrained into Frisco's gross motor function the technique shooters called a "Mozambique," or "failure drill." The term originated from a Rhodesian mercenary who engaged a target at close range and shot two rounds at center mass and still didn't drop his objective. The third round, fired toward the head, severed the spinal cord of his target, killing him instantly. The technique later became a standard modern shooting method.

Da! ... Da! ... Da!

Frisco fired three more rounds, one in the head of each yakuza to confirm the kills as a "security round."

"Stu, quick, get the injured SAT guys out of here," Frisco ordered. Six bodies lay on the ground, two of them injured police officers. Both men appeared to be alive but just barely. Stu grabbed the men and dragged them toward the back door leading to the alley.

"Captain Tanaka!" Frisco yelled up the stairs. "It's Frisco!" He crept toward the stairs. He raised his weapon and hoped for a response.

CHAPTER 38

SDR

TOKYO, JAPAN

"We need to talk about what happened," Naomi said as their taxi hustled through the vacant streets. "I have some things I need to show you—"

"No time. I understand that we need to unpack, well, a lot. Especially what happened at the lab tonight, but I need to focus on the here and now. Frisco and Stu are in trouble."

"What is going to happen? What do you know?" Naomi asked as she looked at Voodoo, who sat beside her. He stared out the window, searching for answers in the periphery of his mind.

"I get specific images at times, but it's normally like major muscle movements. My brain is summarizing the important points as opposed to giving me specifics. I guess the best way to describe it is like speed-reading."

"Speed-reading?" Naomi asked. The taxi took another turn.

"Yeah, if you sound out every word when you read as if you are speaking them, you read much slower even though the brain can process information faster. It's kinda like that. My brain is processing concepts as images and general feelings as opposed to every single event. I know where we need to go. I'm just trying to figure out how to help them get out."

"Get out of where? The pachinko parlor?" Naomi asked.

"No, by the time we get there, they won't be in there anymore. We need to clear a way for them to get out. To do that, we need to find two things—a radio jammer and a sniper."

"Did you say we need to find a sniper?" Naomi's face said everything about how she felt about that.

"Well, not necessarily we. There's going to be an armored SAT vehicle where you'll be safe. You'll wait there while I find him."

"No. I am going with you." She glared at Voodoo.

Voodoo looked over at her and nodded with a slight grin.

"Wait, you knew I was going to say that. You just wanted me going with you to be *my* idea." Naomi's glare shifted to a snarl. "*Zurui yatsu da na...*" she said, mildly disgusted. Voodoo's smile grew. She let out a light giggle and hit him in the arm. "Fine. Guess I helped cause that ability. So, what is the plan?"

"Ever heard of an SDR?" Naomi shook her head no. Voodoo reached into his bag and pulled out a small metal device the size of two decks of cards made of aluminum. It was ribbed with heat sinks and had gold-colored screwlike adapters on the ends. He pulled out two black antennae, like the ones that go on a Wi-Fi router, and screwed them to the device.

"An SDR is a software-defined radio," Voodoo said as he held up the small device. "You can buy these online. These are like the modern-day version of an amateur radio. Hobbyist communities are really into them for detecting radio waves." The taxi came to a stop at a streetlight.

"What are you going to do with it?" Naomi asked.

"I've done some work with machine learning myself. Instead of images, I use statistical models to find radio waves that are out of place. I get the strong impression we're going to need this once we get there."

"So, there is some kind of radio we are worried about?"

"Yeah, the jammer. We need to find it but also find the sniper who's pinning down the officers outside. I plan to make that guy uncomfortable."

"Are we going to fight him or something?"

"If my equipment works, we won't have to do much. The problem will take care of itself," Voodoo said as his thoughts and emotions convolved.

The taxi came to a stop two blocks away from the *shotengai*. Naomi paid the driver. Pachinko alarms, people screaming, and the intermittent pops of gunpowder reverberated through the streets as they stepped out.

"*Daijobu na no kana?*" the driver of the taxi asked curiously.

"Somebody must have hit the jackpot at the pachinko parlor," Naomi replied in Japanese. The driver nodded. She closed the door and the driver moved on.

Voodoo cinched his messenger bag tight across his chest and eyed his surroundings.

"Stay close and move quickly. You're gonna have an important job to do in a minute."

Naomi nodded in response, and the two set off.

• • •

Captain Tanaka's men applied a tourniquet to his injured officer as he analyzed the scene.

More rounds popped from downstairs.

Comms were jammed.

He had men down, and he was neck-deep in a trap.

It was clear the girl running from the building was bait and he'd swallowed it whole. Now he was cornered upstairs between converging fields of fire.

What else did they have planned? he wondered.

He searched the room for signs of explosives or booby traps. He saw nothing.

Perhaps we're in the wrong room.

"Captain Tanaka!" a voice yelled from downstairs. "It's Frisco!"

Captain Tanaka blinked.

Those crazy bastards.

"Captain, it sounds like the Americans are downstairs," one of his men said.

"I want to be mad, but they may be able to help us get out of here," the captain replied. "Prepare to break out. I need two men to cover the hallway so we can shoot our way to the bottom of the stairs—you two grab Ichiro and follow me."

"*Hai*," the men responded collectively. The SAT officers lined up at the door in preparation for the hasty maneuver.

They made their move.

They sprinted down the stairs, their guns anticipating another trap. Instead, they found the floor littered with bodies. Three yakuza and a young girl lay dead. Frisco held his gun barrel toward an empty doorway in the back of the building while Stu cared for the two downed SAT officers.

Stu waved them toward the blasted entry that led out to the alley. An SAT member assertively ran over and stepped out.

BA!

The open-air crack of a rifle rang out, and a round nicked the officer's helmet. Stu yanked him back inside.

"We're pinned. We need another exit!" Stu yelled to Frisco, who looked around the room. There were four potential egress points. The alley was not an option. If they fought through the melee on the pachinko floor and went out the front, they'd be in direct sight of the sniper. Going back up the stairs led to a dead end. There was one last route: the back doorway and a long tunnel. There was no telling where it led. Or what they might face.

"Captain Tanaka, this seems to be our only option," Frisco said. Captain Tanaka stepped up beside Frisco; they looked at each other and nodded.

• • •

Voodoo and Naomi searched for a stairwell with vertical access to an apartment building. Japanese apartments and commercial buildings often use roofs as open space for tenants to use as gardens or for drying clothes.

They spied a fire escape and ascended. At the top, Voodoo assessed the dimensions of the building and its elevation. A 1.5-meter wall provided cover and outlined the roof of the complex.

They positioned themselves by the wall and peeked over. They were six stories up. The pachinko parlor was diagonally in front of them on the right and only fifty meters away.

He opened his laptop and plugged in the software-defined radio. On board the computer, an advanced graphics processing unit hummed, ready to chew through the machine learning algorithm Voodoo prepared. Voodoo selected the appropriate radio frequency band and initiated the analyzing tool.

The ability to scan for radio waves is what made SDRs popular to home hobbyists. The original hackers were people manipulating commercial telephone landlines to create chat rooms back in the '70s. Illegally tweaking the tone on commercial phones opened access to switches and international connections hackers used to communicate for fun. The "fun" ended when one of the most notorious telephone hackers, Captain Crunch, was arrested.

This same curiosity led to the modern cyberhacking communities as the internet came online. Now people used SDRs to return to seeking radio waves floating in the open air. At first glance, Voodoo appeared to be doing little more. In truth, Voodoo was about to create an energy weapon.

"What are you looking for?" Naomi whispered.

"I need to find a constant signal filling the bandwidth where I think the normal radio waves should be," he replied. Naomi looked at the screen.

"It looks like the output from the EEG I had strapped to your head," she said.

"That's because it's not far off," Voodoo replied. "Neural activity in the brain is just another waveform, like radio emissions." Voodoo watched the monitor as scratchy green lines hopped up and down, indicating sporadic traffic. Other lines created flat plateaus that covered wide frequencies, showing steady emissions. "We're looking for that," Voodoo said as he pointed to the screen.

Just above 400 megahertz, a steady signal emitted as a flattened plateau of squiggly green lines.

"That's what a jammer looks like. White Gaussian noise filling up the spectrum." Voodoo pointed there and at another similar plateau at 2,100 megahertz. "That lower one is blocking the police radio frequency, and the other one is blocking the cellular band."

"Now what?" Naomi asked.

"We find it." Voodoo reached into his bag and pulled out an object that looked like an isosceles triangle with a cable sticking out of one end. He removed one of the small black antennas and connected the SDR to the triangular device. He angled it over the top of the wall and watched the screen.

"This is a Yagi antenna. It's directional, so I can use it to find where a radio signal is coming from. Watch the screen," Voodoo said as he moved the Yagi slowly from left to right.

As he pointed the antenna near the pachinko parlor, the signal became strongest. He pulled out a phone with the thermal imager, turned it on, pressed some buttons, and paired the video feed to the femto projector in his contact lens. He held the camera up to the edge of the wall. Voodoo kept his head down and searched for the bright thermal image of a human body.

"There, just on that ledge on the building across from the parlor. That's our guy. He's hidden behind some dark material. I need you to hold the camera while I mess with my computer," Voodoo said to Naomi. She reached up and held the phone in place, her arms outstretched to keep her body low behind the concealment of the wall.

Voodoo knelt and pulled out the sizeable 6S LiPO battery and the ceramic power amplifier, rearranged cables, then tweaked the graphic user interface on the computer.

"Ready?" Voodoo said finally.

"I guess. What for?"

Voodoo sat back on his right foot and looked at Naomi. He had a broad mischievous smile smeared across his face.

"Pure Frickin' Magic."

CHAPTER 39
Overwatch

STARLIGHT PACHINKO PARLOR
TOKYO, JAPAN

"I always hated pachinko parlors," Ryu's voice crackled from the cell phone Taro had placed beside him. "I'm glad I'll never have to see one again."

Armed with a North Korean AKM Type 68 rifle, Taro stalked the egress points of the pachinko parlor with the crosshairs of his Nikon scope. He perched behind an apartment window, a dark blanket obscuring his silhouette. The positions of the fabric and the orientation of his weapon created a facade of empty darkness along the window near a fire escape. Multiple windows on the corner of the building gave him direct line of sight to cover every avenue of approach directly across from the pachinko parlor.

Taro processed the insanity exploding on the gaming floor. "I figured they'd create some kind of diversion once we intercepted that email to SAT. Good thing we knew they were coming," Taro replied. The scar on his upper lip curled. Across the street, the pachinko machines released their bounty to the soundtrack of Japanese boy bands.

"I'm experiencing latency issues with the video. Let me know when to initiate the loop."

"*Arratda*," he replied into his cell phone with a Korean radio confirmation. Tattoos on his arms peeked from behind the black military-style clothing camouflaging him in the darkness—a constant reminder of his commitment to the great charade of his life as a sleeper agent.

Ryu and Taro arrived in Japan cut from the same cloth—or deprived of the same childhood may be a better way to put it. As children in DPRK, they barely survived the most difficult struggle of modern North Korean history—an event his comrades knew as the "Arduous March."

In the mid-1990s, after years of sanctions, their country degraded into a famine. Western estimates put the deaths around half a million—not even close to the three million lives that just withered away. Like their parents. And Ryu's sister.

Taro and Ryu went from playing in the tributaries of Wonsan Harbor to eating straw and frogs to survive. Fate eventually led them to the military, where vengeance drove them toward Special Operations. It was there that they became trained as infiltrators, eventually using specialized training in logistics, finance, and computers to extort and cajole their way into the yakuza.

This allowed them to secretly hide their true intentions as active sleeper cells, manipulating Japanese commerce via businesses and waterways throughout Tokyo. They smuggled and trafficked, sabotaged and undermined. They infected everything they touched. They were an epidemic the Japanese conceded as status quo in the form of organized crime. Even the yakuza failed to grasp their true evil intentions.

In all the time Taro spent training, honing his craft, he never thought the day would come when he would be given the green light to actively engage the Japanese police or Americans with kinetic force. Taro was given both in one day.

Taro picked up a small push-to-talk radio. "Release the girl." Through his scope he watched the helpless package sprint out the back door only to be snapped back.

He adjusted the grip on his trigger hand, shifted the butt of the rifle against his shoulder to optimize the seating in anticipation. The SAT team wasn't far behind.

His crouched position allowed him to move but wasn't nearly as comfortable as being prone. However, if he lay on his stomach, he wouldn't be able to see over the ledge. The half-kneeling position would have to do. During sniper training, he became very accustomed to uncomfortable positions.

Years had passed since those long days stalking through the mountains of his homeland, training with the Amphibious Sniper Brigade. It all came down to this one night, one moment to make it all worth it.

"Sir, are you ready to initiate?" Taro asked.

"Standing by."

Through his scope, armed black figures shuffled through the *shotengai* and prepped the back door for entry.

"Execute."

"The loop is active," Ryu replied. "I'm retrieving the archived video of the package escaping and deleting that as well. Are you ready to go black?"

Taro knew that once he gave the confirmation, he would never speak to his mentor again. Ryu was on his way back to the fatherland. Taro, upon mission success, would be reassigned.

"Good luck, comrade. Visit Mount Baekdu for me." There was a pause on the line.

"Music is on." And with that, all radio communications ceased as the jammer hidden within the pachinko parlor went active. His phone lost connectivity.

Taro focused on his breaths.

BAM!

In a puff of smoke, the back door of the pachinko parlor blew open. Taro merely waited—a gargoyle crouched in the shadows.

Gunshots inside the building.

Movement to the left. Two more figures dressed in black sprinted down the path to the front of the *shotengai*. Unarmed. Taro glanced through his scope to confirm. Taro blinked and adjusted his view. The faces that stared back through magnification weren't Japanese.

They were stupid enough to come along!

He fidgeted like a cat readying to pounce. The same white demons that attacked his men and became famous on Japanese news were now rushing headlong into his trap.

A shot of adrenaline heated arteries in his arms and legs.

Breathe. In... Out...

When the SAT team and the Americans became sufficiently entrenched, he would know. Because Ryu would know. And Ryu would act.

More of the familiar pops and cracks of firearms rang out. The goal was for his men inside, all *Anmoku-dan*, to pin them down in the hallway and kill them. Taro focused on the alley entrance the SAT team blew open in the event someone tried to escape.

A black helmet emerged.

BA!

Taro fired a quick 7.62x39mm bullet.

The head disappeared.

Taro held his rifle steady. *Just a little more time.*

More heat snaked through his body. He'd never felt adrenaline like this before, but he'd never had such an opportunity before either.

In... Out...

He stared through the crosshairs at the alley, waiting for an explosion and burning bodies to pour out so he could finish them off with North Korean–manufactured lead.

Something scraped inside his eyes.

Taro squinted. He rubbed them with his nontrigger hand. Instead of a normal eye irritation like a hair or a bug, his eyes burned, like they were being cooked from the inside. His vision warped. He clenched his eyes tightly and his skin flushed with heat too. He kept his eyes shut and covered them with his hand.

The intensity receded in his eyes, but his hand heated up. He pulled it away to shake it only for the pain to return to his eyes, which now filled with water. Then a sharp stinging pain pierced his ears.

Taro pushed himself to his feet, stepped back from the window, and staggered, realizing he couldn't see.

What's happening to me?

He pivoted his body to the right and the burning pain moved to the back of his head. Something penetrated from his left, from the other building, something burning him.

Taro stepped away from the window and retreated into the tiny apartment where he hid. Within a few moments, the pain receded. He wiped his watery eyes and collected his thoughts. He needed to hold his position to maximize casualties. That was the mission, even if he became one of them. Across the street, the music and alarms continued, but the gunfire fell silent.

Where's the explosion?

In... Out...

Taro brought his rifle to the ready. He rotated around to the edge of the windowsill to confront any human silhouette.

He stepped deep and fast and scanned the rooftop and saw only a stick with a small flag sticking off it.

BAM!

The door behind him flew open. Taro collapsed sideways with shock. In the doorway, a man in a hoodie hurling a ball of fire.

A brick-like object slammed Taro in the chest with a thud. But Taro stood fast, preparing his AKM to deliver vengeance. Even with the stinging pain that lingered in his eyes he was still lethal.

But what came next even more so.

There is a unique smell that comes from burning hair. It's the keratin. But keratin is not *just* in hair. It's in skin and fingernails and when they burn, they all smell the same. And in Taro's case, it didn't matter which part of his body the smell came from. His whole body was on fire.

Taro's rifle slipped from his hands as he flailed. The searing pain of a blowtorch scorched his foot to the bone. He high-stepped and thrashed about the room.

He lost his balance.

Glass shattered.

As the air rushed about him, Taro realized too late—he was falling.

CHAPTER 40

Landslide

TOKYO, JAPAN

To a combat operator, that moment between the known and the unknown is the entire reason for becoming a shooter. It's a mouth salivating before a bite. It's the moment a boxer's opponent lets down his guard. It's the last inch before a first kiss. It's existential Russian roulette where the bullet fires or fails at the same time. With each step, Frisco and Captain Tanaka took another spin.

"Push forward," Frisco whispered. "There's gotta be a way out."

"*Mae, susume*," Captain Tanaka ordered, echoing Frisco.

Up a narrow stairwell, they found a door and passed through.

"We must be in the building on the opposite side of the alley. Is this a hotel?" Frisco asked. Captain Tanaka nodded in rudimentary understanding.

It became readily apparent the door was a concealed entrance to the parlor's brothel. The opposite side blended into the wall. In front of them, shapes of women backlit a rice paper door.

Captain Tanaka raised his left hand and made a fist, signaling to everyone behind to halt. He reached out, pointed his rifle at the crack where the doors met, and slid the door open.

A large room with traditional tatami flooring split off into four sections. Several other doorways led to more private rooms. What lay in the center immediately captured Captain Tanaka's attention.

Captain Tanaka, Frisco, and the rest of his men snaked into the room, sweeping their weapons in search of threats, seeing only one massive object in the center that brought them all pause.

Bound and gagged, five Filipino girls and a boy sat quietly in a circle with their backs to each other. As the SAT team spilled into the room around them, each of their faces repeated the same helpless expression of dread.

Frisco lowered his weapon and pulled the gag from the first girl's mouth. The other men followed suit. The girls' and boy's chins quivered, bodies shook, tears fell, but they remained devoid of movement. Frisco took a tactical pause and assessed the scene. It took only a moment for him to see it.

The cell phone was the first giveaway. The cabling soldered to the circuit board of the phone was the second. The explosives were the final and most prominent.

Frisco saw way too many wires for even the most experienced of EOD technicians to figure out quickly. Captain Tanaka also looked closely at the phone and mumbled something to his colleague, who translated.

"The jammer seems to be working still, so as long as it stays on, no one can detonate the explosives," the officer said.

"Yeah, but who has the jammer, and what's keeping them from turning it off?"

• • •

Voodoo walked to the windowsill. Naomi's little head popped up, barely clearing the wall on the roof across the alley. Even at night, Voodoo could see the horrified look on her face as a man burned on the ground below.

Moments earlier, Voodoo only had seconds to let Naomi in on his plan.

"I changed the radio setup to the SDR," he had told her. "We're no longer receiving signals; we're sending them. You're shooting radio waves right at that dude."

"What will that do?"

"Well, it's transmitting at 2.4 gigahertz. That's the same as Wi-Fi routers and...microwave ovens."

"Wait...I am not...am I?"

"Microwaving him? Yeah, like a chicken nugget."

"Excuse me?!" she whispered angrily. "Like I am cooking him?"

"Hopefully."

Naomi hadn't been too pleased to learn that fact. Voodoo didn't understand the concern. The real kicker came when he sent his LiPO battery into thermal runaway and nailed the sniper with the flaming battery.

Voodoo stepped up to the window and took in the sight of Taro's body burning on the street below. Voodoo nodded before sending Naomi a thumbs-up. Naomi used a different finger in response.

• • •

"Please, help!" one of the girls said in Tagalog-accented English. "They left us here hours ago."

"Who left you here?" Frisco asked. He squatted low to show the girl he meant no harm while using the opportunity to examine the threat.

"The men with the masks," another one of the girls said. They whimpered and pleaded quietly in desperation. On the girl beside him, Frisco recognized scars of rope burns.

"Hang on," Frisco said. "Shh...I need you ladies to stay calm. Everything is going to be okay. We just need to figure some things out first." He spread his hands and lowered them slowly. "Where are you from?"

"Zamboanga, Mindanao."

"Cebu City."

"Davao City."

The girls rattled off cities from all over the Philippines. Frisco recognized the names from a previous deployment to the island nation.

"How did you get here?"

"A man came to our house offering money for work, and my father took the money and drove me down to the docks where I got on a ship. Every time the ship stopped at another port, more girls came on board. We eventually ended up here working for...that...man," the oldest girl said.

"Which man?" Frisco asked. Behind him, he could hear one of the officers translating to Captain Tanaka.

"The evil one...the man that tells everyone what to do," a girl on the far side said.

"The man that makes us...do things with his guests." Frisco didn't need her to elaborate.

"Do you know who his guests were?"

"I think I heard the word 'inspector,'" one girl said.

"The one that looked like a pig," the boy added. His eyes shifted slightly toward the older girl beside him, who wilted as she heard the reference. Once again, Frisco didn't need specifics.

"Do you know any names?"

The girls shook their heads.

Frisco turned toward Captain Tanaka. "I don't think these are the kidnap victims you were hoping for." One of his men translated and Captain Tanaka responded.

"He said he is still glad we came. We wouldn't have known they were here otherwise. He is wondering, though, how long they have been tied up and whether their captors gave them any instructions."

One of the girls looked up at the ceiling and gestured with her chin for Frisco and the officers to do the same. Frisco followed her eyes and stood as he saw it. In each corner of the room, cameras peered down at them like perverted eyes distended from their sockets.

The red light on the camera was all that Frisco needed to see.

"Stu..." he said, slowly stepping back and away from the girls. "Landslide!"

In the event of a house-born improvised explosive, there is only one thing to do. Without hesitation, Stu hefted the two wounded officers onto his back and bolted out. Frisco herded the officers near him toward the door.

"Move, move, move!" he ordered.

"Help us, please! Don't leave us!" the girls yelled. They kicked and shook in their chairs.

Captain Tanaka sidestepped hesitantly with each shove from Frisco, unwilling to accept the inevitable reality before him. Captain Tanaka stared at the girls; Frisco knew the look because he felt the same way. They knew what had to happen.

That was when they heard it.

It first came as static. Radios chirped back to life. Phones vibrated.

Frisco yanked Captain Tanaka by the back of his black body armor out the shoji doors, leaving the girls to fate. He prayed against all the odds that he was wrong.

Experience taught him otherwise.

• • •

Voodoo bolted back to meet Naomi and gathered his equipment before descending back to the street level. With no direct path to the pachinko parlor, they rushed around the backside of the building to the main road two blocks away from where they saw the armored police vehicle parked in the street.

"Quick! Head to the armored car, tell him who you are, and get inside!"

"Voodoo—"

"Just do it, dammit!" Voodoo yelled as he sprinted ahead. She peeled off.

Voodoo wasn't sure what to do next. The voice of his instructor urging him to do something nagged at him. Pangs of anxiety flowed through him.

If I don't know what to do, how am I supposed to stop it? he asked himself.

Voodoo decelerated his run to a walk before settling motionless.

I don't, he realized. *Because I can't.*

The lights of the pachinko parlor fifty meters away glowed as they did in the vision. Until...

BOOM!

A bright white light flashed as a massive explosion erupted from the hotel. Windows shattered and fire blew from inside the building. A second detonation ruptured from the pachinko parlor. Alarms and music morphed into shattering glass and concussive blasts followed by a shock wave that passed right through Voodoo, sucking the air from his lungs and bringing him to a knee. He shielded his face with his left arm as supplemental sparks burst light bulbs and scorched fabric.

Voodoo's hands trembled. Voodoo knew from years of training the reverberating blast of compressed air most likely caused microtears in his internal organs.

He fought to stand, to regain his constitution, but he couldn't look, couldn't believe it.

It was exactly like the dream. Nothing changed. Everything that Voodoo had done made no difference at all. There was nothing he could do even with the relative omniscience he gained from the algorithm.

He won, Voodoo thought. *I couldn't stop him.*

Voodoo knelt on empty ramen cups and food particles as the orange flames from the explosion angrily shot into the open air.

A door at the bottom of the tiny hotel smashed open, and men dressed in black fatigues poured out. Voodoo immediately recognized the abnormally large figure in the front. Stu carried two men, followed by Japanese SAT, and trailed by Frisco.

A momentary spike of relief plummeted to guilt. He was supposed to stop this. He was supposed to find a way for everyone to make it out alive. He should've been here sooner. He should've been more aggressive.

Kneeling in self-pity, Voodoo heard Stu call out to him.

"Voodoo!" he said as he ran by. "Get your ass up. We've got wounded." Stu didn't have time for introspection.

It was almost 4 a.m. The hotel and pachinko parlor burned bright in the night. Plumes of jet-black smoke poured out of the structure like the industrial soul of the complex escaping to the other world beyond. Mingled within, the lives of Ryu's helpless captives and the unsuspecting patrons of the pachinko parlor vanished from existence.

CHAPTER 41
NLP

The black and white infrared image displayed a shivering body, curled in a fetal position. The captive rubbed her legs with her good arm and quietly hummed to herself. Ryu leaned back in his chair and monitored the video feed from the comfort of his stateroom. What little semblance of humanity that existed in Ryu's childhood had long since morphed into hatred for the world around him, for the capitalism and greed of Japan and the West. He drank in the image of Dr. Hawkins's pain, seeking to find joy in her anguish.

He subconsciously rubbed his knee, mimicking the action of his captive. A different emotion nagged at the recesses of his soul. It wasn't remorse. He felt no pity for the American woman. He felt no desire to set her free or relate to her in any way. He merely grasped for the very thing she appeared to be clinging to.

Ryu wanted hope.

The ship gently pitched in the waves and jostled Ryu in his chair, breaking his hypnotic fixation. The sound of the Chinese crew further anchored Ryu in reality, their voices echoing through the passageway of the ship. After years in Japan embedded with the yakuza, Chinese sounded significantly more foreign than he would like. The evil language of the Japanese reminded him of nothing more than the atrocities the people of Japan inflicted on his ancestors only one generation earlier.

The Chinese voices also placed Ryu on edge, and something didn't feel right about Toyotomi kowtowing to Xin Jishu International in this way. The Japanese adamantly protected the rights of Japanese workers in their fleet. Perhaps the chairman had more power than Ryu assumed?

Over the past day, the ship meandered up the eastern coast of Japan toward an ambiguous destination the chairman designated that Ryu would soon change. The moment had almost arrived and only a few more pieces of the puzzle remained to be put in place.

Ryu stood up from his chair and exited his stateroom. He traveled through the ship's passageways, down several ladders past the main cargo hold below deck to a darkened section of the vessel. A red light flickered on the edge of the hall where a guard, dressed in black, sat waiting.

Ryu gave the man a nod and walked toward one of the metal doors. He pulled the latch. The door clanked and then groaned as it opened. The stench of vomit and urine mingled with fish wafted from inside the room.

He stood at the entryway to the dark cell that he had spent hours watching on-screen. Dr. Hawkins lay on the deck, quietly moaning.

He looked down at the pathetic mess of a person writhing in confinement. Even in the darkness, her left elbow appeared swollen. She trembled and pushed herself up to address her visitor.

Ryu's figure created a black silhouette surrounded by fuzzy red light hiding the hint of joy on his face. He didn't speak. He waited to allow the silence between them to deepen and her thoughts to fill the void of inaction.

This was the first moment since her capture that anyone stood before her without a mask. Her voice croaked as she spoke.

"Please, the pain is getting worse, I can't hold anything down," she said. He already knew this and said nothing. The sloshing of water against the hull that seemed thunderous moments before his arrival faded into the absence of sound between Ryu and his captive. Unlike his victims, silence couldn't hurt Ryu. Since the death of his sister, he hadn't had a moment of real respite. He *liked* to listen to the incessant voices in his head.

"What do you want! Dammit! Just tell me what you want!" She curled into a fetal position and shivered. Like the American military, Ryu received extensive training on managing captivity. He knew how to deal with capture shock, sensory deprivation, shame, the cliché "good cop, bad cop" routine. Since the war in Iraq, he knew how America softened its perspective on what they called "enhanced interrogation" and the media called torture. Ryu wasn't interested in these techniques because Dr. Hawkins wasn't here to be interrogated.

Not yet, at least.

Ryu stepped forward, his hands in the pockets of his black utility pants.

Her pain is the beginning. Soon, they will all be in pain, a voice said in his head.

Ryu pulled out a pack of cigarettes, placed one in his mouth, and lit it up. The reddish-yellow flame flickered. Dr. Hawkins looked up just as the fire went out and Ryu took a drag.

"Dr. Hawkins, I hope you have enjoyed your stay," he said in Japanese, smoke floating up from his mouth in the reddish light around him.

"What're you talking about, you sadistic bastard?"

"I've come to ask you a few questions," he started. "But first, we really must discuss your friends." He held the cigarette between his index finger and his thumb with the ember down toward his palm. He waited patiently for her response; the voice in his head danced between laughter and taunting.

"What've you done with Dr. Ichikawa?" Taka-chan asked from her position on the ground.

"Technically, he's with us on this ship right now."

"What does that mean?" She propped her body up with her good arm and looked directly at the outline of his head where his face hid.

"He's here. I'm trying to get inside his head," Ryu said.

"Is that why you're here now? To get inside my head?"

"Eventually...yes. I have the God Algorithm and the vials of serum left in the safe in your office. I want you to help me understand it."

"How...how did you get the vials?" She recoiled against the bulkhead, her buttocks on the deck, her knees against her chest. He waited to allow her imagination to fill in the gaps.

"How do you think? Dr. Ichikawa helped me. He has an eye for secrecy."

Interrogators, human intelligence specialists, and pickup artists all know about something called neuro-linguistic programming (NLP). Most people know this as a poker face or body language, but there is much more to NLP. The average person doesn't control their emotional or verbal responses to the world around them. Humans physically react to statements with nervous laughter, furrowed brows, or revulsion. Expressive people perpetually communicate via NLP. Interrogators use NLP to know what questions create an emotional response from their subjects, and pickup artists use it to find what lines are best to flirt or to draw in a would-be partner's attention.

Ryu, even through the crimson ambiance of the makeshift prison cell, could still read Dr. Hawkins's response. Her imagination filled in the blanks. She knew Ryu used Dr. Ichikawa's eyes to get into the refrigerated safe where he kept Tsuru's blood.

"Did he suffer? When you killed him, I mean? Did he suffer?"

"No more than anyone else is going to suffer. Nor more than the people of my country suffered."

"And what country is that?" she asked.

"*Choson Minjujuui Inmin Konghwaguk*," he replied in Korean.

"What's that mean?"

"Democratic People's Republic of Korea. Your future home." He finally permitted himself to smile and took a drag from his cigarette, allowing the embers to light up his face, his dark eyes drilling into her.

"No, no, no, no! You can't take me to North Korea!"

BAM!

Ryu slammed his fist against the bulkhead. His whole body filled with rage.

"Never call the fatherland that ever again!" He leaned toward her aggressively.

Hit her! Punish her! the voice barked in his mind.

Taka-chan screamed.

She buried her head.

She shook.

She sobbed.

"I'm sorry, I'm sorry!" she pleaded.

Ryu took a deep breath and stood over her, motionless.

He waited—his chest heaved in and out as he let the shock settle in.

He stepped back to the door.

Ryu had several weapons to draw from. Noise amplified silence. The abrupt application of sound with silence disturbs the human mind. It creates sympathetic nervous reactions. Compared to the silence between statements, Ryu knew his violent outburst awakened Dr. Hawkins's imagination. Fear flooded her thoughts. Now, silence would etch away her psyche; it would make her will pliable and weak. He stepped out the entryway and turned to give her one last look as her body shuddered on the deck of her metal dungeon.

"If you aren't truly sorry yet...you will be. And then you will be grateful it is all over."

• • •

There was a locking sound as the solid metal clinched shut, and the reddish glow from the passageway diminished to a fragmented crack in the door. Dr. Hawkins shivered. The man had managed to bring more darkness to her confinement.

North Korea, she thought. *Why on earth am I going to North Korea?*

The idea of the isolated nation brought a horrible fear to her soul. Her thoughts wandered to a future in that nation. She knew very little other than the secluded borders and peculiar, movie villain–like dictator.

The voice from her dream returned:

The crane's blood flows in your veins. Dark eyes are watching. Fast feet will fail a midnight flight. A steady mind in the darkness will find the light. When the blind warriors emerge, lie down and say your name.

This time, with the words, she saw images of faceless men in the rain, isolation, and darkness, then angelic light. She compared the imagery with what just happened. Faceless men had watched, then pursued her at night and took her, and now she sat in isolation and darkness.

A steady mind in the darkness will find the light.

The answer is right in front of me if I just have faith. But faith in what? The dream?

Ichikawa had dreams too, she thought. *Look where that got him.*

Yet his fate, his future, his dreams must have told a much different story. A story that made him run headlong into the demon of his dreams, the very beast that invaded her room just now to flex his metaphorical muscle.

But my dreams give me a hopeful outcome.

She wiped her eyes and took a deep breath, as if she had regained her composure. Her heart beat with fear but she held steady her act. For she had seen enough documentaries on interrogation to understand what her captor was doing: watching her, waiting.

A quote from Clausewitz, a Prussian general noted as a military theorist, framed her memories like a movie subtitle. "If the mind is to emerge unscathed from the unforeseen, two qualities are indispensable: first is an intellect that, even in the darkest hour, retains some glimmerings of the inner light which leads to truth; the second, the courage to follow this faint light wherever it may lead."

A steady mind in the darkness will find the light.

I've been through hell before, she thought. *Ironically, his attempt to make me weak will make me stronger. For I have now seen my enemy, and I, too, will be watching and waiting.*

And soon, very soon, the blind warriors would arrive.

CHAPTER 42
The Aftermath

"How did this happen? I thought DZ was supposed to distract them enough for the SAT team to get into the back and find the intel we need?" Frisco said. The wail of ambulances and fire trucks arriving on the scene flooded the urban canyon of the surrounding buildings with red and blue light.

Voodoo looked up from his position on the curb beside the armored vehicle. "I wish I could explain to you how I thought things were going to turn out, but I'm not sure what it all means at this point," Voodoo replied. His bloodshot eyes and sullen face epitomized dejection. He sat just out of sight of the emergency personnel arriving on the scene.

"Come on," Captain Tanaka said in Japanese. "I need to get you all off the scene." Frisco reached down to Voodoo and gripped his elbow then helped him to his feet. Voodoo nodded in agreement as they all climbed into the back of the SAT armored vehicle. Of the original eight officers, three were injured and loaded into an ambulance as the other five offi-cers remained on the scene to handle the emergency response vehicles. They also stuck around to coordinate the final report of events with specific instructions to "forget" to mention the Americans on the scene. Captain Tanaka intended to clean that up personally.

The vehicle shook with the ignition of the armored car's diesel engine and Frisco, Naomi, Stu, and Voodoo sat on the seats lining the walls facing each other. Captain Tanaka rode shotgun with the driver, who had remained in the vehicle during the entire drama.

"You said you knew this was a trap," Frisco started again. "What exactly did you see?"

"I saw several jumbled images and outcomes, but the main thing I saw was a sniper in position getting ready to shoot you, then something forcing him to get out of the way. Then I saw the buildings exploding. I came up with an idea because I knew there was a jammer, and I knew that a bomb would go off in the building. I was convinced that I could change the outcome of what I saw. But...I can't help but wonder if we caused this whole thing. I mean, if we hadn't... If I hadn't..." Voodoo's body screamed contrition as he sat in a humble position like a man at prayer.

"Wait, you saw the sniper move away in the dream, and the explosion still happened, right?" Naomi said.

"Yeah..." Voodoo replied.

"Well, what you saw was the outcome of *your* actions. Not the actions of everyone else involved," Naomi said.

"What do you mean?" Frisco asked.

"Listen, predictions are about agency. Free will. Individual agency is tricky because it is just that—individual. Throughout our research, I put a lot of thought into how the God Algorithm works. You were dreaming of what actions *you* should take and what *you* wanted to happen. That aspect of agency only goes so far. Other people also have a say in the matter. It is probabilistic. Your dream weighed the potential outcome of your agency and presented the result based on the amount of time you have. Which, in this case, meant you were never going to be able to stop all of it. You'd seen the bombs going off anyway. The only way to guarantee that *none* of it happens is not to try at all."

The foursome pondered her words for a moment.

"So, basically, I can do what I can, and the prediction will come true. If I do nothing, the prediction is anyone's guess, but the images in the dream are a representation of the best possible outcome based on my desire?"

"Yes."

"So, I wanted to save my friends, and I did."

"It seems that way. The sniper would have taken them out as they ran out of the building otherwise."

"What about the kids? Why wouldn't I want to save them? They deserved to live just as much as anyone else," Voodoo asked.

"And the monster that killed them had a say in the matter as well, and you were in no position to stop him."

Voodoo nodded before burying his face in his hands, then pulling them down as if he were washing his face in the sink.

"Where does that put us now, then?" Frisco asked. "We just got our asses kicked." Knowing that he sprinted away from those children and left them behind to die kept sinking into his conscience in slow increments, with each wave hitting harder and harder.

He imagined his daughters. He pictured them being kidnapped and abused only to be used as pawns in some sadistic game of cat and mouse. His parental paranoia shifted to complete rage, and he gritted his teeth and tightened his fist. He slammed one down on his knees in frustration.

"Did you see anything at all in there?" Voodoo asked.

"Nothing," Frisco replied. "Just that those kids were from the Philippines."

Captain Tanaka turned around from the front, where his driver seemed to be translating the conversation. He spoke through his translator.

"We learned that a police officer had been there earlier. An officer that looked like a pig," Captain Tanaka's driver said.

"Does that help us?" Naomi asked in Japanese.

"It *does* actually. I am very confident I know who they are talking about."

"Well, that's something but not much," Frisco said. "I hoped to find some kind of actionable intel." On the opposing bench, Voodoo intensely scoured his phone for something. After a minute, he finally looked up to see everyone staring at him.

"What are you looking for?" Naomi asked.

Voodoo stared at the screen. He used his index and middle finger to zoom in and out of a location before finally responding.

"The Kuril Islands."

"What's so special about that?" Frisco asked.

"That's where Dr. Hawkins is going to be in less than twenty-four hours. That's where we need to be if we're going to save her."

"How do you know?" Frisco asked.

"I saw it in my dream. There's gonna be a battle there one way or another. It's our only chance to save her. If we're not there... If we do nothing, we lose her for sure. If we at least try, we have a chance of saving her."

"What are the Kuril Islands? Where's that?" Frisco asked.

"North of Hokkaido. The northernmost point in Japan. The Kuril Islands are...how shall I say? Full of complications."

"Of course. What are they?" Frisco said. The vehicle driver spun the steering wheel to take a corner.

"Since the end of the nineteenth century until the end of World War II, Japan and Russia have fought over who owns the Kuril Island chain. They extend south from the Kamchatka Peninsula. The islands are not that far off the coast of Hokkaido. I saw in my dream that a ship carrying Dr. Hawkins is going to be there. But she won't be alone. It's gonna be a mess."

"I can tell you're holding back, Voodoo. Spit it out."

"I told Sparks to catch a flight to Hokkaido with the BIB. I'm assuming he made it on the flight because I haven't heard from him since I told him to get moving. I intend to do whatever I can to save Dr. Hawkins. Otherwise, she's toast. I've seen the best-case scenario, and even that isn't pretty. I just need to find a way to get up there and then get onto the Kuril Islands."

"What is this 'I' stuff?" Naomi said. "There are four of us here, Voodoo."

"Listen, Frisco, jump in anytime here, there's no way Buck is going to go for this. We have no actionable intelligence. Any evidence of North Korean or Chinese involvement just exploded in the pachinko parlor. Xiphos just got hacked by Division 121. We have no rear support and no leverage. The only thing we have left are my dreams, which aren't all that reliable, and we can't go at all if Buck doesn't approve it."

"He's right. Without an approved CONOP—"

Naomi waved her hand in front of Frisco's face.

"Oh, sorry. A CONOP is short for 'Concept of Operations,' an order specifically detailing everything we intend to do, the intelligence that led us to why we're doing it, and how we're going to get out in case something goes south. Basically, we'd have to write up a report requesting to conduct a hostage rescue mission in contested Russian territory with no intelligence to support it other than some random guy's dreams. It would be utterly and completely unprecedented. Buck would have to be willing to risk an international incident based on nonsense."

"It is not nonsense!" Naomi raised her voice in annoyance. "I know what the God Algorithm can do. I know what Voodoo sees is the truth. It is *going* to happen if Voodoo is there. The only thing we do not know is what will happen if we are *not* there..."

"*We* believe you, Naomi. Buck won't. There's no way that old bullfrog is gonna go for this," Frisco said.

"Why can the Japanese Self-Defense Force not go?" Naomi asked.

Captain Tanaka's driver listened to his boss speak and then translated.

"Because the Japanese are even less willing to risk an international incident with Russia. We have territorial protests with Russia, South Korea, and China, and each one of them is a powder keg. Whenever we unintentionally agitate one, we upset the others. It's a domino effect."

Frisco nodded. "We can't go without Buck's approval, and the Japanese can't go to the Kuril Islands in our stead. I recommend we tell Buck the truth and do everything we can to convince him and the ambassador to use diplomatic channels. Perhaps the chief of station can help us. I'm sure he has resources we haven't tapped into yet. What do you think, Voodoo?"

Voodoo looked ready to explode.

"Buck would rather let Dr. Hawkins die before risking his career. And can you blame him? It's the ranting dream of some 'enabler'!" Profound frustration poured out of Voodoo. All the years of having to abide by the permission of some shooter bubbled to the molten surface.

"Figures. I stare down the barrel of my nightmares, relived my wife's death. I even relived killing...killing that kid in Iraq before ultimately watching more innocent children die."

Even with the rumble of the armored vehicle, the pause in Voodoo's monologue created a vacuum of sound as his words struck.

"Is that what this is about, Voodoo? That op in Iraq?" Frisco asked. "Listen, man, that wasn't your fault. Anyone of us could've killed that kid—"

"NO! I know for a *fact* that it was me. I took that kid's life, and it's haunted me every day of my life ever since." Voodoo's manic shaking escalated.

"Voodoo, it's war. You know that. We all wanna say that we stepped onto the battlefield and did everything right, but we'd be lying to ourselves. That's the part about war nobody tells you when you're dreaming of some glorious, noble battle. Every time we pull a trigger, we take that risk. That's what makes you different, brother. You raised your hand and took that risk. You sacrificed your very soul for the men beside you."

"That's the messed-up part about this whole thing, Frisco." Voodoo's words sharpened with intensity. "I did what I did to make things right. I fought and continue to fight to make things right. And now we have intel, but there's no way Buck is going to listen.

"I spent years trying to convince every platoon in the Task Force to listen to the intel, listen to the nonshooter, but they always had to learn the hard way first. I've seen too many people die from hubris. I'm not going to watch another!"

Naomi tried to catch Voodoo's gaze. "Voodoo, are you alright? What are you saying?"

"I'm saying, Naomi, that... I'm saying...if anyone chooses to do this...we're on our own."

"We already are, are we not?" Naomi said.

"That's not what he's saying," Frisco explained. He rested his head back against the side of the vehicle. "Voodoo's saying that we're gonna have to go without Buck's permission. If we're gonna do this, we have to risk our lives and our careers on Voodoo's dreams."

Naomi slowly nodded and sank into her seat. Voodoo rubbed his elbow.

"So...Taka-chan is lost. She is gone..." Naomi said quietly.

"No...I'm gonna find a way. I'm going," Voodoo said. "Alone. You all have families at home. I have..." His voice trailed off, then returned with conviction. "Frisco, you have a wife and kids that need their father. Even if you survive, you'd get court-martialed. It's suicide."

Frisco genuinely did *not* want to go. He didn't want this mission. He didn't know Dr. Hawkins or Dr. Ichikawa. This was a long way from a platoon of operators kicking down doors in the Middle East. This was an international cold war over the future of artificial intelligence.

Complete nonsense.

Suicide, just as Voodoo said.

For all the years that his family feared the worst, he owed it to his wife and daughters to fight his way home to them. He owed it to his team to be a real leader and make the hard decision even if it meant letting Dr. Hawkins die so his men could fight another day—a choice just like the one he made moments earlier to leave those kids behind and save his men from a bomb, even though it meant losing young lives in the process.

Frisco made up his mind. America was already full of statues celebrating the ultimate sacrifice men made on missions that never should have been. This would not be another.

Suddenly, Stu spoke for the first time on the entire ride in the armored car.

"This is a dead hooker moment."

Naomi's eyes jumped over to the giant. "Excuse me?"

Frisco and Voodoo looked at Stu and immediately caught the reference, merely bobbing their heads.

"How is this a 'dead hooker moment'?" Naomi asked.

"I'm sorry if this sounds crude, but in our community, there's kind of a saying. When we want to give an example of how loyal we are to each other, someone ends up saying, 'I'd bury a dead hooker for him if he asked me to,'" Frisco explained.

"When would this kind of conversation *ever* come up?" Naomi looked at Frisco and Voodoo in utter disbelief. They looked at each other and shrugged.

"Not literally. It's a metaphor for—"

"Shut up, Frisco. I got this," the Stu-Bear said as he turned to Naomi using his massive hands to explain. The sudden animation in his expressions made the horrifying topic intoxicating. "Your buddy makes a mistake, and for some reason, he caught a body. And he's gotta deal with it. If you're truly his bro, you help him take care of it. Dig a hole or something. Either way, you're part of the deal too. You're all in. And the two of you accept the consequences."

With all the sincerity Frisco had ever seen from Stu, he looked at Naomi but pointed with his left hand at Voodoo sitting right across from him. "We fight and bleed for each other. We'll go to hell and back for each other. With every fiber in our soul, every muscle in our bodies, we'll kick and tear and punch our way through the darkest, vilest pit for our brothers." He turned and looked at Frisco sitting beside Voodoo and stared him down. "No demands, no complaints... No questions."

And with that, Stu looked at Voodoo, who lifted his head and met Stu eye to eye. Stu didn't say another word. He merely put his hand on Voodoo's shoulder and gave Voodoo the most significant thing he had ever given him. He gave Voodoo the one gesture that meant everything to those who knew Stu.

He gave him a sincere and deliberate nod.

Voodoo's eyes watered.

The one nod meant Stu was willing to fight to the ends of the earth with Voodoo, and Frisco felt ashamed he didn't immediately feel the same way.

Being a shooter is not a decision you make once and then change your mind. Being a shooter meant making that decision every day. It meant choosing to be there for the men and women beside you. It meant fighting to be greater than the person you were the day before. In Frisco's case, it meant even being greater than the person he was five minutes ago.

"I'm in. We're in," Frisco said to Voodoo. "You're one of us. Let's do this."

"I'm in too," Captain Tanaka said through his translator, his driver shocked by the sudden participation. "I can't help you in the way you think, but I can get you the resources you need once you get to Hokkaido. You just need to find a way to get up there."

Voodoo asked, "Why are you helping us?"

"You saved my men's lives tonight. We bury dead hookers for each other too."

Frisco, Stu, and Voodoo burst out laughing.

"Yeah!" Frisco shouted as he shook his fist.

Naomi sat back, as equally offended by the morbid and inappropriate metaphor as she was grateful that these men would sacrifice themselves for this cause. They raised their hands to risk their lives for strangers when others cowered. These were warriors and, regardless of their gallows humor, their intentions were brutal *and* righteous. Frisco looked over at Naomi, and her conflicted emotions hardened into resolve.

"We just have one problem," Naomi said. "How are we supposed to get to Hokkaido by the end of the day? The media is still going to be harping about that video of you beating up the police officers. You will not be able to use the Shinkansen or the airports."

Voodoo suddenly regained his devilish grin as an idea popped in his head.

"I think I have a solution for that."

"What is it?" Naomi asked.

"Any of you guys like Korean pop music?"

CHAPTER 43

Index!

DOWNTOWN SAN DIEGO, CALIFORNIA, USA

THURSDAY 5:58 P.M. PST

> **DZ**: I'm ready to deliver the payload. Is the network ready?
> **Janet**: Primary Xiphos network is online.
> **DZ**: Stand by.

I t was close to the end of what should have been a typical working day at Xiphos AI. Janet and Andy stared at the command-line interface and streams of code. Generally, the sight represented the joy of working in a startup developing technology that helps the average person get back at the tech giants of the world. Instead, they were in the middle of a fistfight with state-sponsored cyberterrorists.

Several years earlier, this same group of hackers, doing the bidding of their Dear Leader, hacked into a major motion picture studio and relieved them of a controversial comedy film. They followed through by holding the video hostage as an example of the price private companies pay when they trifle with a rogue regime like North Korea.

"When we started this company, did you ever think we would end up in something this heavy?" Janet asked. She had dark bags under her eyes. An oversize cup of cold brew coffee barely held her together.

"Never. We've stumbled into a perilous game. The thing that keeps running through my head is the fact that we were playing this game already and just didn't realize it."

"What do you mean?" Janet asked.

The code on his screen reflected off Andy's eyes as he faced the monitor. "I mean, when XJI tried to invest in us initially, they did so because they saw our company as an asset. Then we immediately became a threat. Now we're a full-on target. I just think we were in denial."

"But this Division 121 isn't XJI. It's the North Koreans."

"How is that different? In our haste, we somehow garnered the attention of not one but two aggressive communist countries for the technology we're trying to offer the free world," Andy replied.

"The free world *and* the American government. Don't forget about that part. That same tool is the one we just used for Naomi to hook Voodoo up to her equipment."

Andy's eyes widened. "Yeah! I've never seen the system process information like that. Every computer we could access was cranking away. That was incredible."

"I found the whole thing horrifying, to be honest," Janet said.

Beside the monitor connected to their network, a new message pinged on the chat application on Janet's laptop.

THURSDAY 6:08 P.M. PST

DZ: The honeypot worked. I have access to their network.
Janet: What does that mean?
DZ: The honeypot is a back door. Now I just need to deliver a payload.
Janet: Like a virus or a worm?
DZ: Sure. In most cases, I would be a lot more subtle. But I want these guys to hurt.
Janet: I'm not sure I like the sound of that.
DZ: Not hurt physically. Some egos are about to be annihilated, though.
Janet: Just as long as it doesn't get back to us.
DZ: Of course.

Janet felt the same way she did when she cheated on her chemistry test in high school. She felt the exhilaration of breaking the rules while hearing the distant sound of sirens racing toward her at the same time. She looked around the room, like a fugitive checking her rearview mirror.

"What's going on?" Andy asked. "You've got that jumpy look again."

"Delta Zulu is about to hack Division 121. I'm not particularly sure what that means for them, though." She paused. "Or for us."

THURSDAY 6:21 P.M. PST

DZ: I'm in. I have access to the primary information they've been tracking. It appears they've been pulling feeds from the Tokyo police. They've been monitoring emails, creating files on police officers... It looks like they have a record on Xiphos.

Janet: What does it say?

DZ: It appears they've been tracking you for a long time. Your files are tagged.

Janet: What does that mean?

DZ: I'm trying to translate it... Here it is. It's labeled the "Chairman."

Janet looked over at Andy and pointed at the screen. "Andy, look."

"That fat bastard. So, *he's* behind this. I knew it was XJI, but I never thought we'd find evidence this went straight up to him."

DZ: I found something else you may be interested in. The CEO of Toyotomi Industries was found dead the other night. It seems he was killed just like Ichikawa. Wanna guess who benefits the most from his death?

Janet: The chairman.

DZ: In one night, he takes control of Xiphos and Toyotomi Industries completely. It only makes sense that he would try to steal the God Algorithm too.

Janet: This needs to be leaked. The authorities need to know about this.

DZ: As they will, but I can't just leak that information, not yet. I did some digging, though. Toyotomi Industries had a shareholder meeting several days ago. I was able to find some security feeds of the event. I'll post the link. Other than that, the information I found won't stand up in court.

Janet: So, what do you have in mind?

DZ: I need to speak with Voodoo.

Vudu: Whatever you're thinking, go with it. Anything else I should be aware of?

DZ: Voodoo! Is everyone alright?

Vudu: Our team is safe...but they knew we were coming and a lot of people are... It's bad.

DZ: They completely infected the police. I can see it now. I'm sorry I didn't do this earlier. I also found these from a shareholder meeting after I heard about the CEO's death.

Two video thumbnails appeared in chat.

Vudu: @DZ Thanks. There's no way you could have anticipated what they would do. I have one more favor to ask of you, but before I do that, I have something to tell Janet.

Vudu: @Janet I want you to know that the God Algorithm worked. I don't have time to explain to you what happened. But we know what we need to do. Thank you for your help. Now let us take it from here.

Janet: What do you mean?

Vudu: I'm about to take care of this problem. I need you to do something vital.

Janet: Name it.

Vudu: INDEX

Janet immediately closed out of the application. In the back of her mind, police sirens blared. She pulled up something on her computer called "Eraser." Janet dragged all the files related to Dr. Ichikawa, the God Algorithm, Japan, Voodoo, anything of relevance, and dropped it into the virtual software shredding tool.

"Janet, what're you doing?" Andy asked. Janet's frantic movements on the computer keyed him in on the answer. "Voodoo passed you the signal, didn't he?"

Janet quickly turned her head and nodded nervously before completing her actions. In less than a minute, any semblance of Voodoo, Naomi, the God Algorithm, and the usage of Xiphos Gov to support them completely vanished.

"What does this mean? Why do you think he did this now?" Andy asked.

"I can only suspect one reason. Voodoo's about to do something hazardous, and he doesn't want us tied to it."

Janet and Andy sat without speaking. Outside their window, the setting sun burned into the marine layer of clouds over the Pacific Ocean. Somewhere, on the opposite side of the world, Voodoo prepared for what Andy and Janet could only assume to be the most dangerous task of his life. In that same instance, they wished him luck and prayed to God they hadn't just damned the future of their company and their own lives in the process.

CHAPTER 44
The Meeting

S hards of morning light in the land of the rising sun stabbed between buildings and pierced the vehicle window. Voodoo sat beside Naomi in a black SUV, courtesy of Captain Tanaka.

"Are you ready for this?" Voodoo asked.

"As ready as I will ever be," Naomi replied. Naomi wore a pair of designer sunglasses and a black trench coat; Voodoo, a set of black fatigues like the ones worn by the members of SWAT.

"We need to be there in thirty minutes. Frisco and Stu should be meeting us shortly and we'll drive over together," Voodoo said as he reached into his pocket and retrieved his phone, glanced at a text. "Here they are now."

A second SUV pulled up and the two vehicles convoyed to their destination.

Voodoo thumbed his phone. The chat feature created by Delta Zulu no longer worked and Voodoo shut off all network connectivity. He *did* download two files before sending the cover term to Janet to erase all network activity.

"I want you to watch this video with me. It's one last gift from DZ. Perhaps you can help me put some pieces together."

Voodoo pulled out some headphones, handed one earbud to Naomi, and pressed play.

Voodoo explained as the video played, "On the day that Kenzo and Taka-chan went missing, there was a shareholder meeting at the Toranomon Hills building. DZ said he was able to amplify the audio before pushing it over to me."

The shareholder meeting took place in the large conference room on the fifty-second floor of the Toranomon Hills building in downtown Tokyo. The building stands at 255 meters in height and is the fifth largest skyscraper in Japan. The three-meter-high windows frame the view of the expansive metropolis of Tokyo. The scene, like a painting, looks down on countless lower buildings as they huddle in architectural genuflection to their great lord.

An ikebana arrangement of pink dahlia flowers and bare stems to represent heaven, man, and earth sat beside a podium in the front of the room with western bouquets lining the walls. The ceiling lighting was comprised of perfect rectangular white illuminated cubes outlined in dark wood. Several dozen taupe chairs lined the meticulously dressed white tables where more than fifty businessmen and women mingled, drinking coffee.

A tall, muscular man with disheveled black hair and a slim-fitting black suit penetrated the room. With his first step, the genial atmosphere collapsed. The glad-handing and schmoozing disintegrated into muffled footsteps, side-glances, and whispers.

It was as if the man wielded silence like a weapon.

He walked to his seat among the many rows of tables in the middle of the room. As he sat, an unseen gravity bound the bodies around him to the earth, fixated and frozen. The rest of the audience took their seats, eyes forward, away from the man in the black suit.

"Any idea who that guy is?" Voodoo asked.

"No idea. It is obvious he has a chilling effect on everyone at the meeting," Naomi said.

The CEO, an elderly Japanese man with a full head of white hair, narrow eyes, and a blue single-breasted suit and tie, moved with an erect and distinguished posture as he approached the podium.

"*Mina-sama, Irrasshaimase,*" he said as he addressed the audience of assembled shareholders.

Naomi paused the video. "A little background that might help: The CEO of Toyotomi was from the postwar era and represented a generation of Japanese attempting to resurrect the warrior code of bushido through modern business. For a time, he was successful. For decades Toyotomi Industries epitomized a growing and dominant Japan in the economic world. Toyotomi became an emblem for a proud nation to rally behind. Things have changed, though. That really is not the case anymore. The company is in disrepair. It is all over the news."

Voodoo nodded. Naomi resumed the video.

"I am hopeful in the bright future that lies ahead and very excited about our recent merger with Xin Jishu International, the Chinese technology venture capital firm," he said with a grand sweeping motion of his right arm.

On cue, a second man stood and addressed the audience with a smirk and a slight bow. His sparse hair was dark, and his portly physique indicated a financially secure and well-fed lifestyle. He had on a sharp silver-gray single-breasted suit and a small Chinese flag lapel pin signifying his membership in the Chinese Workers' Party.

"That looks like the guy from the video on Kenzo's private server," Voodoo said.

Naomi gasped and covered her mouth with a hand. "I think I know who that is."

"Who is it?"

"Keep the video going so I can be sure."

The man in the black suit in the middle of the room leaned back in his chair. The familiar click and snap of a lighter shot through the room as he lit a cigarette. In his periphery, a woman adjusted her seat and straightened her posture. The silent bodies around him stiffened, unable to ignore his insolence. Yet they appeared too terrified to speak up about his open offense of smoking. He took a drag and a puff of smoke wafted throughout the room.

The CEO carried on about economic figures, investments, and market trends while the man flicked ashes onto the pristine carpet.

"With that, I would like to introduce one of our more aggressive projects," the CEO continued, motioning to a man at the side of the room. From the back of his head, Naomi immediately recognized the man approaching the podium.

"That's Kenzo!" Naomi shook her head and looked out the window, her eyes starting to water.

As Kenzo turned to the side, Voodoo could see he wore clear rimless spectacles, his hair was slicked back with thick gel and beads of sweat formed on his brow as he uncomfortably adjusted the microphone. Compulsory and mildly enthusiastic applause greeted him.

A screen descended from above, and an overhead projector displayed the beginning slide of a PowerPoint presentation.

"It's an honor to be here today," he said in Japanese. "I am Dr. Kenzo Ichikawa. I am the head of neurology at the University of Tokyo. I am here to present the great successes we are having in our research because of the generous funding we have received from Toyotomi Industries." He proceeded with an overview of one of their projects, discussing work to quell pathological neural activity in the brain via exciting new techniques in the field of optogenetics.

Dr. Ichikawa continued for a long while before returning to his seat. The meeting paused for a break. Kenzo stood, thanked the CEO, grabbed his bag, and made a professionally discreet beeline for the elevator.

Voodoo turned up the volume.

The man in the black suit put out his cigarette on the table in front of him, dragging a black smudge across the white tablecloth. He approached the heavyset man from XJI and gave a slight bow before shaking hands.

As soon as they released, the man in black slipped something into his pocket.

"Did you see that?" Voodoo asked.

Naomi nodded, her brow intensely furrowed, one hand still covering her mouth. The man in the black suit then headed to the open entryway near the elevator.

Dr. Ichikawa pressed the button to the elevator over and over as the man approached.

The video ended and Voodoo opened the next. This one was apparently taken from inside the elevator as the doors opened.

The man in black stood between Kenzo and the elevator. His body was motionless with his hands in his pockets, and his head canted slightly, his black eyes transfixed.

Voodoo remembered the very same vision in his dream.

"The time has come, hasn't it?" Dr. Ichikawa said. He pushed his glasses up his nose and swallowed. "I can't... I'm not ready."

The man's cold eyes said nothing.

Dr. Ichikawa lowered his head. He subtly squirmed as if he were an animal trapped before capitulating.

"You'll have it," Dr. Ichikawa said quietly.

The doors shut.

"You think that man was the minor shareholder of Toyotomi that Kenzo was talking about?" Voodoo asked.

"He must be. He looks like yakuza."

"Most likely *Anmoku-dan*. Which means he's North Korean. That's probably Ryu—Dragon. That's the guy that took Taka-chan."

Naomi put her other hand over her mouth and shook her head over and over.

"We'll get her back, I promise," Voodoo said.

"No, that is not the only thing I am worried about," she said. "It is the other man in the video. The man who slipped the order to Ryu...the man from Xin Jishu International."

"What about him?" Voodoo asked.

"That is the chairman of Xin Jishu International."

"The chairman? That dude tried investing in Xiphos AI. After they turned him down, we're pretty sure his contacts in the Chinese government tried to hack into Xiphos and steal their intellectual property. The North Koreans beat him to it last night, though."

Naomi nodded.

"There is one more thing he wants... Taka-chan."

"Why would he want her specifically?" Voodoo asked.

"Because he is a controlling, manipulative bureaucrat who will stop at nothing to gain as much money and power as possible. He wants to take control of the Chinese government someday. And if he has her..."

Voodoo removed the earbud from his ear and soaked in the intense look on Naomi's face.

"He has so much power. How are we supposed to stop someone like him?"

Voodoo's gaze drifted to the city waking up around him.

"We certainly can't do it alone."

CHAPTER 45
Perks

"I thought they were staying in Tokyo for another performance?" the copilot asked.

"You know the drill. PrivaJet sends us a secure email with a flight schedule and passenger manifest and then we make it happen. We need to head north to a place called Nakashibetsu for a quick turnaround. The flight manifest says that there will only be four passengers. One of the band members and three of her security guards."

"Any idea which one? I have a tough time keeping them straight."

"It says it's...Min So-ri," the pilot said, referencing the email from PrivaJet corporate on his tablet.

"That doesn't exactly clear it up for me. There are way too many of them. I mean, a band with twenty members is ridiculous."

Cheers and jubilant fanfare outside indicated their guests had arrived. It was nearly 8 a.m., and fans tarried around the fence of the tiny Japanese airfield east of Tokyo hoping to catch even the slightest peek of their beloved K-pop band. A black SUV and a police escort pulled to a stop, and an attractive woman wearing large sunglasses and a trench coat stepped out of the vehicle with three men. All three members of her security detail wore black fatigues and sunglasses. One of them was a massive block of Caucasian muscle.

"Take a look at the size of that guy!" the copilot said, craning his neck to see outside the cockpit. The man in question was more than twice the size of the other two men following behind the starlet.

A fan lurched forward and protracted a desperate hand at Min So-ri. The colossal security guard intercepted the man with a stiff arm, harshly rejecting his overzealous affection.

"Whoa, that dude means business. We'd better get this bird ready to get in the air," the copilot said.

Within moments the beautiful starlet scaled the steps onto the plane and acknowledged the pilots with a flirty wave.

"*Annyong Haseyo!*" the Canadian pilot said. His feeble attempt at Korean did not impress anyone.

The starlet smiled, then retreated to the aft cabin. The copilot gawked at the celebrity, sauntering away only to have the sight interrupted by the enormous snarling bodyguard who slammed the cockpit door shut.

The pilot and copilot needed little more motivation to complete their final preparations. Within minutes they radioed to the tower, and the Gulfstream G600 pressed off the airstrip toward its northern destination.

• • •

"I am not going to lie, that felt incredible," Naomi said. "Optogeneticists are not lauded by the public very often."

"Remind me to buy DZ a beer," Frisco added.

Stu immediately gawked at an extensive array of food spread out in a secure position on the table to keep it from sliding during takeoff.

"We gave strict instructions not to be disturbed and have food ready for us," Voodoo said. "Like what you see, Stu?"

The Stu-Bear demolished a protein shake, then grabbed a bare handful of Korean bulgogi and rice and tore in like a famished beast.

The other three grabbed plates of kimchi, rice, eggs, and other Korean fares as they relaxed in the G600's elegant leather seats. Voodoo's knees popped like Rice Krispies cereal from the strain of a long night as he sat back down with a plate of food. The lactic acid buildup in his muscles left him aching.

Nobody spoke as they gorged themselves.

Voodoo reached into a cooler and pulled out a large energy drink and downed it before retrieving another.

No one needed to say a word and didn't for nearly fifteen minutes. They merely ate, occasionally releasing mild groans of gastronomic satisfaction. Stu sat in the front of the cabin and passed out. He had bulgogi sauce smeared across his face and hands. Despite being a killer, and a monster of a man, Stu had his moments, like this one, where he looked like nothing more than a chubby birthday boy.

Behind their sunglasses, they all hid bags under their eyes. Naomi was the only presentable one in the bunch, but she also had a ton of makeup on to appear like an active member of 4UBaby. Slight bruising peeked out on the left side of her face where the assailant struck her.

"Alright, Voodoo, what's the next step?" Frisco finally said. He adjusted his position and slouched, interlacing his fingers across his stomach with a drowsy yet content look smeared across his face.

"Well, we should be arriving in Nakashibetsu around 12:30. Sparks still has one layover in Tokyo, another flight, then a one-hour drive to Rausu. Assuming everything goes as planned we won't see him until close to 9 p.m.

"We need to meet up with Captain Tanaka's contacts in Nakashibetsu this afternoon if they come through. We also need a contingency plan if they don't. We'll have to go into combat using only the resources in the BIB. We'll also need to steal or rent a boat to get us across the water from the Shiretoko Peninsula to the Kuril Islands. Kunashir Island to be specific."

"This is ridiculous." Frisco sighed, shaking his head. "I honestly can't believe we're doing any of this."

"How did that conversation with Buck go?" Voodoo asked. Stu snored in the front seat.

"Well, after we split up so you could go buy supplies and coordinate with Delta Zulu, Stu and I went back to the embassy. I got a hold of the rest of the platoon and told them to head south to Yokosuka. I told Buck that the police got a lead after their raid, and that I felt it was a good idea to head up north to meet with the Japanese military units training there to coordinate. I told him we'd use a military air flight out of Yokosuka to get up to Misawa or somewhere closer."

"Did he give you any grief?" Naomi asked.

"Not at all. He was more than happy to get me out of the city before the crowds started up with their protests, and he seemed even more stoked that the Japanese officials were cool with us again."

"I am surprised it was that easy," Naomi said.

"Buck's not a hard-ass all of the time. Just most of the time. I can tell he hates everything about this mission. But when I presented him the idea that we could help from a distance and that Captain Tanaka found Naomi, he looked relieved."

That confirmed everything for Voodoo. Buck would have never gone for this rogue operation. He would sooner let Dr. Hawkins die than risk his career.

Even though Voodoo knew they were making the best decision, a sinking feeling nagged at him. More than an emotion, the words of his dream repeatedly passed through his head, reminding him something was off.

An old friend will be lost, an old friend regained.

Voodoo considered the meaning of the words. An old friend lost. Did that mean one of Voodoo's old friends? An old friend regained must refer to Naomi losing Dr. Hawkins and getting her back.

The sinking feeling alchemized to lead in his belly. Two of Voodoo's old friends sat with him now on this plane. An old friend lost.

Am I going to lose one of my friends? Will I be forced to trade one of them to get Naomi's old friend back? Voodoo thought. *Did I just convince one of my friends to join me only for them to die?*

Frisco spoke up. "Naomi, I've been thinking about something. You know how they discovered the CEO of Toyotomi and Kenzo both murdered in the same way?" His words snapped Voodoo out of his introspection.

"Yes, and?" Naomi replied.

"Is there some kind of symbolism behind seppuku itself that we're missing? Captain Tanaka felt these murders were symbolic."

Voodoo leaned forward with piqued interest.

"Unlike the West, the Japanese believe the heart may be your emotions, but your *hara*, or belly, is your soul. So, when someone commits seppuku, they are releasing their soul. The head is removed to save face, to keep the performer of the act from crying out in pain."

Voodoo's face lit up with an epiphany. "I get it now!" Voodoo snapped and wagged his index fingers. "The murderer took Kenzo's head and left a Korean weapon inside the CEO's belly, correct?"

"Yes," Naomi and Frisco said in unison.

"Toyotomi is a source of economic wealth, the modern-day samurai class of Japan. His death is like the death of Japan's soul. Leaving behind the Korean jingum is how the murderer intended for us to put the pieces together. Also, not telling us who to blame, but who is taking credit."

"And Ichikawa's murder?" Frisco asked.

"The murderer took his head, right? Well, he robbed Japan of their greatest thinker. In one night, he took Japan's soul...and their mind."

Frisco slowly shook his head in disbelief. "This whole thing is getting really dark."

Naomi's lip curled in disgust, and her eyes wandered the cabin until they rested on a small opening in her bag, where a tan folder lay inside.

"Voodoo, I need to show you something," she said, apparently remembering the blood tests from the lab. Naomi reached into her bag and pulled out the manila folder. "These are the results of the blood work we did at the hospital."

Voodoo reached out and stopped her just as Naomi prepared to open the folder.

"I know what you're about to tell me," he said.

"Did the dream show you?"

"A little."

"What do you know then?"

"Ichikawa injected me with the serum years ago when I was sleeping."

Naomi blinked.

"That explains the proteins. What did the dream show you?"

"I saw him sitting beside a river, pouring ashes into the water from a metal container. Then he walked over toward a raft... I was sleeping on that raft. That's when he injected me. I think he had a computer on him too."

"How long ago was that?" Naomi asked.

"Almost twenty years ago. I was only nineteen. I was working as a river guide on the Colorado River at the time. The funny thing is that I saw other memories of his as well. They had to be his memories; I was asleep at the time. Like how I saw cranes flying over my head and a raging river before he injected me. I could feel they were *his* memories."

"Did you see any other memories?"

"Dozens, maybe hundreds. At one point, it was like every possible outcome of the near future played out before my eyes. How was I able to see his memories?"

Naomi looked out the window of the Gulfstream. Fields of rice and wheat worked by hand passed below as the aircraft traveled north.

"Remember what I said about Project Kawa? He was merging his intuition with yours, but this feels like more. I have a theory, and I need Dr. Hawkins to help me figure it out to be sure. What I am thinking is that perhaps the algorithm learned from Dr. Ichikawa as we used the machine with him. Maybe the algorithm triggered similar memories between the two of you."

"Is it possible the algorithm 'remembered' his memories?" Voodoo asked.

"As if it stored them? I am not sure. The algorithm is designed to learn from every use and build a knowledge base of its user."

Frisco leaned forward. "Voodoo, are you saying that you saw the memories of Dr. Ichikawa when you were at the hospital?"

"Seems like it."

"This thing is significantly more powerful than we realized," Frisco said.

"What do you mean?" Naomi asked.

"Imagine if you have as many people as you can with the protein who all then interface with the AI. All of them synchronizing their collective thoughts into one shared consciousness. Imagine what you could do with that information..." Frisco trailed off and looked out the window.

"I was expecting some quippy statement, buddy. What're you getting at?" Voodoo asked.

"Well, think about what Naomi said earlier about being able to see only how to get what you want. The God Algorithm ties into your subconscious to help identify the best path for you to accomplish the thing you want to do most."

"Yeah...and?"

"Now imagine everyone is connected—"

Naomi jumped in. "And now you all can work out a way to collectively accomplish the same task. You could have entire military organizations, politicians, civilians, everyone coordinating the outcome together."

Voodoo nodded. "You could own the future. You'd be creating your own luck..." Then Voodoo added, "Right after we were attacked at the hospital, I had a thought. I didn't say it out loud, but now I understand what it means."

"Wait, you were attacked at the hospital?" Frisco asked.

"We have a lot to catch up on, Frisco," Voodoo said.

"What were you thinking after the attack, Voodoo?" Naomi asked.

"No one should have this kind of advantage. I'm beginning to fear what it can do. I believe now more than ever that we need to stop Ryu."

"And the chairman," Naomi added.

"Ryu? The guy from the pachinko parlor? Who's the chairman?" Frisco asked. Voodoo pulled out his phone and played the four videos DZ sent him from the shareholder meeting and Ichikawa's log.

"*Ryu* is the Japanese word for dragon," Voodoo said. "Somehow the chairman is involved as well."

"Why wasn't he a bigger suspect?" Frisco asked.

Naomi leaned in. "We did not know his link until we found the videos."

Voodoo nodded then said, "He knew about Ichikawa's work, Ryu later invested in it, killed him, then kidnapped Dr. Hawkins."

"Bold move. Because he wants to give it to North Korea?" Frisco asked.

"Apparently. I wonder if the chairman thought Ryu was just yakuza and not really North Korean. We thought this was all China manipulating the US and Japan and it turns out it's North Korea stealing from everyone else."

Voodoo took a swig of his energy drink. "But I get the feeling Ryu is double-crossing the chairman for his own gains."

"Voodoo, I know that you are aware that Dr. Ichikawa gave you the protein, but there is more to these results that we need to talk about," Naomi said.

"Like what?" Voodoo asked. Frisco sat up in his chair and tried to look at the paperwork more intently. The Stu-Bear slipped deeper into hibernation.

"Look at these sheets. On this page, you will see the genes of Tsuru. And on this, you will see yours."

Voodoo held the paperwork with its black, white, and gray lines indicating genetic markers.

"They look similar," Voodoo said.

"Voodoo, where is your mother from?"

Voodoo looked up from the paperwork at Naomi.

"She met my dad in Hawaii, where I was born, but she was originally from Tokyo if I remember correctly. Her family were really conservative and didn't approve of their marriage, so I never met my extended family."

"And?"

"She died when I was ten. My father said she had Batten disease. I can't remember for certain because it didn't make much sense to me when I was little."

"I looked it up, Voodoo. She did not die of Batten disease or whatever they told you." Naomi paused as she prepared to deliver the final blow. "Voodoo, she had the same disease as her niece, Tsuru...and so did you."

"Her niece? Disease? What do you mean by 'did'?"

"Yes, Ichikawa and your mother were brother and sister. You share the same genes as Tsuru."

Voodoo blinked, trying to absorb it all.

"Did you ever have headaches when you were younger? I mean, terrible headaches?"

"Yeah. Migraines. They went away when I was nineteen. When I was..."

"When you were a river guide," Naomi supplied.

"The image of him giving me the injection in my dream—"

"That was the night that Dr. Ichikawa saved your life, Voodoo. The very same night he said goodbye to his daughter, he set all of this in motion. He had lost his daughter and sister to the disease, and even though he most likely did not know you had the disease, he felt it was worth the risk."

"And used me as an experiment... What gave him the idea to use me in the first place?"

"Tsuru. The poem she recited was about the river," Naomi said.

Frisco jumped in, "Naomi, remember that video Miles Johnson showed us at the embassy of Dr. Ichikawa and Dr. Hawkins arguing? Do you think these two things are connected?"

Naomi took a deep breath. "I think she found out about Kenzo testing the protein and Project Kawa on Voodoo. I am very confident the dream you had about your wife years ago was the first time we ever tested Project Kawa. I would not have participated had I known. I doubt Taka-chan would have either. I am very confident that is why she quit."

Frisco's face tightened. "We're missing something. Why didn't Kenzo just try and seek Voodoo out? Why did he have to sneak the protein into your bloodstream and not just say, 'Hey, take this, or you'll die'?" Frisco asked.

Voodoo looked over at his friend. "Because he didn't want to get close to me in case it didn't work. If he could observe from a distance, he could save my life *and* continue Tsuru's legacy."

"Kinda cowardly if you ask me," Frisco said under his breath.

Naomi leered at Frisco. "Do not start, Frisco. He was a lot of things, but I would never call him a coward. He owned up to his mistake, knowing he would die, and still tried to save his friends."

Frisco raised his hands in surrender. "I'm sorry. I didn't mean it like that."

Voodoo put his hand on Naomi's shoulder. "We're still missing pieces to the puzzle. Let's just stay focused."

Naomi took a breath and softened. "You are right. There is only one person who can help us fill in the blank spaces." Naomi smiled. "We will just have to ask Taka-chan."

Frisco grinned at Voodoo, who smiled back, but in the back of Voodoo's mind, he heard the words of his dream surface once again, pecking away at his resolve.

In one day, an old friend will be lost...

The mechanical arms of the clock in Voodoo's mind engaged once again. *Tick, tick, tick, tick...* Voodoo took a mental picture of Frisco and Stu content on a stolen Gulfstream G600, flying over a foreign country on their way to conduct an unsanctioned combat operation on contested soil. Voodoo knew they stood on an existential precipice, their toes dangling off the edge between heaven and hell. They all felt that same rush of endorphins, high on hope, excited for the future, casting aside fear while engulfed in doubt. Voodoo soaked the moment in a little longer, praying that on the backside of this existential puzzle, life waited for Stu and Frisco.

Voodoo only knew that if anyone had to give his life on this mission...it would be him.

CHAPTER 46

The Chairman's Plan

38.972658, 142.987076
SOMEWHERE EAST OF JAPAN

The ripples of the ocean fractured the reflection of stars scattered across the June sky. The cargo ship cut through the waves, and in its wake, green bioluminescent life activated in the aerated water. Ryu leaned against the railing of the vessel and smoked his cigarette, standing between two worlds of eternity.

As Ryu's thoughts wandered, an image of his sister's bloated stomach and sunken eyes, desperate for death's reprieve, appeared in his mind. He fought to morph the memory to something joyful. He tried to remember her laugh. He tried to remember the games they played. Instead, he saw only the cessation of life and inhaled the stench of corpses emptying their bowels in his tiny home in Wonsan as his family members died. The empty, dry flavor of straw filled his mouth.

It tasted like death.

Ryu's lips snarled at the repugnant memory. He dragged the top of his tongue across his front teeth to scrape off the disgusting flavor. He cleared his throat and expelled memory-filled phlegm off the side of the ship before he took one last drag of his cigarette and then yanked it from his mouth, flicking it into the ocean. The orange ember drifted off in the wind before extinguishing in the ocean's expanse. One moment the light burned bright, the next it was gone, just like the lives of those he once cherished, as well as the lives that got in his way.

It was late. Ryu needed to sleep, clear his mind for the task ahead: staging his death and the end of the *Kuroshio Maru*.

Several years earlier, while conducting his first act as a shareholder at Toyotomi Industries, and a yakuza plant performing *sokaiya*, the Japanese version of internal corporate blackmail, Ryu met the man who would change his role as an infiltrator, his mission, and his life forever.

After a decade of preparation, Ryu arrived at the shareholder meeting of Toyotomi Industries armed and ready to blackmail and cajole his way into surreptitious power. He came with only one goal in mind. In Toyotomi's recent financial decline, their fleet of ships depleted, Ryu wanted nothing more than for the fleet to sink to the bottom of the ocean, but not before he had the chance to drive one back to Wonsan Harbor and deliver it to his people like the severed head of his foe.

Traditional *sokaiya* usually involved dramatic outbursts or embarrassing disclosures that focused on theatrics to gain the attention of the attending board members. Ryu preferred a more subtle approach.

During an intermission, his target, the CFO, rose to his feet and walked toward the bathroom. With compromising pictures of the CFO with an escort in hand, Ryu stood and made his move.

"Tanigawa-san," a voice said. "A moment if you don't mind." Ryu paused. Behind him stood a portly Chinese businessman speaking perfect Japanese. The interruption stunned Ryu. This man knew his name, or the name he used, rather. Ryu surrendered to his curiosity.

With one quick glance Ryu knew he hated this man. Ryu hated the way the Chinese carried themselves. They were arrogant and loud. They reminded him of the Asian embodiment of America. Their only saving grace was their adoption of communism in addition to their massive industrial might.

"I know who you are," the chairman of Xin Jishu International said as he leaned in. He smelled like gyoza and bar soap.

I doubt you do, Ryu thought. Though part of him suddenly panicked. Perhaps the chairman did.

"I know a yakuza when I see one. I also know the Tokugawa-Kai well."

Ryu stared at the man's chubby face and his heavy-lidded eyes.

"I think there may be a way that we can help each other," the fat communist continued.

"How is that?" Ryu asked. He pulled on the cuffs of his black jacket to straighten the sleeves.

"I have some interests here with Toyotomi. I also have some, let's just say, more aggressive investments I'm looking into making. Investments that someone like you may want to consider."

Ryu took the bait. "What kind of investment?"

The chairman motioned for Ryu to step toward a corner of the large conference hall. Ryu turned his head to scan the room, hoping to track the CFO.

"What exactly are you proposing?" Ryu asked as he dressed down the chairman with a sharp judgmental glance.

"There is a scientist who will be here later today seeking funding for research. The CEO intends to support him. I want you to offer him more money toward more aggressive efforts."

"Why can't you do this yourself?" Ryu said with a single eyebrow raised.

"Well, the research he is doing is...vital. The problem is that important projects like this take time through normal means. Time we don't necessarily have. If he were to receive money from a separate donor, he might be willing to expedite his research."

"How do you know this? What is he working on?"

"We all have our sources. Let's just say Dr. Ichikawa is very sloppy with his computer security. And we have history. His colleague Dr. Hawkins is the key to all of this, in my opinion. She is quite brilliant and building a powerful algorithm. And I intend for you to get it for me. You may even need to take her in the process." The aged face of the chairman conveyed wisdom and cunning. Part of Ryu started to like him. The other part knew not to trust him. Ryu realized he needed to keep the chairman close.

"What's in this for me?" Ryu asked.

"What do you want?"

"I want the *Kuroshio Maru*. It's a ship in Toyotomi's dying fleet. I need it for...shipping packages."

"That can be arranged within reason. The ships must maintain their current schedules. You must let me know where you need the ship to go, and I will confirm. This is, of course, if the CFO decides to keep them. Rumor has it he intends to sell them all."

"I have a feeling he is about to change his mind."

"So, it's agreed then. You will help me fund Dr. Ichikawa and his work, and you will get access to the *Kuroshio Maru*. I will have an associate at Toyotomi operate as an intermediate for you, to further obfuscate the deal with Dr. Ichikawa. That way, he won't make the immediate association with you personally...and will never know I am involved at all." The round man smiled, exposing his gray, tea-stained teeth.

"Is there anything else I should know about this Dr. Ichikawa?" Ryu asked.

The chairman let out a nervous laugh. "No. Is there anything I should know about how you want to use the *Kuroshio Maru*?"

"No."

"If this arrangement works out well, perhaps we can find other work for you, Tanigawa-san."

In that one short interaction, Ryu usurped control of the ship he coveted, the *Kuroshio Maru*, and also the Japanese Tokugawa-Kai syndicate gained control of a global drug smuggling and human trafficking operation. And all of this was under the cover of the well-respected Toyotomi Industries' legitimate logistics division.

That all changed when, through his own efforts with Division 121, Ryu discovered the God Algorithm, the serum, and its powerful potential. He also discovered the real reason the Chinese chairman wanted Dr. Hawkins—the chairman was a control freak. Dr. Hawkins represented the greatest asset he could never control: the future.

It seemed that the gods of the old world had decided to die at last, and Ryu would usher in the future filled with new deities, modern gods living on the top of Mount Baekdu, the birthplace of the Dear Leader.

When an unseasonably early typhoon pushed north toward the Korean Peninsula, Ryu knew his time had come. Coordinating via couriers and indirect contacts, Ryu contacted the chairman to move the ship north instead of south along its regular route. Once the boat left port, the chairman would have no way of stopping it, especially with Ryu and four of his men on board to take over the bridge if need be.

Ryu awoke many hours later. The sounds of movement in the passageway and the intermingling of Chinese and Japanese voices ripped him from his overdue slumber. He looked at the clock—nearly 8 p.m. Only hours remained between now and the death of the *Kuroshio Maru*. Typhoon Nabi seemed like way too perfect an opportunity for Ryu to steal or scuttle the ship and disappear in its wake. If there could be any more significant indicator sealing Ryu's victory, he didn't see it.

Ryu arose, dressed, and stepped into the passageway to find food in the galley. Rounding one of the many corners to the upper deck, he heard a clang and arguing voices. The Chinese banter caused him to pause. He held his position and listened as a familiar clicking of metal echoed through the passageway. Ryu knew that sound. It was a distinct click and clack he heard day in and day out growing up in Korea. He became particularly familiar with it during his training with Special Operations.

It was the sound of a bolt driving forward on an AK-47—a weapon that Ryu knew should not be on board this vessel. It seemed the chairman had plans of his own.

CHAPTER 47

A Fool's Errand

NAKASHIBETSU, HOKKAIDO, JAPAN

Roughly 400 kilometers east of Sapporo, on the island of Hokkaido, the tiny town of Nakashibetsu is home to the easternmost and northernmost airport in all of Japan. The area of roughly 24,000 people wouldn't ring a bell with most Japanese. Rural areas like this are called "*inaka*," or the countryside. This particular town is little more than farmers, ranchers, and fishermen living a quiet existence away from the hustle and drama of modern Japan.

So, when a white man with fiery red hair stepped off a small plane at Nakashibetsu Airport, locals took notice. Wearing the civilian uniform of his shooter counterparts, Sparks strolled through the minuscule terminal dressed in a flannel shirt with a large Garmin watch on his wrist. He had blue jeans and brown Merrell hiking boots on.

Everything about Sparks looked foreign, and against the kind nature of the local Japanese, the few people that happened to be at the airport gawked at the muscular white man. Sparks strutted over to baggage claim where something more peculiar waited for him.

Sparks stood at the baggage claim with a black backpack carrying a day's worth of clothes. His luggage was about to arrive, and with it, a lot of confused glances from the audience of native Japanese craning their necks to see what this white man was doing in their sleepy village.

"Dis is a pen," a little Japanese boy said, pointing to Sparks as he walked by. Sparks, unaware that all Japanese children say this to foreigners as it is the first English phrase they are taught in schools, raised an eyebrow.

"Thanks for the tip," he replied.

Sparks saw an attendant holding a sign next to the baggage claim and the words "oversize luggage" written in English.

That's definitely me, Sparks thought.

"*Davidson-san desu ka?*" the attendant asked.

"You got 'im," Sparks replied.

The attendant gestured behind him, where several men struggled to slide two very long gray Pelican cases.

"Oh, I got this," Sparks said. He walked over and grabbed the cases, each of which weighed around 150 pounds. Sparks grabbed them by the handles on the side and picked them up, one in each arm.

The struggling skycaps' jaws dropped. The cases looked large enough to hold a body inside. From the looks on their faces, that was what they were thinking. The sight of Sparks picking them up, one with each hand, and lugging them across the airport baffled the onlookers.

Sparks immediately recognized a familiar face.

Voodoo jogged over to Sparks with a huge grin. Naomi followed shortly behind.

"Brah! That was one heck of a trip!" Sparks started.

"I'm so glad you made it on time. Sorry we're a bit late. We need to hurry. I can update you on the ride out. Did you have any trouble at customs?" Voodoo asked.

"*O ki no doku sama*," an older Japanese police officer said to Sparks as he passed by.

"I'm keen on duck and salmon to you too!" Sparks replied to the officer with a wave before turning to Voodoo. "People have been saying that to me everywhere I go. Is that some kind of greeting here?" Sparks asked.

"They think those are coffins," Voodoo whispered to Sparks, leaning sideways to muffle his voice. "Pretend to be sad. We don't need this guy's attention."

Sparks pretended to whimper.

"Man, Steve was such a good dude. I can't believe he's gone," Sparks said with a sniffle.

"Who is Steve?" Naomi asked.

"I said pretend to be sad not...never mind," Voodoo reprimanded.

"*Arigato gozaimasu*," Naomi thanked the officer for his condolences. She gave a humble bow. The officer bowed in return. The officer drew closer, obviously curious about the foreigners at his isolated country terminal. Just then, a Toyota truck pulled up, and Stu jumped out. The officer lurched back at the sight of the giant, his mouth agape.

"What's up, burrito man?" Stu said as he grabbed the coffin-like cases and slung them into the bed of the pickup truck. The officer remained motionless in the background as the foreigners carried on with their business.

"'Sup, man?" Sparks replied to Stu before turning back to Voodoo. "So, what's going on?"

Voodoo put his arm around his protégé. "International conspiracies, hacking, espionage, murder, a hostage crisis."

"Oh, so...the usual."

• • •

A microconvoy of two Toyota Hiluxes found a small, abandoned fishing home beside Highway 87. Mount Iou towered to the west on the Shiretoko Peninsula as they pulled over one hour north of Nakashibetsu in the tiny town of Rausu.

"Holy crap, Voodoo. That's a lot to process," Sparks said as he stepped out of the truck, the hour-long drive giving them ample time to go over all the intel and the dire circumstances hanging in the balance.

Doors slammed behind him as the headlights of the trucks darkened. Voodoo walked from the driver's side of the vehicle, where Naomi, Stu, and Frisco rallied around them.

"This sounds like a dead hooker moment," Sparks said. Stu immediately slapped Sparks across his shoulder with the back of his hand.

"That's the smartest thing I've ever heard you say, Sparks," Stu said with encouragement. The silhouette of Naomi shook its head in disapproval.

"I'm not saying you have to come with us, Sparks. I've put you in a tight spot as it is by just bringing the gear under pretenses," Voodoo said.

"What excuse did you use to bring the BIB out here anyway?" Frisco asked.

"I told our leadership that we're conducting joint training operations with the Japanese Self-Defense Force, and our chain of command didn't seem to care because they knew Voodoo was out here already."

"That's not entirely untrue," Frisco replied. "They are indirectly supporting us in this operation." Frisco looked back toward the trailer attached to the Hilux, where a rigid hull inflatable boat (RHIB) sat on top of a trailer.

"Explain that to me again," Sparks said. "Where does that gear come from?"

"Captain Tanaka, the SAT guy, was former Japanese SOF. He reached out to some of his buddies stationed up here, and they were able to find some equipment that was about to be DRMO'd."

"DRMO'd?" Naomi asked.

"Defense Reutilization Management Order. It's how the military throws things out," Sparks clarified.

"Like I said, Sparks, you don't have to come with us. You can very well stay here on the beach with Naomi and—"

"Are you kidding me, Voodoo?! You're about to engage in a unilateral operation on disputed territory to conduct a hostage rescue based on dreams you had after being connected to the internet! There's no way you're keeping me from going. I'll swim behind the boat if I have to!"

"I like this kid more and more," Stu said, his huge hand smothering Sparks's shoulder in approval.

"Right. So, the pucker factor is gonna be pretty high on this one. I get it. What did we get from our friends in the Japanese military?" Sparks asked.

Frisco reported, "RHIB, three M4s, magazines, smoke grenades, M240 with enough ammunition to support."

"Roger that. How much extra ammo do we have? I need to start prepping the—"

"Way ahead of you, Sparks," Voodoo interrupted. "We've already disassembled several dozen bullets and removed the gunpowder so we can load them onto the drone payloads."

"Sweet. That saves us a bunch of time. There was no way I was even gonna try bringing the BIB through customs with drones carrying explosives, even if they're only gunpowder."

"What kind of payloads did you bring?" Frisco asked.

"Let's get the birds ready, and we can discuss."

The small team broke apart and set to the task of preparing their equipment. Frisco and Stu found a small put-in for the boat while Sparks and Voodoo pulled out the coffin cases and assembled the Business-in-a-Box.

The electric, fixed-wing vertical takeoff and landing (eVTOL) aircraft slid together in a matter of minutes. Four small quadcopter drones attached upside down to a payload bay underneath the plane where landing struts kept them from scraping the ground.

The eVTOL aircraft had four motors for vertical flight and a push motor in the back to propel it forward. This allowed the aircraft to launch from any location that could support its wingspan, then accelerate to eighty miles per hour at up to 15,000 feet.

Voodoo pulled two of the quadcopters aside and packed gunpowder into payloads that attached to the front.

"I took the liberty of renaming the drones," Sparks said to Voodoo. "I felt inspired after doing a little study of Japan."

"What did you name them?"

"I kinda want it to be a surprise. It'll be pretty obvious when you see it displayed in your HUD," Sparks said.

"That reminds me. Did you bring contact lenses for everyone?"

"'Did I bring contact lenses?' he asks. Who do you think you're talking to, Voodoo? Of course I did. Check the back of that case."

Voodoo opened a second compartment in the Pelican case to find a treasure trove of technical gear.

The sound of a 350-horsepower engine motored on the water behind them as Voodoo dug through the kit. The lack of lunar illumination intensified the darkness as Stu steered the boat up to an old wooden dock. Frisco moored the watercraft to a cleat. His boots thumped on the dock as he and Stu headed over to meet Voodoo, Sparks, and Naomi.

"Alright, I need to go over some of this gear with you guys," Sparks started. He stepped over to the compartment that Voodoo opened and began digging through gear and handing it out. "First off, each of you is given a phone. The phone case allows you to strap it to your chest, but you shouldn't need to look at the screen because you'll be wearing these."

Sparks turned on the light from his phone and illuminated a pair of contact lenses, a watch-like device, and clear eye protection. Another item caught Stu's attention.

"Is that a log of dip?!" Stu asked with palpable excitement. "If it's wintergreen, you're in the club, bro."

"'Is it wintergreen?' the chief asks. Of course, dude," Sparks replied as he grabbed the log, removed a can of chewing tobacco, and handed it to Stu.

Stu immediately slapped his index finger against the top of the can and unscrewed it, ripping the seal before removing a hefty pinch. Even in the darkness, everyone could feel Stu's joy. Sparks looked over at Voodoo and pumped his eyebrows.

"I see you've taught this one well," Frisco said to Voodoo approvingly.

"Moving on. The contact lenses and the eye pro look redundant, but they're not. The contact lenses display a monochromatic image. You'll receive basic input via that interface. The watch allows you to control the drones or applications on your phone through gestures. The glasses have a multispectral camera attached to them as well as a supplemental HUD in case you need it. They're also IP 68, so you should be able to get them wet."

"Don't freak out about any of this," Voodoo chimed in. "Sparks and I will be controlling the drones and the payloads. We just need to get you accustomed to using the menu so you can pull the video feeds from the main aircraft. Let us support you in whatever you need."

Frisco and Stu inspected the contact lens case.

"What's the deal with this camera you told us about?" Stu asked.

"Oh, the multispectral camera. It allows you to see outside of visual light ranges. This will come in handy if we drop one of the White Dwarfs," Sparks said.

"Like the star?" Naomi asked.

"Exactly. A super bright ball of light we built at the Directorate. Nonlethal but debilitating. If we decide to drop one of those, all you have to do is close your eyes really tightly. The camera will automatically adapt and project an image on your eye that will allow you to see in any spectrum even if your eyes are closed."

"This is insane," Frisco said to himself as he inspected the glasses.

"This will all be connected via LTE to the eVTOL bird, which will be supplying us comms relay like a flying cell tower."

"Got it," Frisco said. "I think we need to go over actions on the objective. Voodoo, run it by us one more time based on your dreams."

"Right." Voodoo pulled out his last girlfriend. The map application on the phone illuminated everyone's faces as Voodoo slid his finger across the screen.

"We're twenty kilometers from Kunashir Island. It's a straight shot from where we are right here to this beach. On a clear day we would actually be able to see it from the mountains behind us." Voodoo pointed to a crescent-shaped formation of white sand. "The dream showed me we need to be right along the edge of this sand at the tree line."

Alongside the beach, grass and brush graduated to a dense forest. Thousands of years of isolation created dense thickets and forests with little human intervention. Just north of that forest, a road traversed the island. On the opposite side, a small fishing and logistics town hugged the Pacific Ocean.

"We were also able to get a bit of intel from our Japanese friends," Frisco said as he pointed to the town. "There's a garrison of Russian soldiers stationed there. Being contested land, this area holds strategic importance for Russia. The only entrance from the Sea of Okhotsk and Vladivostok is straight through these islands. The Japanese have had these waterways monitored with sensors ever since the Cold War. In response, the Russians have increased their presence as well."

"So, we have to worry about the Russians now too?" Naomi asked.

"Well, I saw four armies battling on the beach. We're one. The Japanese aren't playing, so they're out. That leaves the Russians, the North Koreans—"

"And the Chinese," Sparks said with realization and concern.

"Yeah. The Chinese have decided to come to play too. I'm not sure exactly how, though. I just know they're going to be there."

Voodoo paused as he focused in on a specific location near the forest, fifty meters from the water's edge.

"This is a special reconnaissance mission. Our goal is to infil to this location near the beach. From there, we'll collect intelligence via our assets with the BIB. The eVTOL aircraft will give us standoff surveillance until we need to go kinetic with the smaller drones. I also have some other ones we'll be carrying on our backs.

"Here is what I know—we stay there and wait until we get the right signal, at that moment we move, save Dr. Hawkins, and boogie on back to the RHIB for exfil. Quick snatch and grab."

"Like a bank heist," Sparks added.

"Yes. Except, instead of money, it is my friend." It was hard to ignore the urgency in Naomi's voice. Everyone's silhouette nodded. The small rocks of the parking lot crunched under Stu's feet as he adjusted his weight to look more carefully at the map.

"So, we infil, conduct some recon, create a diversion, then bolt the second we find her. Sounds basic enough, right? Frisco and I have already planned the ingress and egress routes. Assuming the reported sea state and map imagery are accurate, we should be good. Exfil is gonna be a pain in the ass if we get bogged down in a firefight. Hopefully, we can create a large enough diversion to keep the other dudes focused on each other for us to vanish."

"Leave the diversions up to Sparks and me," Voodoo said.

"Roger that," said Frisco.

"Check," affirmed Stu. "I'll be running with the M240. Frisco's the ground force commander, Voodoo's running lead navigation, and Sparks, you're coordinating the air assets and intel. You'll also be the backup taxi driver in case something happens to Frisco or me, assuming you can drive a RHIB."

"Good to go," Sparks replied.

Sparks quickly changed clothes to match the other three. They dressed in black military fatigues they received from the SAT teams with woodland camouflage H-gear that strapped across their chest. The harness carried black plastic magazines called "p-mags" full of 5.56 ammunition or drums of 7.62 bullets for Stu's enormous M240 machine gun. Small cases strapped to their chests held their cell phones.

Unlike any mission they had ever been on, they were not carrying body armor or helmets to protect them. There was no quick reaction force standing by in case of an emergency. No Black Hawk helicopters, A-10 Warthogs, AC-130 gunships supplying air support. They were four rogue operators, fighting against their better judgment, but fighting for something greater than themselves.

The early summer air grew crisp as the mild waves pawed at the pebbles of the beach, and the RHIB rolled as it waited on the pier. Frisco and Stu walked over to the boat as Sparks and Voodoo conducted final flight preparation on the BIB before following them over.

Voodoo handed Naomi a phone from the BIB.

"You can use this to track our position via satellite. You'll also be able to pull video from the main bird, see blue dots for our position, and you'll be able to see our communications via text. You'll know when we're on our way back. You're the closest thing we have to reinforcements."

Naomi nodded, took the phone, and held it close to her as she addressed each member of the team. She hugged them in an act of affection contrary to her reserved nature. Naomi embraced Frisco and Sparks first. Then the giant knelt and swallowed the little lady in his arms as she kissed her protector lightly on the cheek.

Finally, she turned to Voodoo.

"Bring back my friend," she started. "But bring all of *your* friends back as well." Her cheek was chilled by the night air, aside from the warm tears that pressed against Voodoo as she hugged him.

They boarded the RHIB and freed the boat from the dock. Moments later, the four men were little more than a dark blur against the undulating water that seemed to extend out into the stars themselves.

Suddenly, the whirring of propellers sliced the air as the vertical motors on the eVTOL aircraft initiated. Like a swarm of bees, the engines increased in speed with a loud buzz until they created enough lift to usher the plane to the sky. There were no blinking lights to indicate heading or orientation. The aircraft was merely a lone zephyr, blindly climbing to the heavens.

Below it, the 350-horsepower outboard motor of the RHIB throttled, and the four men embarked on fate's errand. Naomi walked back to the trucks and leaned against the side of the Hilux, hugging herself. She rubbed her arms and waved to the unknown in one last gesture of hope, like a yellow ribbon praying for a safe return. Beyond, the four men rushed headlong into uncharted territory. Their faith and loyalty anchored only in the dreams of a friend...to save the life of a stranger.

CHAPTER 48

No Ordinary Seaman

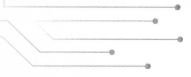

43.545221, 145.619022
SOMEWHERE NEAR HOKKAIDO, JAPAN

Ryu took a deep breath. If Toyotomi crew members carried weapons, that meant all of the Chinese might be plants working for the chairman. Ryu needed to know their numbers, and only the captain on the bridge had that information.

It didn't take long for Ryu to conduct a personnel muster of those loyal to him. Most of the *Anmoku-dan* remained in Tokyo to destroy the pachinko parlor. He had only four men on board, including Ryu, which meant five men against a crew of armed Chinese. At the time they'd departed, he felt four men were enough for what lay ahead. Now it appeared he might be outnumbered ten to one. Knowing the chairman and his connections, these men were most likely People's Liberation Army Navy commandos. They called themselves the "Sea Dragons," if Ryu remembered correctly.

Gunmetal clanked as bolts slid shut, followed by cases clipping closed. Outside the room in the passageway, Ryu opted to pretend he heard nothing. He glanced in the room as he passed by only to see several men sitting on a black case snacking on squid chips and watching the most recent iteration of *Wolf Warrior*, China's uber-patriotic equivalent of *Rambo*.

Ryu's boots gripped the grating of the ladder and squeaked on the tile floor as he headed to the bridge. Instead of the captain, Ryu found the XO, an original Toyotomi employee, manning the helm along with two other merchant marines.

"I need a copy of the ship's manifest," he ordered in greeting. The XO turned to see Ryu. He slid out of the captain's chair, pulled up a clipboard, and thumbed through the papers. He rolled several over the top of the clipboard and handed it to Ryu.

Ryu ran his fingers along the names and assessed the numbers. Fifty personnel—almost all Chinese. Ryu's men, of course, were not annotated.

"It says here that there are nearly forty personnel on this ship with Chinese names. Is that correct?"

"Yes, sir. Some of the men are capable seamen while others...I'm not even sure why they're here."

"Who are the ones we can rely on?" Ryu asked, pecking the clipboard with his first two fingers.

"Well, uh, if you're asking what their skills are, they are listed on the manifest."

Ryu scanned the occupational specialties marked on the manifest and quickly identified a pattern. There seemed to be an extremely high number of individuals labeled "OS."

"What is this?"

"Oh, that stands for ordinary seaman. They're all new to the merchant marine occupation. It's an entry-level position," the XO said.

Ryu counted nearly twenty names labeled OS.

"Where are their berthing assignments?"

"They're assigned to the forward berthing. Ordinary seaman is the lowest-paid rank on the ship."

Ryu had the information he needed. Twenty potential Sea Dragons slithered on his vessel on the chairman's orders, standing by to abduct Ryu's cargo as soon as they received the word.

Ryu knew what *he* would do in this situation if he were the chairman. *He* would extract Dr. Hawkins, kill everyone else on board, and scuttle the ship. Typhoon Nabi would do the rest. The chairman would walk away with Dr. Hawkins, and the algorithm, and Ryu would be removed from the equation as if he were never there. This would be accurate because the man named Ryu Tanigawa never really existed in the first place.

That also meant the chairman planned to extract Dr. Hawkins during the transport, not upon docking, which meant another ship may very well be on its way.

Ryu needed to move quickly.

Ryu slipped out of the bridge and headed aft. The vessel intended to arrive at the target location off the Kuril Islands near 1 a.m. Whatever the chairman planned, it would need to take place soon; otherwise, the chairman would lose his advantage.

Near the cargo hold of the ship, Ryu found one of his men standing guard.

"Gather the other men and meet me here," he ordered.

Within moments Ryu's four men stood assembled below deck; the light of the dark subcompartment of the vessel canvassed them in a red glow.

"At least twenty of the men on board this ship are Chinese special operators," Ryu started. "I don't know what they plan. I can guarantee you they have no intention for us to arrive at our destination."

"What do you want us to do?" one of the men asked.

"How are we supposed to know which twenty out of the fifty crew on board this ship?" said another.

"We're not. There's only one way to solve this. Gather your gear. Grab the package out of the cargo hold and get to the bridge."

"*Arassubnida*," they replied collectively. The cluster of bodies burst, seeping into various compartments of the ship to carry out their orders.

Ryu returned to his stateroom. The satellite equipment and computers were no longer necessary now that he had destroyed the pachinko parlor. There were only a few items that Ryu needed—the serum and the remains of Kenzo Ichikawa being the priority. Of course, these also required careful handling and needed to be refrigerated.

You know what has to be done, the voice said in his mind. *You don't know which twenty are the ones you can't trust...so you must kill all of them.*

The flavor of straw filled his mouth.

Ryu grabbed a garbage bag and stuffed Dr. Hawkins's computer inside, then tore the hard drive of his computer tower out. He opened the refrigerator and looked at the contents. A bowling ball–shaped object wrapped in plastic rested beside two vials of blood. He cogitated, the cold air of the freezer wafting out onto his forearm.

There's a refrigerator on the bridge. You have to go there anyway, the voice advised knowingly.

Ryu grabbed the object and the vials and stuffed them into the garbage bag. He wrapped the contents tightly before applying a healthy amount of duct tape to seal it shut.

Ryu pulled out a black duffel bag from his locker and shoved the contents inside before zipping it shut. Slinging the bag over his back, he bent over and reached under the rack he slept on and retrieved his final items—a long jingum and a North Korean Type 70 pistol.

Similar to the more famous Walther PPK brandished by famous British spies, the North Korean weapon fit well in Ryu's calloused hands. He stuffed the gun into his pocket and placed the sword inside the duffel bag, situating the handle in such a way to make it accessible but unseen.

Ryu gave one last glance at his stateroom before turning back toward the passageway. A Chinese crew member stood just outside, staring at him.

Ryu's black eyes inspected the man. The Chinese sailor stood as if his feet were bolted to the deck plates. The sailor had already seen too much.

Let it begin, the voice said.

At first, there was silence, two men locked in an uncomfortable moment between life and death.

And then there was death.

In one fluid motion, Ryu drew his sword and pierced straight through the man's chest, pinning him against the bulkhead. In a wrenching twist, Ryu extracted the weapon. Gravity flopped the body into his stateroom. Blood from the man's severed aorta puddled on the ground. Ryu grabbed the man's clothes near the calves and flipped the legs into his room and closed the door behind him. Ryu sheathed his sword back in the bag. After a quick cursory check in each direction, Ryu made his way back down to Dr. Hawkins's cell.

Quickly! Get the scientist to the bridge. Take control of the ship, the voice instructed.

Below deck, his four men stood waiting with their gear.

"Grab her. Let's move," Ryu ordered.

The cell door creaked open. Even from five meters away, the pungent odor invaded Ryu's nostrils. He turned away to survey the approach for any would-be attackers as he evaded the scent.

"Where are we going?! Ow, let go of my arm! How many times do I have to tell you!" A hard slap reverberated from her cell. Dr. Hawkins shut her mouth.

"Let's go," Ryu said as he took point.

Tight quarters. Stay in close quarters as long as possible. Do not go into the open. Use your sword.

Guiding along the engineering section, then near the infirmary, around the galley, Ryu led his men. Dr. Hawkins submissively dragged her feet between the two men carrying her. Faking or weak, she wasn't running her mouth or fighting back. Not yet at least.

Ryu entered a long passageway. On the other end, a supposed ordinary seaman waved his right hand up and down, gesturing to someone inside a room beside him to come out.

Ryu sprinted forward.

The ordinary seaman stepped aside, and a Sea Dragon with an AK-74 burst out of the room ready for a fight.

Ryu had already bridged the gap. A downward slice relieved the AK-74–wielding Sea Dragon of his hands; an upward slice slit his throat.

With a horizontal stab, Ryu thrust the angular tip of his sword into the ordinary seaman's mouth.

Behind him, swords slid from their sheaths. Ryu's men stood ready to meet their enemy in close-quarters combat.

Sea Dragons dressed in the blue uniforms of Toyotomi sailors poured into the passageway. Ryu slashed and stabbed his way forward, his men slaughtering behind him. There wasn't enough time for the Sea Dragons to retrieve their weapons before Ryu was upon them, lightning-fast flurries of his blade filleting skin and severing arteries. The metallic scent of fresh blood filled the air in squirts and sprays. Heavy droplets splattered throughout the passageway.

Soon ten bodies lay bleeding out on the passageway as Ryu pressed on. His hapkido- and Tae Kwon Do–trained team of assassins in tow, he prepared to excise vengeance on anyone else who dared stand in their way.

Ryu and his men arrived at the bridge. Still manning the helm as part of his watch, the XO dropped his jaw in horror as Ryu and his four men flooded the room, fresh blood covering their clothes.

"What on earth happened? And who is that woman—"

Ryu extended his arm and the XO stopped speaking. Inches away from the XO's face, the razor-sharp jingum cast a blood-speckled sheen across the bridge. The XO's eyes widened.

"Lock the doors!" Ryu ordered.

Ryu's men immediately slammed the doors behind them. "Call the captain and tell him to get up here now. Do *not* alarm him."

The XO held a phone up in his shaking hand, ready to call, but stopped. An incoming call had just blinked on.

Hesitantly, the XO answered then said, "It's for you."

Ryu held the phone up to his ear.

"This wasn't the plan, Tanigawa-san," the chairman said calmly. "You're on the wrong side of Kunashir Island."

"I have a delivery to make."

"Not until I get what I want."

"I will kill her if you interfere. I know everything about what she was working on."

There was a pause on the line.

"Then I regret what comes next," the chairman said. "Her gift is now a risk. As are you."

The line went dead.

Ryu nodded to his men, who dropped Dr. Hawkins onto the floor of the bridge and drew weapons from their bags.

"Load and make ready for a gunfight. Our countrymen will be here soon enough."

CHAPTER 49
Special Reconnaissance

RAUSU, HOKKAIDO, JAPAN

Every time Voodoo put on his uniform, he knew a moment like this would come—a moment when circumstance, and the severity of the outcome, were not respecters of men. His late wife asked him once if he ever second-guessed his decisions. She specifically wondered if he was ever afraid when he gripped a fast rope and stepped out of a helicopter, knowing that his grip was the only thing keeping him from a quick sixty-foot descent to death.

"When you're standing on the helo, and it's your turn to grab the fast rope, that's not the moment for thought. That's not the moment to question how you got there. That's the moment to grab the line and go," Voodoo told her.

The rigid bow of the boat punched through the peaks and troughs of the waves. Frisco manned the helm while Voodoo, Sparks, and Stu crouched behind the inflatable tubes, the barrels of their rifles aimed at the growing expanse of dark water.

There was no moment of doubt, no second thoughts. All four held their weapons, gritted their teeth, and raced headlong in search of their fate.

Behind them, the lights of the Shiretoko Peninsula lined the water below a large mountain. The distance grew between their small craft and the settlement of Rausu, a town that derived its name from the Ainu, the indigenous people of Hokkaido.

The tiny town's name comes from the Ainu word "rausi," which means "the place of men with beast-like spirit." Tonight, that same spirit manifested itself on the dark waters as the four men catapulted themselves onward.

"I still can't believe you got a microwave kill," Sparks said to Voodoo from behind him, just loud enough for Frisco and Stu to hear. "Damn, that's almost as cool as that dude that got a toaster kill."

"That was me," Stu admitted as he crouched near the bow of the boat, pointing his M240 skyward.

"What! You're the guy that got a toaster kill? You've gotta tell me the whole story," Sparks said like some kind of shooter fanboy.

"My gun jammed, the other guy's gun jammed too, so I grabbed the first thing I could see. There happened to be a toaster right there in the kitchen, so I hit the dude with it. And then he died."

"That's the coolest story I've ever heard." Sparks leaned in close to Voodoo and whispered, "Just between us girls, Stu's kinda lacking in the dramatic storytelling skills, isn't he?"

Voodoo laughed.

"I have a critical question to ask," Sparks continued. "When we find Dr. Hawkins, what are you gonna say? I've already picked out a line."

"Here we go..." Voodoo said like a verbal eye roll.

"Just asking. What's the best line? I'm gonna say, 'Uber for Dr. Hawkins?'"

"That's terrible," Voodoo replied. "You've gotta come up with something better than that!"

"Top it then."

"Welcome to Fantasy Island!" Frisco tried.

"Boo!" Sparks heckled. "Whatcha got, Voodoo?"

"Is that a ship?"

"That's stupid—"

"Shut up! Look!" Voodoo pointed, quickly realizing the darkness limited their ability to see his hand.

Voodoo twisted his left wrist with a quick snapping motion, and menu options appeared in the corner of his eye in a dim white augmented reality display. Voodoo toggled the menu and enabled the shared augmented reality features. In that instant, the same list appeared on the screen of every team member.

"Look up, and you'll see the drone," he instructed. Everyone shifted their gaze upward and saw a blue box overlayed on a moving object in the starry sky. Voodoo toggled the options, and four more boxes appeared, each representing the drones attached to the bottom of the fixed-wing aircraft. With another adjustment, labels appeared under the boxes with the names Hachiman, Amaterasu, Apollo, Raijin, and Thor.

"Nice touch, Sparks," Voodoo said.

"I thought you'd like that. You can tell what the drone does based on the name of the god. Simple as that." Even in the darkness, Voodoo could feel how pleased Sparks was with himself.

Voodoo toggled the menu and selected Hachiman, the god of war, the eVTOL mothership hovering in orbit above at 7,000 feet. The infrared camera feed of Hachiman appeared in everyone's heads-up display as a monochromatic streaming video in the lower right corner of their eyes.

"What the hell is a 'hachi-man'?" Stu asked; the corn-fed, white giant sounded particularly twangy.

Voodoo chuckled. "Japanese god of war. Supposedly the deity that brought the kamikaze, or divine wind, that saved Japan from the Mongol invasion in the thirteenth century. Kinda like the Japanese version of Mars."

"Yeah, and apparently his symbol is a dove, a winged messenger that's supposed to bring the end of war," Sparks said, still pleased as punch.

Voodoo imagined the egrets flying along the Colorado River, guiding the rafts to safety, and the cranes circling the skies in his dream.

"I hope that's true. Sure does feel like we're about to start a war tonight and not end one," Frisco said.

"We'll find out soon enough," Voodoo said as he took manual control of the gimbaled camera and slew the look angle, searching for the ship he thought he saw in the distance. Less than eight kilometers north, he found a large cargo ship limping along in the water. The infrared lens keyed in on disparities that presented heat in white.

"Is that where she is?" Frisco asked, holding the RHIB steady while watching the video feed in his contact lens.

"For the time being. That will all change soon. We need to get to the beach."

Frisco increased the throttle and pushed the boat closer to thirty knots, smacking the waves as the RHIB pushed on toward Kunashir Island.

Sparks said, "Alright guys, I need all of you to turn on the cameras on your glasses just like I showed you. I want to make sure you're all comfortable with it because it's the closest thing we have to night vision."

They all toggled a switch on their glasses, and a separate video feed popped into focus. The video was black and white but comparable to a degraded variant of the modern white phosphor NODs they would typically wear on a mission like this.

Tethered via the LTE network, with his teammates' multispectral cameras now active on their glasses, Voodoo could select their feeds and see through the cameras on other people's heads. It had a disembodying effect like being able to see through someone else's eyes.

"Good. It looks like everyone is up. Remember, if we choose to drop one of the White Dwarf payloads, be sure to close your eyes. The multispectral camera will immediately adapt to the brightness."

"We're getting close, gents. Time to get bro-fessional. Button it up and stand by." Frisco eased up on the throttle, and the boat slowed.

Creeping closer, the flat beach of Kunashir Island extended out like a sleeping giant. Gentle waves lapped up onto the shore in a convenient slack tide, and Frisco timed the boat to match it, pacing with the flow to drive the RHIB onto the beach.

The boat scraped to a stop. Voodoo, Sparks, and Stu leaped into the shallow water and onto the dry sand. The three took a knee and created a small arrow with Stu in the center with his M240. They scanned the perimeter with the barrels of their rifles, searching for the glow of heat signatures.

Stu carried an M240: a massive fifty-inch-long, twenty-five-pound gun with a twenty-four-inch barrel that is generally used as a crew-served weapon mounted on vehicles. As Voodoo followed Stu onto the beach with his six-pound, fourteen-inch-barreled M4, he realized that, for the first time since he met Stu, Stu was finally carrying a weapon proportional to his size. Voodoo remembered how old-school shooters used to take the M240 into combat, and only the biggest guys in the platoon were given the task. They were even called "pig gunners" because of the weight of the enormous weapon.

Frisco followed behind, pulling a rope and an anchor to dig into the beach to hold the RHIB in place. Frisco dug the anchor into the sand and tested the resistance on the line. Even in the light waves, the boat tussled and drifted left and right. If they pulled the raft too far onto the beach, they risked being unable to get into the water quickly during the rescue, but not enough anchorage and they risked having no means of escape awaiting them when they returned.

Frisco watched the RHIB for only a moment before making an executive decision. He tapped Sparks on the shoulder as he knelt beside him.

"Sparks, I don't trust leaving the boat here. I don't like this at all, but we stand a much better chance if someone stays with the craft."

Without a word, Sparks turned and grabbed the anchor, coiled the line, and pushed the RHIB back in the water before hefting his muscular frame on board. In seconds the boat was moving slowly back out to sea until sharply turning about and cruising to the open water.

Frisco positioned himself at the tip of the three-man spear and gave a knife-hand gesture to move out. Voodoo stood first, followed by Stu, each covering a field of fire to the left or right, scanning the beach and the tree line for potential threats.

Five kilometers remained between their target location and the amphibious infiltration point. They intended to move north, parallel to a dirt road, keeping clear of two small homes most likely inhabited by Russian or Ainu fisherman. They planned to stay close to the forest, using the brush to hide their silhouettes. Once they reached their destination, they would hide in the grass and microterrain along the forest to conduct surveillance.

They clipped along at a light jog. Two kilometers in, they arrived at the first indigenous home. The lights were off, but Frisco's camera keyed in on a glowing object. He put up his left hand in a fist. Everyone stopped and picked a field of fire, left, right, or behind to scan their perimeter.

Frisco observed the house, checking for movement before recognizing the object in question. A dog.

Frisco pointed with his index and middle finger toward his own eyes and then forward, alerting them to keep their eyes out. In any other circumstance, a silent 9mm bullet would solve this problem. Tonight was a different story—they had no silencers. Camouflaging their movements and sounds was a given. Now they needed to mask their scent as well.

Frisco directed his fire team toward the water. They would be exposed on the beach, but the waves and sea spray would mask their scent in the northerly wind.

They quickly discovered the beach to be more compact in this section, and an eroded bank offered cover behind a terraced ledge of short grass. The hard-packed sand supported their feet as they picked up the pace.

The Milky Way scattered across the night sky as the three men sprinted north, the chill northerly wind calming their nerves as it brushed across their faces.

As they ran, Voodoo held his weapon at high combat-ready with the barrel diagonally across his chest. He occasionally let go with his left hand to manage the menu of the HUD.

Through the video, Voodoo noticed a deviation in the ship's course. The wake beside the vessel spread, and the bioluminescent light brightened in the aerated water behind it.

Twenty minutes later they nestled themselves near the forest edge. They dispersed with a three-meter spread. Stu was on the far right with Voodoo in the middle and Frisco on the left.

In the grass and natural deviations of the earth, they found concealment and enough elevation to view the upcoming battlefield. Stu oriented the M240 and his field of fire north, covering the road that traversed the island from the beach toward the Russian garrison. The coniferous trees behind them were an apparent blind spot, but they quickly realized that the dense brush, broken branches, and tinder made for a clamorous perimeter. Anyone using it to sneak up would make a ton of noise.

Frisco covered south while Voodoo focused on the beach to the west. They lay prone, and the moist earth cooled their bodies after the five-kilometer movement up the beach; five kilometers they knew they would have to run back down with three armies at their heels if everything went right.

If anything went wrong...well, no one had any intention of things going wrong.

"Radio check," Voodoo said, checking the cellular connectivity of the LTE tower flying above their head. Below the video feed from Hachiman in their HUD, text appeared, dictating the words next to Voodoo's call sign.

"Good check. How me, over?" Stu replied.

"Lima Charlie," Frisco replied in the universal term meaning "loud and clear." The words of each team member annotated on their augmented reality feed.

"Lickin' chicken," Sparks added from his position alone in the darkness.

"That ship is moving much faster now. Way too fast to be headed to a beach," Voodoo observed. The three men on the ground, and Sparks from the RHIB, watched the minicargo vessel increase in speed, cutting a heavy wake as it tore through the ocean.

"If they hit land moving that fast—"

"Whoever is on board is gonna get messed up," Voodoo finished. "But all we can do is wait."

Near the forest on Kunashir Island, the three men dissolved into their surroundings. Their bodies cooled, anticipation grew, and Voodoo's thoughts wandered back and forth between reality and the dreams he braved the night before. Behind them, the trees creaked in a choreographed routine thousands of years old. Liana vines gnarled up the birch and pine and protected the flank but also stood as shapeless sentinels, barricading against escape.

The three men lay still, observing. All four spent the next moments watching the video feed of the ship. It couldn't have been more than fifteen minutes before they could see the ship with their naked eyes, preparing to drive itself into the contested land of the southernmost Kuril Island. The 8,000-ton vessel barreled toward them like a juggernaut. Within minutes, they would witness the dramatic death of the Toyotomi Industries workhorse.

"Did anyone order a male stripper?" Stu asked suddenly.

Frisco and Voodoo lifted their heads from their weapons and looked over at Stu, completely confused.

"Now that's what you say when you save a hostage!" Sparks cheered.

CHAPTER 50
Leap of Faith

NEAR KUNASHIRSKIY STRAIT
KUNASHIR ISLAND

ap. Tap. Tap.
Without the red glow outside her cell or the rain pouring down around her, Taka-chan saw her captors clearly for the first time. Tattooed, muscular, and covered in blood, they stalked about, salivating like caged tigers hungry to eat their captors.

The mild lighting of the bridge navigation monitors and computer screens speckled the room in blues and greens. The sun set just after 10 p.m. and plunged the world outside their island of metal into darkness. In the ambient light, Taka-chan's eyes darted between her captors and the pitiful crew members trapped with them on the bridge, hoping to anticipate their intentions. After hearing the man on the phone wanted her dead, the smartest thing she could do was be compliant, at least for the time being.

Tap. Tap.

The man everyone called Dragon barked orders from the center of the bridge at the crewmember manning the helm. The ship pulled hard to starboard, and the entire vessel listed sharply. Taka-chan propped herself against the bulkhead, gripping metal components to keep herself from sliding across the deck. The men in black and the crew spread their feet, leaned forward, and braced themselves. Drops of blood rolled in rivulets across the tile floor.

For a moment, the clink of metal against the glass window on the bridge doors stopped. The ship leveled out. The crewman increased thrust from the cargo ship's engines and pressed all forward at twenty knots.

Taka-chan mustered the courage to peek through the window of the locked bridge door. On the opposite side, Chinese crew members, clad in blue overalls with the Toyotomi Industries logo embroidered over the left breast, menacingly hovered outside, rifles at the ready. With each rap on the glass, they taunted the Dragon, reminding him he had no escape—a piranha in a fish tank.

Tap. Tap. Tap.

Taka-chan, recently torn from her isolation, had no understanding of how these events transpired, or why the Chinese sailors wanted the Dragon dead. She only knew the contemptuous men on the opposite side of the glass windows had no idea who they were messing with.

• • •

The southernmost Kuril Island, Kunashir, shares the muddled climate of its neighbors to the north. Warm and humid winds from the south or a Siberian chill from the north normally lead to fog, drizzle, and overcast skies. The people of Kunashir say,

"If you want to know the weather for tomorrow, ask the day after tomorrow." Tonight, the sky remained uncharacteristically clear, empty.

Voodoo and his fire team lay prone in the microterrain surrounded by thick grass, moss, and the occasional pink sundew, a carnivorous plant. The cold beach lay in front of them to the west with the Sea of Okhotsk beyond.

"Kunashir" is an Ainu word that means "black island." The name seemed appropriate, as the behemoth cargo ship, named after the black current, sustained its advance toward the beachhead.

"Sparks, we're getting close to go time here, buddy. I think it's time we call in the reinforcements," Voodoo said quietly. Beside him, Stu slipped another pinch of tobacco into his lip.

"Say no more."

Voodoo looked skyward—the blue box designating Hachiman split. Up in the dim twilight, four quadcopters mounted upside down to the belly of their mother ship disconnected from their mounting bays. The pull of the earth gently freed them from the fixed-wing aircraft, and they fell. The internal accelerometers detected movement, while the magnetometers responded to the increase in gravity. The onboard computers activated the electronic speed controllers and the motors fired. The quadcopters, one by one, self-righted and commenced a controlled descent from 7,000 feet to the upcoming battlefield below.

Raijin, Thor, Amaterasu, and Apollo, appropriately named for their unique payloads, arrived on scene—soldiers in Hachiman's army descending as a divine wind.

Voodoo thought of his most recent dream while attached to the Xiphos network.

Old gods and new will battle on contested lands.

Well, there are the old gods, Voodoo thought. *Who are the new?*

Voodoo accessed the newly deployed drones through his HUD. He sent Amaterasu to loiter at several hundred feet above the road to the north, its infrared camera directed at the path approaching from the east. Voodoo pushed the video feed to Stu's contact lenses.

Voodoo sent Thor south along the beach, covering their avenue of escape, and assigned the video to Frisco. Finally, he placed Apollo and Raijin directly over the beach, standing by.

Each member of Voodoo's team now monitored their battlefield with multiple video feeds, literally controlling the gods in the sky with mere gestures of their hands.

We are the new gods, Voodoo realized in a sudden epiphany.

In front of them, the ship showed no sign of slowing, anticipating impact, or deviating from its path.

Just then, Voodoo noticed a variation in color in the water near the beach. Sloshing with the incoming waves, an amorphous object materialized in the water. At first, it appeared like a glitch in the video caused by cavitation, then it multiplied. One body became two, then three, followed by a fourth. Finally, Voodoo understood the apparitions before him.

"Gents, I think we've got company." Voodoo swiped and sent the feed to all four members of his fire team.

"Those look like..." Sparks said before trailing off.

"Those're frogmen," Frisco clarified. "This is a rendezvous point. They're about to conduct a pickup."

The four frogmen multiplied to eight. Frisco, Stu, and Voodoo slightly lifted their heads from the obscurity of the lush terrain to get a better view of the beach two hundred meters away.

One by one, the silhouettes of men emerged from the water. Through the infrared cameras above and the multispectral cameras on their HUDs below, Voodoo and his team identified eight amphibious assaulters. Donned in black wet suits, dive masks, and compact assault rifles, they formed a half circle, a U-shaped formation of gun barrels surveying the beach and distant tree line.

"I'm going to look for their transport," Sparks said over comms. Frisco, Stu, and Voodoo remained silent, motionless eyes peering through the salty sea air as the first visitors arrived at a soon-to-be hectic beach party.

An enormous wave rolled behind the frogmen as the Toyotomi ship made landfall. The frogmen on the beach sprinted inland and created a small cigar-shaped perimeter, standing by to welcome the leviathan ashore.

The bulbous bow of the *Kuroshio Maru* sliced through the water potentially for its last time as the sea surrendered to land. Voodoo expected some dramatic crash, an earth-shaking impact as the ship hit the island. The metal hull screeched against the crystalline and volcanic sand as the ship became one with the soft beach ahead of it.

In the absence of a dramatic crash, a bubble of a wave poured out across the beach like a microtide as the ship slid to an anticlimactic yet jerky halt.

For a moment, Voodoo was disappointed.

Then the firefight erupted.

• • •

From the floor of the bridge, Taka-chan studied the face of the man she knew as Dragon while the ship steamed forward. The chilled tile beneath her buttocks absorbed her body heat. Every time she adjusted her position, the cold floor against her skin reminded her not to get comfortable. Her moment was about to arrive.

Taka-chan's captors didn't waste time tying up her hands; her broken arm and anemic body constricted her enough. She did well to hide her actual strength. She bid her time until the right moment—the opportunity to run or fight.

Suddenly, the men around the room fell into a frenzy, yelling at each other with wide eyes toward the ship's bow. They hunkered down as if bracing for impact.

We're about to crash!

She didn't hear a huge thud. No explosions. But when eighty tons of steel stops, even semi-abruptly, inertia carries anything not strapped down like a slingshot.

A high-pitched scream from the ship's hull vibrated through the air. The entire vessel scraped like it was rubbing against a massive block of sandpaper before snapping to a halt.

Then the slingshot fired.

Outside the bridge, the figures tapping at the window disappeared in a blur. Dr. Hawkins's body compressed against the bulkhead with twenty knots of force. To her: a mild car crash. Heaven knows what it felt like to the men outside the window catapulted forward onto the ship's deck.

Hands grabbed Taka-chan by her arms. She winced and let out an uncontrollable whimper as their grip dug into her swollen dislocated elbow. Two men drew her to a stand. The Dragon clenched a small handgun at the ready. With a clang, he released the clamps pinning the bridge door closed. He flung it open and aimed.

Pop! Pop! ... Pop! Pop! Pop!

Taka-chan's escorts dragged her straight into a slaughter, not unlike the one she experienced less than an hour earlier in the passageway.

Only now, they were outside on the deck of the ship. The cold night air and the salty smell of the sea filled her lungs. New darkness swallowed her. She could barely discern buildings in the distance and thousands of stars in the sky.

Her escorts yanked her along the deck toward the bow.

Da! Da! Da! Da! Da! Da!

Machine-gun fire blasted behind her. An escort went limp and toppled over, dragging her with him.

Da! Da! Da! Da!

Another barrage of bullets eliminated the other one, and his body collapsed on top of her.

Bullets whizzed. The deck beneath her grew warm and wet with a viscous pool of her captors' blood.

I can't believe this is happening...

With every ounce of heated North Korean blood that flowed, a gallon of frigid horror filled her veins.

Screeching bullets ricocheted off the metal, Chinese and Korean voices roared. Japanese crew inside the bridge moaned and ranted. For the moment, Taka-chan held her tongue as the soulless flesh of her former captors grew cold and pinned her to the deck of the *Kuroshio Maru*.

• • •

Hachiman scanned the heat of flashing barrels in infrared as a firefight erupted on the deck of the vessel. Glowing bodies darted across the ship, seeking cover, angling for tactical advantage.

"Sparks, get us some eyes on that deck," Voodoo ordered quietly, his voice masked by the pops of gunfire. Voodoo glanced up to see the illuminated boxes of his drones maneuvering. Raijin adjusted its look angle over the aft of the ship looking forward from several hundred feet, its whisper-quiet propellers outside of earshot. The machine-gun fire and yells further masked the low-level buzz from the drones.

"Uh, guys, are you seeing this?"

"Show me, Sparks," Frisco said.

Sparks shifted the angle of the Hachiman camera and zoomed in on the water.

"Is that a speedboat?" Voodoo asked.

"I was doing some research online before the trip. I think it's a North Korean infiltration craft. It's a speedboat that can submerge ten feet underwater at minimal snorkel depth," Sparks said.

The tiny vessel maneuvered up to the aft of the ship.

"It looks like they're trying to board," Sparks said.

Through the video feed, more North Korean frogmen appeared and extended shepherd's crooks twenty feet up and onto the pitched aft deck of the ship. North Korean infiltrators connected caving ladders and commenced their attack on the beached vessel.

Voodoo and his team could do nothing more than watch as six more fighters entered the battle, sneaking up behind the other glowing figures competing in a high stakes battle for the future.

"If we wait any longer, they'll have a whole platoon out here," Stu said as gunfire continued on the ship.

"Just wait. Our moment will come," Voodoo said.

"I only see two armies here, Voodoo. North Korea and us. Where are the other players?"

"I'm pretty sure one group is on the ship fighting the North Koreans," Voodoo said.

"The Chinese? The North Koreans are fighting the Chinese?" Frisco asked with alarm.

"Looks like it."

The frogmen on the beach dispersed, establishing fields of fire.

"Gents, I've got movement to the east. Vehicle lights," Stu said. "Any way I can get a closer look?"

"On it," Sparks said as the video feed from Amaterasu pushed to the east one kilometer, loitering over the Russian garrison. Nearly thirty Russian soldiers poured out of the building shlepping rifles and helmets. They moved as if responding to an invasion.

That wasn't far from the truth.

"Looks like our dance card is about to be filled, boys. Whatta ya got, Voodoo?" Frisco asked.

"Just stand by. Any moment now."

• • •

The gunfire over Taka-chan shifted aft. With her dead captors' weight draped over her, she wriggled her head free. Bursts of gunpowder focused on the rear deck, away from her position. *Where is Dragon?*

A large hand hooked her armpit and yanked, dragging her out from under the lifeless flesh decaying on top of her.

Taka-chan immediately recognized the Dragon's calloused hands. Her legs kicked to shuffle her body along the deck to relieve the pain as he clenched her skin. Her cloudy mind groped for context in her strange surroundings.

I need to fight. No, be smart. I need to escape. She hoped for some sign amid this growing battle under the night's umbrella.

Then she saw it.

Just over the bow of the *Kuroshio Maru*, her answer, the real answer, lay in the distance.

A steady mind in the darkness will find the light.
Headlights!

The Dragon had her alone, frantically dragging her across the deck toward cover.

An angry body appeared around the corner. The Dragon drew his sword to engage, dropping his bag and Dr. Hawkins in the process.

This is my chance. She needed to get to the headlights, and off the ship.

I can't be more than fifteen meters above the water.

Fueled by nothing more than her will to live, Dr. Hawkins snatched the black duffel bag and sprinted to the port side of the ship.

The Dragon's sword and his opponent's gun barrel crashed in close quarters combat.

Taka-chan reached the edge. With the bag slung over her shoulder, she hastily climbed up the railing and perched over the metal precipice. The calm ocean wind gently nudged her back in encouragement, and below, the unknown spread its arms to embrace her.

She jumped.

CHAPTER 51
The Blind Warriors

KUNASHIR ISLAND

Above the men jockeying for victory, the white-hot infrared eye of Hachiman fixated on an isolated display of reckless abandon.

"Someone just jumped off the port side of the ship!" Sparks said. Voodoo and his fire team monitored the video feed from a femto projector less than a millimeter from their cornea.

The drones autonomously rearranged their positions for visual optimization while avoiding collision in a choreographed aerial dance.

Amaterasu followed the inbound Russian troops from the garrison while Raijin angled to view the body that just threw itself from the *Kuroshio Maru.*

The North Korean boarding party confronted the Sea Dragons on the deck of the dead cargo ship. Between storage containers, the trained special operatives tactically maneuvered in an exchange of lead bullets traveling at 710 meters per second.

Raijin dipped in altitude to view the water on the port side of the ship. The *Kuroshio Maru* dramatically angled upward as the bulbous bow covered in barnacles and chipped red paint ballooned onto the beach. One-quarter of the ship now rested on the soil of Kunashir Island.

"Whoever just threw themselves off that ship got pretty damn lucky. They barely landed in the water, and it couldn't have been more than a few feet deep. They must be pretty jacked up. Hang on, they're moving."

A body emerged from the water like some Darwinian quadruped, clawing at the sand with a bag strapped to its back. Having jumped off the port side, the person remained invisible to the North Korean frogmen situated to the south, spread across the beach.

"They're moving. I'm not sure what to, though," Sparks said. The frogmen fanned out, seeking the small troughs in the sand to conceal themselves.

"I do," Stu said. In the video feed from Amaterasu, a convoy of Russian forces drove toward them. "I count six vicks with about five to six pax per vick. We're looking at two platoons of Russian infantry headed our way. ETA two mikes."

The headlights of the trucks reflected off the ship as the vehicles approached.

Meanwhile, the singular figure crawled across the beach, moving inland toward the Russian troops advancing on their position. Sparks widened the aperture of the Hachiman lens to increase their view.

On board the ship, the battle raged on.

On the beach, eight frogmen lay waiting.

On the road, two platoons of Russian infantry raced toward them.

All the while an unknown person struggled in the sand.

The piston slap and exhaust of diesel engines, rubber tires gripping dirt, and bright headlights heralded the arrival of the Russian troops. Stu trained the iron sights of his M240 on the lead vehicle as doors opened, and Russian military-issued leather boots hit the ground.

Soldiers dismounted from their vehicles and dispersed on both sides of the road in search of cover as they heard the discharging AK-47 rounds on the deck of the *Kuroshio Maru*.

Russian voices called out, coordinating movement, gravel crunched, and twigs snapped.

Frisco, Stu, and Voodoo slowed their breaths, rubbed their thumbs along the familiar knurling of their weapons' safeties, their index fingers hovering over their triggers, and stood by.

Just then, the crawling amphibian on the beach evolved, sprinting on two feet toward the Russians, toward Voodoo and his team. Four of the North Korean frogmen leaped to their feet and rushed after, serpentining across the sand like agitated cobras.

"Is that her, Voodoo? Is that her?" Sparks asked.

Amaterasu hovered directly above them now, still tracking the lead vehicle of the Russian convoy. Voodoo adjusted his position and pointed at the drone. Through his lens, the blue box labeled "Amaterasu" switched to green as Voodoo asserted control. With the mere articulation of his fingers, Voodoo initiated the payload, and a green arcing augmented reality line extended from his hand. A circle appeared on the beach that indicated the target location to activate the cube-shaped object attached to the belly of the flying robot.

The figure raced toward them.

The frogmen pursued.

The Russians stood ready.

Voodoo clenched his fist, and the green circle turned red just behind the desperate figure running for their life.

Above everyone's head, the Amaterasu drone pitched hard right and yawed, changing its hover to an eighty-miles-per-hour descent.

There was no warning when it finally happened, no sudden pop or explosion. The payload on the drone didn't emit the stereotypical bang of a kinetic weapon.

Because that's not what this was.

On the beach, the frogmen strained to capture the escapee charging toward the Russian soldiers staging for a fight. All parties fixated on the one person desperately racing to freedom.

"Let there be light," Voodoo said over the radios.

Then...that's all there was.

• • •

Taka-chan leaped off the deck of the *Kuroshio Maru* into the arms of oblivion. Just as the wind of free fall welcomed her, she hit the water with a whoosh and a muddy thud. The frigid water ripped the air from her lungs. She instinctively bit down, and her arms and legs collapsed into a fetal position.

The numbing water embraced her skin. For the first time in days, she felt free as a frothy two-foot wave escorted her weak body beachward.

She surfaced. In the distance, she saw the headlights.

A steady mind in the darkness will find the light.

Get up! Move! She swiped the salt water from her eyes as she trudged on.

The malnourishment and constant pain left her fragile and breaking.

But she was far from broken.

Taka-chan crawled, clawing at the sand before standing. She limped into a run as the hard, wet sand gave way to soft. She pressed forward toward the headlights, the distant glow waving her forward as a beacon of hope. Gunfire and Korean voices mingled with Chinese.

They drew closer; her legs pumped faster. She pushed through the excruciating pain, deep bruises, and the memory of hopeless isolation. She raced to the freedom promised her in the prophetic dream.

Then, ahead of her, shrouded in the headlights of military vehicles, Slavic voices growled in the shadows.

Where the hell am I?

A stab of fear and betrayal pierced her chest.

She slowed. There was movement behind her, kicking up sand and drawing close. Panic flooded her mind as she accepted the lesser of two evils and pushed on again toward the Russians. Toward the light.

Then a mechanical hum descended upon her.

Dr. Hawkins heard what she thought to be a swarm of bees before a lightning-fast Doppler shift buzzed behind her and ended in a loud slap on the earth. Specks of sand splashed across her back.

That's when it finally happened.

Behind her, the brightest light she had ever seen incinerated the night. Taka-chan's negative world of silhouettes flipped to positive, nothing but a blazing, aural white glow. She covered her eyes with her hands and peeked through a crack in her flesh. The light enveloped her like a blanket of alabaster fire, blasting forward toward the tree line and piercing the eyes of the Russian soldiers she now saw so clearly.

Shrill Russian and Korean voices cried out in torment as the light burned into their eyes.

Taka-chan became a statue, trapped in space and time, terrified of what may come next.

• • •

Just as it was supposed to, the White Dwarf payload detonated the moment Amaterasu reached target altitude. In the final moments of its descent, the tiny quadcopter did a 180-degree horizontal flip and dove straight into the ground to give its payload optimal dispersion.

The sun itself shines on the earth at close to 126,000 lumens. For thirty seconds, the White Dwarf is capable of tripling that number, completely blinding anyone who dares put eyes upon it.

In the instant before it detonated, the North Korean frogmen and the Russian soldiers searched the darkness with their fully dilated naked eyes. In that same moment, blinding light stabbed straight into their optical nerve, permanently blinding the unlucky ones.

Voodoo, Stu, and Frisco remained silent. All three men slammed their eyes shut.

Their multispectral cameras, operating outside of the optical spectrum, ignored the brightness of the White Dwarf. They saw the world around them via a pass-through video feed, their contact lenses literally allowing them to see with their eyes closed.

When the light of Amaterasu protects you, rise and face the eastern threat.

Voodoo whispered, "It's time," and the text appeared in everyone's HUD. Slowly, the witch doctor and his cult members rose to their feet.

• • •

The world was bathed in angelic light.

She couldn't move.

Something stirred in the tree line. Then, the grass came to life.

Three armed men emerged as if summoned from the earth itself, angling toward her with stealth and purpose.

Their eyes are closed!

She fell to her knees.

Korean, Chinese, and Russian soldiers screamed all around them. Waves hit the beach in mild crashes, but Taka-chan could hear only the voice from her dream speaking to her as clearly as the first time she heard it: *When the blind warriors emerge, lie down and say your name.* The blind warriors pressed forward, and the man in the middle pointed his rifle skyward and extended his hand.

She surrendered to fate and fell forward. At the top of her lungs, she cried out, "My name is Kerry! My name is Kerry Hawkins! I am Kerry Hawkins!"

CHAPTER 52
The Dragon and the Witch Doctor

KUNASHIR ISLAND

Ryu cast the barrel of the AK-47 aside with a deflecting strike, leaving him exposed to the butt of the rifle. The Chinese soldier struck Ryu across his cheek, sending him reeling to the guard rail of the ship. Ryu drew his sidearm and fired, grazing the Sea Dragon's shoulder with the first round, drilling a hole through his forehead with the second. Blood, brains, and bone splattered across the metal bulkhead.

The Sea Dragon collapsed lifelessly to the deck. Ryu's eyes watered from the blow. He forced his eyelids open and shut to regain his bearings. Around him, rounds ricocheted off thick metal. Muzzle flashes lit the deck like an erratic fireworks display.

Ryu spun about to check on his cargo.

She's not here! the voice in Ryu's head bellowed.

Searing anger filled his body. His silent calm exploded into a violent rage.

You can't go home if she's gone! the voice nagged. *She stole the bag!*

Ryu tightened his grip on his sword in one hand and the North Korean Type 70 pistol in the other. He leaned back and shouted at the night sky; his arms quivered as he flexed all the muscles in his body. Veins protruded from his neck like roots from a tree trunk. His face burned hot with blood.

He paced the deck, stomping his feet in frustration just as a shimmer of headlights cast his shadow against a nearby bulkhead.

Ryu ran to the front of the ship and that's when he saw her.

On the beach, sprinting toward the oncoming vehicles, Dr. Hawkins raced for freedom. Ryu scoured the deck for a way to descend. Then he saw his men on the beach, breaking formation to chase her down. Their quick response breathed hope back into his lungs.

Ryu redirected his focus to the aft of the ship, to the fast attack craft the other frogmen used to board the vessel.

Ryu acted without thinking. His legs carried his body forward as if possessed with the 122.5-meter-long vessel, the open deck, and the firefight all nothing more than a blur as he zipped aft. Three Sea Dragons appeared behind a Conex box and presented the barrels of their AK-74 short-range automatic rifles, homing in on the moving mass advancing on their position.

Pop! Pop!

Ryu fired and strafed sideways, transitioning to a dive roll before firing again.

Pop!

Three shots. Three dead. Ryu pressed on.

His legs pumped with his weapons at the ready. Another Sea Dragon emerged from behind cover facing away from him.

In one fluid motion, Ryu sliced the back of the Chinese soldier's neck, severing his spinal cord, the resistance on the blade confirming the finality of the cut.

Then, just as Ryu anticipated another target, a luminescent white glow filled the beach to his rear. The ship's cabin behind him shielded him from the full intensity of the light. Ryu skidded beside a cargo container and froze. On the beach below, he could hear the agonized shouts of his countrymen.

"My eyes!" he heard them scream. The bright light burned with an intensity greater than anything he had ever seen. Ryu felt as if one of the stars in the heavens had fallen to their earthly world below.

In front of him, one of his countrymen stood, slack-jawed and confused. Ryu grabbed him at the shoulder by his black neoprene wet suit and dragged him to the rear of the ship, where the caving ladder remained attached.

Below, the semisubmersible North Korean infiltration craft was still in the water, bobbing in the mild waves.

Ryu mounted the ladder and his colleague followed.

On the beach, the light vanished just as quickly as it appeared, and another explosion of gunfire filled the vacuum it left behind.

• • •

Enveloped by blinding light, Kerry Hawkins remained motionless on the beach, accepting the bizarre fate unfolding around her. The smell of kelp and salt grounded her to the cool sand beneath her.

Footsteps displaced the wet sand and she felt the presence of the blind warriors beside her.

"Fate is a river. We just have to make it through the rapids."

I know that voice. That voice spoke those very same words to her nearly twenty years ago.

Her mind flashed with her memory of the river, the rescue, and walking away from Gavin.

And now here she was. That same voice, the same man, once again, arrived to pull Persephone from the grips of Hades. And just like before, drawing close and full of anger, Charon, in the form of vengeful frogmen, waited to escort them all to the underworld.

Before she could raise her head, strong arms scooped underneath her weak body and hoisted her off the ground.

• • •

Voodoo and Frisco pulled the pins of their smoke grenades. With a wide arc, they tossed one toward the beach and the other toward the convoy of vehicles. The grenades popped and fizzed. Thick black smoke filled the air. The blinding light and the dark fog coalesced like a celestial nebula trapped on the terrestrial world with four human bodies huddled in the center.

Stu scooped up Dr. Hawkins and placed her on his back in a fireman's carry, taking careful consideration of her broken limb. With one arm, he steadied the precious life of Kerry Hawkins on his shoulder. And with the other, he held the fifty-inch-long M240 ready to lay waste to any who dared get in their way.

Without hesitation, they broke into a dead sprint. The light wouldn't last long, and they knew it. If they moved quickly enough, they would be out of sight long before the North Koreans or the Russians realized what happened. If they were swift, the other armies would start shooting at each other, and no one would ever know the Americans were there.

They didn't have such luck.

The light vanished. In its place, a fire combusted as the White Dwarf payload overloaded its power source. The lithium-polymer battery incinerated the remaining components of the drone once called Amaterasu.

In response, bullets from the beach and the road fired blindly into the smoke and confusion. Several North Korean frogmen still able to fight popped up, their instruments of war now trained on Voodoo's fleeing team.

Frisco swerved, knelt, and aimed.

Dap! Dap! Dap!

A frogman fell limp as another shot back. Bullets snapped by Frisco's head. On the other side of a dense cloud of smoke, the Russians fired indiscriminately toward the beach.

Dap! Dap!

Frisco fired at the other frogman and missed.

Voodoo, pulling up the rear behind Stu, knew another distraction was in order. He glanced at the sky to find Raijin and Thor.

"Stu, gimme some suppressing fire!" Voodoo yelled to the one-man ambulance in front of him. Voodoo dropped to a prone position flat on the beach as Stu brought the M240 about.

Ba! Ba! Ba! Ba! Ba! Ba! Ba! Ba!

The 7.62 rounds of the M240 blasted from the pig in a stream of orange lights.

Dap! Dap! Dap! ... Ba! Ba! Ba! Ba! Ba! Ba! ... Dap! Dap! Dap! ... Ba! Ba! Ba! Ba!

Frisco joined in with his M4, offsetting the silence between automatic bursts. He balanced the dead space, taking turns between the barrage of fire, doing what shooters call "making them sing." Frisco and Stu set the mood with their music as Voodoo prepared for the climax.

With one green arc aimed at the frogmen on the beach and the other at the Russian infantrymen on the road, Thor and Raijin rocketed into kamikaze attack runs.

BAM! ... BAM!

The drones detonated their conical energetic payloads several feet from their intended targets. The shadows of men dropped to the earth on the beach and on the road to the north.

Gunfire ceased.

Frisco and Stu abruptly disengaged, swiveled around, and stepped right back into a dead sprint along the hard-packed sand of the beach. Voodoo paused to cover their six.

The frogmen and the Russians were stunned, but Voodoo wanted absolute certainty of a successful exfiltration.

He pointed at the last remaining drone, painted a target right in front of him, and clenched his fist. In seconds, Apollo burst into another extraordinary ball of light.

The battling armies, struggling to make sense of the chaos, didn't see Voodoo jump to his feet. They only saw another angelic visitor, "blessing" them with its presence.

Blind, bewildered, and completely overmatched, the remaining forces crumbled in defeat.

The white blast surrounded Voodoo, lighting his path forward as he accelerated south. There was no bag of chicken bones poured out on the ground and no insurgent to drag home for questioning. There was, however, a witch doctor and his cult vanishing in a spectacular display of "Pure Frickin' Magic."

CHAPTER 53
Dreams Don't Lie

KUNASHIR ISLAND

"**S**parks, you got our position?" Frisco called out over the radio between breaths, the balls of his feet driving him forward. Sweat poured down his face.

"Trackin'. I'm one klick offshore. Where do you want me?"

"I'm dropping a point on the map just south of a tiny peninsula," Frisco huffed. "Meet us on the back side."

Voodoo caught up just as Apollo gave up the ghost, and their world plunged back into darkness. A dog barked in the distance, but it didn't matter now.

Moments later, the rumble of the 350-horsepower motors of the RHIB jumped off the waves and into their eardrums. A spark of elation filled their chests.

Voodoo knew better than to celebrate now. They still needed to get back to Japanese soil—uncontested Japanese soil to be specific.

Frisco, Stu, and Voodoo high-kneed their way into the shallow water as Sparks pulled the boat close. Frisco tripped and fell beneath the waves as the beach dropped out to deeper water, only to resurface quickly. They hooked the side of the RHIB one at a time, and Stu carefully rolled Kerry onto the front of the boat, where she flopped onto her back. Then the men flung their bodies into the maritime shuttle.

Sparks quickly spun the wheel and forced the throttle forward. It stabbed through the incoming waves as the RHIB headed back out to sea, retracing their path toward the place of men with beast-like spirits.

"It took you long enough, Gavin," Kerry said, lying on her back. Frisco and Voodoo sat on each side of her; Stu manned the bow with his M240.

"Who the hell is Gavin?" Sparks asked.

It had been a long time since anyone called him that—a different life. A life Voodoo desperately hoped to find again.

Frisco chuckled. "That's Voodoo, Sparks."

"Really, Voodoo? Your name is Gavin? I always figured your parents were a cell phone and a Yagi antenna."

"They call you 'Voodoo'?" Kerry asked as a quick chuckle shifted to a chunky cough. "Do you practice witchcraft too now?" Kerry's weak face gave a wry grin. Her dark hair crusted against her head in a matted mess.

"Something like that," Voodoo replied.

"Do you guys know each other?" Frisco asked.

"Something like that," Kerry replied.

Voodoo quickly introduced the team of rescuers.

"We have about an hour to get back to Japan," Voodoo said. "How's your arm? Are you gonna be okay?" He pressed a bottle of water against her lips, and she took a drink.

"I can make it. At least we're outside. I'd rather be on the Colorado, though."

"I hear that," Voodoo said.

"How did you know about my arm?"

"We have a lot to catch you up on. For now, sit tight. We're not in the clear just yet. What's in the bag?"

"The guy that kidnapped me had it on his back. I stole it before I jumped off the ship," Kerry said as Voodoo unzipped it and reached inside, revealing a garbage bag wrapped in tape. He pulled a knife from his pocket and cut it open. Computer hard drives, a laptop, and two vials of blood Voodoo knew from his dreams sat on the top. But a horrifying discovery lay beneath them.

"Is that a head?" Stu asked, looking over his shoulder, his body and weapon trained forward.

Kerry reeled in shock, her good hand cupping her mouth. "That son of a... I can't believe... I've been carrying around..." Kerry's head shook, and she started to cry. Voodoo quickly covered the contents back up and zipped the bag closed.

He placed his hand on Kerry's shoulder, who pulled herself up, embraced Voodoo, and fell on his neck, weeping. She still wore only yoga pants and an Iron Maiden T-shirt. Her body shivered in the night air as the RHIB bounced on the waves. She smelled of fish, vomit, and body odor, but Voodoo didn't care. He felt the muscles in her back, weakened from her captivity but still firm. He could feel her breaths stutter as she sobbed before calming. She prolonged the embrace.

"I'm sorry," Voodoo said. His mind flashed to the last time he saw her, standing in the dirt parking lot of Vagabond River Expeditions. The warm summer sun was setting over the red glow of the sandstone canyon surrounding Moab. He never expected to see her again, just like every other customer. He had no intention of this encounter suffering the same fate. He had too many questions.

She sniffled and pulled away.

"Rest. Keep your head down. We have a long ride ahead of us," Voodoo said as Kerry leaned back against the side of the RHIB. Frisco handed Voodoo a scratchy green military blanket from the back of the boat, and he wrapped Kerry up in it.

The boat bounced hard in the chop as they ferried across the twenty-kilometer-wide strip of water between the Kuril Islands and the Shiretoko Peninsula. It normally would take an hour to cross in agreeable conditions, but it appeared the weather planned to put up an argument.

They had been on the water only a short time before the waves and wind picked up. Voodoo remembered the typhoon preparing to push east across northern Hokkaido.

The boat bounced and slammed harder until Sparks throttled back on the engine, slowing to fifteen knots. "Gotta take it easy and get back in one piece."

Frisco stood beside Sparks at the helm to look at the sea ahead then checked their six. The distance grew between their boat and the chaos on Kunashir Island.

"Good idea. Let's stay frosty. We're in the home stretch," Frisco said with encouragement.

A message from Naomi appeared in everyone's HUD. "I have been watching the Hachiman feed. It looks like something is heading toward you."

Voodoo accessed the menu in his HUD. Only Hachiman remained in Voodoo's army of gods. Its camera still monitored the battlefield they left behind. Voodoo widened the camera angle and established the RHIB as a new waypoint. A bioluminescent trail appeared in the ocean like railroad tracks.

Tracks mean a train, Voodoo thought. *There must be another boat.*

He slew the camera toward their RHIB and searched the vicinity. The aerated water which activated the bioluminescent life pointed straight at the RHIB only to vanish a hundred meters away. *No railroad tracks?*

Electric spiders crawled underneath Voodoo's skin as his hairs stood on end.

"Sparks," Voodoo started. "Did you say that those North Korean infiltration boats are semisubmersible?"

"Yeah, gray fast-attack boats with a covered central cabin that can slide open. They normally carry about five people. They can snorkel at like ten feet underwater according to what I could find online."

Voodoo stood and looked at the ominous ocean around them.

"Hit the throttle, Sparks! Now!" Voodoo yelled.

Too late.

BAM!

With a hard jolt, the RHIB rolled hard to port as a huge speedboat jumped out of the water. The gray hulled craft had an enclosed cabin on the top that slid open. The peaked bow of the North Korean vessel punched the front of the RHIB. Stu absorbed part of the impact as the reinforced fiberglass frame struck his head.

Stu toppled beside Dr. Hawkins.

Frisco and Sparks fell toward the middle. The black duffel bag flew into the water. Voodoo instinctively high-sided on the raft, his subconscious mind defaulting to his years of training as a river guide.

The high-speed motor of the North Korean craft increased power as the two vessels leveled and came alongside. Frisco and

Sparks struggled to get to their feet while Voodoo searched for his rifle.

An old friend will be lost...

Time slowed as the words from his dream washed over his mind like a tide. The boats rubbed and screeched. The shadows grew. Stu wasn't moving with Kerry trapped underneath him as Frisco and Sparks scrambled.

I can't lose them, Voodoo thought. *I won't let the dream end like this.*

A bag brushed against Voodoo's right foot, and he immediately knew what hid inside.

The boats bounced in the choppy waves and collided again as the driver of the North Korean craft remained dead set on keeping close to the RHIB.

Voodoo reached into the bag, grabbed the object inside, and forcefully chucked it into the air.

The accelerometers of the drone immediately recognized the shift in inertia, armed itself, and fired the motors. With a quick snapping motion, the drone popped into a loiter and locked on to Voodoo's position.

One of the North Korean infiltrators prepared to jump off the fast attack boat onto the RHIB. Voodoo pointed straight at the man with his left hand. The man halted.

For a moment, as if no one else around them existed at all, Voodoo and the dark figure locked eyes. Palpable energy pushed and pulled between them like magnets with the wrong polarity. A silent, dark matter passed between them as if their determination itself became a tangible object.

The black figure drew a sword high above his head. Even in the darkness, Voodoo could see a smile on the man's face as he prepared to strike.

Voodoo, still pointing at the man, smiled back...and clenched his fist.

The sound of a swarm of bees zipped toward them.

BAM!

The North Korean infiltrator launched at Voodoo just as the drone detonated on the deck of the speedboat.

Voodoo weaved to the right, avoiding the sword-wielding attacker as a slashing strike whipped through the air.

An old friend will be lost...

Voodoo spun just as the North Korean infiltrator collided headlong into Frisco.

With a splash, Frisco and the attacker were gone.

CHAPTER 54
Silence

44.0424126, 145.6378468
OFF KUNASHIR ISLAND

The stun of impact, coupled with the frigid temperature, ripped the air from his lungs. The black liquid invaded his mouth with an overwhelming flavor of briny saltwater. His muscles tightened. For a moment, he lost all grasp of his whereabouts. If it weren't for the salty seawater stinging his eyes, he'd know no difference between the world with his eyes open or closed.

Finish the fight, the voice said.

Ryu recognized the hilt of his sword in his right hand, and in his left, he felt wet cloth. It moved with a mind of its own. Ryu pulled it closer to him, and he felt his body float across the liquid expanse, drifting through the void toward the shifting mass.

It was a body. It was a man, rather. Not the man he intended to kill, but this one, whoever he was, also needed to die.

A hand gripped Ryu's arm at his biceps and another hand groped at his throat.

Ryu thrust his blade forward. Again and again, he stabbed into the abyss as the hands tightened their grip on his throat. Ryu shoved down and to the side, failing to make a purchase. The assailing hands squeezed tighter.

Up! the voice yelled.

Then Ryu realized, his opponent floated upside down. He stabbed up and made contact—the familiar rip of flesh communicated through the blade like Morse code to Ryu's murderous soul.

The hands released as a boot kicked him in the face. Ryu reached out with his left hand and stabbed again with his sword.

His opponent vanished.

The familiar burn of hypoxia ignited in his lungs, and Ryu kicked with his legs to surface. Suddenly, hands grabbed his feet and limbs. He flailed.

Two limbs multiplied to four as legs wrapped around his body like coordinated boa constrictors. The harder Ryu fought, the tighter the serpent tightened its coil. A constricting limb slithered around Ryu's arm and head, immobilizing his sword, twisting his wrist, yanking the weapon from his hand.

Kill him! Kill him! the voices cried in Ryu's head.

Then suddenly for the first time, the sounds Ryu heard in his head fell silent, confused and overwhelmed, as if they knew what was coming.

Ryu knew death itself awaited in the waters around him. The ghosts he called with nascent whistles and casual prayers decided now to rise from the depths and drag him down to hell.

But Ryu had never been one to give up that easily.

● ● ●

Voodoo's body pierced the water like an arrow as he dove after his brother-in-arms. The cold water shocked his system, but years of training in the Pacific Ocean made swimming in the unknown second nature.

He breached the surface and trod water, searching for signs of Frisco and the attacker in the growing whitecaps hopping around him.

Something rubbed against Voodoo's neck. He instinctively reached up and found his glasses dangling. A retention band around the back held them around his neck. They must have fallen as he jumped in the water. Voodoo angled them back onto his face, and he pressed the button on the side, activating the multispectral camera.

They're supposed to be waterproof, Voodoo thought.

An image appeared in Voodoo's contact lens with blues, reds, and oranges differentiating objects, giving Voodoo sight in the darkness. He held his breath and slipped under the surface; illuminated infrared light extended his vision in the depths but not by much. The Bluetooth connection dipped in and out, making his image choppy.

Just barely below the surface, a blob wriggled. Voodoo swam closer, and his camera helped him identify the edges of two bodies grappling underwater. One floated below the other.

And one held a weapon.

Voodoo swam deeper, breast stroking with his arms and frog kicking with his legs, thrusting and gliding through the water toward the armed swimmer.

Voodoo pulled at his legs, hooked the man's head, isolated his arm, and then twisted his position in the water in a wrestling move called a "grapevine." The man shook and twisted, writhed, and kicked, but Voodoo arched his back and interwove his legs like a snake. Voodoo's arm hooked around his head and crushed his opponent's neck in a guillotine.

Bubbles of air vomited out of the man's mouth. The armed man released garbled underwater screams that failed to find an audience.

It was almost over. *Keep squeezing!* Voodoo's lungs burned. Could he hold on long enough to finish the job?

Images of the pachinko parlor exploding in the night sky, the lost children, Naomi's attackers, even the child in Iraq streamed through Voodoo's mind.

Now is my chance at redemption. Even if it kills me. I will not let go...

• • •

Frisco sharply inhaled as he breached the surface. Wave caps greeted him with heaves and shoves. Ripping pain along his back urgently reminded him to find safety.

"Frisco! Voodoo! Is that you?" a voice yelled in the darkness. The sound of motors filled his ears. His legs rotated like eggbeaters beneath his body, thrusting his torso out of the water as he raised his arm.

"I'm here!" he yelled back.

Sparks steered the boat to his location, and strong hands ripped Frisco out of the water. Sparks dumped him into the middle of the RHIB. Frisco's spent muscles surrendered to the safety of the RHIB as he fought for breath.

"Where's Voodoo?" Sparks asked. Frisco could barely make out his face in the darkness. The alkaline sting of salt water obscured his vision. He could see the silhouette of Stu lying near the bow with Dr. Hawkins trying to revive him.

"I never saw him," Frisco admitted between deep breaths and coughs. "I didn't know he went into the water with me."

Da! Da! Da! Da! Da!

Submachine-gun fire interjected as Sparks ducked his head. He slipped around the helm toward the bow, searching the floor of the RHIB.

Frisco lifted his head to see the North Korean vessel maneuvering toward them.

Sparks popped to his feet, M240 in hand, leaning into the weapon as if it were a spear ready to pierce the hull of the boat with a single thrust.

Ba! Ba! Ba! Ba! Ba! ... Ba! Ba! Ba! Ba! Ba!

Orange strings of light leaped from the RHIB across the dark expanse to the North Korean boat. Sparks put one foot on the inflatable tube of the RHIB to reinforce his stance.

Sparks could see the North Koreans through the eyes of Hachiman, watching from above.

Ba! Ba! Ba! Ba! Ba! Ba! Ba! Ba! Ba! Ba!

Sparks held down the trigger and refused to let up. Instead of pausing between bursts to let the barrel cool, Sparks let the weapon loose. The belt of 7.62 bullets dumped into the machine gun, unleashing a steady string of punishment out the barrel. Glowing hot brass sprung out the side, hopping across the RHIB's inflatable tube and into the water.

The North Korean boat veered hard, but Sparks refused to ease up. One way or another, Sparks intended to win this fight.

The chain of orange rounds shifted from the interior cabin toward the aft, directly into the motors. Within seconds, sparks ignited a fire.

BOOM!

The engines of the infiltration craft exploded. Debris cast from the boat littered the water in burning fragments and fiberglass flotsam, leaving the vessel adrift.

"Nice shootin', Sparks!" Stu said as he sat up, rubbing his head.

"Welcome back, Sleeping Beauty," Frisco said from the aft of the boat, a breath of relief drifting from his lungs.

Sparks pointed the M240 skyward. The barrel was white-hot and warped from the excessive number of rounds Sparks blew through it.

"Well, they were supposed to be DRMO'd anyway. I just figured I could blow out the barrel, and nobody'd care."

Stu let out a hearty laugh.

"You're my kinda guy, Sparks."

Sparks discarded the spent weapon into the water, the warped barrel making it nothing more than dead weight to them now.

"Where's Gavin?" Kerry asked, her head spinning left and right for any sign of her rescuer.

Sparks gestured with his left hand, slewing the camera of the eVTOL aircraft overhead searching the water for heat. Then, on the opposite side of their boat and the smoldering remains of the North Korean vessel, the heat signature of a human body surfaced.

Everyone held their breath as Sparks brought the boat about and quickly realized...it wasn't Voodoo.

• • •

Ryu flexed and writhed, twitched and squirmed, scraped and punched. Before he blacked out, Ryu's lungs burst aflame with hypoxia. The burning sensation is the literal buildup of carbon dioxide poisoning the lungs, screaming at the nerves in the human body to breathe, to extinguish the torturous fire scorching the life-sustaining organs in his chest. His body instinctively inhaled, and, for the briefest of moments, the alkaline seawater extinguished the fire in his lungs before they seized, and his body panicked.

Ryu convulsed.

The strangulating grip mercilessly denied him any reprieve, any hope for salvation. Ryu's attacker was relentless. Ryu felt the claws of the devil's servant gripping him in the deep.

The dark underworld grew quiet.

The voices in his head stopped.

Ryu's mortal frame lost the will to fight.

And just as he did, just as he surrendered to the finality of his existence, she came back to him.

A girl's infectious giggle softly echoed.

Ryu found the reprieve he sought all these years. Aside from the joy he had with his sister, Ryu truly wanted only one thing, one gift denied him every day of his life since his family died.

And he finally found it.

Silence.

• • •

"It's not Voodoo!" Sparks said as he poked the dead body. "Doesn't look like the dude who attacked us either. I think this guy fell out when the drone hit the boat."

Fire crackled and burned on the adrift North Korean vessel as it wandered away in the waves. Kerry Hawkins, Stu, Sparks, and Frisco scanned the blackness around them. Sloshing water nudged the boat. The motor idled.

"We can't lose Voodoo..." Frisco's teeth chattered as he lay on the floor of the boat, nursing his injury. "Where are you, old friend?"

Each second drew out like a blade, cutting into hope. The wary team of fighters remained silent; their hearts beat tightly as if their chests shrunk with each passing second.

A minute passed.

Then another.

"How long has it been since he jumped?" Kerry asked.

"At least five minutes I'd guess," Sparks replied. "Too long... He swam a bit on the surface too but... I dunno, man. What do we do if he's lost? I mean...what do we do if Voodoo's gone?" The loyal sled dog searched for his teammate, his mentor.

A message from Naomi appeared in everyone's HUD. "There is activity on the beach. They may be able to see the fire on the boat."

Sparks, Frisco, and Stu gave each other a sharp glance.

"We need to get moving," Frisco said reluctantly. Everyone understood the weight of his words. "Voodoo would want us to get her back safely."

Sparks and Stu said nothing, merely nodding their heads. It was for the best. Voodoo would want them to finish the job.

Sparks manned the helm. His hand shook as he gripped the throttle.

Suddenly, with an enormous gasp and splashing arms, a swimmer broke the surface of the water.

"Holy crap!" Sparks yelled out. "You crazy bastard, Voodoo!"

Voodoo breathed deeply. Each gasp for air sounded like the first he had ever taken as Voodoo returned to the land of the living.

Everyone on board inhaled a similar breath, reigniting hope.

Sparks adjusted the boat and pulled Voodoo in. His body collapsed on the floor as he struggled to regain his breath. Kerry crawled over to him as Stu, Frisco, and Sparks knelt.

"Scared the hell out of us, bro-chacho."

"Let's get outta here," Voodoo advised between breaths. "I've had enough of these dudes."

Everyone let out a laugh of relief. Even Stu seemed ready for this one to be over.

"It's good to have you back, old friend," Kerry said to Voodoo.

He coughed violently. "What did you say?"

"I said it's good to have you back, old friend." Voodoo stared at her. "We thought we lost you just now."

"Yeah, I suppose *you* did."

CHAPTER 55
Credit Where It Belongs

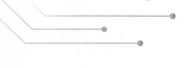

"Tell me what you see in these photos," the chief of station said as he slid a printed satellite photo across the table.

"Looks like a bright light on some island." Commander Buck Buchanan wasn't much for games, and he could feel the chief of station setting him up. "What is it?"

"These were taken last night over the Kuril Islands. I must say these are the craziest photos I've seen in a long time. I want to be upset that you didn't bring me in on your plans. But your boys did some incredible work."

My boys? Buck thought. He opted to remain silent and let the moment ride before opening his mouth. Behind him, a junior officer from Buck's platoon stood by, notepad in hand.

The chief continued, "After they found Dr. Hawkins, a North Korean infiltration craft washed up onto the shore near the town of Rausu in Northern Hokkaido. I haven't seen the Japanese this excited...ever, really. This is incredible."

Buck grit his teeth against the snarl he felt building. Frisco lied to him. Buck never authorized any operation. Hell, he didn't understand half the words the chief of station said.

"We keep picking up chatter about how the Chinese and North Koreans attacked the Russians on the Kuril Island, but with the typhoon hittin' the island, it's likely most of the evidence is gonna be washed out to sea. All except the Toyotomi cargo ship, which, wow, that's a different mess." The chief of station couldn't stop smiling. For a career intelligence operative, this was the perfect scenario.

"We also received a tip this mornin'. I had some of my analysts in DC dig into the intel and it all seems to be on the up and up. Ever heard of Delta Zulu?" the chief of station asked.

Buck slowly opened his mouth. Before words could fill the vacant hole in his face, the chief of station answered for him. "Whether you have or not doesn't matter. They have a long history with the intelligence community. They sent me the intel this morning, and now we have evidence that the North Korean cybergroup, Division 121, in conjunction with XJI and the Chinese government, hacked into Xiphos AI as they worked to support your operation. Long story short, not only did we recover Dr. Hawkins, we have evidence as to who was behind her capture and the death of Dr. Ichikawa."

The chief of station pointed to the picture again.

"I believe the Directorate calls this a White Dwarf payload if my sources are correct. Three times the brightness of the sun at a short distance but only lasts for thirty seconds. Just long enough for us to see it and nobody else."

Buck waited for the other shoe to drop. He anticipated the "but" statement to shadow any front-loaded positivity.

"But…" the chief of station said.

There it is, Buck thought. *Damn that Frisco. He'll pay for this.*

"We don't have the God Algorithm and Dr. Hawkins seems to be missing her laptop."

"And you're wondering if my guys have it?" Buck probed.

"Well, yeah. Do they?"

Buck considered lying. He still didn't understand this conversation, but Buck couldn't appear uninformed. He needed to own this room just like every room he walked into. What would cause fewer new questions he couldn't answer?

"You know what I know." End of story.

"That's unfortunate. That would have been the greatest outcome in this whole scenario—getting the God Algorithm into some of our people's hands back in the States and putting it to some real good."

Buck released a healthy ball of tobacco spit into a plastic bottle as he sunk deeper into the chair, the light above reflecting off his finely shaven, bald head.

"Yeah. It's unfortunate," Buck agreed. A piece of tobacco buried itself between his top incisors. It was just like these intel guys to worry over some computer AI thing, he thought.

"Regardless, I certainly hope you all recognize the heroism of your men. Let me know if there is anythin' I can do for you. I'll be sure to let your admiral know exactly how impressed I've been with your leadership in this endeavor, the help you've been to the US embassy, and our relationship with the Japanese government."

No other "but"? A successful mission, his leadership praised. Buck started to relax—

"And those four men we saw in the image need to be commended."

Buck panicked. *Four men?* He needed to get ahead of this and quickly. Had Frisco worked with or for someone else? Couldn't be. He wouldn't let it be. He needed to make sure everyone knew that he was the one managing this successful Task Force from start to finish.

Buck lifted himself to his feet. The chief of station stretched out his hand, and Buck crushed it, never forgetting the age-old adage that you always show you have the firmer handshake, no matter what.

Buck and his junior officer stepped out of the chief of station's office into the hallway of the embassy.

He snarled at the junior officer, "Get me Stu and Frisco. Now. They have some explaining to do."

"Weren't there four guys on the op, sir?"

"Right. But they weren't shooters. If Frisco and Stu decided to let someone else tag along, that's on them. They should be happy they aren't dead or getting court-martialed. Not yet, at least. For the record, my shooters executed the whole mission start to finish. Classified history will remember it that way. You heard the chief of station, this was a Task Force mission. And if I remember correctly, I'm the Task Force commander."

CHAPTER 56
The Lost Hawk

NAKASHIBETSU, HOKKAIDO, JAPAN

" Confidential sources within the Japanese National Police Agency have had a break in the case regarding the murder of renowned neurologist Dr. Kenzo Ichikawa. Last week, Dr. Ichikawa was found murdered at the Koishikawa Korakuen Gardens. Less than twenty-four hours later, the CEO of Toyotomi Industries, Kosuke Oota, was also found murdered in his home. Both men, apparently the victims of seppuku.

"Sources close to the case have revealed that the same weapon, a Korean jingum, was used to murder both men. Investigators at NHK have discovered that the recent merger between Toyotomi Industries and Xin Jishu International may have played a role in this twisted plot. A federal indictment is currently in place for the chairman of Xin Jishu International, Mr. Hwang Li-Liang. Mr. Hwang is under suspicion for his potential role in the murder as well as blackmail, human trafficking, and espionage.

"In other news, Inspector Noriyuki Yoshimoto was arrested today along with several other members of the National Police Agency after an anonymous tip sent video evidence of sexual assault, rape, and child molestation to police headquarters. His arrest is also linked to the recent destruction of Starlight Pachinko Parlor. Inspector Yoshimoto is being held without bail pending a hearing. The superintendent general of the National Police Agency refused to comment as other investigations are still underway."

"That is enough of that," Naomi said as she pressed the power button on the remote control. The television in the hospital room went black just as Voodoo entered wearing a pair of jeans and a casual button-down shirt. Any semblance of the man in black fatigues commanding drones with his hands no longer existed.

Stu, Frisco, and Sparks followed closely behind. Stu and Frisco looked like Ivan Drago and Rocky Balboa at the end of *Rocky IV*. Frisco had bandages across his back from his stab wound while Stu had his head wrapped. Sparks gnawed on some teriyaki chicken on a stick like a happy kid at a carnival. The bruises on Voodoo were less visible but fatigue echoed in his eyes. After the explosion at the pachinko parlor, the rescue operation on Kunashir Island, and the literal underwater knife fight, Voodoo felt his age.

Dr. Kerry Hawkins lay on her hospital bed, her left eye black and swollen shut, her left arm in a cast, and her right arm connected to an IV drip.

"How goes the recovery?" Voodoo asked.

Kerry stabbed a ball of takoyaki with a toothpick and popped it into her mouth before wincing slightly.

"I can see out of my left eye again," she said between chews. She nodded to the side at her friend. "Naomi brought me some takoyaki from a guy selling it out of the back of a van, so I'd say things are looking pretty good." Kerry's smile warped under the swollen features on her face as she swallowed.

"I did not have time to get you anything better. Nakashibetsu does not have a whole lot of food options," Naomi said with the slightest embarrassment.

Kerry reached out with her good arm and touched Naomi's hand. "It's great," she said with her morphed smile. "No complaints here."

Frisco spoke up. "I just found out word got back to my CO that the God Algorithm was lost. Do we want to keep it that way?"

"The people in this room are the only ones that know the truth about the God Algorithm," Voodoo said. "Yeah, we lost the bag with Kerry's computer, but we still have the algorithm and the protein." Voodoo crossed his arms. "I don't know if I can speak for everyone, but I don't feel like this is something that anyone should know about. I certainly don't know if the God Algorithm is ready for some government to have access to it."

"What do you mean?" Frisco asked.

"Frisco, I don't think anyone truly understands what this can do, and until *we* do, we should keep it tight to our chests. Let the world think it's gone," Voodoo said.

"But think about the good we can do with it. Look at what we were able to accomplish!"

"Look at how many people died in the process," Naomi interjected. "Kenzo Ichikawa became obsessed with it, and that led to his death—one wrong decision that led to more. Yes, he saved Voodoo's life, but the people at the pachinko parlor, all those soldiers on the island, and Kenzo himself all dead because of something he could have walked away from years ago. His desire helped him create dreams that he chased to his death."

"I have a greater fear," Dr. Hawkins said. "People always think of AI as the ultimate development of machines that can think—AI that becomes self-aware and all that other *Terminator* junk. Yes, machine learning can automate processes that may lead to weapons deciding who lives and dies. But there's more, something even more dangerous, less controllable. The algorithm that I helped build is like a highway of information between humans and machine. My concern is what happens when *humans* can all become enhanced through machine learning? We've already seen that nations are ready to kill for it."

The room fell silent as Dr. Hawkins's words hung in the air.

Frisco agreed, "I see what you mean. As far as anyone is concerned, we found Dr. Hawkins based on intel we gathered from a variety of sources and logistics logs from the ship, and that's how we ended up on Kunashir Island. At least, that's what my CO is buying. We have to fill in some gaps with pretty vague answers, but Buck seems on board as long as it makes him look good."

Voodoo said, "That's why we keep this whole thing a secret, so we can figure out the best path for it. I mean, considering that whole conversation you had at the embassy about an AI war, I get the feeling that things are just getting started." Frisco nodded in response. Voodoo turned to Frisco and Stu. "Are you going to be alright flying back to Yokosuka?"

"I think we'll be good now that I know for a fact that my CO isn't going to court-martial us. At least, not yet."

"What do you mean?" Naomi asked.

"Word of our little excursion got back to the chief of station, and he was stoked with the way that things turned out. So, of course, our CO is taking all the credit and making sure that everyone's story is straight, as if *he* is the one that approved everything."

Frisco glanced over at Voodoo. Voodoo knew that face. It was the face he received after most deployments when he watched other people take credit for his work or the success of another person. It shouldn't be this way. But that was always how things managed to turn out.

Voodoo didn't care. He never really did. If he came into this job hoping for the credit to always get to the right person, he would live his life like a bitter victim. And that just wasn't him.

"Kerry, I'd like to ask you some more questions, if you're up to it?"

"Go for it," she said as she chewed another ball of takoyaki. "Better yet, let me start." Kerry swallowed. "I'm guessing you're wondering about how this all happened?"

"I wish I had known earlier that you were the same person from the river all those years ago. I've put a lot of it together on my own but—"

"Allow me to explain. I didn't realize it until much later, but the rafting trip on the Colorado was *not* the first time we met. Do you remember visiting Japan when you were little?"

Voodoo cocked his head slightly. "Vaguely. My mother brought me to Japan once when I was, like, five."

"So, I'm sure you don't remember why you were there."

Voodoo shook his head.

"You visited a park and played with two girls. That was Tsuru and me. We were young so it's no surprise you forgot about it. However, Kenzo *did* tell Tsuru who *you* were. And Tsuru couldn't let it go. She didn't have any siblings, so she latched on to the idea of a cousin. Her father told her about your family, Gavin. And everything you did. Tsuru was obsessed with you. Once she found out that she had a cousin in the United States and that your family were river guides, she talked about it constantly, studied the Colorado River, the Grand Canyon.

She was saving money to come to meet you. Then she got sick. I moved back to the States when I was fourteen, got wrapped up in my own life. That was three years before Tsuru died."

Voodoo listened carefully. "I wish she had reached out earlier. This could have been a very different story..." He paused and picked at his fingers. "I think I have a good grasp of what you were doing with Project Tsuru and Project Kawa, but I also had a dream on the plane to Japan when I know I wasn't receiving signals through my phone from the God Algorithm. How do you explain that?"

Kerry smiled through her bruised cheeks.

"We call those 'echoes.' Kenzo would get them from time to time. Your subconscious mind is powerful. The same as you may see any impactful dream more than once, God Algorithm–derived dreams may instantiate multiple times. In your case, it was holding on to the words from the night before."

"What about Tsuru's first dream? Kenzo's initial algorithm was very rudimentary. I also saw one of Kenzo's logs. The one where Tsuru wakes up and then recites the words that set this all in motion. How did she know that you would be the key to creating the God Algorithm?" Voodoo asked.

Kerry Hawkins made a face. "What do you mean?"

"Her dream said, 'On the rough river, the guiding crane will go to the sky, and the lost hawk is the path to the return to the nest.' You're the lost hawk. She's the crane that returned to the sky."

Kerry nodded and then smiled. "I am *not* the hawk she referred to."

Voodoo's face grew warm. "Of course you are. Kenzo took her to the river to spread her ashes and regain a relationship with you. You're the one who fell out of the boat. You're the lost friend...right? If you're not, then who is?"

"You know, part of me thought the same thing. Then I really thought about it. Tsuru loved the idea of the river. She loved the idea of her cousin. She especially loved your name." The room fell quiet as Naomi and Voodoo leaned in more carefully. "Gavin. It seems like a simple enough name, right? Do you know where it comes from?"

Gavin shrugged. "It's English, I think. I never put much thought into it."

"Well, names always have meaning in Japanese. You know that. Westerners come to Japan and they are always asked what their name means. When they don't know, it throws people off—not knowing the meaning of your own name is such a foreign concept to them.

"So, Tsuru, just like anyone else in Japan, wanted to know the meaning of your name. Gavin comes from 'Gawain.' It's a Welsh name." Kerry smiled. "It means 'white hawk.'"

"Wait, what?"

"You're the lost hawk that would be the path back to the nest. Tsuru wanted to bring her family back together. At least that's what she hoped. It wasn't a premonition; it was a desire. Instead, her father took that as inspiration to create an algorithm that could see the future. It saved your life, but also turned you into a long-term experiment that we unknowingly took part in."

A tear fell down Naomi's cheek. Voodoo glanced at her and back at Kerry, who started to cry as well. "We're so sorry, Gavin. It all started with the hallucination of a dying girl who wanted nothing more than to meet her cousin. But, just like that day in the park, we were together again on the beach of the Colorado River...when the crane went to the sky."

Warm hands on Voodoo's heart squeezed it so tight it broke. A tsunami of emotions slammed into him. Sorrow for

Tsuru and Kenzo. For his mother. For Kerry and Naomi. For his wife. For the kids in the pachinko parlor and that poor child in the window. For so very many caught in the deadly currents of his life. And maybe most of all for having hid his dream of Frisco and Stu, knowing they may have died. Every emotion he had welling up inside of him just burst out and Voodoo folded into a heap on the hospital room floor.

Part of him had hoped there was a higher purpose behind the messages he received, a greater voice speaking to him in his sleep, guiding him forward like some holy spirit. Instead, it was the selfish machinations of his disturbed uncle and the creative genius of a woman he hardly knew.

He wanted to be angry but felt no hate. Instead, he just felt alone, weak, broken. The way he did each morning he awoke in his bed without his wife—reaching out to find no one there. He missed out on a life filled with a mother, a cousin, an uncle, a wife, children. *Now I have nothing... I am nothing.*

A hand rested on his shoulder. Then another, and another. He looked up to see Frisco standing above him extending a hand, pulling him to his feet. Stu and Sparks were there too. Stu gave Voodoo a nod. Naomi stepped up. And Kerry reached out.

"You're not alone, brother," Frisco said. "You may feel like you've lost everything. You may feel adrift. But you've had our six ever since the day I met you. It's time we had yours."

• • •

The seven weary travelers tarried in the room, sharing their lives for one last moment before breaking away. Voodoo and Frisco clasped hands and shared a gentle bro hug, and Voodoo gently patted his wounded friend, keeping the heterosexual exclamation points small. Sparks, Stu, and Frisco left to join up with several members of their platoon. But not before promising to keep the space between them narrow, the interactions often. Naomi escorted them out, keeping particularly close to Stu-Bear, who didn't seem to mind her presence.

It was late. Amaterasu made her exit. Dusk faded to evening in the land of the rising sun. Voodoo remained beside Kerry in her hospital bed. Her medication set in, and she drifted off. Voodoo looked at the face of the woman he once knew, a face he thought he would never remember but never forgot—a strong young woman shaken by the power of Hades Canyon, baptized and reborn, a fighter battling to find the light.

She wasn't the only one who had changed.

Gavin, who was once the new kid, fighting to prove himself with a misfit band of river guides and semihomeless vagabonds, rested beside her, once again, as a rescuer. He braved the fluted metamorphic rock of Vishnu Schist, where fish had their brains dashed on the canyon walls. Gavin, who became known as Voodoo, the outcast, the enabler, the help, who led platoons of special operators from the tip of the spear but still sat in the back, picking up brass with the new guys.

They called him tech, enabler, misfit, gaijin. He called himself weak, unworthy, murderer, a failure. And through it all, through the insults and misfortune, he picked up his gun and covered their six. Gavin, Voodoo, digital ghost, and witch doctor. A person is the sum of the whole, not the label at the moment. And at any time, you can be better than the person you were five minutes ago. Voodoo was a man hoping to make his life worthy of the great gift given to him by the family he never knew, and a cousin who gave her life to create it.

Voodoo sat in the chair beside Kerry's hospital bed, choosing this time to not let her walk down US Route 191, never to be seen again. But instead, to remain at her side, to brave a different canyon. And together, he would allow the crane to guide them wherever the river of fate chose to take them.

Voodoo closed his eyes and, for the first time, imagined a life where silence and dreams were not weapons. He pictured a time when dreams that started on the water could end there too.

Voodoo felt the hands of his wife, encouraging him to enjoy the present despite knowing the end, and reminding him that he was not alone.

Voodoo saw Frisco's eyes giving a supportive smile, and Stu giving him a nod.

Voodoo finally saw his life away from the nightmares. He left his mental armor and fears behind, embracing the welcoming light of rest. And at that moment, Voodoo slept...and Gavin dreamt.

The AI war is just beginning.

Visit www.jlhancock.com to join Voodoo
and the Directorate on the next fight.

ACKNOWLEDGMENTS

From the time I first came up with the plot of this book in October 2019, to the day it was published, my friends and family have been by my side. I cannot express enough how much that has meant to me.

I would like to thank my wife and daughters for putting up with my late nights writing and my perpetual distraction as I fixated on vexing plot points.

I'd like to thank my co-workers, you know who you are, for listening to me rant and for not admitting me into an asylum.

Most importantly though, this book is dedicated to Chief Petty Officer Christian Michael Pike who gave his life serving his country in the mountains of Afghanistan in March, 2013. For one moment, I have never pitied Chris, I envy him. He gave his life doing what he loved most. There is nothing more beautiful than that.

Not a day goes by that I don't think of Chris. His sacrifice motivates me to dig deeper and push harder. I see him every day in my friends and family who supported me along the way in writing this book. May his memory forever serve as a guiding light, reminding us that we should never ask for lighter burdens but build broader shoulders.

I miss you, brother.

Made in the USA
Middletown, DE
21 July 2022

69774438R00281